T0009480

Apoca Lips

Apoca Lips

A XANTH NOVEL

Piers Anthony

OPEN ROAD

INTEGRATED MEDIA

NEW YORK

All rights reserved, including without limitation the right to reproduce this book or any portion thereof in any form or by any means, whether electronic or mechanical, now known or hereinafter invented, without the express written permission of the publisher.

This is a work of fiction. Names, characters, places, events, and incidents either are the product of the author's imagination or are used fictitiously. Any resemblance to actual persons, living or dead, businesses, companies, events, or locales is entirely coincidental.

Copyright © 2023 by Piers Anthony

ISBN: 978-1-5040-6693-8

Published in 2023 by Open Road Integrated Media, Inc.
180 Maiden Lane
New York, NY 10038
www.openroadmedia.com

Apoca Lips

Chapter 1

BATON

Nolan saw it coming: a kind of wand with bat wings. He knew it had no substance because it flew right through the branch and foliage of a nearby acorn tree without colliding. It was imaginary.

It came up to him and tapped him on the shoulder, but there was no actual contact. Then it hovered close.

"I don't know what you're up to, spook," he said to it. "But I know I can't touch you any more than you can touch me. So I will ignore you until you go away."

The baton did what looked like a double-take, bobbing in the air. It was surprised?

Intrigued, Nolan clarified the situation. "Okay, I will explain. I am Prince Nolan Naga, son of King Naldo Naga and Queen Mela Merwoman. Yes, she of the plaid panties. That's why my hair is plaid, and my scales." He did a quick switch to his naga form with bright plaid scales, then back to human form. "Yes, I am a crossbreed, half human, quarter serpent, quarter fish. We aren't supposed to have talents other than changing between our forms, but the stork must have messed up, because I did get a small one. The ability to see imaginary things, like flying batons. So I do see you, not that it does either of us any good. Are you satisfied?"

The baton had no real head, but it nodded with its upper bulb. So it understood him.

"So now you can be on your way, because I have no use for you. I have a date to swim with my mother, as we do each afternoon, because she gets tired having to wear feet for too long and needs a good daily splash to refresh. Begone."

But the baton continued to hover, not flying away.

"What's with you?" Nolan asked. "You have no purpose here, other than maybe to annoy me. The fact that I can see you should be irrelevant, since you are imaginary."

The baton shook its nonexistent head no.

This was arousing Nolan's curiosity. "You claim you do have a purpose here? What is it?"

The baton shrugged, unable to answer.

"Oh, so it's to be a game of nineteen questions?"

It nodded.

Nolan would have been annoyed if he were not getting seriously curious. So he played the game. "You have to tell me something?"

It hesitated, then shook no.

"Not exactly tell me? But there is something I might want to know?"

It nodded yes.

The mystery was intensifying.

"Show me something?"

Again the hesitation, followed by no.

Nolan got a minor inspiration. "Make me understand something?"

An emphatic nod. Yes!

This was getting really interesting. Nolan was reasonably smart for his species, for all that he was a meld of at least three species, and he liked to know what was what. There had to be a reason for this visit by an imaginary thing.

He kept questioning the baton, but each time he thought he got close to the answer, he lost it. Finally he came to the nineteenth question and knew that if he didn't get it this time, he would forfeit the answer. His prior questions had established that the baton was not here to give him any special power, or put him in danger, or grant success, or provide enlightenment. The news seemed neutral yet had to be significant. Whatever could it be?

Then he got an idea so brilliant that the light of its flash illuminated the nearby landscape. "I'm the protagonist!" he exclaimed. "Of an adventure."

The baton nodded, evidently relieved that he had finally caught on.

"You brought me the viewpoint because I'm about to have a significant experience that is story-worthy, so it can be recorded in the annuls of Xanth."

Yes.

"Does this happen to all protagonists? I mean, that you bring it to them? But they don't know that because they can't see you?"

Yes. Yes. Yes. The nineteen questions were over, but once he got the answer, all else was mere detail and dialogue.

"So you're going to stick around until my adventure is done, then you'll move on to the next protagonist?"

Yes.

"But you can't or won't tell me what my great noteworthy adventure is going to be?"

Yes.

"So I might as well ignore you anyway."

Yes.

Nolan walked to the nearby inlet of the sea. He stooped to touch the water with his finger. Sure enough, he felt the familiar vibration of his mother as she swam toward him, right on schedule. He waited, not changing form yet.

The surface of the sea rippled. Then her head popped out of the water, her greenish hair turning yellowish in air. "There you are, Nolan!" she called. "Why haven't you changed yet?"

"I want to talk before we swim."

"Oh." She swam to the shore, formed her flukes into legs, and heaved herself onto land. She was full-breasted, as merwomen were, much better endowed than freshwater mermaids. That didn't bother Nolan; he was used to seeing his mother natural. "What about?"

"I'm to be the protagonist of a story."

She firmed up her legs and walked to join him, nude of course. She did not come close to showing her age, which was seventy; she claimed that the seawater preserved her, but he suspected that she had found a secret source of youth elixir. "How do you know?"

"I got tapped by the Baton of Protagonism. It is hovering beside us now."

Her awareness of company caused her to inhale, putting on her best front. "Ah. You can see it."

"Yes. It took me nineteen questions to ascertain its mission, but it is definitely here. So I must have a big adventure coming up. I'm not sure what to do. I haven't played this role before."

She nodded. "I was a protagonist once. That's how I met your father."

The baton nodded, remembering.

"After donning plaid panties and freaking out the landscape," Nolan agreed. That bit of family history was well known.

She smiled reminiscently. "Don't demean it. Those panties are reflected in your hair and eyes. They truly impressed your father, and it shows in you."

"To be sure. I am properly proud of my heritage. But I doubt that can account for my selection as a protagonist. Apart from my hair, I'm just an ordinary crossbreed, the son of two crossbreed species. That's not very exciting."

"Ordinary folk can make good protagonists. So can crossbreeds, or even aliens."

"I suppose. But what great adventure can be approaching me, to warrant my selection for this honor?"

"Well, you are thirty-two years old. Past time to find a bride and generate grandchildren."

Of course she would think of that. She had been after him for a decade to get on with it. It seemed that parents did not feel completely legitimate until they were grandparents. "But I have found no suitable woman," he protested. "All the viable attractive crossbreed princesses are taken." He glanced at her slantingly. "Unless you wouldn't mind if I took up with a sexy commoner? There are some very personable lower-class maidens in the vicinity, not to mention the mermaids who innocently sun themselves within sight of the castle."

She froze in horror. "Don't even joke about it, son! You must have a royal match for the time when you assume the naga throne. She doesn't have to be naga, just royal. Those mermaids are hardly innocent; they know exactly where the castle is, and who is in it, and they make certain of the line of sight."

To be sure. They could also be quite affectionate, off the record. But Mela did have a point: he needed a royal bride. "So how do I find the perfect woman? That is to say, both royal and sexy? That seems to be quite the challenge." Because of course royals of either gender were not necessarily young or sexy.

"Indeed," she agreed. "That must be your coming adventure: finding and winning your ideal bride."

He hadn't thought of that. Still, he argued the case. "Princes find princesses all the time, and they aren't all protagonists. What's different about me?"

She considered. "Maybe you had better ask the Good Magician. All protagonists do."

That was another thing he hadn't thought of. Well, why not? He did want the right woman, and the Good Magician should be able to tell him who and where she was. He glanced at the baton, which still hovered close, its wings slowly flapping. "What do you think?" he asked it.

To his surprise, it nodded affirmatively. He realized that it might be getting bored here, and wanted to get on with the adventure.

"Let's swim," he said to Mela.

"I thought you'd never ask." She launched herself at the sea, her legs reverting to tail in the process. He followed, shifting to his fish form so that he would not have to stay within range of air. He did enjoy these family exercises.

Nolan approached the Good Magician's castle at a fast slither. He was in his naga form, with a snakelike body that enabled him to move swiftly through thick brush. That saved him some hassle when traveling. But as he got close, he reverted to human form, delved into his magic pouch to recover his clothes and sword, and paused to consider. He knew there would be three requirements, or Challenges, each navigable provided he figured out its spot mystery, and that he should get through well enough if he kept his common sense. He knew that his talent would not help, and maybe not his shifting forms: he was likely limited to the form he used to enter the grounds. Probably human was best for that anyway.

The baton had paced him throughout, always hovering close. It didn't seem to be getting bored. Yet.

The castle seemed placid, with a pennant flying from the highest tower. That was surely deceptive. It might be peaceful inside, but first he had to reach it, and that could be harrowing.

"What do you think?" he asked the baton. But it only shrugged. Probably it wasn't allowed to help him navigate the Challenges. That would be cheating.

Well, either he would get through or he wouldn't. So he walked boldly toward the edifice.

And found himself on what seemed to be a battlefield, level and barren. There must have been a recent battle, because things were strewn around, such as a helmet here, a sword there, and a gauntlet somewhere else. He needed to get across it and out of the way before there was any more action.

So he had triggered the Challenge but had no idea how to get past it. So much for his commonsense approach. He glanced at the baton. Was it smirking?

He stepped forth—and almost tripped over a pile of discarded leather armor. It was visible, but he hadn't noticed it. A soldier must have worn it years ago, then maybe outgrown it and discarded it. Not that it mattered now. Nolan stepped around it.

But the moment he set foot on the field, he heard a distant cry. "Charge!" He looked and saw a line of soldiers double-pacing toward him. He tried to back off but discovered that somehow he was now in the middle of the tract, too far from the edge to escape before the vanguard caught him.

"You know, if I don't make it through the Challenges, I won't learn who my ideal woman is and won't have that adventure," he reminded the baton. "You'll be wasting your time on a failed protagonist, while the other batons oversee real novelty." He was guessing that there was a covey of the things, to handle multiple adventures.

The faceless smirk faded. That confirmed his guess.

He focused on his situation. Well, the old leather armor was still beside him. Could he don that and fight his way clear? It did look as if it would fit him. He viewed the charging army and knew he would be hacked to pieces in half a moment or less.

There had to be a way through, if he could only figure it out in time. That was the nature of each Challenge. He knew that if he failed, he would not actually be killed; he would just be washed out of the Challenge and never get in to see the Good Magician. That prospect annoyed him. Maybe he could find his ideal woman without the Magician's help, but chances were that he would find a lesser creature. He wanted exactly the right one, no substitute, and she could be anywhere or even halfway to nowhere.

The army was getting distressingly close. In fact, they saw him. There was a "Tally ho!" cry as they oriented on him. Now he was really in trouble. Even the baton looked concerned.

Well, he could at least fight, and maybe take out a soldier or three before being overwhelmed. There would be some small satisfaction in that, though they wouldn't die any more than he would. They would merely have balked his passage.

The armor might help. He scrambled into it, knowing how it should fit. It was complete with boots, gauntlets, and helmet. There was even a scabbard with a serviceable sword, so he put his own sword back in the pouch. But there was something about this whole apparatus that he didn't understand. Why was it made out of leather instead of steel? Why was it not scarred with prior sword strikes? It seemed pristine. Had it never been used? That seemed unlikely, because it was here on the field, with wear marks and creases. It had to have been used, just not battered.

The vanguard was almost upon him. Nolan drew his sword, which he did know how to use. He would go down fighting. "Stay clear," he warned the baton. "I don't want to accidentally slice you in half."

The baton hastily moved out just beyond sword range.

Still, the situation bothered him. What was the key to escape that he had missed? It had to be here somewhere. He hated being stupid almost as much as he hated washing out of the Challenge. A suit of leather armor, instead of steel, that must have been used yet not battered. Where was the sense in that? The answer was mischievously hiding from him.

He got half an idea. The mystery of the hide was hiding from him.

Hide. Hiding.

Then he got it in a flash he hoped would not alert the converging troops. This was a hide suit. He sheathed his sword, then stood perfectly still. The baton hovered close again, uncertain what he was doing.

The troops arrived. They milled about, not attacking. "Where did he go?" one asked.

"He just disappeared," another said.

"He found the armor," a third said.

"Oh, bleep!"

Then they all vanished, and Nolan was free to continue across the field. But he remained still, just in case they had hide suits of their own and were trying to trick him into revealing himself.

Then he found himself beyond the field and without the armor. He had indeed prevailed. "So there," he told the baton. "I made it." The baton nodded. Maybe it had known he would.

He was in what seemed to be a labyrinth of tunnels leading every which way, plus a few extra. Some went up, some down, some crosswise. He probably could navigate any of them if he were careful, but he suspected that few if any actually led out of the chamber to the surface. Maybe he would just have to follow each one, and if it dead-ended, return to follow another. In time he should find the right one.

There was a line of ants crossing the chamber. A beetle bug challenged their right of way. The lead ant loosed a bolt of fire that burned the bug to a crisp. These were fire ants! Not creatures to mess with.

But they seemed to have a problem. They were milling about uncertainly. What was the matter? "What's your take on this?" he asked the baton, but it did not respond.

Then he saw that there was liquid dripping rapidly from the ceiling, forming a dirty puddle below. Before long the forming pool would overflow its rocky banks and start flooding the lower passages. Then the upper ones. If the correct route out was a lower one, he would need to find it soon.

So would the ants. Water was anathema to fire creatures—except for fire water—unless they could burn it dry in the manner of salamanders. As far as he knew, ants could not. So why were they staying around instead of moving on out?

Well, that was not his concern. He needed to select a path and find his way out. But how? There were so many to choose from! He needed better information.

He looked around some more, knowing that somewhere here there was likely to be a clue. He just needed to pick up on it, and more efficiently than he had the last one. He knew he had lucked out on that battlefield.

Then he saw a large swing hanging from so far up that the ropes disappeared into the gloom. Who in Xanth would want to swing here?

The ants were milling directly below the swing. Was that coincidence?

Now Nolan was curious. That was dangerous, because once he focused on a mystery, he might not be able to let go of it until he solved it.

"I think I need to talk with those ants," he told the baton. "I suspect you have some limited telepathy, because you need to understand any protagonist you get sent to, human or inhuman. Who knows, you might even have to associate with a fire ant someday." Because as he understood it, anyone or anything could be a protagonist. Not necessarily a good one, but still a main character for a while.

The baton nodded.

"Now, those ants may have a problem. I am curious to know what it is. Would it be cheating if you helped me converse with them, as fellow travelers, as it were?"

The baton nodded. Yes, it would be cheating.

Nolan sighed. He would just have to figure it out for himself.

He considered the fire ants. It was almost as if they wanted to get to the swing, but there was no way, as they were not a flying variety. They could surely climb the wall, but there was no guarantee that would touch the ropes of the swing. But why would they want to take a swing anyway?

There was a draft that tousled his hair in passing. Air was passing through the cave, going who knew where. It tugged at the swing, making it move slightly. The ants stirred as if concerned. Were they afraid they could be blown away?

Then he got a notion. Could the ants want to swing on the swing? It might be a rare experience for them.

He looked at the baton, but it was studiedly neutral. Still no help there.

Well, bleep. He could help the ants, if they were of a mind to accept it. It was just possible that they could communicate, as ants had antennae that enabled them to talk with one another. Why not with him?

He sat down and put his right hand on the cave floor, fingers down, close to the throng. If they attacked by burning him, he would rise up and stomp them to stains. He suspected they knew that.

The ants paused, as if considering. Then a large one approached his hand. It looked to be the queen ant, because she wore a fiery little crown. She did not fire at him. Instead she climbed carefully onto the back of his index finger. Her antennae seemed to spark.

Hello.

She was talking to him! She surely couldn't understand his verbal speech, but maybe his thought could reach her through his skin. "Hello," he said, focusing his thought to match.

I am Queen Antonia Fire Ant. Who are you?

"I am Prince Nolan Naga, presently in human form."

A naga prince! What is your business here?

"I am seeking the Good Magician, so he can find me my ideal woman, preferably a sexy princess." He smiled. "Not an ant princess, I think. No offense. How about you?"

We are performing our Service for his Answer to our Question. But that's irrelevant. We are part of the Challenge at the moment. We will toast you if you take the wrong path.

"But I don't know the correct path."

Indeed. That is the Challenge.

There had to be more to it than that. The rising water would mess him up as readily as the ants. "Why should we quarrel? I bear you no malice. I just want to get safely out of here."

Indeed.

She might be following a script. He just needed to learn it and find a way to turn it to his advantage. "There has to be a way we can help each other. Why do you want to reach that swing?"

Once a year the cave wind passes the swing and generates swing music. We like to celebrate the event by dancing on it. We call it the Swing Dance. There was supposed to be a vine trailing from it that we could climb, but some idiot setting up this scene must have forgotten that detail. Now the wind is rising and we can't get there in time. It's a great disappointment.

Ah. That was the script. They had to reach the swing in time to dance to the music of the wind. "You need to reach the swing. I need to find a safe route out of here. You surely know all the passages. How about a trade: I will help you reach the swing if you help me find the right path out. Deal?"

She didn't play coy. The wind was rising. *Deal.*

The baton remained neutral.

"I believe I can just reach the swing with my hand. You can climb up me to get there. Promise you won't burn me."

She made a mental laugh. *Promise. Despite your lack of interest in an ant princess.* Then she scrambled off his finger to rejoin her troupe and give them the word.

Nolan stood. He reached up and touched the bottom of the swing with the tip of his longest finger. Close call!

The ants swarmed to his feet and scrambled up his trousers. There was no fire. They climbed to his neck, up along his lifted arm, and to the bottom of the swing. They clung to the wood and went on around to the seat of it.

The last to pass was the queen. *You may delay to watch our dance if you wish. Then I will assign a minion to guide you out of the cave.*

"Thank you, Queen Antonia."

You are more than welcome.

It seemed that she liked him, now that they had made a mutually beneficial deal. She moved on up to the swing.

Nolan lowered his arm, which was tired, and stood back to watch the dance. The cave wind was rising, and the swing swung back and forth when his stabilizing finger left it.

Then he realized that he couldn't see the dance because it was on the upper surface of the seat of the swing, which was out of his sight. Fortunately that was not difficult to deal with. He walked to the curving edge of the cave, climbing the wall as it were. Then he was able to see across to the upper surface of the swing.

The baton watched too. It lacked eyes, but it was orienting itself toward the swing.

Now the air current blew in earnest. It caught the swing and drove it forth and back. As it moved, it rocked a bit and formed lilting notes in the wind. Not only did the ants hold firm, they danced, forming patterns that swung in and out in time with the motion of the swing. It was pretty.

Then they shot out their fire. The jets of it intersected above them and curled into fiery smoke, which wavered in the wind like a living thing in itself before it dissipated. It was beautiful.

Nolan was enchanted. He had never seen art like this before, enhanced by the music. When the show was done he applauded. The baton nodded and beat its wings in time with the claps of his hands: it appreciated the show too.

The wind died and the swing settled back to stillness. The show was over. Nolan returned to the swing and stretched up his arm to enable the ants to descend, but instead they dropped to the cave floor. They were so small that such a fall did not hurt them. It was only the ascent that had been beyond them.

Then one ant dropped to his hand. Surprised, he lowered it toward the floor. But the ant demurred. *I am Aurora Ant. I am no princess, but I am one of the rare ants with the talent of contact telepathy, like that of the queen. I will guide you out of the cave.*

Oh. He had almost forgotten their deal. Fortunately the queen had not. "Thank you, Aurora." He moved his hand to his shoulder so that she could be more secure there. He realized that not just any ant could help him; there needed to be communication. The queen had made sure of that.

The baton nodded smugly. It seemed it had not forgotten. But neither had it reminded him. Its studied neutrality was starting to annoy him.

This way. The ant made a mental arrow, pointing.

He went that way. Soon she made another arrow, and he took a side path he would not have recognized alone. Then another.

While they moved, they talked. "I am Prince Nolan Naga, going to ask the Good Magician for information about my ideal woman."

I must confess that I, too, have a mission, she replied. There was something about her mind or tone that he liked. It was almost as if she were a pretty girl.

I am a pretty girl, she thought. *For an ant.*

Oh. "Sorry."

The baton nodded smugly. So it could hear her thoughts despite the lack of physical contact, just as it heard Nolan's thoughts.

My mission is to find a suitable location for our tribe to move. We were defending a farmer's field from moles, but then the ungrateful wretch fired us. So we need to move. That's why we came to see the Good Magician.

"Oh, of course. I hope you find a suitable new home."

I suspect that you will go there, in the course of your travels. That's why the Good Magician put us together.

He realized that this could be so. "Welcome to travel with me, then." Her pretty-girl mind made him continue to enjoy her company.

She directed him through the labyrinth, until at last they emerged into daylight. He was through the second Challenge . . .

Only to face the third. The path ahead led directly through fields of plants to a giant pair of hairy stakes that completely blocked it. Briar bushes grew close by the sides so that he could not get around the stakes.

He glanced at the baton. It nodded. He was on his own again, to figure out the nature of the impediment, and the way to get past it. Probably the baton had no better idea than he did.

This is interesting, Aurora thought. *A whole other setting.*

He looked around. The bushes formed a nearly solid wall. He looked back. He saw that he had passed by a large field growing some kind of crop of vegetables or fruits. In fact they looked like pineapples.

That made him pause. Pineapples were dangerous; they could explode violently, wiping out anything close.

The baton had not warned him about that either.

That baton is not very nice, Aurora thought.

"You can see it?" he asked, surprised.

Our dialogue is mental. I can see what you see, when I am with you.

Oh. "Good enough."

What was the connection between the hairy stakes and the field of plants? he wondered. There had to be one, this being a Challenge.

He returned to the stakes and peered closely at them.

"What do you think you're looking at, oaf?"

Nolan was startled. Where had the voice come from? There was nothing but the stakes. "Where are you?" he asked.

"Right before you, dullard."

The stakes were talking? So it seemed. "But you have no mouth. How can you talk?"

"The same way you can generate the illusion of thinking without a brain, clod."

No help there. The baton seemed amused. "Are you a Challenge?"

"Of course we are, dope."

Neither are those stakes very nice, Aurora thought.

Then he made half a connection. "You look like the calves of a giant man. But I don't see the rest of the giant."

"We are the ankles of a giant, dimwit," the stakes corrected him. "An invisible giant. We are the only part of him that is visible. There's nothing else like us. We are a legend among body parts."

An invisible giant. Now it made some sense. He was standing on the path, only the lower part of his legs visible. Nolan wasn't sure how to proceed, so he stalled by rephrasing a question. "How is it you can talk? Normally body parts are silent."

"Normally invisible giant body parts are invisible and silent. But we became visible and also audible, idiot. Any fool understands that."

That did seem to make a certain sense, if he strained at it. "Why isn't the rest of him visible?"

"He worked too hard and got tired. Too tired to maintain his invisibility all the way down to his feet. Now he's too tired to move out of your way. So you're stuck, imbecile. Go back where you came from."

So this was the real Challenge. To get the invisible giant to move out of the way. Except that he was too tired to move.

How could Nolan make the giant untired? That was the question.

He cerebrated for a while, then considered, then pondered while the baton rolled its eyeless eyes impatiently. Maybe he was indeed guilty of the illusion of thinking. Nothing came.

So he gave it up for the moment and went back to look at the field of plants. Then he saw a little sign: solar farm. The pineapples might be the farm crop. Maybe they got their dangerous energy from sitting all day in the direct sunlight.

Still, why were they here? Their tremendous energy could be dangerous for a giant, too, if he accidentally stepped on one and set it off. They would be like land mines.

The baton hovered patiently, waiting for his illusion mind to come up with the obvious. He was glad it couldn't speak, because it would have said something sarcastic.

Solar farm. Giant. What was the connection? The giant was probably getting hungry, waiting on the path. It must want him to get on with it, either succeeding or failing, so it could get off duty and go eat a snack.

Then he got it, maybe. "Those are power plants!" he said. "And big fruits. Maybe the giant eats pineapples for energy. This is the giant's garden."

He went to the nearest ripe pineapple and put his hands carefully to its sides. He pulled it ever so gently out of the ground. It did not detonate. So far so good.

He carried the pineapple back to where the giant stood. "Back again, moron?" the ankles inquired.

He ignored them. "Hey, Invisible Giant!" he called as loudly as he could. "Are you hungry?" He hoped the giant did have enough energy to talk.

There was a giant-sized pause. Then a voice came from the sky. "Yes."

Victory, maybe. "I have brought you a ripe pineapple. Can you reach down and take it?" He held the fruit up over his head, hoping that the giant's arms were not as tired as his legs.

Something took it from his hands. It flew on upward. That would be the giant's invisible grasp.

You figured it out, Aurora thought. *Congratulations.*

Nolan liked her better and better.

"Oh, beans," the ankles muttered.

"Not beans, dunce," Nolan retorted. "Pineapple."

You told them.

There was a giant slurping sound above. The invisible giant was eating the pineapple.

Then the ankles started fading. The giant was regaining his strength and becoming fully invisible.

"Noooo!" the ankles cried.

"You thought you were a legend among body parts," Nolan said smugly. "But instead you were just a leg end."

There was no response. The ankles were now invisible and silent.

Then he stood before the castle entrance. He had conquered the third Challenge.

The door opened. There stood a middle-aged woman. "Hello, Prince Nolan," she said. "Hello, Aurora Ant. I am Wira, Magician Humfrey's daughter-in-law. I will take you to the Designated Wife."

Nolan remembered. The Good Magician had five or six wives who alternated, because he was allowed only one at a time. "Thank you."

Weird.

Wira ushered him into a pleasant room, where a rather pretty young woman waited. "Prince Nolan, this is MareAnn." She looked like a teenager.

"Hello, Nolan," MareAnn said as Wira faded out. "We are so glad you made it through." She showed him to a seat, then sat opposite him and crossed her legs. She had nice legs, and they showed to advantage.

"Uh, I thought you'd be older. Weren't you the Good Magician's first wife?"

She laughed. "Not exactly. We first met 175 years ago, when we were both fifteen and fell in love. But my talent was summoning equines, including unicorns, and I feared that if I lost my innocence I would no longer be able to fetch the magic equines. So I regretfully declined to marry him. But much later, after I died of old age and went to Hell, I discovered that Hell was almost as hard on innocence as marriage. So I was the last to marry him, in the Xanth Year 1090. It was a small ceremony, so we consider me to be only half a wife. Now it is Xanth Year 1123, thirty-three years later, so he has a half-wife of thirty-three years."

Nolan suspected that there was a bit of humor there, but he wasn't sure what it was. Aurora seemed to get it; she was amused. "But you don't look a hundred and seventy-five, or even thirty-three. You're more like fifteen."

"Yes. We have youth elixir, which I use regularly to restore myself to that age. This way I feel as if I am in first love again, and he rather likes me this way too."

Nolan, observing her legs, could appreciate one reason why.

"I see the Baton of Protagonism is with you," MareAnn remarked.

"You can see it?" he asked, surprised.

"Here in the Good Magician's castle, magic can't be concealed. You are unusual in your ability to see it."

"That's my talent: to see imaginary things."

"Ah, of course. That gives you power over them. You can make the baton obey you."

"I can?"

"To a degree. You could, for example, require it to move on and make someone else the protagonist. But I don't recommend that."

"Why not?"

"Because protagonists have interesting lives. They are always the center of the action, and nothing really bad happens to them. That can be a useful protection when there is danger."

"That's interesting. I have found the baton somewhat unresponsive."

"You may not have addressed it properly. Simply say 'Baton, turn a somersault,' and see what happens."

Nolan looked at the hovering thing. "Baton, turn a somersault."

It somersaulted in air. Point made.

Wira returned. "The Good Magician is occupied today. He will see you in the morning."

MareAnn rose, taking her legs out of display mode. "I will show you to your room."

Soon he was safely ensconced in a nice bedroom. Then he was summoned for dinner, where he had a nice meal, and Aurora had one too, her size. It was a single fresh seed of some sort, which she toasted with a small jet of flame. The baton did not need to eat, being imaginary.

He turned in and slept, only to dream of a woman who had fiery hair and legs like MareAnn's but was really someone else. "Who are you?" he asked her. The baton seemed curious too.

She laughed. "Don't you know me? I'm Aurora."

Now he recognized her voice, which in his dream had become vocal. "Oh, hello, Aurora. I didn't feature you in human form."

"This is how I would look as a human girl. I have fewer legs." She lifted her skirt waist-high to show him that there were only two. He might have freaked out had he not been asleep. He realized that she was teasing him. It seemed that girls of any species knew how to do that to any man.

They chatted amicably. Then his dream moved on, following its own random course, and she was gone.

In the morning he washed up and dressed, and Aurora rejoined him, perching on his head. She now had all six legs. *But you are free to imagine me with two*, she thought, *limited as they may be*. She was teasing again.

Then he thought of something. "If you spend any significant time with me, Aurora, you will be with me when I transform to one of my other shapes. What will you do when I shed my clothes?"

She resumed her imaginary bare human form, inhaling. *Too bad we are not of similar species, or we could have some fun together without clothes.* The teasing was intense.

Nolan did not care to admit that he liked the show. "I'm not joking. You don't want to drown when I become a fish."

She sobered. *Good point. What happens to your accessories when you change?*

"I have a magic pouch that sucks them in automatically." He touched the belted bag he wore around his midsection.

Then I will simply ride your shirt into the pouch and peek out through the fabric.

"That will do," he agreed. Then thought of something else. "You are speaking in italics, but in the dream you talked normally. Can you do that when I'm awake?"

"I think so," she said, surprised. "It's just a matter of translation. But others won't hear me, unless they are telepathic, as it remains mind talk."

"That's fine."

In due course they met the Good Magician, who looked mainly like an ancient gnome dwarfed by his huge Book of Answers. "Who and where is my ideal woman?" Nolan asked.

"She is Apoca of the Lips tribe, currently residing in the Queendom of Thanx. You will find her there." The owl eyes blinked. "Your Service is to ameliorate the Curse of Talents. You will need Apoca's and Nimbus's help."

"The what? With whom?"

But the Good Magician was already back in his book. Nolan had been dismissed. He remembered that obscurity was one of the gnome's defining traits.

"Maybe Apoca will know," Wira suggested. "She is a pretty savvy woman."

"I don't even know what she looks like!"

She brought him before a magic mirror. "Apoca," she said, and a woman appeared there. She was extremely shapely, with outsized lips. Weirdly, what looked like a nickelpede perched on her shoulder. But what he mainly noticed was her hair, which was plaid, matching his own. Well, now!

"I like her already," he said. "The Good Magician must have known about the hair."

"Of course," Wira agreed.

They returned to the living room and MareAnn. "My ideal woman is called Apoca," Nolan said.

"She has been here on occasion. She is a formidable female."

"But she seems to have a—a nickelpede on her shoulder."

"Oh, that's Nimbus. She's a companion, much like Aurora with you. She is another rare individual with contact telepathy."

Oh. That did make sense. Then he got an idea. "If Apoca and I are to work together to handle this Curse of Talents, she may be in danger. I want to protect her."

"She's safe enough in Thanx. They are militant feminists."

"Still, I want to be sure. It seems that protagonists are protected. Could I send the baton over to her? Make her the main character, with its benefits?"

Her eyes widened. "That's some notion! But yes, you can do it. You understand, you will lose the magic safety of protagonism yourself."

He touched the hilt of his sword. "I can handle my own defense."

She smiled. "Why not?"

Nolan looked at the baton. "Baton of Protagonism, go keep Apoca Lips company. Make yourself apparent to her, so she knows what it's about."

"Good idea," MareAnn agreed.

The baton didn't argue or balk. It had been commanded. It spread its wings and flew away.

The scene faded, as there was no longer a protagonist to animate it.

Chapter 2

APOCA

Apoca paused, her hair turning yellow for mystery. Actually, it was translucent, reflecting her thoughts, which lit up her skull beneath it, but she could control it when she had to. "What is that?"

Her friend Nimbus looked. "A bat-winged baton hovering in front of us."

"That's what I thought I saw. But does it make any sense at all?"

"Maybe it's a toy, like those wind-up flyers Mundane children have."

"Let's find out." Apoca stepped forward and grabbed the center of the rod, her hair turning a neutral gray. She had a certain feel for danger, based on hard experience, and this apparition seemed harmless.

Her hand passed through it without resistance.

"It's an illusion!" Nimbus said, surprised. "It looked real."

Now the baton flew forward and tapped Apoca lightly on the shoulder. Then it retreated, hovering before them again.

"Something odd here," Apoca said, the yellow returning.

"Extremely odd," Nimbus agreed.

"Well, we seem to have no use for it," Apoca said. "So let's move on." She took a step forward, carrying Nimbus Nickelpede on her shoulder.

The flying baton moved with them, hovering just beyond arm's reach.

"It seems to want our company," Nimbus said. She didn't actually speak; her proximity enabled contact telepathy so that the two could talk comfortably with each other. It seemed like ordinary dialogue.

Apoca knew that nickelpedes were regarded generally as a scourge, because when they attacked living flesh they gouged out nickel-sized chunks. But Nimbus was her friend; any gouging she did would be of something else, in defense of Apoca. She was actually a nice person, once befriended.

Apoca laughed. "I could use the company of a good man, not a bulbous flying rod, suggestive as that may be if you have a dirty mind." Her hair was turning green for positive, with a bit of humor.

"My mind is filthy," Nimbus said. "I could use a rugged male 'pede similarly."

"But we've both been busy organizing our folks' places in the wonderful Queendom of Thanx," Apoca said, continuing a dialogue they had had before. Girl talk never got old. "But who is worthy of us?"

"Nobody, almost by definition."

"Almost." They laughed together, not completely amused.

"Which is a problem in a matriarchal community," Nimbus agreed after half a moment. "Thanx is really Xanth spelled backward, and it's fine that it reverses the archaic male dominance of other medieval kingdoms, but it does tend to repel the he-man males."

"Which leaves some of us who aren't turned on by effeminate males dry and high," Apoca said. "In addition, since I am a queen in my own right, I really should seek a king or prince. That further rarefies my prospects."

"Most of the good human and 'pede princes do seem to be taken. We're not getting any younger."

The baton angled forward, almost as if nodding. They both looked at it, startled. "It's almost as if it understands us," Nimbus said.

Apoca was direct, as usual. "Ghostly Flying Baton, do you understand our dialogue?"

The baton nodded again.

"This is interesting," Nimbus said.

"Indeed." Apoca focused. "Are you here for a reason?"

Another nod.

"Is it something to do with us?"

Nod.

"Is it important?"

Emphatic nod.

Apoca and Nimbus shared a mental glance, because a physical one was impractical. "We'd better get help," Nimbus said. "Privately, in case this is someone's magic joke on us."

"Vinia?"

"That's my thought."

There was a stirring ahead. Someone was coming toward them.

"Vinia, of course," Apoca said. Her hair was green for welcome; she liked the girl.

"It's not coincidence, with her," the nickelpede said. "She follows her paths."

"True. Her paths are like my hair, in a manner. The colors may even match."

Nimbus nodded her tail. "Green for positive, blue for negative, yellow for doubt or mystery, yellow-green for humor, gray for neutral, and black for doom."

"You are really sharp on that," Apoca said, surprised.

"I have made a study."

"Hello, Apoca! Hi, Nimbus!" the girl called as she came in range. "Do you need me?"

"I think we do," Apoca said. "Did the paths lead you here?" She knew they had.

"Yes. There's a really green patch right in front of you."

That was because Vinia's hidden talent was to see colored paths to the future, as they had been discussing. Green was the best color. It had originally led her to Apoca a year ago, and they had done each other considerable good and now were fast friends. Vinia was still technically a child, thirteen, but verging on the allure of early maidenhood. She had dull brown hair, brown eyes, and an open talent of telekinesis. She was betrothed to Prince Ion, a year younger than she, but a full Magician in his own right. So she would be a princess in due course, though she never acted like one. Everybody liked her; she had many friends, human and non-human.

"There's an illusory winged baton in that spot," Apoca said. "Here, take my hand so you can see it." She extended one hand. Physical contact enabled mental contact.

Vinia took it. "Oh my," she gasped as she shared Apoca's vision. "I have no idea what it is, but I know it's important because of the intensity of the green. Do you have any idea what it means?"

"We hoped you would be able to see a path to the answer," Apoca answered.

Vinia nodded. "There is a new path."

They followed the new path, though only Vinia could see it. It led into the heart of Thanx, and to the door of Queen Demesne Demoness, who ruled the queendom. Apoca and Vinia were fast friends with her, as was Nimbus.

But it was her husband, Queen Consort Demon Grossclout, who answered. He was a fearsome figure with short, gnarled horns; a swishing, tufted tail; and a built-in glower. "Mesne is busy today. Will I do?" He had for centuries been the terror of the Demon University of Magic, his talent being Intimidation. But Demesne had pretty well tamed him, and he regarded Vinia somewhat like a daughter and Apoca as a former lover, unsurprisingly.

"You'll do," Vinia said. "You're solid green."

He knew exactly what she meant. "Thank you, Vin." Then he looked directly at Apoca. "Well, Lips Queen! So you're now the protagonist."

"I'm the what?" Apoca asked, taken aback.

"The protagonist. The main character of the current scene. Vin was it last year, for a whole novel, and now it seems you're it. You will surely have an interesting story to tell, in due course. You even have the protagonist baton with you."

Apoca looked at the winged baton. "You can see it?"

"Of course I can see it, Hot Lips. Magic is my domain. The baton conveys protagonism to whomever it selects." He squinted. "But there is an asterisk. It seems to be only on loan to you, sent by the real protagonist. I haven't seen that restriction before."

"I'm a fake protagonist?"

He smiled, his awesome fangs flashing momentarily. "Not fake, merely temporary, until it returns to the original protagonist."

"And whom might that be?" Vinia asked brightly.

The demon focused. "That would be, let me see, Prince Nolan Naga, who has the talent of seeing imaginary things that wield real power. That gives him power over it, and he sent it to you, Poca. He must have told it to make itself visible to you."

"A naga prince!" Vinia exclaimed. "A human-serpent crossbreed."

Grossclout focused again, delving into his memories of all things magical. "Not exactly. He's not a pure crossbreed, oxymoronic as that term may seem. He also has piscene ancestry. An unusual combination."

"But why?" Apoca asked, bewildered. The explanation for the baton was as perplexing as its presence.

"Why else? He wants you to have the temporary protection of protagonism." The demon had never had much patience with limited words, and mauled them into the necessary applications. Apoca quietly admired that.

"And why does he want me to have that? We have never met."

The demon focused once more. "Nolan is coming here to court you, Poca."

She was astonished. "To court me! Whatever for?"

"That means he wants to marry you," Vinia explained helpfully. "So he can do Adult Conspiracy things with you. He must think you're sexy."

Apoca shrugged that off so violently that the concept bounced off the wall and almost collided with a passing bird. The bird looked startled but intrigued, probably having not encountered that before outside of mating season. "I mean, why does he want to marry a woman he has never even met? One who could kiss him into love slavery?"

The demon chuckled. "He must like your look. Men are notorious fools about the appearance of women. I happen to know. Mesne wraps me around her little finger, or whatever." He pronounced the name "Meen" despite the spelling.

She was not much amused. "This is ludicrous!"

Grossclout added yet another focus. "There is a caution. The prince incurred a debt to the Good Magician, payment for the Answer to his Question about his ideal woman. He must ameliorate the Curse of Talents. If you associate with him, that may become your mission too."

"A curse?"

"I am not clear on that myself. It must be quite recent magic. But perhaps Vin can help you locate it."

"Maybe I can," the girl said. "There's a path." She started following it. Now that she could clearly see the paths, she was eager to follow them before they faded.

Apoca's head seemed to be spinning. "Thank you," she told the demon, and hurried after Vinia. What a day this had suddenly become!

This path led to the residential section of the newly forming Thanx community. A number of the assertive immigrant women had married obliging men and made comfortable homesteads. They were by no means anti-male; they just liked to be in control. Apoca knew exactly how that was.

They arrived at a nondescript door. Apoca knocked. In two-thirds of a moment it was opened by a muddy woman. Her hair and clothing were a rich and drippy brown. "Can it wait?" she asked. "I'm about to take a bath."

"I think it needs to be now," Vinia said. "She's drenched in green."

"I'm drenched in mud," the woman retorted. "Junior somehow got into a pile of it. I've got to get us both in the tub to soak it off before it cakes."

"This seems inauspicious," Apoca said. "Maybe tomorrow?"

"No. Right now," the girl insisted. "Before the green fades."

"What are you talking about?" The woman's temper was understandably strained, if not mud-soiled.

Apoca quickly explained. "I am Queen Apoca of the Lips tribe. I received a, er, warning about a Curse of Talents, but I don't know what that is. This is Vinia, who can see special paths leading her to the right places. Her path led her here. So we think the answer may be here."

"The Lips women. I've seen your section, and of course you've got the mouth. You're the ones who can kiss a man into oblivion."

"That's us," Apoca agreed. It was true that her lips were outsized compared to those of routine women. They were infused with the potent magic of her kind.

"So the neighboring men don't bother us anymore. The bad ones get kissed."

"Now they behave better, yes."

The woman considered half a moment. "Come in, look around. If you see your answer, let me know. Meanwhile Junior and I will wash."

"Fair enough. Thank you."

They entered. There was a baby boy reveling in mud. More was appearing in his hands.

"He can conjure mud!" Vinia exclaimed. "That's his talent!"

"And it's a curse," the woman said as she picked him up and stepped into a filled tub, clothing and all. She was being practical.

"Solid green."

Apoca was not satisfied. "A talent is a talent. Some are messier than others, but that's not exactly a curse."

"That depends on your sense of cleanliness," the woman retorted as she scrubbed at her child and her soiled clothing. The tub water was turning thick black, coming to resemble soup on the way to pudding.

"Yet it must relate," Vinia said. "Or the path would not have led us here."

"I wish your talent could talk," Apoca muttered. "Maybe it could explain."

"There's a new path." Vinia started to follow it.

"Thank you for your cooperation!" Apoca called to the woman as she followed.

"You're welcome," the woman called back wryly. "Do visit again if you're ever short of mud."

The new path led to another home in the same section. Apoca knocked on the indicated door.

Another mother answered, holding a baby girl who was in turn holding a wedge of apple pie. "Yes?"

They explained as efficiently as was feasible.

The woman shrugged. "My daughter's talent manifested a few days ago. It's no curse. She conjures apple pies. They are delicious."

"The green is strong," Vinia said as she looked at the baby.

But they were unable to figure out how this could be a curse. They thanked the mother and went on after enjoying slices of newly made apple pie. No curse at all! Which left the mystery intact.

The third path led them to another baby. This one had somehow gotten into a pile of manure. The smell was awful, and his mother was distraught. "He's been such a good little boy, until today," she exclaimed. "Now somehow he's reveling in sh*t!"

Apoca was intrigued by the way she pronounced the word, but that was beside the point. She did have a problem.

"This does smell like a curse," Vinia remarked, wrinkling her nose.

Even the baton seemed to be distressed; it shuddered in place, as if trying to hold its breath.

"Ha. Ha. Ha," Apoca said, distinctly unamused. "But then why did your paths lead us to the other two babies? All they have in common is conjuring."

The light of an idea flashed over the girl's head. "They all conjure pies! Mud pies, fruit pies, cow pies! It's the same talent!"

Apoca saw it, amazed. "The same talent. That's not supposed to happen."

"Which is maybe why it's a curse. The Curse of Talents!"

"And this Nolan Naga has to handle it," Apoca said grimly. "While courting me."

"Someone has to handle it," Vinia said sensibly. "We can't have every baby delivered with the same talent. Things would get dull in a hurry."

"So do you two have anything to say to me?" the woman inquired tiredly.

Oops! They had forgotten her in the throes of their revelation. But Apoca had a notion. "If the talents are all the same, conjuring pies, maybe you can convince your boy to conjure something other than cow flops. See if you can get him to fetch an apple pie."

The woman looked extremely doubtful, but she grasped desperately at the faint hope. "Bobby," she said carefully to the baby. "Fetch a nice apple pie."

The boy looked at her. Then a pie appeared in his hands.

Victory! They had not only verified the curse, they had maybe solved the woman's problem of sh*t. Why would the baby bother with manure when he could have apple pie?

"Thank you," the woman sighed, vastly relieved.

"You are welcome," Apoca said, and hastily retreated.

Back by themselves, as they walked toward the Lips section, they found their relief short-lived. "That's an awful curse," Vinia said. "But maybe it's limited to those three."

"Maybe. Check your paths to see if there are any others."

The girl checked. "Oh no! There are paths going every which way."

"Which likely means that every new baby here has the same talent. We just didn't know it because it takes a while for a talent to manifest."

"That's a disaster! Xanth has always had all different talents, or at least variations. Whose fault is it?"

"Baby talents are Dwarf Demon business. Nobody messes with a capital-D Demon of any type."

"Nobody except Squid." Squid was the alien land cuttlefish who thought of herself as a girl, who had somehow managed to nab the horrendously powerful Demon Chaos as her boyfriend and saved the universe. Apoca suspected there was quite a story there.

"Nobody else," Apoca said. "But you know, your paths might lead us there to that Demon, if we were foolish enough to try it."

"They might, not that we'd ever be that foolish."

"Better to leave it with Nolan."

Vinia glanced at her. "Do we think he's smart enough to handle it on his own?"

Apoca frowned. "He's a man. He's bound to bungle it."

They laughed. It was a standard joke in the feminist community.

Then they sobered. "Do you think a challenge as great as this one is bound to be, should be left to a man?" Vinia asked.

"With all the women of Thanx and maybe Xanth, too, hostage to his success?"

They looked at each other and shuddered in unison. "We maybe do have to do it ourselves," Vinia said.

Apoca sighed. "Nolan wants to woo me. He had better be one handsome lout."

They laughed again, but it was a weak one. Apoca really did want to find a suitable man before she got much older, but the fact that one liked her look was no guarantee that he was the right one.

"Maybe you should check him out in the magic mirror."

Now, why hadn't she thought of that herself? She hardly needed to guess at the naga prince's appearance; the mirror would show her. Not that how he looked was really that important. It was character she sought, and a decent magic talent. "I'd better." Not that even this would prove anything that mattered. Maybe she was overly cynical about men, having fought them so long.

Then it came to her. She didn't have to commit to the man in order to accompany him on his mission, which did require competent performance. She could phrase it as a trial association, by the end of which she would decide whether to consent to his suit. That would provide her time to properly assess his character.

Because though many marriages were made when little hearts flew between two people, that was not always the case. Apoca was too complicated a person to be defined by such a signal. She needed to really know a man before she decided.

Reassured, she walked on.

They did visit the magic mirror that Thanx had obtained from Prince Ion, who used it to stay in touch with his parents and was happy to share once Vinia had pointed out the advantages of regular communications. Vinia was already being wifely to him, and it made him a better person. Men of any age required proper management. The looking glass was useful for searching out lost folk, exploring one's suppressed emotions, and for communication with the dignitaries of other kingdoms. "Hello, Mirror," she said.

"Hello, Queen Apoca," it replied. "And Vinia." For the girl was standing beside her. "What brings you to consult with me?"

"Prince Nolan Naga is coming to court me. Is he a suitable prospect?" It wasn't what she had meant to ask; she must be more nervous than she thought.

"Yes."

Just like that? She did not fully trust this, but it was useless to argue a case with the mirror. "Show him to me."

The picture appeared in the mirror. It showed a man exactly her own age with startling plaid hair and eyes. Yet, apart from that, he was reasonably handsome. Then it changed to his serpent form, with plaid scales. Then to his fish form, also with plaid scales. "Oh my," she breathed.

"Your hair is turning plaid," Vinia said.

"It does that when my reactions are mixed. I didn't realize he was a shape-changer, though of course as a naga he would be, at least to the extent of his ancestral components. He actually is handsome."

"He sure is," the girl agreed. Her dawning maidenhood made her interested in appearances, though she was of course completely committed to young Magician Prince Ion.

Apoca had one more question for the mirror. "Why does he want to court me?"

"He likes your plaid hair. His mother has plaid panties, which compelled the attention of his father, so plaid is in his makeup."

"But that's ridiculous! He doesn't even know me."

The mirror was silent; she had not asked it a question. Anyway it generally limited any person to three answers, and she had used hers up. Was Nolan suitable, what did he look like, and why was he courting her.

"Thank you, Mirror," she said, suppressing her unjustified annoyance.

"You are welcome, Queen Apoca." The mirror went blank.

"So I guess we are committed," Vinia said.

"To the mission, yes," Apoca agreed. "Not to the man, for me. Actually, it's not something you need to do."

"Yes, I do."

"Why? You know it could be dangerous."

"Three reasons. First I'm your friend, and I want to support you in danger as well as in safety, and I can choose the safest paths. Second, the job really needs doing, and I know I can help. Third, the paths indicate I should; they become sour the moment I think about turning away. Fourth, I was the protagonist for the last adventure, which led me to you, and I guess I'm not quite used to being a background character again, so if you're the protagonist now, I want to stick with you to maybe halfway share the feeling of it. Does that make any sense?"

Apoca just hugged her, pleased with her support regardless of the number of her reasons. "What else do your paths indicate?"

Vinia looked. "We need more people, to make it safer and get the right things done."

"Now, how do mere colored paths show a thing like that? It's not a direction, it's a concept."

The girl smiled. "When I thought about going ahead as we are, the path I am on dimmed a little. When I thought about adding someone, it brightened."

"So it seems that your talent is maturing as you grow, and you are getting better at interpreting its nuances. It's not just direction but quality."

"I guess. I am getting more comfortable with it as time passes."

Apoca nodded. "A Quest, which is really what this is, normally requires one protagonist plus about five supportive Companions. Nolan Naga and I may share protagonism, and you can be a Companion, so there are several slots available. There must be a way leading to a good additional Companion. Go for it."

The girl set off, following the invisible path. This led, surprisingly, to the haunted house that several Mundanian ghosts had refurbished, making it look every bit as haunted as it was. And to Ghorgeous Ghost, whom Vinia had helped by enabling her to solve the mystery of her own murder so that not only was justice served but she and her ghost friends had been freed to come to Thanx. She remained as stunningly beautiful as she had been the day she died, except that features like her hair, eyes, and figure were now changeable. Apoca knew that Vinia envied the woman's appearance, though she was becoming increasingly esthetic herself.

"It's good to see you, Vinia," Ghorgeous exclaimed mentally so that it seemed almost like verbal speech. At the moment her tresses were sky blue, with a smattering of tiny white clouds. "You too, Queen Apoca. What brings you to our humble neck of the whoods?" She tended to add ghostly *h*'s to stray words.

"My paths led me to you, just as they did last year," Vinia explained. "We must go on a maybe dangerous Quest, and we need Companions who can help."

Ghorgeous made a ghostly laugh. "I doubt I qualify. I'm dead. Remember? If you get stuck in a bog, I can't pull you out. You need someone solid."

"The paths don't lie. We need you."

"There are ways you might help," Apoca said. "If I got stuck in a bog, you could fly to tell Vinia so she could organize a rescue. Actually, you could fly ahead to spy out the terrain and warn us about the bog so we wouldn't run afoul of it."

"Um, maybe so," the ghost agreed thoughtfully.

"And you could wrap around me to make me look different," Vinia said. "In case we encountered brute men who wanted to catch me for I can't imagine what. Maybe like an ogress."

Apoca exchanged an adult look with Ghorgeous. The girl plainly had half a notion what brute men do, maybe even three-quarters. She was verging on teen-pretty. Some men preferred that to adult comely and weren't fastidious about age. She might indeed need protection.

"I could facilitate some illusion," the ghost agreed. "And maybe spook a foe into retreating. That might even be fun." She expanded into a fearsome figure with glinting gimlet eyes and horrendously long fangs.

There was most of a pause. "So?" Vinia prompted.

"Unless you have other commitments," Apoca said. "This may be quite a distracting adventure and take some time."

The ghost decided as she reverted to normal. "Actually I'm bhored out of my ghourd. We have refurbished the house, and others know we're harmless. We even have children's nights for spooky stories. All ghood clean fun, but I have a frustrated taste for nhaughty adventure. This could represent a nice break. I will join your Quest."

"Oh, thank you!" Vinia exclaimed, hugging her by making a loop of her arms around the place where Ghorgeous hovered.

Apoca suspected that this would be the first Quest with a ghost Companion. But why not? Ghorgeous was a good person, regardless.

She glanced at the baton. It seemed resigned. So did Nimbus, who had stayed out of the dialogue.

"There's another path," Vinia announced.

"Follow it," Apoca said. This might even be the first Quest wherein they selected Companions in advance, rather than letting them accumulate naturally. Nolan Naga might be surprised to discover what he was walking into.

This one led to the slum section of a neighboring kingdom. There were no border guards or other defenses because nobody cared about the rabble here.

"Uh-oh," Ghorgeous murmured. "This looks to be heading toward Phun Ghent."

Apoca shuddered but did not comment. Maybe it was orienting on someone else.

"Who?" Vinia asked.

"Phun Ghent," Ghorgeous repeated. "Pun Gent to you. It's a medium-length story. We ghosts know it well, because it involves a witch and a pariah, things we relate to. No need to bhore you with it."

Vinia came to a stop on the invisible path, and the others had to pause also, as they did not know where it was leading. "There's something weird about this. The path is turning yellow. That means doubt. But it flashed green when you mentioned Pun Gent, so that is where it leads. I think we'd better figure it out before we get in trouble."

"Good thinking," Apoca agreed. "Give her the background story, Ghorgeous."

"It is this," the ghost said. "Ghent was an ordinary man, very nice and polite, with the talent of killing wheeds. Folk traded him favors for his service in clearing out the wheeds in their yards. He was handsome, and girls were interested in him. He had a bright fhuture."

"But something happened," Vinia said wisely.

"Yes. It was a shame. He got mixed up about an address and didn't know he had the wrong house. There was a six-sided yard solidly clogged with witch grass. So he focused, and in an hour cleared it out to the last nhoxious blade. The yard was nhothing but bare dirt, ready for something better to be planted. The witch grass would never come back. That was part of his talent. When he abolished a wheed, it stayed ghone. He had done a good job."

"So what went wrong?"

"Then the witch returned. Her name was Craft. She had carefully cultivated that garden for her own purposes, as there are special magic properties in that particular grass that are essential to assorted potions. That's why it is named as it is; witches depend on it."

"Uh-oh."

"Exactly. Witch Craft was furious. She thought he had dhone it on purpose to spite her. So she phunished him with a nhoxious hex."

"The yard!" Vinia exclaimed. "Six-sided. A hexagon."

"Yes, she specialized in hexes. Others call them curses. She was as good at her specialty as he was in his. All because of a misunderstanding."

"What was the curse?"

"To speak only in phuns, until he finds the phundit who could tell him how to stop it. Since then he has become a pariah, because his presence gives others phundigestion and they can't stand the stench of it. His life is a shamble, and his future is past."

"Punish," Vinia said, working it out. "Pun-ish. With puns."

"Exactly."

"And the path is taking us to him, to have him join our Quest."

"So it seems," Apoca said.

"But why would we need him? How could endless puns possibly help the mission?"

"That is the question of the hour."

"Your paths," Ghorgeous said. "Can they show you the way to answering that qhuestion?"

"Maybe. I don't know."

"Think about our doing the mission with Pun Gent," Apoca suggested. "See what lights up. Then think about doing it without him. Something else is bound to show. Then tell us what the difference is between them. That may clarify it."

The girl concentrated. "Without him"—she shuddered—"the paths are black. That means doom."

"Ouch," Apoca and the ghost said, almost together. The mission could not be accomplished without the punster?

"With him"—she looked half surprised—"right into the pundemic zone."

The pundemic zone. That was a huge region that had formed when puns had multiplied uncontrollably following the unpun plague. They had had to bring puns out of storage to replace them, and it had gone too far. They had averted pundemonium only by magically wafting them into a largely unsettled region, where they festered on their own. Nobody went there voluntarily, except maybe criminals who knew they would not be pursued there. It had become a no sane man's land.

"And there we have our answer," Apoca said. "We need the punster to navigate the pundemic without losing his mind."

"Or ours," Vinia said, making a face of distaste.

"Because the satisfaction of the Qhuest must be there," Ghorgeous said.

The three of them shuddered in unison. This was bound to be bad. Nimbus and the baton remained silent, but it was clear with barely a trace of cloudy that they were not much thrilled either.

Yet it seemed it had to be done. They nerved themselves and moved grimly onward.

Soon they reached Gent's house. It looked like an ordinary run-down hovel, except that there were no weeds. Apoca suspected that even the local rabble avoided the occupant. *He must be a lonely man.* She had a notion how that was, because of her position and her double talent. That latter was one of the things that she and Vinia had in common, though their talents were completely different; they would always be fast friends.

"This is the place," Vinia said.

Apoca knocked on the door. In half a moment a handsome young man opened it. "Watt mae eye dew four yew?" he inquired politely.

He was speaking in homophones! That might be considered a form of punning. If that was the worst of it, they could handle it.

"You are Pun Gent?" Apoca asked, making quite sure.

"Aye AM." That was AM as in PM, hardly even a homophone.

"I am Apoca of the Lips tribe, with my friends Vinia, Ghorgeous Ghost, and Nimbus Nickelpede. We have come to invite you to join us in an important Quest."

He frowned. "Ewe cant bee serial."

And some words were simply wrong. It seemed the curse prevented him from using the right words, one way or another, even when it had to stretch credulity.

"I am serious," she said firmly. "I know that you suffer from a witch's curse and can't speak sensibly. But can you nod or shake your head as I talk?"

He nodded, looking relieved. Effective communication had to be an issue with him.

"It appears that Thanx, and maybe Xanth itself, is suffering from a kind of curse that causes all newly delivered babies to have the same talent, that of summoning pies. Apple pies, mud pies, cow pies, whatever. It gets messy. Our mission, as we interpret it, is to rectify this problem before too many more babies are spoiled. Vinia here has a touch for finding the right route to lead us to the solution. Unfortunately it leads right into the pundemic zone. We don't think we can handle that ourselves."

"Eye aim knot gooing their!" Gent protested. "Ime slick oaf pens!"

"But we nheed you," Ghorgeous said.

He looked at her. "Isle bee candied. Aye loaf lee wombat lake yoo cud charnel mee unto ding eat wit aye keys, butt yore knot reel."

Apoca stifled a smile. He had tried to call her a lovely woman, but it had come out "loaf lee wombat," and doing it with a kiss had become "ding eat wit aye keys." A curse indeed. This might take some getting used to.

"I am rheel," Ghorgeous said as firmly as her ethereal state allowed. "Merely without my late body. I can firm up small parts of it at need. I could kiss you if I focused."

"Bout your steel uh goose."

She nodded. "But I am still a ghost," she agreed. She seemed to have no trouble understanding him. "I'd love to have a handsome man like you to charm, but I know my limitation. Still, you should out of common decency consider our proposal."

He shook his head. "Eye fuel bat abate at, butt eye cant facet moor pains."

"You feel bad about it," the ghost translated. "But can't face more puns."

"Yew canny union staid meal!"

"I can understand you," Ghorgeous agreed. "Because I am mostly reading your mind to get your meaning, as I do for the others." She quirked a trace of a smile. "Being discorporate has its minor points."

"Yeast."

"Yes."

"We have a problem," Apoca said. "We really do need you to handle the abominable puns." She glanced at Vinia. "True?"

"True," Vinia said. "All the other paths lose their green, and some are downright black."

"Watt ism tis groin?"

"What is this green?" Ghorgeous translated. She looked at Apoca. "Can we safely answer?"

Apoca was firm. "Not unless he joins the mission. We do have privacy issues."

"Eye aim knot journeying yore misting."

"Bleep," Apoca swore. She could express herself more effectively, but not in the presence of a child. "Am I going to have to kiss you?"

He laughed. "Eye no yore Lisp clams. Eye donate bereave theme."

So he was a skeptic about the love-slave properties of the Lips kisses, the more fool he. "You would kiss me?"

He nodded. He thought that a Lips kiss was just a smooch. She would have to make him a believer.

"I wouldn't," Ghorgeous said warningly.

"Eye wood."

"Then do it," Apoca said, stepping up to face him closely. She knew she was an attractive woman, and she had seen him eyeing her, as he had Ghorgeous. He was foolishly interested.

He didn't hesitate. He truly believed that the Lips talent was fake. He took her in his arms and soundly kissed her mouth. He probably hadn't been able to do that with a willing woman since the curse.

The Lips folk didn't have to kiss for effect; they could be normal when they chose. In regular family relationships they were just like regular women. But this was a special occasion. She put her magic into it, kissing for effect. She felt the power of it passing from her lips to his, and on into him. He was done for.

Gent fell back, half stunned.

"Uh-oh," Ghorgeous said for him.

"You are now my love slave," Apoca said, knowing that her hair was turning plaid because she was concealing any emotions she might have had. This was a necessary process. "My whim is your command. We will not be lovers. You will merely gladly obey my every command. I shall not be a harsh mistress, and I will let you go when my need for your services is over."

He nodded assent. It was not in him to oppose any wish of hers. He had become a believer the hard way.

"You expressed aversion to entering the region of the pundemic," she continued. "But we need your help there. I regret putting you through this, but it is necessary to facilitate our larger purpose. I can if necessary direct you to suppress your aversion, and that should abate it, at least to an extent."

He nodded again, amenable to whatever she wanted.

"We do have some trouble understanding your speech, so when you have to talk, Ghorgeous will translate. When you need to find something, such as a safe place to sleep, Vinia will show you where. Trust her; she knows."

He nodded once more.

"Do you have any questions?"

Now he spoke. "Yeast. Wren dew oui startle?"

Ghorgeous smiled. "When do we start?" she translated.

"Within a few days. So organize your home for your absence, and prepare a knapsack with supplies for yourself, as we can't be sure we will always be near pie plants or blanket trees. Ghorgeous will notify you when we are ready."

He nodded once more and retreated into his house.

Apoca glanced at the others. "Now we should do the same for ourselves."

"Adventure, here we come!" Vinia exclaimed with youthful enthusiasm. Apoca refrained from commenting, being less thrilled by the prospect.

They organized. Vinia clarified things with Ion and his sister Princess Hilda; Ghorgeous informed her ghost friends, and Nimbus let the nickelpedes know. Apoca and Vinia packed food and supplies, and Vinia fetched a chip of wood from the haunted house so that Ghorgeous would have it to orient on, as otherwise she would have been limited in range. The ghosts were no longer absolutely bound, but they got uncomfortable too far away from the house. Apoca explained things to Queen Demesne, who was happy to have a competent team on the case. They were ready.

The next morning, Ghorgeous appeared before Apoca. "Vinia says he's coming within the hour! There's a bright-green path to where we can meet him. She's rousting out Gent now."

"Thank you. Tell her to swing by here so I can join you." Apoca was already appreciating the usefulness of the ghost in coordinating things.

Soon they were together. Apoca knew her hair was bright plaid as she suppressed her horrendously mixed feelings about this whole adventure. She wanted to save the talents for the babies, yes, and she was intrigued about being seriously courted. But the whole thing was such a challenge!

It seemed like just a moment before they were organized as a unified party and heading out to meet Prince Nolan. There across the field was a male figure. Apoca saw the plaid color of his head. That was him!

Apoca gritted her teeth and marched forward. She hoped, ridiculously, that she was looking suitably regal. Or at least attractive. Or something.

Chapter 3

PUNDEMIC

Nolan saw the approaching party: a woman, a girl, and a man. Who were they?

"See the plaid!" Aurora exclaimed in his mind. "That's the one!"

Now he saw it: the woman had plaid hair. She was the one. Indeed, the Baton of Protagonism was flying from her. It had done its job and was reverting to its home base: him.

Suddenly his knees felt shaky. He had used the protected paths to make his way to the Queendom of Thanx, intent on catching and wooing his ideal woman. He hadn't thought much about the details of interaction. And there she was. With another man.

"There are men in the queendom," Aurora reminded him. "She can work with them without committing to them."

Oh, of course. He had to beware of unfounded assumptions.

"That's right," the ant said. "In fact, it's probably just as well I'm along. You don't seem to know much about handling women."

She had him dead to rights. He had interacted with women all his life but never courted one before. Suddenly he cared about this one's personal reactions.

"I will whisper in your ear, as it were, so you don't foul up too badly."

"Thanks," he said sincerely. He had not realized before how much difference female guidance could make in a situation like this.

"All part of the deal. I need to keep you on course so you can find us a suitable location. That won't work well if you alienate your desired woman at the outset."

She was right, again. Her mind was as fiery in its fashion as her burning talent.

"Thank you." He felt her pleasure. But he would have to watch his incidental thoughts, lest he inadvertently annoy her.

"You are catching on."

He walked on.

The other party walked on too. In barely three and a half moments they came together. "Hello, Nolan Naga," the woman said. "I am Apoca Lips." She indicated the girl. "This is my friend Vinia, who will assist us in locating and traveling safe paths through the wilderness." She touched her own shoulder, where a deadly bug perched. "This is my friend Nimbus Nicklepede, who will assist with tangled terrain and with liaison with others of her kind." She indicated the man. "This is my love slave Pun Gent, who will help us handle the clustering puns." She gestured to an empty space. "This is Ghorgeous Ghost, who will help with communications. Ghorgeous, present yourself to him, so he knows you."

There was a flicker in the air before his face, and the translucent face of a marvelously lovely woman formed. "Hello, Nolan," she said via a projection to his mind. "And Aurora Ant." She faded out to a faint flicker.

"Hello, Ghost," Aurora thought, surprised. "So you are telepathic!"

"Not exactly. I am amorphous. I touched the two of you with my invisible substance and picked up your thoughts. Without that contact I could not communicate well."

"It seems they already have the Quest organized," Nolan murmured in a thought, taken aback.

"They're women." That of course explained it. Women liked to organize personal details. "Now graciously acknowledge."

He opened his mouth. "Uh—"

"Well spoken, Prince," Apoca said. "Shall we be on our way?" She glanced at the girl.

"Vinia," Aurora said in his mind. That was just as well, because Nolan had lost track in the welter of introductions. "Ghorgeous updated me. She sees paths."

Vinia nodded. "The greenest path is right now."

Apoca looked at Nolan. "Green is best. We can't see the colors, but she can. We will follow her."

Just like that, they were on their way, with the baton hovering near Nolan.

"Apoca makes the decisions?" he asked the ant silently.

"Well, Apoca is a queen," Aurora said. "Accustomed to command. No fainting flower. Is that the kind you like?"

He realized that he had not had any real expectations about the woman. He had been compelled by her plaid hair, which it was now apparent was a temporary color; at the moment it was green, which he presumed was positive. Regardless, she remained a most intriguing woman. "She has a fine figure."

"I will take that as a yes," Aurora said, amused.

He found himself walking beside Apoca. "Not coincidence," Aurora said. "She is curious about you. This is your chance to make a good initial impression."

"Well, fancy meeting you here, Prince," Apoca said.

"Say something clever," the ant advised.

"Uh—"

"I understand you came to court me because of my hair."

This one he could answer. "Not exactly. The Good Magician told me you were my ideal woman."

"The current question is whether you are my ideal man."

Aurora made a mental picture of a man fending off the thrust of a spear. "Don't respond to that directly. She's poking at you to see how you react."

He rallied to the challenge. "Then I saw you in a magic mirror, and your hair was plaid, like mine."

"And for you that was sufficient."

"Trap!" Aurora warned. "Don't agree."

"No," he said. "I liked that your hair seemed to match mine, but I had to get to know you personally before I could judge your fitness for me."

"So you could verify my figure."

He didn't even need the ant's warning. Apoca had one of the finest figures in Xanth. But it annoyed him to be tested like this. He was, after all, a prince. So he gave an answer calculated to annoy her also. "That too."

She laughed. "So you do have some spunk."

He had to smile. "Some," he agreed.

"Maybe we'll get along."

"We will if you so choose."

She nodded and was silent.

"Good riposte," the ant commented. The baton nodded as well.

The ghost appeared. "Something magic this way comes."

Vinia looked, surprised. "But the path is green."

"Prince Magician Ion and Princess Sorceress Hilda," Ghorgeous clarified. "They're green too."

Something appeared in the sky, approaching them. It turned out to be a small flying carpet carrying two people, male and female. "Oh, I forgot to say goodbye," Vinia said ruefully. Then she explained. "I love Ion, and will marry him when we grow up. But we do spend time apart so as not to get on each other's nerves. He is the Magician of Immunity to All Elixirs, and she is the Sorceress of Sewing. She sewed that magic carpet, for example. They're both nice people."

The carpet landed ahead of them and the girl got off. She was a child of twelve with dark hair through which a white stripe passed. She carried a ball of wool. "We forgot to give you the vac scene," she said, handing the ball to Vinia.

Vinia looked at it. "The what scene?"

"The vac scene. Fortunately Ion has a supply. It will make you immune to the pundemic. You don't want to get infected, get pundigestion, and start emitting foul puns so that nobody can stand to be near you. That's too much punishment."

"We don't," Vinia agreed, mortified. "I never thought of that."

"Neither did we. But Benny did. He has a caprine mind, delving into places it shouldn't. I love it, especially when we are truly private. So we flew to intercept you."

"Benny is Hilda's human-goat half-breed boyfriend," Ghorgeous clarified for Nolan. "A nice guy, though he has some private billy-goat thoughts."

"Which must be what Hilda likes about him," Aurora said.

"Nice girls do like naughty boys," the ghost agreed.

"Thanks," Vinia said weakly to Hilda. "Um, how does it work?"

"It's a vapor. Get in the ball and pop the vial open and breathe, and it's done. But there is a side effect, which is why it's not more widely used."

"Side effect?"

Hilda whispered something in her ear.

Vinia blushed. Nolan suspected she was getting better at it as she approached maidenhood. "I'll warn the others."

"In due course. Right now you have to take it, because I need to take the ball back. There's too much good yarn in it to waste."

"But—"

Hilda handed her a vial, then touched the ball. It expanded explosively and became a large sphere with a round opening in the side. "Time for your vac scene," she called to the others. "Get in the ball."

Impressed by the princessly tone of command, Nolan, Apoca, and Gent followed Vinia into the ball, and Ghorgeous joined them. "I dhon't want to get infected either," she explained. "Puns are best left to themselves, especially the foul ones. That mheans most of them."

The inside of the ball was a surprisingly spacious chamber; they all fit comfortably. Light filtered in through the stretched fabric. *This must be another example of the princess's impressive sewing,* Nolan thought. The entrance irised closed.

Vinia broke open the vial. Vapor spread out. They all breathed it, having no choice, and all except Gent and the baton went into uncontrollable laughter that continued until stifled by coughing fits. Nolan had never heard an ant or nickelpede laughing before. *Oh, that must be the side effect!* It passed in about a moment and a third but felt like twice as long. Laughing without humor was like vomiting from an empty stomach. Gent was unaffected because he already had pundigestion, and the baton was not a person but an imaginary symbol.

"That must be the reaction that will be stifled when we encounter the puns," Aurora said as she recovered her poise.

"I didn't know ants laughed."

"We don't. We don't even breathe. This is a first for me. It must be for Nimbus too."

"And for me, as a ghost," Ghorgeous said. "I prefer spooky laughter. That is potent stuff."

"But worth it if it protects us from being like Gent," Nolan said. Their dialogue was silent, so Gent was not being insulted.

The iris opened and they stepped out. "You have had the vac scene," Hilda said.

"Thank you," Vinia said as the ball compacted.

"Just fix the talents," Hilda said as she returned to the carpet. "I don't know which is worse, babies conjuring stinky cow pies or friends vomiting laughter."

Vinia ran to the carpet to plant a surprisingly mature kiss on her fiancé. Then she returned to resume her identification of the green path as the carpet took off.

"Prince Ion is lame," Ghorgeous said. "He must either ride a carpet or get help walking, so he mostly stays put."

"There's something we weren't told," Aurora said. "I distrust that side effect."

"A little laughing fit won't hurt us."

"If that's all it is, why didn't the whole queendom get vac scened?"

"Maybe there's not enough to go around."

"Maybe." The dialogue lapsed, as it tended to do when not prompted. But she had planted a seed of doubt. Was there something else? Some reason folk didn't like to use the vac scene? Were they being unreasonable, or did they know something? Nolan would be alert for it.

In due course Vinia paused. "We are at the fringe of the pundemic zone," she said as the others caught up to her. "We don't know exactly what to expect. The paths show the route, but they don't explain it. It is probably best to take our potty breaks before we get into it. This spot is safe from puns and other threats, but I don't know how far out that's true."

"So stay close in," Apoca said. She plainly had no fear of the wilderness. Nolan liked that. In fact, he liked everything about her, so far, even her reservations about him. She was very much her own woman. The naga folk would surely accept her as their queen, in due course, though she was no crossbreed.

The small group scattered into the surrounding bushes. Nolan noted where Apoca went, then chose an adjacent path. He didn't want to spy on her, but he liked being near her. He did his business, then paused. Something was hovering before him.

Then Aurora caught on. "The ghost, Ghorgeous. I feel her mind."

"Hello, Ghorgeous," he murmured. "I didn't know you liked to spy on the privacy of stray men."

The ghost laughed and became more visible, presenting a scintillating outline. "You're a handsome lout, but that's not my purpose at the moment. I ranged outward, just checking, and spied some maenad types in the area near where Apoca is pausing. I thought you might want to know."

Maenads. Nolan knew of them. They were a species of nymph in the form of naked, raging women, insatiably violent and bloodthirsty. He had encountered some on occasion, quickly discovering that though they had marvelous bodies, they were not ideal girlfriends. They might pretend to be amenable to a man's interest, but it was only a ruse to get close enough to take a bite out of him. They were bad news. "Thanks. But I don't want to intrude on Apoca's privacy. Live women can get upset about that sort of thing."

She laughed again. "Dead women, too, if we had functions. But those maenads are armed with stick-hers. Those are sticks used only by girls on girls. There are five 'nads. She's likely to need help."

Surely so. "Can you lead me there?"

"Now." She floated into the brush.

He followed. "How can you range out anywhere?" Aurora asked the ghost as they moved. "I thought ghosts were bound to their haunts."

"Vinia has a chip of wood from our haunted house. I have to stay within a comfortable range of it, or I lose coherence."

Nolan was interested. If by some mischance they lost Vinia, they would lose Ghorgeous, too, unless someone recovered the chip. They did need to stay together.

In no more than another moment and a half they heard a scream close ahead. It was not the gentle scream of a surprised woman but the exultant sound of a predator closing on prey.

Nolan changed to naga form, becoming a serpent with a human head. His human clothing snapped into his magic pouch as it was spelled to do, carrying his sheathed sword and Aurora Ant along. He slithered rapidly toward the sound.

In another half moment he burst upon the scene. There was Apoca with a club of her own, about to be beset by the maenads. She might take out one or two or even three, but not all five. She was a queen, not an Amazon. That was, of course, why the maenads hunted in a pack.

Nolan roared, calling attention to himself as he charged. The maenads would have trouble attacking him, because his coils were low and writhing, and because their stick-hers would be ineffective against a male. But mainly because if there was one thing a maenad feared, it was a big, aggressive serpent. There was something about his sinuous masculine shape that freaked them out.

"I wonder what that could be?" Aurora asked rhetorically, amused.

The maenads screamed in horror and fled. In three-quarters of a moment they were gone. That was just as well, for them, because he would have laid them out in short order and eaten one or two of them. Or worse, had Apoca not been present.

Apoca faced him, not at all affrighted. "Well, thank you, prince. You saved me an awkward encounter."

"You saved her from getting bludgeoned and eaten," Aurora said. "And she knows it."

"I doubt it," he answered her silently. "The ghost could have spooked them off by assuming the semblance of a zombie ogre hungry for live meat."

"Then why didn't she?"

"She was setting it up for me," he said, realizing. "So I could properly impress Apoca."

The ant nodded mentally. "You owe Ghorgeous one."

"I do." The ghost had faded out when the action started, leaving the scene to him.

"Oh, go ahead and change back," Apoca said, mistaking the reason for his pause. "I know what men look like."

She surely did. He had hesitated because the pouch magic was one-way. It brought in his clothing and equipment as he changed forms, becoming a sealed band about his middle, but could not reverse the process.

Nolan reverted to human form, standing briefly naked as he fished in the pouch for his apparel. It helped that he knew he had a good human body in all its parts.

Apoca neither flinched nor stared as he fished his clothing out of the magic pouch and donned it, but her glance was appraising. "And you didn't even need your sword. Nimbus says you look good enough to eat."

For the moment he had forgotten the nickelpede who traveled with her, just as Aurora traveled with him. "Thank you, Nimbus." The bug raised her tail in acknowledgment.

Aurora was not impressed. "The bug knows I'd toast her if she tried to chomp you."

The baton nodded. Nolan hadn't thought of the fire ant as protection, but she was.

Apoca smiled. "We are glad you were close enough to help."

"Ghorgeous told me the maenads were coming, so I hurried."

"Ah. She is helpful." She quirked a smile. "Maybe there will come an occasion when I rescue you similarly."

"She is flirting," Aurora said. "Hinting that you might see a flash of her naked, as she saw you."

"I look forward to that," he said aloud.

Their dialogue ran out of fuel and puttered to a halt as they returned to the invisibly green path. Apoca walked closer to him now. He had indeed impressed her, thanks to the ghost. It also suggested that Apoca had no concern at all about his being a crossbreed.

Soon the group re-formed and resumed traveling. In due course they entered the nefarious pundemic zone. They could tell by the scenery, which somehow looked worn out, as if by too much groaning. Closest to the path there was a row of dresses with arithmetic symbols.

They continued walking, but somehow made no progress. It was as if their feet were pushing back an invisible moving belt. What was happening?

Apoca seemed to understand. "Gent," she murmured.

Now Pun Gent called out the sights. "Add Dress," he said, pointing out the one with a large plus sign. "Minus Dress," with the minus sign. "Multiply Dress" with a big X. "Divide Dress" with its sign. All of them were attractive, apart from their signs.

Nolan suppressed a groan. How bad was this going to get?

"They might fit me," Vinia said. "When I come of age."

"There have to be better places to window shop," Apoca said.

Yet now they had passed the dresses. "Each abysmal pun has to be recognized before we can pass," Aurora said. "I remember now."

And that was why the punster was with them.

"Did you notice Gent is no longer talking in homonyms?" the ant asked. "He is in his element now, so the curse may be irrelevant."

"Good point."

Then Nolan noticed that Apoca was looking at him with surprise. He glanced down. His posterior was bare. His clothing was intact, yet had become translucent in that area. What had happened to it?

There was something else. Apoca's own midsection was similarly exposed. And Vinia's. And Ghorgeous's. Only Gent's clothing was opaque.

Apoca saw his look and glanced down. "Oh, beans!" she swore. Apparently that word was not bleepable.

"I meant to warn you," Vinia said. "It seems the side effect is em-bare-ass-ment."

Nolan kept his mouth shut. The fact was that both Apoca and the ghost had very nice behinds, and Vinia's was showing early promise, with or without clothing.

"This is bleep on modesty," Ghorgeous lamented. "I thought I'd be immune to any physical effects."

The baton seemed amused.

Nolan pieced it together. "When we run afoul of awful puns, our posteriors show. Embarrassment."

"Hilda didn't give us time to consider," Vinia said, trying to cover her midsection, but it wasn't working. "She knew we might balk if we knew."

"Which would have been too bad," Apoca said grimly. "Because we do need to accomplish the mission."

Nolan tried to direct his gaze elsewhere, but it resisted. Gent, who was fully covered, was attempting the same, but the ghost's fine form had a lock on his eyes.

"Oh, gho ahead and look," Ghorgeous snapped, completely aware of their gazes. "We're all in the same bhoat, as it were. It's the price of the protection." Apoca nodded agreement, though hardly pleased. Some boats had to navigate rough seas, or "sees" as the pun would have it.

That did seem best. What else could they do?

But in barely (so to speak) half a moment, opacity returned to the clothing. The show was over.

They breathed a collective sigh of relief and walked on, following the green path.

The next section was no better. There was a stick of wood lying across the path, in the form of giant red lips. Beyond it was a tree branch with a similar configuration, and indeed a whole tree resembling a face with a mouth puckered as if for a kiss. Nolan did not know what to make of it. Neither did the others.

"Lip stick," Gent said, kicking the branch out of the way. It made a bzzzt sound as if giving him a raspberry; indeed a red raspberry popped out. He indicated the branch. "Lip branch." The lips formed into a kiss. Then the tree. "Lip tree." The other branches moved forward as if to embrace him, but he avoided them. "Mouth stick, face stick," he concluded. "Not even very good puns. This is a weed tree." Now the branches tried to smite him for the insult, but he was already out of their range.

So they had passed another pun cluster. Nolan was coming to appreciate the man more.

The bare-bottom show was back. Walking next behind Apoca, Nolan realized that there were incidental benefits to the side effect. She had a very nice walk.

"But what about when she walks behind you?" Aurora asked.

"She's as interested in your butt as you are in hers," Ghorgeous said.

She was? That was interesting in another manner. But then the effect faded. It seemed that even an egregious collection of puns could embarrass them only so long.

They came to a big sign: weap. "Uh-oh," Gent said.

"What does it mean?" Apoca asked.

"This marks a region of weap-puns," Gent explained. "They can be dangerous."

And the show was on again. It was now clear why the people of the Queendom of Thanx weren't using the vac scene. It made for too much scenery.

"Oh, come now," Apoca protested. "Puns can be obnoxious, sometimes sickening, giving you pundigestion and all, but they are dangerous only to your sanity, temporarily. We'll just have to grit our teeth and get through, and maybe wash off the stench of them afterwards." Her gaze flicked downward, as if there were some dirty looks she'd like to wash off too.

The thought of stripping and washing with Apoca appealed to Nolan, but he had the sense to keep his mouth shut.

"Just as well," Aurora said. "She would not be amused."

Gent was adamant. "Not merely sanity, in this case. We'll have to make a detour around it."

Nolan realized that the man might be her love slave, but he did have a mind, and enough will of his own to be sure of protecting her.

Apoca glanced at Vinia. "The best path goes this way," the girl said. "But there are less convenient alternates."

"So we'll make slower progress if we detour?" Apoca asked. Obviously she wanted to get beyond the pundemic miasma as quickly as possible.

"Yes. And encounter worse puns."

Apoca turned back to Gent. "Exactly what is dangerous?"

"The bombs."

"What kind of bombs?"

Gent pointed to a cloud in the shape of a mushroom. "The A-bomb, for one. It can vaporize you, and those it doesn't destroy it douses with unhealthy radiation. They found that out in Mundania. The pun version might not be as lethal, but we don't want to mess with it."

"He is making sense," Nolan said, forcing himself to focus on something other than her midsection exposure.

Apoca looked at an empty space. "Ghorgeous, you're Mundane. Do you know anything about the A-bomb?"

The ghost formed, faintly, as if trying to fog out her nudity. It didn't work; the side effect would not be denied. "It's the most terrible weapon of all. They never should have used it."

"But what about a pun bomb?"

"That would be the P-bomb. The A-bomb is not very funny."

Apoca turned back to Gent. "What else is in this section?"

"The F-bomb."

"What is that? Another mushroom?"

Gent opened his mouth and swore a blue streak. A jet of blue fire shot out, singeing the nearby foliage. Vinia's ears turned blue-red, and Nolan recoiled from the foul heat of it.

Gent took a fresh breath as the noxious blue smoke cleared. "That was an F-bomb. Mine was relatively mild, because the presence of a child caused the worst of it to be bleeped out, but the real thing would be significantly worse."

"He is making sense," Nolan repeated. The man was cursed, but he was sensible.

Apoca was fazed. "Any more bombs?" she asked weakly.

"The H-bomb, and others not yet defined. We won't like them."

"The path seems to go uncomfortably close to the bombs," Vinia said. "I think it just wants to get us there, without being much concerned about our emotional states."

Apoca finally gave up. "Take a detour," she told Vinia with bad grace.

Nolan realized that he was seeing the woman in a bad moment. That didn't bother him; it meant she was human.

They took the detour. The abysmal puns continued, clarified by Gent so they could pass, but no bombs. Their progress was slow and uncertain, as well as explosive, but relatively safe.

Then they came to a house. It was an odd one. It seemed to be squatting on giant chicken legs, though it clearly was no chicken. When it spied them it jumped up, tilting dangerously, spilling small round things from its open windows. One fell near Vinia, who bent to pick it up. "It's a nut!" she exclaimed, surprised.

"It's a nut house," Gent explained.

Nolan and Apoca groaned almost together, turning completely naked. Identified, the house settled back down and let them pass.

Then they came to another oddity. It looked like a Mundane car that had been in a bad accident. Its front fender was dented, one wheel was twisted askew, and its windshield was fragmented. It was a derelict, yet strangely animated, as if fearing yet more damage. Their approach seemed to make it shudder. They were unable to pass by it. What were they missing?

"It is a nervous wreck," Gent said.

Oh. Nolan and Apoca shared another groan and siege of bareness, this time joined by Vinia.

"This is not the place to build our new anthill," Aurora remarked. "Even though our ant abdomens are always bare anyway."

The sky was darkening. "We had better make camp for the night," Nolan said. "Daylight puns are bad enough; we don't want to navigate midnight puns."

"Agreed," Apoca said, slightly surprising him.

Vinia explored her local paths. "This area is safe," she reported. "Deep green throughout. Room enough for us all."

Nolan was coming to appreciate her talent in a new way. She was quite useful on an excursion like this, and not merely to find the best route.

"Which is of course why Apoca picked her as a Companion for this Quest," Aurora said.

This irked him for some obscure reason. He paused to run it down, and caught it. "It's supposed to be my Quest, not hers. The Good Magician gave it to me. I'm supposed to pick my Companions."

"You are courting her, right? Do you want to tell her that?"

And have her get mad and depart, just when he was really appreciating her revealed qualities, physical and mental? He sighed.

"You are better off without the illusion that males run things," the ant continued. "You don't now, never have, and never will truly govern. We females allow you to think you are in charge, to make you halfway docile, is all."

He feared she was correct.

There was a shimmer beside the tent he was pitching. A pair of lips formed in the air before his face. "Mind if I join you?" Ghorgeous Ghost inquired.

"Not at all," Aurora answered without consulting him.

Nolan kept his mouth shut. It wasn't as if he could stop the visit, even if he wanted to. Besides, he owed her.

Soon they were in their tent, with Gent's tent adjacent and Apoca's beyond that. Vinia's tent was nearby. The ghost was lying invisibly beside him.

"So what's on your vaporous mind?" Aurora asked.

Translucent lips formed. "That side effect. Gent was lhooking at me."

"So was Nolan. And you looked at them. You agreed you might as well."

"Nolan lhooked more at Apoca than at me."

"Men do look; they can't help it." It was as if Nolan wasn't there.

"They do," the ghost agreed. "I'm used to it. But here's the thing. I'm lonely. I lost my fiancé over a decade ago, back in Mundania, and he has moved on. I wish him well. But I wish I could have at least a bit of the life I had before. The flirting, the dating, the nhaughty feels, the censored dialogue. I miss it."

"Nolan's not available," the ant reminded her. "He's courting Apoca."

"Yes. But Gent is available."

"And he's halfway normal, here in the pun zone. You've got his interest. But there's a problem. You're a ghost."

"This about that: Ghosts can do more than some folk think, when we try. I can make my face feel solid, so I can kiss."

"What about the rest of you? Men like to get their hands on the soft stuff."

"I can firm that up, too, one place at a time. It works best in the dark, so he can't see my face disappear when I focus on my chest, or wherever. I can give him a good time, piece by piece. That's not the problem."

Nolan realized that it was Aurora the ghost had come to visit, not him. Still, this was interesting. He hadn't realized how much females knew about males, whatever the species.

"Then what is? You know he'll go as far as you enable him to."

"It is whether it is appropriate. There can't be anything permanent. For one thing, he will inevitably age and die, in time, while I will always be twenty-one."

"Still, you could give him several decades."

"But I couldn't marry him. I would be distracting him from whatever living woman might want him. That would not be fair."

"I see your point. But ants don't marry, so I can't advise you on that. You'll have to ask Nolan."

Suddenly Nolan was in the dialogue. "You can do it. Just advise him at the outset that it is only a passing fling, subject to termination at any time by either party. That he should consider living women, and you will fade out when he finds one he likes."

"I hadn't thought of that! But would he really want to make out with a ghost? I mean, looking is one thing, but seriously touching is another. He might be turned off."

"I don't think so. Men like touching even more than looking."

Her eyes grew large and lovely, with deep-blue irises and long lashes. "Would you touch as well as look?"

Oops. "I am oriented on another woman," he said uncomfortably.

"Clarification," Aurora said. "She is not propositioning you. She is asking your opinion as a man."

Oh. "Yes, I would touch."

"Are you sure?"

"She remains uncertain," Aurora said. "Kiss her and pass judgment."

This might be dangerous terrain. "I don't—"

He was cut off by the contact of the ghost's firm lips against his. She kissed him deeply and tenderly. His emotion flared. What a smooch!

She drew back, releasing him from a near freak-out.

". . . see any reason why not," he finished breathlessly.

"Thank you, Nolan."

"You're welcome." He still felt as if he were floating.

"I'll go broach him now." She faded.

"You did well," Aurora said.

"She could have seduced me if she tried. If she had a firmer body."

"That was apparent. You gave her the answer she needed."

"I suppose I did. Now, if only it was as easy with Apoca."

"Well, you might ask her."

"That might turn her off."

"It might," the ant agreed.

They went silent, drifting off to sleep. But the kiss lingered. If Ghorgeous could do that with her mouth, what might she do with her chest? Her legs? She could indeed be a man's lover in the dark.

"But she's not Apoca," Aurora said.

"I envy Gent."

"Surely you do. Now, sleep."

But he couldn't sleep. He kept feeling that kiss.

"You're not even interested in the ghost!" the ant exclaimed.

"True." But the kiss remained.

"For shame's sake! You're all up in a heaval. We've got to erase that kiss!"

Indeed. "How?"

"There's a way. Apoca can do it. She doesn't have to enslave a man; she can do an ordinary kiss when she chooses. She can overwrite the ghost kiss."

"But I don't want to turn her off by appearing to be interested in another female."

"She kissed you."

"But the kiss smote me."

The ant considered. "Apoca should understand. It has to be risked."

That seemed to be true. "Still, she might think I was just trying to sneak one in."

"I will handle it. I will talk to her. Stay here." The ant jumped off his shoulder and hurried into the night. Fortunately Apoca's tent was not far away.

Now it was the prospect of Apoca's kiss that held his attention. What a dream that was! He had been fascinated by her ever since seeing her image. Yes, her lips were huge, but that was her species. She remained a remarkably attractive woman, and surely the right one for him.

Someone approached his tent in the darkness. "Aurora explained," Apoca said. "I understand." She got down on the ground before him. He was aware of her more by sound than sight, but did see the faint plaid of her hair, indicating her mixed thoughts. "This is only a corrective measure, not a commitment. You're courting me. If you are going to be distracted by a kiss, it had better be mine. Besides, I owe you for saving me from the maenads."

Perversely, he tried to argue. "Yes, but Ghorgeous could have—"

Her face intercepted his, downside up. She kissed him.

The ghost's kiss had made him feel as if he were floating. Apoca's kiss lifted him literally off the ground so that his back nudged the roof of the tent.

She ended it after an eternal instant. "That should do it." She got back to her feet and departed.

"Now you can sleep," Nimbus said as he slowly sank back to the ground. She had evidently transferred to him during the kiss.

Nimbus? "Where's Aurora?" he demanded, alarmed.

"Peace," the nickelpede said. "She's getting to know Apoca, just as I am getting to know you. We are all on this mission together and need to know each other well, in case there's a complication." She communicated by contact telepathy, just as Aurora did.

That did make sense when he considered it. This could also be a source of information about Apoca's real feelings toward him.

"Ha! I will never tell you about her suppressed interest in your lean bare butt, just as Aurora will be silent about yours in her plush butt. It wouldn't be ethical."

"What do nickelpedes know or care about ethics?"

"Very little. It's an advantage."

It seemed that they would get along.

He did sleep, in due course, and dreamed of Apoca, butt and all. He woke later and thought about it. It was true: Apoca's kiss not only had not hurt him, it had extirpated the ghost. He was getting smitten by Apoca, but this was natural. Yes, her kiss helped, but not compulsively. He knew why she had not used her power on him: she wanted an independent friend, not a love slave.

"Naturally, I will not divulge that her interests and dreams parallel yours," Nimbus said.

"Naturally," he agreed.

"Aurora is a beautiful ant. I like her. I am beautiful too, for my kind." She flashed a translated picture of a lovely human woman with outsized gloves covering her pincers. He was reminded how nickelpedes could gouge out nickel-sized scoops of flesh.

"You are," he agreed. It was amazing how nice even the most formidable bugs could be, once he got to know them.

"You could make a handsome nick stud, too, with the right translation."

He laughed. "Thanks."

"Care to dream with me?"

Nickelpedes dreamed? "How?"

"Like this." Her sightly human image kissed him on the mouth. There was a surge of passion, but it rapidly faded. "I know better than to put too much oomph in it. That's what Ghorgeous did."

"Thank you," he said weakly. He certainly didn't need more kiss complications.

"You don't," Nimbus agreed. "Fortunately, ghosts and bugs are incidental. Apoca is the one for you."

"Yes." He had always thought of nickelpedes as the nastiest of bugs. That would never be the case again.

"To be sure."

They both relaxed. Again, he had no trouble sleeping.

In the morning the humans ate from their packs, not trusting the local pies, handled natural functions, and resumed their journey. The bugs foraged for themselves, then rejoined their original companions. "How did you like Nimbus?" Aurora inquired.

Diplomacy was best. "She's almost as nice as you."

The ant laughed. That was another thing she had learned from her association with humans. "I know she kissed you. She likes being naughty."

"And you don't?"

Aurora formed her own dream image, and kissed him, low voltage with just a tinge of rapture. Clearly naughtiness was a quality the bugs shared.

He had now been kissed by four different females within the past night and day. A ghost, two bugs, and a woman. Four completely different types, but a similar command of flirtation. Maybe the ladies really did rule.

"And don't you forget it."

Gent looked surprisingly satisfied. He was technically Apoca's love slave, but it seemed that a little fling on the side was not out of order. Nolan had a notion how that could be. He was no longer obsessed with the ghost's kiss, but he remembered its power.

They came to a cornfield, forging through the head-high plants until progress stopped. "We are up to our ears in corn," Gent said. Fortunately their flashing posterior nakedness was mostly concealed by the massed stalks.

The sun became bright. Vinia found a patch of cap plants and harvested a cap to shield her eyes. But when she put it on, fluid drenched her head, and there was a strong smell of fuel. It seemed that her paths did not cover incidental items.

"Gas cap," Gent said.

Annoyed, the girl shed the rest of her clothes and headed for a nearby pool to wash herself off. She grabbed for another cap as she passed it.

"I wouldn't," Gent warned. "That's a screw cap."

"A what?"

"Don't put it on!" Apoca snapped without explaining.

Vinia reluctantly let it go. She jumped in the pool, rinsed her hair, then harvested a smock to wear.

They came to a clearing where there were many loaves of bread scattered about. The moment they entered it, music played and the bread started dancing.

"A bun dance," Gent said.

Nolan got the pun. "Abundance." With plenty of bread doing it. He didn't bother to look down at his nakedness because of that awful pun.

They skirted the dance and came to a solid stake set in the ground. But the moment they approached it rapiers projected sharply from it.

"Fencepost," Gent explained. "As in fencing."

There was a collective groan, and of course they were all bare again.

But they were taking it in stride, as it were. Clothing no longer mattered as much.

Nolan found himself walking beside Apoca. Was that by her design, or his? Did it matter?

"Nimbus kissed me." So that he was not hiding anything from her.

"I told her to."

That set him back. "Why?"

"So I could verify whether you would tell me."

"Why?"

"I am intrigued by you, but I prefer complete honesty between us."

Did she really? "Do you want me to tell you what I'd like to do with you in bed?"

She laughed, not at all abashed. "Not that complete. Not yet."

"Then when?"

"When I'm ready."

"Not when I'm ready?"

"You're courting me. You've already made your decision. I have not yet made mine. Therefore the option is mine."

"Are you playing hard to get?"

"I'm flirting, my way."

He found that he liked her way. She was a fiercely independent woman, and he preferred that type.

They came to a kind of forest gallery with several alcoves. They knew it was a gallery because it was ringed by a platoon of dancing gals. One alcove had an old-fashioned lamp from whose spout smoke was issuing. Gradually it formed into a floating Demon, who looked languidly at them, his eye lingering on Apoca, then eased back into the lamp. They watched, unable to move on.

"Slow djinn," Gent said.

They flashed naked again. "I got the pun but refused to give that Demon the satisfaction of seeing my clothing fade," Apoca said with muted pride.

"He was undressing you mentally anyway," Gent said.

"Oh, fudge!"

The next alcove had a male and a female zombie shambling together. They embraced messily and kissed, pushing in each other's faces. They seemed to be much taken with each other. That was all.

"When two zombies fall in love, it is necromance," Gent said.

Their clothing had not yet healed from the prior pun, but now it puffed into smoke.

The next alcove had a man drinking from a glass labeled WORMWOOD. Then he stared at a picture of a fair young woman.

Nolan didn't get it, and he saw that the others were similarly blank. But until they did get it, they were unable to move on.

"Absinthe makes the heart grow fonder," Gent said. "This is an ad for wormwood as an aphrodisiac."

They all groaned as the smoke of their clothing caught fire.

The next alcove had a mathematician with numbers all over his cloak as he worked a balky device consisting of circular pegs mounted on horizontal poles. The pegs refused to stay in the places he put them, and he was swearing blue streaks. There was no sound, but the streaks were crisscrossing the alcove. What was the pun?

"That's an abacuss," Gent said. "A swearing mathematician."

The smoke blew away in the breeze, as they tried unsuccessfully to suppress their groans.

Then at last they emerged from the gallery, leaving the gals behind, and found a broad field. "This is our first important stop," Gent announced.

Nolan was uncertain whether to feel relieved or worried.

A female animal was grazing there, wearing a vest with the word "dolly" on it. That was all. This was important?

Nolan spied the baton hovering close by. It occurred to him that a female protagonist might be able to handle this curious situation better.

"She might," Aurora agreed, bemused.

Why not? "Okay, get on over there," he told the baton.

Chapter 4

DOLLY LLAMA

Apoca saw the baton flying closer to her. She was to be the protagonist again? So be it. "Let's find out what's happening here," she said, walking toward the animal, which looked like a sheep with a long neck. "Hello, Dolly!" she called.

"Hello, Apoca," the creature replied.

Apoca paused, startled. Had the animal really spoken her name?

"She did," Nimbus said. "The way I do, mentally, though it seems she doesn't need physical contact to do it."

"And hello, Nimbus."

Meanwhile the other members of their party were reacting as if hearing their own names, mentally. Simultaneous telepathy?

"This is Dolly Llama, a noted local sage," Gent said. "She is a pun on the name of the Dalai Lama of Tibet, Mundania, but she is not at all frivolous. Neither is the original Dalai."

Their clothing became un-opaque at the revelation of the pun, but the llama seemed not to be concerned. She was, after all, an animal. "Thank you, Gent," Dolly said. "I am not into prophecy but can see that your punishment curse will have an unexpected termination, in due course."

"Thank you, Dolly," he said, gratified.

"And hello, Baton of Protagonism. I have not seen you here before."

The baton bobbed acknowledgment.

Apoca was coming to realize that this was no ordinary talking animal.

The llama's attention focused on Vinia. "And your green paths led this party to me, Vinia. That's interesting. It suggests that we may be able to do each other some good."

"I suppose we could lead you out of the pundemic zone," Vinia said.

Dolly shook her head. "No. I am not interested in departing this pasture. I came here to escape the constant appeals for advice from sundry and all. My life was devolving into pundemonium. Now I follow the example of the Good Magician, isolating myself to a degree and requiring recompense for my service. I reside in a virtual island within the pundemic zone, where the puns are reduced, though it is completely surrounded by them. Very few folk care to traverse this region, for a reason you understand, and fewer desire commentary rather than straight directives."

"You give answers!" Vinia exclaimed. "That's why the paths lead to you."

"I proffer perspective. That is not the same."

"Whatever," Apoca said. "The paths do seem to know what's what."

"Perhaps. I represent one avenue among many, not necessarily the most useful one for you. You may prefer to pass me by."

"Maybe," Apoca said. "I am inclined to consider what you offer versus what you cost, then weigh the alternatives before making a decision."

"You are an eminently sensible woman. Your suitor is fortunate that you are more than a pretty figure. What you desire is imponderable, while what I require may be dangerous even if feasible. This makes for vague parameters, which in turn require careful consideration."

Apoca glanced at Nolan, but he was staying clear, leaving it to her.

"First things first," she said. "What are you asking for your commentary?"

"I mostly graze this fine field. But it has a fringe of excellent pies, or technically pi's, that I very much like to ingest when I relax in the evenings. But recently there has come a pie rat that consumes them before I can. I want to be rid of that rat."

"Pie rat," Gent said. "As in pirate, one who steals physical or intellectual valuables."

There was a muted groan from the group.

"You said pi's," Nolan said. "What kind are those?"

"They are number pies. They contain all the numbers of the pi ratio, in order."

"Um—"

"The ratio of the circumference of a circle to its diameter. It's a magic number, invaluable. I love to digest the unique parts of it. I can't do that if the pie rat steals the pies before they properly ripen. I have knowledge of many things, but this requires a physical process."

The group shared a confused glance. None of them understood exactly what she was talking about. Did it matter, really? The point was that she needed to be rid of the rat.

"There are ways to eliminate rats," Apoca said.

"I do not want poison, as that could affect me also. Nor do I want strenuous mechanisms such as Mundane firearms. I simply want that rat quickly, cleanly, and permanently gone."

Apoca looked at Nolan. He shrugged. "Show me the rat."

"I must advise you that it is a cunning brute, with friends among the neighbors. If you chase it, it will lead you into trouble."

"I can handle trouble."

Apoca had seen him do it. But the rat was probably more devious than the maenads. She was not sure she liked the smell of this.

"Over there," Dolly said, pointing with her nose.

Sure enough, there was a big rat foraging among the growing pies at the fringe of the field.

Nolan transformed to his serpent form, becoming a big rat snake. His clothing disappeared, all but the pouch belt he wore around his middle. Now it was around the middle of the snake, seeming not to inhibit it at all. He took off after the rat, slithering with amazing rapidity.

The pie rat saw him coming and scooted away. But the snake was gaining on it. Could Nolan catch the elusive creature?

The rat sped up. The snake accelerated, closing the gap.

The rat veered to pass close to a bush with silvery disks. The disks dropped off, developing giant pincers.

"Those aren't flowers," Nimbus said. "They are resting quarterpedes. They are like us nickelpedes, only five times worse. Nolan shouldn't mess with them; they'll relentlessly gouge out quarter-sized chunks of his flesh."

There was a flash, and the nearest quarterpede jumped up, flipped over, and landed on its back, a scorched husk. The others immediately scurried away from the snake, who passed the bush unmolested.

"What happened?" Apoca asked, surprised.

"Let me check. Aurora and I have gotten to know each other. We are on the way to becoming friends, because of our unique associations with you flesh folk. We understand each other. We have established a telepathic rapport. I will ask her."

"You can do non-contact telepathy?"

"Some friends can, though it is unusual between species." There was half a pause. "Ah! Aurora fried it. She's a fire ant, remember. The other quarterpedes got the message and skedaddled."

Apoca nodded. "She's protecting him, the way you would protect me."

"Yes. She likes him, the way I like you. She even kissed him, after I did."

"He is kissable," Apoca agreed.

"You are falling for him."

"I suppose I am. But I have a way to go before I land."

They saw the rat plunge into a river. A number of colored fins oriented.

"That water is infested by loan sharks," Dolly said. "They'll take an arm and a leg if you let them. The rat has a deal with them, sharing my stolen pi's. The sharks love the numbers. So they will not bother the rat. But they will chew up Nolan if he ventures there."

"Maybe not," Apoca said, remembering how he had scared off the maenads. The man had resources.

The snake plunged into the water. The sharks converged. The snake changed as it splashed in, becoming something else. The sharks veered away.

"What happened?" Dolly asked, surprised in her turn. It seemed that she knew a lot but was not clairvoyant.

"Aurora says he transformed into a big fish. He has fish ancestry, so can assume the form. It's not his talent, merely part of his makeup."

"But the sharks saw it happen," Apoca protested, impressed despite her caution. "They know he's a shape-changer chasing their rat friend. Why aren't they attacking him?"

Nimbus checked with Aurora. "Oh, my! He became a sell-fish."

"A pun on selfish," Gent said. "A sell-fish doesn't borrow, it sells, so the loan sharks can't touch it."

"He can choose the type of fish he becomes?" Apoca asked, becoming more impressed despite her caution.

"Yes. Aurora says he practiced as a youth, so he can do different fish, different serpents, and even different men, as long as they are part of his ancestry. They all have the same mass; he can't become a whale shark or a sardine, the way a true transformer could, but it serves him well enough."

"That is impressive," Dolly said.

Apoca could only nod. She was determined to judge the man objectively, but he was swaying her feelings without even trying to. He was just naturally doing what he was equipped to do.

"Oh, my!" Nimbus repeated. "He just changed forms again. Now he's a rat fish, the kind that eats rats."

"I would like to see that," Dolly said.

"Let me see if I can put it on holo." A three-dimensional picture appeared of a fish swimming through river water. "It's not photographic, because Aurora is in the magic pouch with his clothing, peering out between the strands. All she can see physically is his fish belly. But she's drawing on his mind, too, and his knowledge of the environment. So this is a composite mental image approximating the reality."

"It will do," Apoca said.

The rat fish closed swiftly on the swimming rat, coming up behind and beneath it. Then the fish leaped out of the water, jaws gaping, and came down on the rat. In barely a quarter of a moment the rat was chomped and swallowed, a meal for the fish.

"That pie rat is history," Nimbus said with satisfaction as the picture faded.

"It is," Dolly agreed. "You have covered my fee and will have my discussion."

Soon Nolan returned. "That was fun. That rat tasted of an endless string of non-repeating numbers."

"It would," Dolly agreed. "Now, if the group of you will park yourselves, I will address each of you in turn."

"Oh, I am just concerned with the fulfillment of my mission to solve the problem of the repeating talents," Nolan said as they formed a half circle before the llama and sat on the ground, or on their friends, or merely hovered in place. "The others are just my Companions in the Quest."

"Which is yours because it is the price of the Good Magician's answer to your Question about the identity of your ideal woman," Dolly said. "Therefore, Apoca is integral to the Quest, because without her it would not exist, or at least would not be for the eight of you. She even carries the name of this volume in the annals of Xanth."

"Eight of us?" Apoca asked.

"Nolan, Aurora, Apoca, Nimbus, Gent, Vinia, Ghorgeous, and Baton. Eighteen syllables. Eight identities."

"She must have eaten some of those number pies despite the thieving rat," Nimbus remarked.

"The baton counts?" Apoca asked. "But it merely conveys the perspective."

"It is nevertheless a significant identity in its own right. It, or another of its type, has accompanied every main character since Xanth history began, though few of them knew it, and without it there would be no stories. Merely a confused mishmash of history, personalities, and devious interrelationships of little interest to anyone. The opportunity for compelling narratives would be wasted. It, too, is integral."

The baton nodded agreement.

A half-perplexed gaze lapped the circle. The llama evidently had her own perspective.

"Proceeding in reverse order," Dolly continued, "Ghorgeous Ghost is considerably more than an incidental presence. All of you represent links in the chain of accomplishment, and without any of you, that chain would break. Technically all links are equally important, but nontechnically Ghorgeous is vital to the denouement. Do not allow her to leave the party."

"As if anyone could lock in a ghost," Nimbus muttered.

"Oh, I'm just here to help out incidentally," Ghorgeous protested. "Because I can check things out invisibly, pass through solid walls, keep guard at night, and spook credulous creatures when necessary. Any ghost could do it. I'm really not important."

"Perhaps," the llama said. There was an undertone fraught with hidden meaning.

Apoca was reminded uneasily of the mock-girl Squid, who was called the most important person in the universe. She had dismissed that out of hand . . . until it proved to be true. What was there about the ghost that was so crucial? Ghorgeous seemed as doubtful as Apoca was.

"Vinia," Dolly said, causing the girl to startle. "A variant of the name Wivinia, meaning 'of the quiet life.' Her life has not been quiet; she was the protagonist of the last story." She glanced at Baton, who bobbed confirmation. "A creature of two powerful talents, telekinesis and seeing colored paths to the future. They work together to make her a future princess. She is essential to this Quest, because only the paths can show the way safely through. Yet there are limits."

"Such as my having little idea what I am doing, here or anywhere," the girl agreed.

"But she is an excellent friend," Apoca said, winning a smile of appreciation.

"Gent, unkindly nicknamed Pun Gent because of the curse the Witch Craft put on him for inadvertently ruining her garden of witch grass. He thought it was a yard overrun by weeds. His talent is killing weeds. Since a weed is by definition a plant where it is not wanted, his better-defined talent is killing plants."

Gent sat up straight. "I never thought of that!"

"Actually, the witch's curse is not entirely what it seems," Dolly continued. "She is not yet through with Gent, but must wait until Apoca releases him from love slavery, which she will do in due course."

"I never want to see the witch again!" Gent exclaimed. "She knew it was an accident, but she cursed me anyway."

"Perhaps." Again the word was fraught, which made Apoca wonder. What was Dolly not saying?

"Are we missing something?" Apoca asked.

"Yes."

"What?"

"I am unable to tell you that, because it might affect your future and make my commentary invalid."

"Oh, the way my paths change once I decide on the one to follow," Vinia said.

"Exactly."

"In fact, they are vague now, as if your comment is putting them in flux."

"Yes. Your decisions have to be your own."

"Then why are we here at all?" Nolan demanded.

"Because my commentary will enable you to achieve your mission, if you handle it correctly. That is a crucial aspect of your unusual situation.

Once you have properly explored your options, you may be able to succeed."

"May?"

"No particular aspect of the future can ever be guaranteed. We exist in a realm of quantum fluctuations."

This was getting beyond Apoca's comprehension again. She had never heard of the magic called quantum. "So we'll just have to take your word for it?"

"Yes. Perhaps someday you will comprehend."

The glance circulated again. "Then get on with it," Apoca said with imperfect grace.

"Nimbus Nickelpede, your companion and friend, is another link in the chain. She is enjoying this excursion, as it promises bloodthirsty action, and might deliver a suitable mate for her."

There was that "might" again. This time Apoca let it pass.

"In fact, one of her contributions may be incipient."

"Oh?" Nimbus asked, surprised.

"I don't know what form it will take, but Nimbus is integral."

The nickelpede flicked her tail in a shrug.

"And Apoca," the llama continued. "She will have some serious kissing to do before the mission is complete. Both kinds."

So Dolly knew she could kiss a man into love slavery, and a woman out of it, or at least out of submissiveness. But it was not the kind of thing she ever did casually. "I'm not kissing Nolan that way."

"Nolan is already half-immune."

That made Apoca pause for another thought. Only natural love made a man immune. Did that mean that Nolan was falling in love with her? He was courting her, to be sure, but that did not necessarily mean love. Princes were notorious for marrying for political advantage while having a flock of prettier mistresses. She did not want that kind.

"And Aurora Ant," Dolly said. "She, too, is vital, and is close to an event now."

Aurora, back on Nolan's shoulder, started. "I'm just scouting for a suitable foraging ground for my home anthill. I'll help out where I can, but I am only an ant, after all." Apoca heard her via Nimbus, who was now in chronic attunement.

"You saved me a gouging by the quarterpedes," Nolan reminded her. He was in similar touch via Aurora.

"All part of the deal." But there was an undertone. They were of wildly different species, but she liked him. That was why she occasionally flashed him with her human-girl dream image. It was fun flirting even if there was no realistic future in it.

"I know how that is," Nimbus said privately. "His kisses have power."

"They do," Apoca agreed.

"Finally Prince Nolan Naga," Dolly said. "Whose handsome aspect enthralls all the females of this Quest."

"That's not true!" Ghorgeous and Vinia said almost together. Then they looked at each other and shared a blush. Nimbus and Aurora were doing the bug equivalent. Only Apoca had both her expression and discomfit under control, though she felt the truth of it. The prince was making an incidental impact. Part of it was because it was clear he had no such intention.

Nolan looked startled. "I never—"

"They understand," Dolly said. "His sole intention is to accomplish the mission."

"That is true."

"Fortunately this sort of thing is harmless," the llama said. "But he will face more serious and less harmless temptations before the Quest is complete."

"I am not looking for temptation," Nolan said. "I just want to save the babies and win Apoca, not necessarily in that order."

"The Quest is needfully complicated, because it relates to a Demon. A man once asked a Demon whether it was true that the ratio of a Demon to an ordinary mortal person was that of a galaxy to a grain of sand. The Demon replied that this understated the case. However, this is merely a Dwarf Demon, so the case is approximately correct. Nevertheless, this is no ordinary challenge. This is the point where you must decide whether to continue or to give it up."

"If we give it up, the babies may never again have individual talents," Nolan said. "And my payment for the Good Magician's Answer will be void."

"If you continue, you will be entering a realm of extreme danger to yourselves and those you hold dear," Dolly said. She glanced at Vinia. "Such as your Prince Ion."

"Oh!" Vinia cried, stricken.

The llama glanced at Apoca. "Such as the Queendom of Thanx."

That struck her like a Mundane safe falling on her head. Thanx was a marvelous feminist community, and Queen Demesne was her friend. She did not want anything ill to happen to it. "Mm."

Dolly glanced at Aurora. "Such as your home anthill."

The fire ant quailed as if drenched.

She glanced at Nolan. "Such as the Naga Kingdom."

Nolan paled but stood firm. "What are the odds of our success?"

"Approximately even, depending on chance and commitment."

He glanced around, evidently shaken but determined. "I mean to complete this Quest, regardless of the risk, but the rest of you are not obliged. I will proceed alone if need be. You are free to go home, but any who wish to join me will be welcome."

Apoca felt herself crossing the nebulous boundary between intrigue and love. This was a man to be respected. She appreciated the formidable risk but cringed at the thought of letting him take it alone. "I will join you, with a similar release of the others."

Gent spoke. "In that case, I too am in."

Oops. "You have no choice, being my love slave. I will free you for that." She walked to him, held him close, and delivered the nullifying kiss she had used to free the women of Thanx of the submission malady. "Now you are free. You may go."

Gent considered as the power of the kiss took hold. "I am free!" he echoed. "I am no longer bound to you. You can no longer compel my unquestioning obedience to your slightest whim. In fact, I respect you, but don't love you. You are not my kind of woman for romance."

"Correct. I enslaved you only because we needed your help navigating the pundemic zone. If the group dissolves, that need is less, and it is only right to free you."

He nodded. "But I am not yet free of the curse, which will manifest when I leave the environment of the pundemic. Meanwhile, you have inadvertently provided me with something I lacked: companionable associates. I value that. I suspect that if the Quest is successful, I will also find the release of my curse. Therefore I will continue, now of my own free will."

Apoca was touched. "That's very nice of you. I hope it works out."

"It will," Dolly said.

"Now it seems we are three," Nolan said. "Plus of course the baton. You four other ladies may depart at your convenience."

"I should toast your butt," Aurora said. "You forget that I am with you because you are fated to pass the ideal place for our new anthill. I will stay with you until that occurs."

"Oops, sorry. I did forget."

"And she's also a bit sweet on him, species be bleeped," Nimbus murmured. "As am I, as foolishly."

"As are all four of you," Apoca said.

"And you too," the nickelpede retorted. Then, for all to hear: "I am staying with Apoca. Someone needs to protect her from foreign bugs."

"Me too," Vinia said. "How else are they going to find the paths?"

"And me," Ghorgeous said. "I want to see Thanx and Xanth maintain their diversity of talents, and I know I can help."

"I am gratified by your continued support," Nolan said. "I could kiss you all."

A soft ripple coursed through the four, and Apoca. "In your dreams," Ghorgeous said, and they all laughed. He might indeed receive some dream kisses.

"So the Quest remains complete," Dolly said, unsurprised. "Now I will acquaint you with the wider parameters, which are formidable."

They settled down to listen. Apoca knew this would not be entirely pleasant.

"Your Quest is to handle the problem of the identical talents of all new babies. Talents are assigned by the Dwarf Demon of Talents, as you know. The question is why he has become derelict, as Demons are largely defined by their positions and will cease to exist if those positions are lost. He could be summarily replaced by a Demon Court if the matter comes to general attention. This would not be to his advantage."

Apoca wondered about that, now that the llama had clarified it. Whatever could have possessed the Demon to put its own existence at risk?

"Demons, both capped and uncapped, along with most other creatures, lack, and seldom care about them," Dolly continued, "but close proximity to souls can evoke a hunger for them that they do not necessarily comprehend. Souls are a mortal specialty, largely limited to the human contingent. This explains the inclinations of the two insectoid members of this party toward the human members. The proximity provides them with a previously unknown satisfaction."

That was interesting. Nimbus had come into contact with Vinia last year, and now was with Apoca. Aurora had encountered Nolan. No wonder they got along.

"His position causes the Demon of Talents to be exposed to the nascent souls of prospective humans. The three dots of the procreative signal spell out the entire new person, including the soul. That evokes the hunger. Only those with souls are capable of true love, but those without souls can begin to appreciate its power when in the near presence of souls. Demon Talents has developed the capacity to love but does not properly understand it. Such understanding is not a matter of intellect but of emotion, another thing most demons and Demons lack. So his reaction is confused and inappropriate. He has developed a crush on a Demoness, a feeling she does not return. Thus he is out of sorts, distracted, and neglectful of his duty. That is why he no longer properly assigns the talents. They are locked on the last one he assigned before the neglect began."

"Wow!" Nimbus said. "That's a whole lot I never dreamed of before, and not just about the talents."

"Dolly really does know her stuff," Apoca agreed, similarly impressed.

"The female is the Dwarf Demoness of Transcription. She translates the embedded message of the three dots to spheres of responsibility, one of which is the magic talent. That portion she relays to D Talents. The other portions, such as physical appearance, mental capacity, and emotional makeup, she takes to the responsible Dwarf Demons. When all are done, the baby is assembled and given to the stork for delivery. The process is complicated, and normally takes about nine months." Dolly made a mental smile. "On rare occasion there is an error, such as extra fingers or the inclusion of two talents in the package."

"Such as your two types of kisses," Nimbus said. "Or Vinia's telekinesis and paths."

"Thus D Talents continues to neglect his duty while pondering how to make an impression on D Transcription. She, being similarly exposed to souls, has developed her own hunger, but not for any tryst with D Talents.

She wants a soul of her own. That makes her desire as futile as his. But she does continue performing her duty."

"So now there are two frustrated Demons," Apoca murmured. "Yet complexer."

"Normally the situation would be resolved when the neglect came to the attention of one of the full Demons," Dolly continued. "But D Talents is cunning. He has cast a shroud of ignorance upon the issue, so that no other Demons are aware of it. The only ones who are conscious of it are the mothers of the new babies, and they, being merely mortals, don't count. However, the Quest could make a sufficient scene to attract the attention of a Demon. Mortals may be as insignificant as grains of sand, but a party of six of them and a ghost coming to beseech a Dwarf Demon to do his job just might do it. D Talents, aware of that, means to see that no such scene occurs. He can't take direct action in the mortal sphere because Demon Policy forbids interference in other Demons' domains. But he can take indirect action that may be effective."

"Such as what?" Nolan asked, looking daunted but determined.

"There are a number of routes leading to the domain of a Demon. Those with souls are capable of traversing them when they have assistance, such as special magic. These may not be entirely physical but may appear so when Vinia's perception of the paths identifies them. You will select and follow the most likely ones. However, the Demon may arrange to nullify whatever path you select, making it become a false path. When you try a new path that has not been falsified, he may nullify that one also. Thus you may search forever without getting anywhere."

"But that would be cheating!"

The llama nodded. "A Demon may cheat if he thinks he can get away with it."

"Are you saying that my Quest is impossible?" Nolan asked.

"No. Merely that you must take a special step to ensure that the game is fair."

"This is not a game to me," he said grimly.

"It is a game to a Demon. Demons, being routinely bored by the immensity of their power, phrase key issues as games with each other. Normally they make wagers on the outcome of unpredictable minor events, such as the decisions of mortals. They do not interfere with the actions of the selected pawns because that would invalidate the randomness of the decisions. You, as mortals, may force a game on the Demon of Talents. That may be the only way you can succeed in your Quest."

Nolan, taken aback, was silent.

Apoca spoke. "You mentioned a special step we must take. What is it?"

"You must enlist the support of a full Demon to guarantee the fairness of the game. He will not intervene but may do that much."

"How can we ever do that? If we can't even reach a Dwarf Demon, how could we ever reach a full Demon?"

"You must go to Squid."

"Who?"

"The alien cuttlefish girl who was the protagonist three stories ago. Her boyfriend is the Demon Chaos."

Now Apoca remembered. Squid, one of the five children rescued from a doomed alternate Xanth. She was said to be a nice girl, for all that she was actually a land-going alien sea creature. If she asked this favor of her boyfriend, who was incidentally the most powerful of all the Demons, he would surely grant it. It had to be her soul that had made him love her, as the llama had explained generally.

"We'll do that," Nolan decided. "Thank you for your clarification of the issue."

"You are welcome, prince. You did rid me of the noxious pie rat."

And she had delivered the most competent discussion they could have found anywhere. The nature of their mission was now scarily clear. Apoca was moved. "Dolly, would you care to be my friend?"

There was a sudden peal of thunder as the sky darkened. A storm had appeared without warning and threatened to soak them.

"That's Fracto!" Nolan exclaimed. "Always looking for a parade to rain on!"

"Cumulo Fracto Nimbus," Dolly agreed. "He hasn't been here for ages. I wonder whether this could be coincidence."

"What else could it be?" Apoca asked.

"An intervention sponsored by the Demon."

Apoca was not the only one taken aback. "The Demon of Talents made a deal with Fracto to wash us out?"

"That would eliminate coincidence. I distrust coincidence when magic is involved."

"I will check this out," Ghorgeous said, and faded. In barely four-fifths of a moment she was back. "Fracto has a Demonic map showing him where to go. It has to be a deal. He is supercharged with water and voltage. We need to get the bleep out of here."

"The paths are suddenly skewed," Vinia said. "They are curling around in spirals. I've never seen that before."

Apoca gazed at the swirling weather moving rapidly toward them, lit by internal lightning flashes. The leaves and small branches of trees were already flying. "This is mischief."

Nolan looked about. "This is a level valley surrounded by the punfestation. It will soon be flooded, and the water could wash us into the sea. I can handle that, but I fear for the rest of you. Nowhere to hide."

"I know of a place," Dolly said. "An invisible mountain adjacent to my pasture. The invisible giants go there to relax. We leave each other alone. They don't step on me, and I don't tell others of their hideout. You must keep the secret too."

"We will," Nolan said, speaking for them all.

"It has grottoes, but vermin inhabit them." Dolly glanced at Nimbus, then at Aurora. "No offense intended."

"Lead the way," Aurora said. "I will reason with the vermin, and if they don't agree to share, I will toast them." She fired a sample jet.

"This way," the llama said, and trotted across her pasture. They followed. So did the raging storm, its savage rainfall pursuing them like an ocean wave.

They came to an invisible rise. The ground beneath their feet was solid, but they seemed to be walking on air.

"Now I know why the spirals," Vinia said. "The paths are looping around the mountain, to climb it!"

The storm struck. Water sheeted down, instantly soaking them all. What bothered Apoca more was the lightning forming into a huge glowing bolt, pointing this way and that as if searching for its target. When it struck, it could blast a boulder into pebbles. As for the rest—she knew her figure had nothing to fear from the soaking. In her youth she had won a wettee shirt contest, and she had maintained her profile. Not that anyone was looking.

"That's what you think," Nimbus said. "Aurora snapped a mental picture as she passed and is sharing it with Nolan."

"Why, that naughty bug!" But actually she was not much bothered. What was the use of having it, if no one ever saw it?

"Aurora says he is salivating."

Just so.

They came up to a cliff, made visible by the rain splashing against it. The path went beside it.

"Here is the nearest grotto," Dolly said, pausing by a dark hole outlined by the absence of plunging rain. "But the vermin may not want to share. They consist of assorted biting bugs and reptiles, all invisible. They can see each other, and us, but we can't see them."

"We will reason with them," Nolan said. "But it may take a moment, and the storm won't wait."

Apoca got an idea. "Will it work?" she asked Nimbus as she flashed the notion.

"It had better," the nickelpede replied.

"We will guard the entrance while you negotiate with the vermin," she told Nolan and Aurora.

Nolan, Aurora, Gent, Vinia, and Dolly crowded into the grotto, while Apoca, Nimbus, and the baton remained outside, facing the oncoming storm. Water poured onto them like a river waterfall, but it was the massive bolt of lightning they watched most closely.

The bolt soon located them. It rose up, looped in the air to gain velocity, and zapped directly toward them.

And sheared away at the last instant, smashing into the face of the cliff to the side. Invisible stone crashed down onto the path, striking invisible sparks.

Nolan looked back. "What happened?" he called, alarmed.

"The lightning bolt missed us."

"At point-blank range? You should have come inside with us."

"We were safe," Apoca explained. "Nimbus Nickelpede is on my shoulder, and her name protected us. Because the cloud is Cumulo Fracto Nimbus, and he can't hurt his namesake. It is in the Big Landmark Unwritten Rules Book. BLURB. Even the Mundanes know of it, though I think they mess up the definition."

"You've got nerve," he said admiringly.

She loved that, and not just because she did have nerve. So, it was apparent, did he.

Now she could focus on what the others were doing in the cave. "Here is the replay," Nimbus said, and put it on.

The group entered the grotto cave. All manner of bugs were there, invisible but evident by their minds, which were intent on mayhem, because they did not like having their home invaded by visible folk. Some also were hungry for blood, literally.

"You can tune in on the mass of minds," Aurora told him. "That's a general haze. Or on individual bugs, because each has a kind of self-image. So you can in effect see them, when you focus."

He focused. Sure enough, he began to make out individuals. His experience with Aurora facilitated the process.

It was time to make his case. "We are seeking temporary shelter from the storm," Nolan said, his message translated to generalized bug language by Aurora. "We want only to ride it out, then be on our way. We will leave you alone if you leave us alone. Peace?"

The bugs flew forward in an invisible mass, teeth and stingers leading. It was to be war.

Aurora sent out a moving shaft of fire that would have had little effect on man-sized creatures, but was devastating to small bugs. Their wings burned off and their bodies shriveled and curled up in the flash of heat. The cave floor was littered with their dead and dying bodies. They were becoming visible as they died.

"I may have neglected to mention that my companion is a fire ant," Nolan said. "I apologize for that omission. She can shoot down anything that flies. Now I proffer my offer again. Peace?"

This time a mass of ground bugs charged, protected from fire a degree by the cool, damp floor. He saw their translucent flickerings as they moved. The ant would soon be worn out trying to burn such a mat.

Nolan stepped forward and stomped the first wave with his boots. In one and a half moments the floor was a carpet of squished bugs. These, too, became more visible as they died.

"Perhaps I also neglected to mention that I am wearing combat boots. I apologize again. I can stomp anything within range of my feet. I proffer my offer a third time, with the caution that if it is declined I will not make it a fourth time, as I will understand that the only way to achieve peace in this grotto will be to extirpate every invisible bug in it. That would be a shame, as I suspect that many of you are decent folk, like some I have known, who would prefer accommodation, but what must be, must be. Peace?"

This time the bugs decided to be gracious.

"We will settle in one corner of the chamber," Nolan said. "Any bugs who wish to visit and converse will be welcome. Perhaps we will discover some common interests." He smiled. "For example, do any of you lady bugs have mental images of how you would appear if you assumed human form? My friend Aurora would be happy to demonstrate the mental trans-lation mechanism. It requires brief physical contact with one of us human visitors but is otherwise not stressful. We might even have a mock party."

The bugs hesitated, then cleared back from one corner of the cavern. Nolan and his company went there.

At that point Apoca and Nimbus entered the cave, and the replay merged with reality. They joined the others in the corner.

Then, hesitantly three doodlebugs approached. "We are at peace, right?" Nolan said. "Or at least an ongoing truce. Nobody tries to bite, nobody fires, and nobody stomps, right?"

"They agree," Aurora said. She was better able than he to pick up on bug thoughts from a distance, being a bug herself. For dealing with him she needed physical contact, but bugs were her type.

"But aren't doodlebugs the larva of ant lions?" Nimbus asked. "They eat ants!"

"These are young, not-yet-mature lions," Aurora said. "And they don't eat fire ants." She breathed a token jet of fire. Indeed, her kind was not prey to their kind.

Nolan carefully put his left hand down on the floor beside the three. They walked over to it and climbed on. Now their thoughts reached him, a confused mishmash of intrigue and trepidation. They had been sent by the bug leader to establish relations but were understandably nervous about this dangerously booted monster.

He tried to reassure them. "You know of BLURB? In exchange for our sanctuary here, we will teach you something nice."

"Like this," Aurora said, her message reaching them now that all of them were in direct contact with him. "You are lovely creatures of your kind, or would like to be, when you mature, right? Here is the equivalent in the human kind." She put on her nice human image, modestly garbed.

The three doodlebugs tried. Their first efforts were grotesque parodies of the human form. That wouldn't do.

"Like Apoca, here," Aurora said. "Start with her, gaze closely, translate, then modify to fit your own preference."

Three images of Apoca appeared, startling her, the original. Gradually they shifted, becoming different women. One had long black hair, another long yellow hair, and the third had long red hair. Then their clothing faded, because bugs did not wear clothing. But the revealed flesh was not accurate; it was in the shape of the external outfit.

"Um, no," Aurora said. "More like this." She projected a properly nude girl, complete with separated breasts and thighs.

It took several tries, as doodlebugs were not mammalian, but in due course they got it right. There were now three lovely nude girls standing before Nolan, projected images. "Very nice," he said.

Aurora sent a signal, and the three blushed fetchingly. The skin of one turned black, another turned yellow, and the third turned bright red. They were still works in progress. However, they soon got their costumes in order and managed to make Gent gaze with appreciation, though he knew their nature. They danced fetchingly together. They began to teach the other bugs the dream-image technique. Soon there was a bevy of lovely human girl images, who practiced by openly flirting with the two men. They were even forming invisible panties to intensify the effect. Apoca was relieved that they were only bugs; otherwise it could have gotten awkward, knowing the weakness of men for appearance rather than reality.

Meanwhile the storm outside raged in frustration. Wind blew rain into the grotto, which soon began to flood. That was bad news for the bugs.

"We need to move to a deeper cave," Apoca said. Nimbus relayed her thought to Aurora, who shared it with the doodlebugs. "I see there is a passage."

The three emulations of her became agitated. "They can't go there," Aurora relayed. "Every cave is occupied by different bugs, and they don't necessarily get along well."

"What kind are next door?" Nolan asked.

"Nickelpedes."

"That's my cue," Nimbus said. "I will reason with them."

"Do nickelpedes usually reason?"

"I was joking. I will speak to them in the language they understand. That is, Nolan will stomp them into goo if they don't back off."

Apoca walked over to the passage. It led to another cave, and there stood the translucent outlines of nickelpede guards in the forefront and a scintillating mass of bugs in the middle-ground. Doodlebugs would not stand a chance against them, and neither would most of the other bugs here. Nolan's boots were another matter.

"Uh-oh," Nimbus said to Apoca. "I can feel their hostility. They don't like their neighbor bugs, but they really don't like visible folk. There are too many of them for Nolan to stomp without many getting through and chomping everyone else. This will be a hard sell."

"I have an idea," Apoca said. "You can seduce their male chief, in the presence of the others. That should impress them."

"More likely that chief will cut off my pincers."

Apoca understood that that would be a dire fate. A nickelpede without pincers would be like a human being without arms, helpless and doomed. "Let me explain. My power to enslave men is not entirely magic. I have a technique that you may be able to adapt."

"Nickelpedes don't seduce the way humans do."

"I understand that. Let's meld minds a moment so I can clarify this in an instant."

"Okay," Nimbus agreed doubtfully.

They melded. It took exactly an instant.

"Wow!" Nimbus exclaimed, impressed. "That just might do it."

Apoca put a hand down, and the nickelpede traversed it and dropped to the floor. She marched up to the chief, who stood to the side, spotting him by the arrogant flicker of his mind. He was Nicodemus, a warrior among warriors. "Hello, big boy. I am Nimbus. Back away, you and your minions, or I will seduce you in front of all your fellows and make you a laughingstock as well as my love slave."

Nickelpedes were not much given to laughter, but this was so preposterous that he couldn't help it. "You're visible!" That was a prime insult.

"So I am, the more fool you, Nicky. You know how humiliating it will be. Now, pay attention, dolt." She lifted her pincers and clicked them in a key cadence. It was the opening of the mating sequence, with a slight but critical modification. It now included some of Apoca's magic.

Astounded, he replied with his own click sequence before he realized; it was an automatic response.

Nimbus followed up with the next clicking sequence, loaded with submission magic. It was the equivalent of Apoca's kiss. He was locked in, and he had to follow through. The other nickelpedes stared; Apoca saw their flickering amazement with her eyes and felt it in their minds. Why was their chief making out with a visible female?

It worked. The third exchange of pincer cadences bound Nicodemus's will to Nimbus's will. This did not mean mating but absolute submission on his part. He would mate with her only when and if she chose it.

The other nickelpedes remained amazed. The visible visitor had somehow ensorcelled the chief!

"Tell your minions to welcome the visitors from the next cave," Nimbus directed in ordinary click talk. "And to offer them every courtesy. Not one of them will be attacked."

Nicodemus echoed her clicks, and the minions grudgingly obeyed. They gave way, allowing the visibles and the bugs to scramble in, including the three enhanced doodlebugs and their bevy of trainees. That was just as well, because the water was rising.

In fact it soon started to flood the nickelpede chamber too. They would have to move to a higher cave.

Apoca and Nimbus repeated their performance, and enslaved another invisible chief, this one a spider, Apollo Arachnid. He kept no web but had a harem of lady spiders with webs who provided him everything he wanted, including myriad progeny. Before long not only was Apollo Nimbus's love slave, the ladies were learning how to entice prey by flashing provocative panties. Apoca wasn't sure how effective that would be, since the whole point of panties was their visibility, but if the spiders were satisfied, so was she. Two-legged panties were impressive; would eight-legged ones be quadruple as alluring? Who could say?

The water kept rising. Fracto was really determined to wash them out, and there might be some covert enhancement of his powers by the Dwarf Demon, who might indeed be cheating. They were in trouble.

Pursued by the water, they came at last to the huge uppermost cavern. "Gina Giantess resides here," Dolly said. "I have had no dealings with her. She seems reclusive. I understand she is waiting on her boyfriend, who is far, far away."

"The bugs assure me that no one dare intrude here," Aurora said. "She could obliterate all the invisible bugs merely by peeing into their caves."

"True," Dolly agreed. "She does not like vermin in her clean residence."

"I will check," Apoca said. This did seem formidable, but they were all too likely to be eliminated anyway by the flooding. Only the topmost cave was high enough to be secure.

Apoca, Nimbus, and Dolly entered the forbidden grotto. The invisible giantess was perhaps ten times Apoca's height, for all that she was lying down, a most formidable creature. It was certainly best not to aggravate her.

"Gina," Apoca said. "We need to talk with you."

The response was furious. "What are you doing in my boudoir? You know you bugs are forbidden."

"I am not a bug. I am Queen Apoca Lips, here on special business. You can see that I am visible. But the nasty cloud Cumulo Fracto Nimbus is interfering, and this is the only place in this region that is secure from him at the moment. I need your help, or at least your forbearance."

The giantess sat up, evidently intrigued. "You are a human queen? Why would you stray here? The puns are horrible."

"They are," Apoca agreed. "It's a devious story."

"Tell me."

Apoca realized that the giantess was lonely. That, in retrospect, was not surprising.

"We honor the BLURB. You know, the Big Landmark Unwritten Rules Book. We will make a fair exchange for your sufferance."

"I know of it. The only thing I want is compatible company," Gina said sadly.

"Let me introduce you to your neighbor Dolly Llama. She is a most interesting person."

"An animal!"

Dolly spoke. "A significant portion of your isolation stems from your failure to utilize what is near at foot. You suppose that only other invisible giants are worthwhile. But a rich companionship is available right here in the mountain. I myself was ignorant of this until recently. For example, the mock dancing girls."

"The what?"

Dolly sent a mental signal to the three doodlebugs, who strutted boldly forward in their human dream images. They danced, twirling so that their newly appearing short skirts lifted, almost showing their invisible panties.

"Oh, if I could do that, my beloved Geode would spend more time here," Gina said appreciatively.

"They will be glad to teach you the motions."

"But they are bugs!"

"They are actresses of the insectoid persuasion. They have learned to emulate the human form, in imagination, and are exploring its parameters. You can do the same."

"Parameters," Gina repeated. "Do you mean perimeters?"

"No. Parameters are to perimeters as giants are to grains of sand: considerably more complicated and variable. There is a qualitative distinction. I can explore this in more detail, but that would require more time than is presently available."

"You are my neighbor?"

"I reside beside the invisible mountain."

"I confess the bugs have become interesting," the giantess said. "But you interest me more. You have a mind."

"I do, for all that I am crafted from a pun. But my present concern is to provide sanctuary for the assorted residents of the mountain, who are being flooded out because of Demonic resistance to a Quest of their visitors. I shall be happy to converse with you indefinitely, as long as you grant them access to a section of your domain so that they can survive comfortably."

"Are you bargaining with me?"

"I am."

"There must be an interesting story here."

"There is."

"And you will acquaint me with the whole of it?"

"I will."

"And the bugs will not sting me or soil my premises?"

"They will not. We have a truce."

"Then let them come."

Apoca saw that Dolly had made the necessary deal with the giantess. Introductions followed, and they settled down to watch the dancing doodlebugs while telling Gina the story of the problem of the talents and the spite of Dwarf Demon and storming cloud. She turned out to be a responsive listener, intelligent and sympathetic.

"I have heard enough," the giantess said abruptly. "Pardon me while I send Fracto away."

She could do that? Apoca wondered how, as the nasty cloud was not susceptible to rational arguments.

Gina got to her feet, picked up a giant fan, and stepped outside the mountain. She waved the fan with such powerful strokes that the cloud was soon blown away by the hurricane force of the wind. "And don't come back!" she called after it. "Or I'll fetch my larger fan."

Apoca suspected that was not a bluff.

Chapter 5

THE KISS

Nolan was relieved. The threat to the assorted bugs and to themselves had been abruptly ended, thanks to the action taken by Gina Giantess. Already the water was draining, since it had been caused by the rains blowing into the lower caves, rather than general landscape flooding. Now they could focus on the next leg of their Quest, visiting the cuttlefish girl called Squid. He did not know her personally, but her reputation was positive. She did not abuse her relationship with the most powerful of all the Demons.

He saw the Baton of Protagonism fly from Apoca to him. He hadn't called it; had it decided that he was more interesting at this point than Apoca? Not that it really mattered.

"Thank you, girls," Apoca said to the doodlebug trio. "You have been most entertaining. Now you can return to your own cave as the water clears."

The three did one more flourish that flashed their panties in a manner Nolan really appreciated; had he not known that they were only bugs, he might have freaked out. They shut down their dream images and became mere doodles again. They had learned well.

"They have indeed," Aurora said.

The invisible giantess glanced at them, her attention attracted by something. "What just happened here?"

Nolan smiled. "Perhaps you noticed the change of perspective. There is an invisible baton that brings it to a person who is engaged in an interesting story."

"So that's what that winged wand is doing! I had wondered."

It figured that an invisible person could see an invisible baton. "Yes. I think it also records and transcribes the stories, suitably clarified and condensed. So you may appear, as it were, in our story, in due course."

"Really?" Gina primped her invisible hair.

"We think so. Unless a rogue editor gets at it and cuts it out."

"I will tromp that editor into a faint red smear!"

Apoca laughed. "That threat should suffice. Editors are not known for their courage. They fear even the threat of a suit made of law, whatever that is."

"A law suit," the giantess agreed, smiling. "Mundanes do have funny apparel."

"I think our business here is done," Nolan said. "We will vacate your domain as soon as the bugs have cleared out."

"No, wait! I have a new respect for bugs, and I find you visible folk marvelously entertaining. Stay the night, and in the morning I will carry you to your next scene."

Nolan and Apoca exchanged a surprised look. This could save them a lot of travel time, not to mention struggling with the puns. Or would it? "You can avoid the pundemic?" Nolan asked.

"Well, no. The puns soil my feet when I step on them, and my toes become fetishes. It's a nuisance. But I like your company so much that I am willing to endure it."

Vinia piped up. "I have some leftover vac scene that might help with that. But it has side effects."

They discussed it, and Gina concluded that the em-bare-assing effect would not be much of a problem for her because her anatomy was already invisible. So she sniffed it, then laughed until she cried. Then she picked them up in a miniature (to her) glass cup and went out to try it on the nearest zone of egregiousness.

It was late in the day, and the sun had sunk so low that it accidentally touched the pundemic zone. It developed a circle of light around it, and looked as if it had a glowing headache.

"The sun has got the corona virus," Gent said.

Gina groaned. But she did not get pundigestion and did not emit foul-smelling puns of her own. Her bare feet did not become foot fetishes. She was indeed now immune to the scene.

Back in the cave, they feasted on incidental visible pies Gina had harvested by accident, and gulped visible boot rear, which retained its kick if not its appearance. Apoca, Gina, and Dolly decided to be a trio of unlikely girlfriends, their relationship based on compatibility and intellect rather than species. Nolan certainly had no objection; if that meant that the giantess and the llama were associates once he won the queen's hand, so be it.

"Good conclusion," Aurora agreed.

The group slept on invisible beds of ferns and had a good night. Aurora and Nimbus emulated the appearance of two of the doodlebug images and did a teasing panty-mime dance in his dream. Then Gina joined in, making a visible-girl dream form in their size. Such a thing could be done only in dreams, because of the considerable difference in their real sizes and forms, but was great fun here.

Nolan woke later in the night. "I just realized that we overlooked a detail. We don't know where Squid is."

"Dolly says she and Chaos are riding in *Fibot*, the Fire Sail Boat."

"And where is *Fibot*?"

"That is the question of the hour. The boat travels all around Xanth, on special missions or just sightseeing. Dolly says not to be concerned about it; an avenue will appear."

"Would it happen to be a green path Vinia sees?"

"Exactly."

He relaxed and returned to sleep.

And woke again. "What of Dolly? Her island is still soaking wet."

The ant checked. "Dolly will accompany us, then return with Gina once we move on."

That did seem to make sense. He slept again.

In the morning they ate, handled natural functions, then got into the cup. There was room for the five solid human-sized folk, the ghost, two bugs, and the baton. Gina set a mesh cap on the top and lifted it high as she strode out of the cave. They peered through the glass and saw the landscape as if they were flying at treetop height. That was an interesting experience in its own right.

"I have not witnessed this scene before from this vantage," Dolly said as she peered down through the bottom of the glass at the slightly shaded pundemic region.

"I have," Vinia said. "We used flying carpets in my protagonism story. They flew much higher, so we could see as the birds do."

"That would be interesting," Gent said.

Nolan saw that when the sunlight struck the glass bottom at the right angle, there was a faint reflection. He wondered whether Apoca's legs would be visible under her skirt.

"Brace yourselves," Gina called from above. "I am about to start striding at speed."

Nolan found himself jammed next to Apoca as the glass swooped forth and back with the motions of the giantess's hand. "Go ahead; put your arm around me, for mutual stability."

"Stability, of course," he agreed as he did it. Was she flirting? Yet Vinia and Gent were holding on to each other as the glass rocked, and they certainly weren't flirting. It was hard to keep one's footing because the surface had no handholds. Only the four-footed llama was steady on her own.

"And if it is flirting, why the heaven not?" Aurora asked. "You both know where you're heading, emotionally."

Meanwhile, the woman's shapely body against his was a delight, regardless.

"Thank you," Apoca said. "You're not bad yourself."

Oops! Of course Aurora was relaying his thoughts to Nimbus, who was reporting to Apoca. At times he forgot he was bugged.

"It doesn't require ants or nickelpedes to pick up on a man's thoughts, regardless," she said. "I saw you looking for the reflection."

"Sorry," he said, embarrassed for a different reason than the vac scene side effect.

"Next time maybe I'll stand with my legs apart." She paused half a moment. "For steadiness, of course."

"Of course," he agreed weakly. Now she was teasing. It was devastatingly effective. He had seen her bareness from the vac scene side effect, but the idea of covertly seeing up under her skirt was electrifyingly naughty.

Then the giantess made a misstep and flailed her arms, and the two of them were flung into the mesh cap. Apoca was plastered against him from neck to knee, marvelously soft in all the right places.

"Kiss her," Aurora said. "She wants it."

Trusting the ant, he found Apoca's face and kissed it. She didn't try to protest. She kissed him back. She did not use her power, but it hardly made a difference; he was near the end of his fall into love.

"You are achieving immunity," Aurora said. "When natural love is complete, the kiss enslavement loses its power."

"That's what I wanted for you," Apoca said, evidently advised by Nimbus. "I don't want an ensorcelled man for romance."

"You wanted me free?"

"Free of love slavery. Not of love."

"But what of yourself? I have been trying to give you leeway. I want you to join me of your own free will."

"When I kissed you before, that was power-free. But perhaps I miscalculated, because the backlash from that kiss smote me. This one nearly finished the job."

This was an amazing confession. He was courting her, but had thought he had not yet made much of an emotional impression. She was not even pretending to play hard to get.

"Um," he said, out of sorts.

"I am not much for pretense."

"Maybe then we shouldn't kiss again, at least until we're sure."

"And maybe we should just go for it."

"But—"

She kissed him. This one had its own power. He reveled in it.

"Look! They're floating!" Vinia said.

Startled, they broke the kiss and looked about. They were indeed floating in the glass, while the others were sitting on the bottom beside the standing llama. The two of them had somehow forgotten that they were not private; all else had been tuned out.

"Floating. I thought I was the only one here who could do that," Ghorgeous said. "Next thing they might even start holding hands."

Everyone laughed. Nolan and Apoca slowly settled to the bottom. There seemed to be no further need for distancing.

Apoca took his hand. That was its own delight.

They looked out, admiring the passing scenery. It seemed that the giantess knew where Squid lived.

"Not exactly," Aurora said. "She is in mental touch with other invisible giants, and they know where things are."

"But—"

"I am relaying the green path to her," Vinia said. "Via the bugs."

That was right; he had forgotten. They would get there.

A vast crack in the landscape opened up below. "What is that?" Apoca asked, startled.

"That is the famed Gap Chasm," Nolan said, privately gratified that he knew a detail she didn't. "For a long time it had a forget spell on it, so few folk even knew it was there, but now it is generally known."

And there above it floated a small boat with a fiery sail. Aurora was turned on by the sail, being a fire ant. But that was it? It was hardly big enough for four people to sit comfortably.

Two people were in it, a young man and a lovely woman. The woman waved as they spied the traveling glass. She had lustrous dark-brown hair and pearl-gray eyes, together with a body so eloquently slender as to make Apoca seem slightly heavyset. Nolan didn't even notice what the man next to her looked like.

"Those are Lydell and Grania, Dell and Nia for short," Dolly said. "They co-captain *Fibot*. She is older than she looks."

"She looks about twenty-five," Nolan said, fascinated.

"Physically, yes. But in life-span she is sixty-five. She got rejuvenated when she had to swim through a pond of youth elixir. It's a separate story. Dell really is twenty-five."

"And they are a couple?" Apoca asked skeptically. As a general rule, men preferred to have the advantage of age; older women were not sought.

"A successful one. She has both the youth and the experience to keep him happy. They know each other well and have no illusions about age. It was integrity that brought them together."

So the man preferred character. That spoke well for him.

Apoca nodded. "That will do."

The giantess brought the glass to the boat and slowly tilted it so they could walk on its side. She popped the mesh off.

"Welcome to *Fibot*!" Dell called. "Do come aboard."

"Um, is there room?" Nolan asked cautiously, eyeing the tiny craft.

Nia smiled brilliantly. "It is larger than it looks. This way, please."

Nolan and Apoca stepped onto the small deck, now holding hands for reassurance rather than romance. They followed the other couple to an open hatch in the center, near the fiery sail. "Beautiful!" Aurora said, staring at the sail.

Dell descended, then Nia. Nolan was amazed, because there should not have been room for such depth.

"You first," Apoca said.

"But if you descend above me . . ."

"No reflection needed."

That was beyond even a tease. He descended to an amazingly capacious chamber below, then watched as she followed. He saw her shapely legs under her skirt then . . .

She jogged his elbow. "Snap out of it, Nolan."

They were standing beside each other on the lower deck. "What?"

"You freaked out," Aurora said.

A panty freak. Well, he shouldn't have looked. But he knew he would do it again if he got the chance. It was a liability of masculinity.

Nia laughed. "I do that to Dell. He has finally learned not to look, at least not in public."

"This way," Dell said, seeming amused. Maybe they made a game of it, pretending accidental exposure. A young man who liked to look, and an old woman who liked to show it off, now that she had it again. And why not?

Somehow they were in a sizable ship with many halls and chambers. How could this be?

"The Fire Sail Boat is larger on the inside than the outside. It is known magic," Dolly said, startling them. They had been so distracted by the phenomenon that they hadn't realized she had followed. How had she navigated the ladder? Beside her were Gent and a lovely, strange woman, together with a small green bird and what appeared to be a mechanical fish on legs.

"I carried her down," Gent said.

"You're not speaking in puns!" Apoca exclaimed.

"The boat has a counter-hex spell. My curse will return when we leave it." He turned to the woman beside him. "And this is Gina. Tata brought her an accommodation spell so she could become small and visible and tour the boat."

"Tata?" Nolan asked.

"The robot dogfish." The screen on the front formed the word HELLO. "And this is the pet peeve." He indicated the bird.

"They largely run the ship," Dolly said. "They are the crew."

Oh.

They came to a larger stateroom, where another couple stood to greet them. The girl had dull brown hair, gray eyes, and was an unimpressive teen. The boy had black hair and eyes and was a similarly unimpressive teen.

"Squid and Larry," Dell said.

Nolan was amazed. He had expected a sort of octopus dressed up to vaguely resemble a human girl, and some sort of scintillating companion. These two were so ordinary as to be almost Mundane.

Squid laughed. "I really am an alien cuttlefish, but I am good at emulation." She lifted one arm, and it separated into two twined tentacles, then re-formed as a human appendage. "I think of myself as a human girl, most of the time. I certainly have human passions that annoy the Adult Conspiracy, because I'm not technically bound by it." She turned to her companion. "And Larry is the male form of my friend Laurelai."

The boy changed form to become a girl in male clothing, which was clearly awkward because of her full-blown figure, then reverted to male. He still looked distinctly ordinary, though his clothing now looked somewhat bent out of shape.

"Larry is the human host for Demon Chaos," Dolly explained. "Normally the Demon doesn't show it, as he is still observing the local ways of mortals and prefers to be mostly anonymous."

Oh, again. Nolan had not before appreciated how a couple with more sheer magic than any other would not want to be the handsomest and prettiest of all, but it did make sense. They preferred to disappear into the crowd.

"Let's go tour the ship while these two couples handle their business," Nia suggested.

"Much as we would prefer to snoop," Gina said regretfully as she followed their hosts.

The peeve hopped to her shoulder. "You're an amateur anyway. Nia's the prime expert on snooping," it said with Gina's voice, for all that she had not yet spoken. "Her talent is to make floating eyes that can peer into anyone's private business."

Nia did not comment, but a pair of eyes formed in the air that stared broodingly at the bird for blabbing her secret. The peeve hunched as if iced. More games among friends.

In a generous moment Nolan and Apoca were alone with Squid and Chaos, apart from the ever-watching baton. And Aurora and Nimbus, who were maintaining complete mental silence. "We understand you have a problem with the Dwarf Demon of Talents," Squid said, "who seems to be neglecting his job."

So word had gotten around, or maybe they had a private source of information, like the outernet. "Yes," Nolan said. "Every baby is now delivered with the same talent. We need a favor from you in that connection."

"You wish to exchange favors, per BLURB?"

"We think so. But we have no idea what favor we might render for folk of your powers."

Squid angled her head in a perfectly human manner. "There just might be something."

Nolan feared he wouldn't much like it, but he kept his mouth shut. They did need the favor.

Apoca cut to the chase, as was her wont. Nolan liked that word, because it seemed either negative or misspelled, yet wasn't. It meant custom. "What something?"

"Well, I'm only fourteen, in human terms. I'm not supposed to know about Conspiracy things like summoning the stork. Actually I have had some experience because we visited another timeline where I was adult, but I hardly remember the details." She glanced sidelong at Larry, whose expression changed subtly. He had quietly become Chaos. "He remembers, but isn't supposed to tell me." She made a brief cute mad face.

And Chaos, who had existed for billions of years, was honoring the local code, Nolan realized, because he was trying to learn mortal ways. He was playing the role of his host, a teen boy.

"And?" Apoca asked.

"And I'm alien, however girlish I may look or feel. So Chaos has never kissed an adult human woman, though we are seriously dating."

Where was this leading?

"And?" Apoca repeated.

"I'd like him to have that experience."

Apoca's face remained neutral, but Nolan began to see a green path forming, for all that Vinia was off exploring *Fibot* with the others. "And?"

"You are adult," Squid said seriously. "And reputed to be a pretty good kisser."

Nolan had to laugh. "Her kiss can enslave a man!"

"Not Chaos."

Suddenly it was clarifying. "You want me to kiss Chaos?" Apoca asked,

Squid was young, and alien, but now she managed a fair blush. "Yes."

"When Prince Nolan is courting me?"

The blush continued. "Yes. So Chaos can finally know what a real mature, womanly kiss is like."

Apoca turned to Nolan. "Would you object?"

He was shaken. "I don't govern you!"

"You did not answer my question."

He pondered it for a good half a moment. How did he feel about it? Then he realized he was curious. How would her potent kiss affect the Demon? "We are both experienced lovers elsewhere, from before we met. You kissed Gent twice. I kissed Nimbus and Aurora in their dream forms. No, I don't object."

"Then I will do it." She smiled. "Squid pro quo."

Both Nolan and Chaos smiled, sharing a trace of male appreciation. Apoca clearly had experience and mind, signals of maturity.

Squid turned to Chaos. "This is a fair exchange, BLURB-style. You guarantee that Dwarf Demon Talents can't cheat. That should not be considered alien Demon interference in the Demon Xanth's domain. You are merely preventing the Dwarf Demon from interfering. In return, Apoca will kiss you with her full power, so you will get a hint of what my kisses will be like, once I get there, except I'll have less potency. Okay?"

Chaos made a small twitch with one little finger. It was a minor gesture, but Nolan felt the power of it rippling outward. Something in the universe had changed. The Demon had done his part.

Now Apoca did her part. She stood and approached Chaos, who stood to meet her. "Put your arms about me, gently. Lower your face to mine. Be prepared for Xanth's most potent kiss."

Nolan knew she was not exaggerating. He had seen its effect and felt its potential when she kissed him while stifling her power. Even her stifled kiss had had a profound effect on him; her powered kiss would be phenomenally stronger. The Demon would know he had been kissed by a mistress of the art.

The two came together and kissed without further ceremony. They merely stood there embraced, touching mouths, but the power radiated instantly and irresistibly outward. The very air seemed to shimmer.

Nolan had no awareness of walking across the chamber but discovered himself kissing Squid, who was kissing him back. It was clear that she had no reservations. She might be technically a child, but she did know how to do it. Both of them were committed to others but were compelled. Yet it was more than that. There was an environment, an awareness, that encompassed the whole of the ship. He was picking up on it and knew that Squid was too. Dell was ardently kissing Nia; no real surprise there, as they were a married couple. Gent was kissing Gina. That was a surprise. He knew that out beyond the ship men were suddenly kissing women, who were not objecting at all. In fact, they moved to intercept the approaching men while getting into the correct position. They were not mere passing pecks; each smooch was passionate. It was in fact Xanth's biggest kiss-off. The child Vinia and the ghost Ghorgeous were looking on with unconcealed envy, being too young or too insubstantial to participate, besides having no males to partner with. What a demonstration of the Demon's peripheral power!

"That's only the beginning," Aurora said. "Nimbus is relaying the essence. Here it is."

Then Nolan, and Squid, felt what Apoca was feeling. They were in her mind. She had normally had complete control over the male response to her kisses, but she had never before kissed a Demon. Especially not this one. If a normal Demon was a galaxy, this one made a galaxy seem like a grain of sand. Chaos was indeed the most powerful of all the Demons, regardless of the mortal shell he was borrowing at the moment. Apoca's power was hardly a ripple in the merest electron of his being. He was half the universe, literally.

More than that. The Mundanes knew of four fundamental forces: Strong, Weak, Electromagnetic, and Gravity. In fact the Demons animated them, with Jupiter the local representative of Strong, Venus the Weak, Mars Electromagnetic, and Earth Gravity. But there were five. The fifth was Magic, represented locally by Xanth. The Demon Chaos was the master of all of it, the raw stuff from which reality was fashioned. It governed the actions of the other five forces, and of the others like Dark Matter, represented by Nemesis, and Mass/Energy, represented by Neptune, and Antimatter, represented by Fornax, and the several Dimensions, represented by Saturn, and of course the myriad Dwarf Demons. All of them were incidental compared to Chaos.

Apoca's mind was stretched in obscure ways that she could not begin to understand, let alone handle. Her feelings were an incomprehensible mishmash. This was one thing that she, as a mortal person, had that the Demon did not: human feeling. He was learning it from Squid and now from Apoca. His abiding curiosity was coursing past her lips and on into her heart. Into her gut. Into her very most private crannies of existence, her secret self. She was being stripped naked in ways that would have appalled her had she even understood them.

Yet that, too, was only the beginning. She was stripping him also, in her fashion. It was the mystery of her soul that truly fascinated him. Demons had no souls, and even passing contact with mortal souls flummoxed them. That was how Squid had corralled the most powerful Demon ever to exist: she had inadvertently touched him with her soul. He could not give up that contact. If the Demons had any weakness, it was their addiction to the nuances of the soul, once they encountered it. That generally meant human contact, though there were exceptions. Squid was one; as the adopted alien sibling of four human children, herself emulating a human child, she had gradually picked up a soul, sharing portions of theirs. They had gladly shared with her, their souls growing back what they gave to her; it had made them siblings in a closer sense than mere family relations ever could. But hers was nevertheless an artificial soul, a composite of four. Apoca represented the first fully natural soul this Demon had encountered. He was for the moment lost in wonder, feeling like a grain of sand himself. This was, perhaps, what Squid had really wanted: not his appreciation of the barely significant maturity of Apoca's speck-of-sand physical body, but his intimate contact with the incalculable majesty of her original soul.

Yes, he had touched humans before, notably Larry, whose body he used as his human host. But that was hardly the same. Larry's physical body was male, but his true gender was female. The Demon actually provided the masculinity for the form. He was thus adjacent to the soul but could not properly understand its essence. The mystery remained. This contact with Apoca, in contrast, lent another perspective: that of quasi-romance. From that orientation he was able to explore her soul spiritually. That made all the difference.

"Souls are complicated," Aurora remarked to Nolan. She, as an ant, had none of her own, but surely appreciated his. He could only agree.

The physical universe was also complicated. Now Apoca saw the galaxies in their clusters, extending outward to the very boundary of reality. They were myriad, infinitely too many to count or even to imagine. Together they formed obscure shapes, each galaxy being a mere atom in a vastly larger structure. Was it some kind of creature? She couldn't tell.

Then she realized that it was the real bodies of the Demons, rather than their local mock-ups, amorphous clouds of matter and force. The largest was a turmoil of seeming nothingness, a chaotic mass of concept and emptiness.

Chaotic? It was the Demon Chaos in his natural form! He animated the mortal body of Larry merely as a device to become tangible to Squid and the other mortals. Because there was no possible interaction otherwise.

She was kissing half the universe.

Apoca was a spirit, touching a male entity who had no spirit. Her form was a matter of opinion. Now she traveled, propelled and guided by she knew not what. She flew at many times the speed of light, which the foolish Mundanes thought was impossible, to a galaxy so distant that its light might never reach Xanth. She plunged into it, passing between stars or through them, unaffected. She came to a world shaped roughly like a scorpion with an elevated tail. Then to that tail, which seemed to grow enormously as she approached it. There were seas and mountains on it, rivers and valleys and weird trees.

On the spreading branch of one tree was a nest, and in the nest was a kind of scorpion, with three legs in front and two more behind, and a raised segmented tail with a deadly-looking stinger on the end. She landed on that stinger, turning out to be tiny compared to it, and took hold of its skin.

And she picked up on the scorpion's thoughts. "Contact telepathy,"

Aurora said. "Scour Scorpion doesn't know we are here, but we can read him."

Scour Scorpion was lovesick. He longed for the acceptance of a lovely female, Scylla, but she was largely uninterested in him. He had been told that he had something that would win her savage heart, but he had no idea what it was. He was just a low-caste imported worker locked into a dull and wearing job that the higher-caste workers wouldn't touch. If he did not perform at par one day, he would be cashiered the next day and sent back to his home tree in disgrace. He had to perform!

He contemplated the day's garden of bulbs. Fifteen of them ready to be stung. The first ones would be easy, as his night's accumulation of serum impregnated them with the trigger for forming the meaty bolus that the top-caste mantises fed on. The middle ones would be doable. But the last ones would feel like running his tail through a wringer.

He glanced at his tail. It was a standard segmented effort, indistinguishable from any other of its type. Its only distinction was the pink copper ring he wore on the second to last segment. He had inherited it from his mother. She had told him to wear it always until he found a female worthy of it.

Which led into another frustration. There was the female he thought worthy: Scylla. She was the collector of the stung bulbs, which she took to the curing oven along with the produce of the adjacent workers. She had the loveliest tail he had ever seen, the segments perfectly aligned. He would gladly give her the ring, but only if they had a relationship. There was no sign that she would ever be amenable to any personal association with him. Still, he mooned and sunned and starred for her.

Well, on to work. He picked up the first bulb and held it firmly high by two of his forelegs, maintaining his balance with the third leg. He swung his stinger over his head. He stung the bulb with the needle point of his stinger, injecting just the right amount of serum. He set it down and waited for his stinger to recharge. Then he picked up the second bulb and stung it also. He shut his eyes and imagined that it was a juicy honeybug that would scream and expire, coagulating into a delicious meal. The third one he pictured as a predator that had mistaken him for a victim. Yow! As it instead got a bellyful of poison. Served it right.

He gave up the joys of imagination as he progressed through the middle range. This was merely wearing work and his tail was tiring. He just wanted to get it done.

Then came the final five bulbs. His stinger was weary and running low on serum. Each one was a worse chore. Finally he reached the last one, but just couldn't sting it. He was out of juice.

Scylla arrived. Oh, no! He didn't have the complete array. She would report him, as she was required to do, and he would be busted and sent home in disgrace. But what could he do? He needed more time to recharge.

"This is sad," Nimbus said. "He's going to wash out, and lose his job and his girl, when he could so readily win both."

Apoca was perplexed. "How so?"

"All he has to do is give her the ring. It will multiply her potency and make her the most influential stinger of her generation. That's why his mother was so great. It works only on females, a female secret, so he has to give it to the right one."

"How do you know this?"

"I know about scorpions. They are compatible scourges. That's how they operate."

Apoca was intrigued. "Too bad we can't tell him that."

"I wonder. We're not ghosts, we're visitors. Maybe we can."

So Apoca tried. *Scour!* she called mentally. *Give her the ring! You have nothing to lose and everything to gain.*

Scour reacted. "What am I thinking? This is crazy." He did not realize that the thought was not his own.

Apoca tried again, boosted by the nickelpede's ability. *It is not crazy. It is your chance to win her. Take off the ring and proffer it to her.*

Meanwhile Scylla Scorpion was entering his area. "All done?" she clicked.

"I—no, not yet," Scour clicked as he tried desperately to think of a suitable stall. "I have one left to do."

She eyed him with all three antennae, surprised. "Why not all of them?"

GIVE HER THE RING!

Numbly, he applied his pincers to the ring and carefully twisted it off his tail. "First I must give you this." He proffered the ring. "It was my mother's."

Scylla was amazed. "Is that what it looks like? A Ring of Power?"

YES.

"Yes," he echoed, fearing disaster.

She took the ring and applied it to her own tail. Suddenly she seemed almost to glow. Her posterior assumed a new vibrancy as the power of the ring infused it. "It is! It really is! With this I will be the most potent stinger in the clan!"

"Yes," he agreed weakly. "My mother was."

She oriented her lovely antennae on him. "Yes, of course I will marry you, Scour, as soon as I deliver these boluses. I will honor your mother's legacy. We have some caste rising to do."

Just like that? "But—"

"Oh, yes, one remains to do." She picked up the last bulb, held it high, and delivered a perfect sting. Then she set it in the trough with the others. "Thank you for saving one for me to verify with."

"Uh, yes, of course."

She pinched one of his pincers in a scorpion kiss that made his whole body reverberate. "Come along, now. There are nuptials to accomplish, among other things."

Apoca and Nimbus lifted off Scour's tail as the happy couple walked toward their sudden future. It seemed that their job here was done.

"We were visiting angels," Apoca said, amazed. "Touching poor mortals."

"We made it happen," Nimbus agreed.

They sailed up, up, and away from Scorpion World. Away from the stellar system. Away from the anonymous galaxy. In a tiny fraction of a moment it was like a grain of sand behind them. They were back in the larger fabric of the universe.

Next Apoca became aware of the other larger reality. "I am still kissing Demon Chaos, back in Xanth proper. Only an instant has passed."

"A romantic instant," Nimbus agreed. "Are we going home now?"

Apoca eyed the zooming galaxies they were passing. Each was unique to itself, grandly rotating about its massive black-hole center with its curtains of stellar spirals studded with novae and supernovae. "I don't think so. We're still headed outward."

"Something is sending us somewhere. Do we know why?"

"I have no idea. Maybe Chaos is up to something."

"What would he be up to, aside from feeling up your soul and fathoming your mature kiss?"

"I have no idea. But there must be something."

They came to a black blob of a dim-starred galaxy and plunged into its fringe. Somehow in that dark fog they found a Stygian system with a gloomy planet barely able to maintain its orbit, hosting giant alien slugs. And on to a colony of slugs basking in muck, then up along a muddy river slogging its way through the meanders of a gloomy forest, and out to a giant cabbage in the quicksand center, where two sodden rafts were moored. There were even moldy signs identifying the river, in a language they had never heard of but somehow were able to read now: STYX.

The River Styx? That bordered Hell? No, it had to be a trick of translation. This would be the alien hell, parallel to the one near Xanth. In a universe as vast as this there had to be parallels.

They flew to a giant gray slug feeding on the cabbage. The smell was awful, but of course that was their Xanthian perspective; it might be like perfume to the natives. They landed on the head section of the slug, which was not aware of their presence. So this was another anonymous visit.

They read the slug's mind. He was Slough, a young male ready to mate and start a family, if only he had a prospect. There was a lady slug he liked, but she had no interest in him. That situation seemed almost familiar to Apoca; maybe it was universal. Her name was Slender Slug, and she was just coming into season. If Slough did not get her soon someone else would. But how could he get her amicable attention when she was looking for an older, better-established, more slimy male? At any rate he had come here to feed because he had seen her come to this cabbage, and he wanted to be near her, just in case. He stayed on the opposite side so she did not know he was there and could not angrily send him away.

"Let's delve," Nimbus said. "I'm not much familiar with slugs, but as long as we're reading his mind, maybe there's something buried in the sludge."

They delved. They found a packet of salve Slough had inherited from his grandfather, of little or no seeming value other than nostalgia. It was supposed to enhance adhesion, enabling a slug to double or triple his stickiness when navigating difficult surfaces. Slough had never needed it, but perhaps in the future he might.

Meanwhile this was excellent cabbage, tasty and nutritious. He finished one large leaf and moved to an adjacent one.

And there around the bulbous body of the cabbage was Slender. She was twice his mass, as a nubile female should be, and thick in proportion. But for a lady slug she was, well, slender. In fact, she was cramming her body full of cabbage in order to put on more mass and be ready for mating and progeny. To be as solid and sexy as she could manage.

And she was in trouble. The leaf she was feeding on had detached from the main bulk of the cabbage and was leaning perilously close to the surrounding quicksand. If she got dunked in that, she would be lost.

Slough was at a loss what to do. He could not even try to help her physically; if he slid to her leaf it would just make the descent faster. In any event, her greater weight would soon slide them both into the deadly sand, never to emerge. He could not pull her clear even if he had a secure leaf to stick to; she was far too heavy.

The salve! Apoca yelled mentally. *Give it to her!*

Slough hesitated, perplexed. Why was he thinking of that?

It is super sticky, Apoca reminded him, pretending to be his own sluggish thoughts. *So she can power her way up and off.*

Oh. That might indeed help. Slough emitted a package of smells, the slug way of communicating. He wafted the little cloud of them toward her. "Take my salve," they conveyed in aromatic detail. "It will enable you to stick much better."

She sent a fragrant cloud back. "I'll try it. I'm desperate."

He brought the package to the surface, then humped his skin, flipping the bundle across to her. It struck her flank and stuck there as it was supposed to. She flexed a fold of her skin and took it in. She would absorb its content internally, then spread it out to her surface.

In barely a moment and a half she felt its impact. "Oooh!" she wafted. "It's working! I can stick much stronger."

Then she slid powerfully up the dangling stem to the safety of the main body of the cabbage. "You saved me!" she wafted. "How can I ever repay you?"

"Mate with me," Slough wafted, hardly believing his fortune. He knew he had to act immediately, while her gratitude was fresh and before any other male winded her readiness.

"Come do it," she wafted.

He slid toward her, his system revving up for the engagement.

Apoca and Nimbus were already up and away, their business here done. "Bleep," Apoca muttered. "I wanted to see how alien slugs signaled the stork." She was flying by the imperative of the kiss, not her own will.

"At least we were able to help, again."

"Yes. It seems we had a romantic mission here also."

"We helped Boy Get Girl," the nickelpede agreed.

Now they were back out in the universe, among the sand grain galaxies. Still amidst the kiss, which had now lasted all of two instants.

"This is really coming to obsess me," Apoca said. "What is the Demon up to, apart from plumbing the very depths of my being?"

"Maybe he owes favors to alien creatures and is using us to handle them."

"With his immense power? It would be easier to do them himself."

"Not if he has trouble relating to tiny souled folk, as the scorpions and slugs seem to be. You would have trouble handling nickelpede or ant affairs."

"I would," Apoca agreed. "But I'm not sure that's the whole of it."

"Neither am I."

"Regardless, Chaos is a pretty good kisser. Squid may be young, but she has taught him well."

"Now he will be better, thanks to you."

"Perhaps."

They came to a giant cluster of young stars that were not exactly a galaxy but were packed so close together they seemed to be almost touching each other. They dived into it. The stars turned out to be farther apart than they had seemed from a distance, whole light-minutes, but the region was a burning blaze of light.

"Aurora would love it here," Nimbus said.

"I would," Aurora agreed. She was in touch, relaying their experience to Nolan.

They were in a dense tapestry of beams of light passing between the closely packed stars. There were flickers throughout it, as if currents were animating it. No, they were beams of colored lights, zipping between stars as if playing tag.

They intercepted one such beam, a blue one, and became an unnoticed part of it. This was Blair Blue, young, bright, and male. He was orienting on Pinkie Pink, a pretty female. If he could catch her he could have her; this was that kind of game, fun but with real stakes. The girls loved to tease the boys but did have to merge beams if fairly caught. However she had little if any romantic interest in him, so eluded him by using clever reflections at intersections that shot her off in unexpected directions. All he could catch were tantalizing flickers of her deliberately narrow escapes. He was becoming quite frustrated, exactly as she intended.

"This kind of teasing is not nice," Apoca said. "She is trying to torment him."

"If there is a way for him to catch her, and our pattern remains, we must know the clue to what he needs," Nimbus said.

"Yes. But what is it?"

"What indeed. As far as we can tell, Blair is a completely ordinary light beam, while Pinkie craves novelty."

"Novelty," Apoca agreed. "Actually we represent considerable novelty, being alien creatures from unimaginably far away. Too bad that doesn't count."

"Unless we make it count," Nimbus said thoughtfully.

That started a mental dialogue. Could they somehow do it? "Maybe, just maybe, we can," Apoca said. "We have become light ourselves, for this interaction, so Blair is slightly longer than he was. If we stab ahead and catch her taillight, we can impress on her our utter alienness, and that will be a full dose of novelty."

"Let's do it."

Pinkie came to an intersection and slowed slightly, something the light beams of Xanth and Mundania were unable to do. Or rather, she was extending her length to make herself longer, seemingly almost within reach. She was playing it invitingly close, intensifying the cruel tease.

Apoca shot to the front of Blair, extending his length just a little.

They caught the tip of Pinkie's tail. *Alien light!* they flashed, letting Pinkie feel it.

The touch electrified her. Here was more novelty than she had ever known! She fell instantly in love. She let Blair advance to overlap her completely, so that the two beams formed a lovely purple that awed all the other beams. Not only were they in instant love, they had spectacularly merged. The experience was illuminating.

And Apoca and Nimbus were vaulting back out of the scene, out of the stellar cluster, out of that entire region of space. They were on their way home.

"Good job, well done," Apoca said.

"But we still don't know why," Nimbus said. "There must be some point to this exercise we are unable to understand."

"Maybe it was just a diversion, so that he could savor our essence."

"Our grown mature female woman essence," Nimbus agreed. "We delivered that in good measure. Any other male would have been seduced into abject love slavery."

"Squid is surely a phenomenally lucky pseudo-girl."

Suddenly Apoca was back kissing Chaos, three instants after she had started. The kiss broke and she took a breath. Physically it had been nothing special, and not much emotionally, but mentally—what a happening!

"Thank you," Squid said as Chaos faded into the background. "The favors have been exchanged. The scales are even. You will be going to see the Good Magician next. He will tell you your spot mission."

Just like that? Nolan, reverting to his own consciousness, was surprised.

Chapter 6

MNEMONICA

Apoca was surprised. Was she the protagonist again? It was getting hard to tell. But there was the baton, hovering beside her. She had felt like the protagonist before, but it wasn't her turn. What had happened?

"I was tuning in on you," Nolan said. "Via Aurora and Nimbus. Then you ended the kiss, and my awareness returned to me. Only to discover us here in"—he paused to look around and spied a sign—"Limbo."

Now Apoca looked around. There was the sign, neatly mounted on the trunk of an acorn tree in otherwise pleasant green scenery. Assorted pie plants grew in patches, and there was a thick-trunked beerbarrel tree nearby, surely filled with boot rear, the beverage with a kick. They would not go hungry or thirsty. Also a shoe tree with assorted slippers, and clothing trees. Even a pan-tree for ladies' underwear. But something was missing. "Where are the others?"

"I am here with you," Nimbus said. "And Aurora is with Nolan."

"That's a relief! But what about the other members of the Quest? And Dolly Llama and Gina Giantess? Not to mention Squid and Chaos and the Fire Sail Boat?"

"We were there with them," Nolan agreed. "Now we're here."

"Squid said we had to go see the Good Magician."

"I already saw the Good Magician. That's why I'm here courting you."

"Something is weird," she concluded. "Maybe it is my turn to see him, though I'm not sure why."

"Someone is coming," Aurora said, with Nimbus relaying it.

"Uh-oh," Nimbus said. "I feel a blanket of silence closing in on me and on Aurora. I fear our participation is not allowed near the Good Magician's Castle."

"But you two are our friends," Apoca said. "We like to compare notes with you."

There was no answer. Apoca saw Nolan glancing at his own shoulder in surprise. The bugs had been silenced. They were still there, in fine fettle, only unable to communicate. Good Magician's rules.

They oriented on the sound of footsteps. In one and a half moments a lovely young woman appeared, making her way cautiously toward them as she passed through a patch of pie plants with a lingering look at a ripe lemon meringue. Extremely lovely. She was in fact the shapeliest black-haired beauty Apoca had ever seen, and she had seen a number recently. She could tell that Nolan was close to freaking out, though the girl was modestly dressed. It was not that he was a lecher but that this knockout was simply overpowering. Every slightest move of her body as she walked hinted at romantic rapture. Even Apoca herself found herself wondering what it would be like to kiss this creature.

She needed to break up this spectacle before it got out of hand. "Hello!" she called.

The woman looked at her. "Hello," she echoed, her voice dulcet. "Do you know where we are?"

Nolan was silent, his mind evidently too full of visual ecstasy to leave room for any other function. He was after all a man; allowance had to be made.

"We do not," Apoca said. "We suddenly found ourselves here with no explanation."

The girl smiled uncertainly, the expression making her even prettier, if that was possible. "Me too."

"Maybe we're dreaming," Nolan said. He certainly looked dreamy.

Enough of this. "I am Apoca, and this is my companion Nolan. We are on a special Quest. Who are you and why are you here?"

"I am Chameleon. I don't know why I'm here."

"Chameleon!" Apoca and Nolan said almost together. "The Chameleon?" Apoca asked.

The woman looked at them, startled. "I am just myself, nobody important. Is something wrong?"

Apoca took a breath. "You're a historical figure!"

Chameleon glanced down at her figure as if making sure something illicit wasn't showing. "I've been told my figure is okay."

Apoca remembered that the historical Chameleon varied with the cycles of the moon, ranging from beautiful and stupid to ugly and smart. "It's okay. I meant you are known from long ago. I am surprised to find you here."

Chameleon focused. "I remember, I think I will marry Bink, and we will live a long time."

Nolan shook himself out of his trance. "You remember your future?"

"Sort of. I remember my past as a village girl, with the men looking at me, and I remember what will happen to me, but it gets sort of vague in the distance. Is that all right?"

"That's fine," Apoca said reassuringly. "This is a strange place. We don't understand it well either."

"Maybe I can understand it better in my smart phase."

Which transition would take two weeks. "Maybe."

"I will try it."

"Uh—"

But the woman was already changing. Her lovely features faded and became ordinary, then ugly. She was now a crone. "Now we shall see," she said. Her voice had a new authority.

"But your full cycle takes four weeks!" Apoca protested.

"And was involuntary," the new Chameleon agreed. "This is evidently not a normal Xanth setting. Somehow my duller self caught on. It seems we have options we lacked before."

"It's Limbo," Nolan said, no longer at all distracted by her appearance. "There's a sign."

"Which means that we have been lifted out of our normal habitats and are in a presumably temporary state of uncertainty. There must be a reason. A purpose."

"Uh, yes," Nolan agreed.

"I saw an indication that the Good Magician's castle is in the vicinity. You said you are on a Quest. Could that relate?"

"We were told we would be seeing the Good Magician," Apoca said.

"Let's not rush it before we get a better notion. I seem to be in a framework that allows me to gain some perspective on the whole of my life. Is this similarly true for you?"

Apoca exchanged enough of a glance with Nolan. "No."

"Interesting. Is one of you the protagonist?"

She was sharp, all right. Apoca glanced at the baton. "Yes. At the moment I am."

"Then I may have been summoned to assist you in your Quest. Perhaps you should provide me with more details of it."

They told her about it, right up to the Kiss. Chameleon caught on swiftly. "So a Demon is involved. He would of course have the power to craft a temporary reality for us and put us here in Limbo. I may have an insight to his intention."

"You do?" Nolan asked. "You are smarter than we are."

"Of course. Which is surely why I am here. You need input beyond your own capacity."

Apoca appreciated the insight but was discovering that she did not like this version of Chameleon as well as the other. She suppressed that attitude. "What are we missing?"

"The Demons are in most respects all-powerful. They entertain themselves by playing Demon games, competing for enhanced status among themselves. They typically make wagers on mortal situations, because these are unpredictable. Their ground rules require them not to intervene, ensuring that the contests are fair. They also have a policy of nonintervention in each other's domains. Thus Demon Chaos will not directly interfere in the Land of Xanth. But since he has obviously been asked to help you, he is doing it indirectly. Thus my appearance."

"He did help us," Nolan said. "He is ensuring that the route to find Dwarf Demon Talents will be there."

Chameleon glanced at him with perhaps a mixed emotion: contempt for his low intelligence and appreciation for his handsome body. "Would that be the limit of Squid's request?"

This time Apoca and Nolan shared a generous glance. They had not thought of that! Squid was a nice girl. She would have asked for more.

"Mortals can't hope to compete with any Demon on any level other than emotion," Chameleon said, seeing that they understood. "You have virtually no chance on your own. So Chaos, to please his mortal friend, and perhaps liking the mature kiss Apoca delivered, is doing more. He can't intervene directly, but there may be an indirect way to help you. By giving hints of your necessary strategy to persuade Dwarf Demon Talents to do your will. The three incidents occurring in the Universe Kiss seem to have a common thread; Boy desires Girl and has the means to win her provided he can recognize and implement it in time."

"Yes," Apoca agreed, half-awed. Why hadn't she seen that before?

"So you may have the means to win your Demon's case, and thus yours, if you can discover it."

Enable Dwarf Demon Talents to win Dwarf Demoness Transcription? What could they possibly offer him or her to enable that? They were grains of sand.

Chameleon angled a shrewd glance toward her, fathoming her concern. "Perhaps this current episode will enable you to figure it out."

"We don't even know what the current episode is," Nolan complained.

"Exactly. This is clearly a crafted setting, controlled by the Demon Chaos. He must be trying to clarify it for you, without being obvious. You will want to pay close attention to details."

The details of a crafted setting? Apoca elected not to comment. She wished Vinia were here to search out a green path.

"We'll try," Nolan said.

"There has to be a reason I was plucked from my ordinary life to appear here," Chameleon said. "I suspect that I will remember none of it when I return to my normal frame. I am here merely to serve my purpose, which I believe is to clarify this process for you. There will surely be others, similarly plucked. The two of you are the protagonists; only the pair of you are likely to emerge from this environ with intact memory. Apply it well."

Environ. Short for environment. In her smart phase she used a more sophisticated vocabulary.

"We'll try," Apoca agreed. She found herself somewhat awed to be in the presence of such a historical figure, even if it was in Limbo.

"Probably the Demon Chaos will guide you through this confusion as you orient on his hidden purpose."

"We hope so," Nolan said.

A figure appeared in the distance. "Ah, there's Bink!" Chameleon exclaimed. "Back to my favored form." She changed rapidly to her comely aspect and ran to meet him, her body flexing in all the right places and her hair flinging back appealingly.

Of course that would be what he liked, Apoca thought. Phenomenal beauty and devotion coupled with barely enough intellect to function. A virtual nymph. Nymphs were typically good for only one thing, which made them highly popular with men. Gratification with no backtalk.

This time Nolan did freak out, though no underclothing showed. Apoca waited until the girl was far enough away to be beyond jiggle range, then touched his elbow. "Wake, dreamer. She's not for you."

He snapped out of it. "Did I get distracted?"

"You did. But that's par for the course."

Chameleon caught Bink in a flying hug. They kissed passionately, the perfect couple. Then she whispered in his ear and walked on beyond him. And faded out, her scene done.

Bink walked toward them. He was a rugged but rather ordinary man. "Hello, Nolan and Apoca. Chameleon tells me I have business with you. How can I help?"

"We're not sure," Apoca said. "It seems we have a sequence to play out, but we don't yet know what it is."

Bink considered. "I seem to have a memory of my past and future, but the two of you appear in it only quite vaguely, and are peripheral. You are not in my family line."

"We are not," Apoca agreed. "Chameleon conjectured that we are here to learn something that will enable us to succeed in our Quest, and that you must be here to help us. Beyond that we have no idea."

He glanced cannily at her. "Was she in her smart stage?"

"Yes."

"Then she's probably right. So I'd better just tag along with you until I find a way to help."

They started walking, going nowhere in particular. They chatted with Bink, who turned out to be an easygoing, likable chap, not at all egoistic because of his historical significance. Of course here in Limbo, he didn't know he was historical.

They came to another sign: GOOD MAGICIAN'S CASTLE.

"That's right," Apoca said. "We are supposed to see the Good Magician."

"That normally means three Challenges to pass, so that he knows you are serious."

"Even in a simulation?" Nolan asked.

"A realistic simulation."

Of course it would be realistic. What had they been thinking?

They gazed at the castle beyond the sign. It was surrounded by innocent scenery and a competent moat featuring a ferocious-looking moat monster. But what drew Apoca's attention was a sinister sparkle in the air surrounding the scene. She didn't like the look of it. "This castle may or may not be legitimate," she said. "But I doubt it is safe to barge on up to it."

"My thought too," Nolan said. He picked up a stone and threw it toward the moat.

The stone exploded in midair, forming a cloud of sand that fell to the ground like rain.

"Presumably we are safe from any real harm here in Limbo," Bink said. "But normally a careless move can wash a person out of the Good Magician's Challenges. He does not tolerate carelessness gladly."

And surely they did not want to wash out of this one. "Um," Apoca agreed.

"In fact he does not tolerate anything gladly," Bink concluded, remembering. "His grumpiness is famous. Or as Chameleon smart would say, infamous."

Nolan picked up a loose stick and threw it in the same direction. It burst into flame, leaving a cloud of ashes that drifted down to coat the turf. Finally he picked up a bucket of water that happened to be sitting beside the path, surely by no coincidence, and heaved a big splash. It puffed into vapor that heated on into smoke as it floated away in the trace breeze.

"This is hostile magic," Apoca said. "Entirely surrounding the castle."

"Then this must be my clue," Bink said. He stepped forward.

"Wait!" Apoca cried, too late. There was no sense in deliberately washing out.

Bink became the center of a conflagration. The magic fire tried to incinerate him, but he stood firm, ignoring it. It tried harder, only to wear itself out. Finally it gave up, all its power expended. The sparkle in the air was gone.

Now Apoca remembered. Bink had Magician-class magic that normally did not show: he could not be harmed by magic. The magic had destroyed itself trying. The way was clear. He had known this would happen.

Another man appeared, walking from behind them during their distraction. "Good show, Bink!" he called.

"Hello, Trent," Bink called back as he dusted off some dying flickers.

The legendary King Trent! Apoca was amazed again.

"What are we up to, friend?" Trent asked.

"We seem to be in a timeless spot simulation for the benefit of Nolan Naga and Apoca Lips," Bink replied. "They have a Quest and need to see the Good Magician."

Trent turned to them. Apoca was struck by his mature handsomeness. "Hello, Nolan and Apoca. I doubt we have met, though I seem to have a faint emerging memory of our eventual association. You are from my future?"

"We are," Apoca agreed, feeling girlish. "To us you are a historical figure. You established the Golden Age of Xanth, after first being vilified as the Evil Magician."

Trent laughed. "Vilifications sometimes lack substance. Let's see what I can do for you."

Bink had disappeared, his link in the chain completed.

They walked on through the recent death field. There was the moat. The drawbridge was up and secured from the other side; no help there. There was a small rowboat just big enough for three. And the horrendous moat monster. It was clear from the nature of its look and slaver that it would regard any reckless folk who tried to row across the moat as its meal for the day.

"This would seem to be it," Trent said. "I will clear the way for you."

"Uh," Nolan said uncertainly. The monster was far bigger than his serpent form, which would be the same mass as his human form. Ancestral forms tended to be more limited than magical transformations.

"Precisely." Trent faced the moat monster. "My friends need to cross this water. You had best turn tail and splash to the far side of the castle to provide them safe access. Do you understand me, snootface?"

The monster clearly understood. It gaped its cavernous maw and plunged toward the Magician, who would make barely one gulpful.

Trent made a gesture with one hand. The monster abruptly shrank into a harmless worm. It fell at the edge of the water and hastily delved into the safety of the muck.

The Transformer had made his case. The way ahead was now clear.

"Hello, love," a female voice said, startling them. Apoca, distracted by the transformation, had not seen the woman approach. She was of middle age but quite handsome.

"Hello, Iris," Trent said. He opened his arms, and she stepped into them. They hugged and kissed, briefly. Then he spoke to Apoca. "It was a marriage of mutual convenience, but in time it became real love. This sort of thing can happen." It was as if he knew of her caution about committing to Nolan. Maybe he remembered from their future.

"And what brings us here out of context?" Iris inquired.

"Nolan and Apoca are on a Quest, and seem to be in a simulation that requires our assistance. They have already met Bink and Chameleon, and now the two of us. It would seem to be your turn next, dear."

Iris turned to them. "Have we met? My memory is vague."

"We seem to be of a later age than you," Apoca said. "But we remember you. You're the Sorceress of Illusion."

"I am." Her features shifted, briefly mirroring Apoca's own. There was no doubt of her ability. But why would they need such high-powered illusion?

"We want to eliminate a problem in our time," Apoca explained. "All our babies are being delivered with the same talent, that of summoning pies of any kind, including mud pies. To do that we need to talk with the Dwarf Demon of Talents. This setting seems to be a bypath on the way there."

Iris nodded. "Mortals don't normally mess with Demons, unless the mortals are the objects of some monstrous Demon game. But the same talent for every child? That's appalling. Of course I'll help."

"The way this scene is going," Nolan said, "there will be something that only you can help us with."

There was a stirring on the surface of the water of the moat. Shapes rose out of the water. They were the heads of some kind of animal.

Apoca suffered a horrible realization. She had seen similar heads before. "Look away! Those look like basilisks or cockatrices! The female and the male of the species. Their gaze is lethal."

"I remember Astrid Basilisk," Iris said. "She assumed human form and was a really nice person. I believe there is a statue of her. But she had to be constantly veiled, lest she wipe out her friends."

"But that does not make much sense," Nolan said. "The moat monster would not have tolerated such creatures in its area. They would have been a constant threat to it. Anyway, they aren't swimmers."

"So they must be illusions," Iris said. "Either the changed appearances of fish in the water, or completely imaginary."

Apoca was not much reassured. "I don't want to meet their gazes regardless. Even the illusion might be stunning."

"It might be," Iris agreed. "But this falls into the area of my expertise."

"Handling basilisks?" Nolan asked.

"Handling illusions. I will change them into more compatible images." She faced the moat and concentrated.

Apoca couldn't help looking, though she squinted, just in case. The ugly faces converted into lovely mermaids in burstingly tight halters, together with handsome mermen.

"I'm impressed," Nolan said.

By the apparent transformation, or the halters? Apoca decided not to comment.

"Go ahead and cross," Iris said. "My daughter Irene will help you next."

And there was another woman, with lovely green hair that matched her green skirt. "Hello, travelers," Irene said as she got into the rowboat. "Thanks, Mom." Iris was already departing.

They got in behind Irene, and Nolan took the oars and stroked the boat out toward the merfolk. He was facing backward, but Apoca knew he would get plenty to see as they passed the figures.

It was time for introductions again. "We are from your future," she told Irene. "I am Apoca Lips—my tribe can kiss men into abject subjugation— and he is Nolan Naga, who can assume the three forms of his ancestry. We are on a mission to save the children of our time from the fate of all having the same talent. This appears to be a simulated setting we must navigate with the help of you earlier folk."

Nolan was silent as he rowed, but not from the effort of moving the boat. The mermaids were swimming in on either side and flashing him with their buxom torsos.

"I am Irene. My talent is to make plants grow. I'm not sure how this will help you, but I will do what I can."

"There must be something," Apoca said. "This is clearly a contrived setting."

They looked back to see what the merfolk were up to. The maids were taking off their halters, while the men were making muscle poses for the women in the boat. Irene shook her head. "Too bad they're only illusion."

Apoca could only agree. But they could have looked like basilisks and cockatrices without Iris's intercession.

They reached the inner bank and stepped onto land. The merfolk evinced disgust and sank back under the water, turning tail, as it were.

But now they faced a seemingly bottomless cleft in the ground, too wide to safely jump across. It was another Challenge.

"Oh look, a little Symmetree," Irene said, peering at a tiny flower.

Apoca knew that her specialty was plants, so she found this interesting. "Uh, yes, it's pretty." It seemed best to be polite.

Irene smiled. "Observe." She pointed to the plant. "Grow."

The symmetree responded by expanding rapidly. Its six crystalline branches became long planks that spread symmetrically across the landscape and also the cleft. Irene got on one and walked across without a problem.

Oh. Apoca followed her, and so did Nolan. How easy it was to handle the Challenges with the kind of help they had!

"Ah, there's Dor," Irene said, and went to hug and kiss him.

Apoca had not seen the man arrive, but that was par for this course.

They separated. "This is my husband, Dor," Irene said. "The son of Bink and Chameleon. His talent is to talk to the inanimate, and it answers." She squeezed his hand. "Of course, there can be disadvantages."

"You said it, sister!" a rock near her foot exclaimed. "I can see up your leg, and that's not all. I can see right up to your—"

Irene lifted her foot and stomped on the rock. It shut up.

"Rocks aren't very smart," she explained. "But a bit of discipline helps."

It occurred to Apoca that Nolan's talent of seeing and interacting with the imaginary might be similar to Dor's dialogue with the inanimate. The two men might have liked to compare notes, were the setting different.

There was a roar. They looked and saw an awful ogre forging toward them, about twelve feet tall and big in proportion.

"Bogey ahoy!" the rock cried.

"Me Oboe Ogre," the creature said with an oddly musical voice. "Who you?"

"You're as ugly and stupid as they come," the rock said.

The ogre paused, surprised. "Thank you."

"Ogres are justifiably proud of their stupidity," Dor explained. "Not to mention their ugliness and strength."

"Your voice is funny," the rock said, catching on to the way to annoy it.

The ogre began to swell.

Apoca smiled at Oboe. "Please, Mr. Ogre, may we pass by? We have to see the Good Magician."

The creature swelled up even larger. "Me smash she!"

Apoca realized that she had been foolish. Of course the ogre's job was to prevent them from passing. She had just asked it to mess up its mission.

"Stomp her!" the rock cried gleefully.

Apoca was coming to appreciate what Irene had meant about disadvantages. She wanted to stomp the rock herself, but that would give it a good view of her own leg under her skirt, up to wherever. She might tease Nolan about that view, but not a loudmouthed stone.

"I think this is a job for our son Dolph," Dor said grimly.

Then somehow Dor was gone and another man had taken his place. "Oh, an ogre," Dolph said. "Their job is to tie small trees in knots and teach young dragons the meaning of fear."

Oboe smiled horrendously and put his ham hands on a nearby sapling about as thick as a man's wrist, then readily tied it into a knot. Then he looked about for a dragon to teach. Finding none he oriented on Nolan and Apoca. He smiled again.

Apoca remembered that as bad as an ogre's smile was, an ogress's smile was worse. She was supposed to be able to curdle milk with it. Once, an actress had played the role of an ogress so well that she had even curdled water.

"Stand back," Dolph murmured.

What did he have in mind? They stood back.

Dolph changed into a roc, the kind of bird that could pick up a Mundane elephant in its talons and fly away with it. Suddenly the stones were singing, loudly and violently. Rock music, Apoca realized.

The roc spread his enormous wings, leaped into the air, and snatched the ogre as he launched up, up, and into the sky. Oboe made a musical note of surprise as he was carried to the atmosphere. The big bird flew to a nearby lake. There was a horrendous splash as he dropped the ogre into the water. Then he flew back, landed, and reverted to his human form.

"Thank you," Apoca said a bit weakly.

There came dreadful screaming from the lake, mixed with musical notes, as of creatures in abject terror.

"That wasn't nice," Apoca said, though she was not too sorry for the ogre.

"Yes. I didn't think of the loan sharks there," Dolph said. "They must have tried to take an arm and a leg, and he didn't let them. Now he's teaching them the meaning of fear."

Oh. The screams were from the sharks. They should have known not to mess with an ogre.

"Hey, I'm back," Nimbus said. "So is Aurora. We have been unsilenced."

"That's a relief. I much prefer your company. The Challenges, such as they were, must be over."

"A formidable creature is approaching, Aurora says."

Now the way was clear to the castle's front gate. A heavily veiled woman with a thick bandanna over her head emerged. "Welcome, visitors," she called. "Do come in."

Dolph had faded out. The rocks were silent. Apparently the Challenges were over. They went to join the woman.

"We are Nolan and Apoca, of a later time," Apoca said. "Together with our friends Nimbus Nickelpede and Aurora Ant. We seem to have been put in this rather timeless Limbo for a reason we don't yet properly understand."

"My husband, Humfrey, the Good Magician, will surely clarify it for you. I am the Gorgon. I mean you no harm; my veil will protect you from my direct gaze. You will not get stoned."

"The Gorgon!" Apoca exclaimed, amazed. "The Designated Wife?"

"Not exactly. That's in the future, when Humfrey goes to Hell to rescue me, and winds up also with his five former wives who are residing there, though they are nice folk. Then we will have to take turns, as Xanth permits a man only one wife at a time."

"Oh. Yes, of course." Apoca had for the moment forgotten that bit of history.

In three and a third moments they were ensconced in a comfortable living room. Nolan had spoken of the Good Magician's daughter-in-law, Wira, but she was not here. This was evidently before her time.

"Hello also, Nimbus and Aurora," the Gorgon said as she removed her bandanna to reveal her snaky hair. The little serpents hissed with pleasure at being freed. "I confess to being surprised by your friendly presence, but this is an unusual setting."

"This is an unusual situation," Nimbus said.

"MareAnn was the Designated Wife when I visited here before," Nolan said. "I mean, later in history."

"I understand," the Gorgon said. "I like her. I remember how we off-wives will confab when not on duty. We do have things in common." She smiled under her veil. "Humfrey is not the easiest person to get along with." Her headful of snakes hissed agreement.

"I like her hair," Nimbus said. "She plainly understands vicious creatures." That was a compliment.

"How did you come to marry him?" Apoca asked the Gorgon.

"My talent and my curse is to turn anyone who meets my gaze to stone. I hated it, but was locked into it. Until the Magician Humfrey came. He used his magic to make my face invisible for a time, freeing me of the curse. I fell in love with him at that moment. So I pondered a while, then made the excursion to his castle to ask him a Question. My Question was 'Will you marry me?' He made me serve a year as his assistant before he gave me his Answer: Yes."

"He what?" Nolan asked incredulously.

"A year's service is his standard fee for an Answer."

"But—"

"Be at peace, naga prince. It did make sense. By the time I completed that year I knew him far better than I had before. I could have changed my mind at any time and gone my way. He was in fact giving me a chance to break it off. But I chose to marry him with full knowledge of his grumpy nature, and I never regretted it."

Nolan spread his hands. "I suppose it did make sense."

"The Good Magician's strictures always do, once you understand them."

"It seems we have a spot mission here," Apoca said. "Which we are about to learn. But I am perplexed by the parade of early Xanth characters. They are all nice, and certainly helpful, but they seem to be just passing through. Is there a reason?"

"There is. You are dealing with a Dwarf Demon whose reliability and honesty have been questioned. The rules of Demon interaction will be enforced, but there might be ways in which the DD could still manage to cheat. He will foil you if he can, because he doesn't want to return to his duty. This show is not for your benefit so much as to remind him that a full Demon is watching."

Apoca was surprised. "Oh. I thought my interaction with the Demon Chaos was essentially over. At least, after this follow-up mission, whatever it is."

"Not exactly." The Gorgon's eyes were covered, but even so something showed in them. Something resembling disciplined chaos. It was very like half the universe lurking under the veil.

That, actually, was reassuring. Just as Squid's kiss had impressed the Demon, his kiss had impressed Apoca. He could have made her his love slave, had he chosen. His sheer power was exhilarating. She was glad to have him along, however veiled. "Uh, thank you."

"Now you will see the Good Magician Humfrey."

In perhaps one point three moments they were in his presence. The gnome-like eyes looked up from his giant Book of Answers. "The four of you will rescue Mnemonica." The eyes returned to the page. So he knew of the bugs.

Back in the living room they felt free to speak again. "Who the bleep is Mnemonica?" Nolan demanded.

"I will look her up for you," the Gorgon said. She went to the bookshelf Apoca hadn't noticed before—had it even been there?—and heaved down a tome, *Xanth Character Database*. She opened it and found the place. "Mnemonica, daughter of Nolan Naga and Apoca Lips."

They stared at her. "But we aren't even married yet!" Apoca exclaimed. "How can we have a daughter?"

The Gorgon nodded. "Remember, this is a sequence in timeless Limbo. Time is not linear here. The presumption is that once you come to know each other well enough, as I came to know Humfrey, you will elect to marry and signal the stork for her. Because that is in your future, you are free to change your minds and eliminate her, sight-unseen. In that event, your memories of her will fade; she will become an alternate character existing somewhere on Ida's moons."

Apoca exchanged a pained glance with Nolan. Eliminate their daughter? Without even giving her a chance? What a horror!

"If we are to rescue her," Nolan said, "we will come to know her, here in Limbo. So we could change our minds if we didn't like her."

"And she would never suffer rejection," the Gorgon agreed. "Because she would never exist, except as a might-have-been. I understand there are a considerable number of them residing on the moons of Ida. She should be in excellent company." Her veil quirked. "It occurs to me that your Demon friend is giving you a unique opportunity."

"It is nevertheless a horror," he said firmly. "We are not child slayers."

Apoca knew in that instant that they would marry and signal for Mnemonica. This was a key point of agreement between them. They would not sacrifice their prospective daughter.

"We feel the compatibility between you," Nimbus said.

"The name," Apoca said after approximately a moment. "It does not echo either of ours."

The Gorgon nodded again. "Men usually have sons, and women have daughters, as signaled by their alliterative names. But you will reside in the Queendom of Thanx, according to my future memory, where women have an independent streak. The girl surely reflects that. Her name signals assisted memory. Perhaps it reflects a special memory ability. She could be a historian."

Apoca found herself liking Mnemonica, despite not knowing her.

"I like her too," Nimbus said.

"What are we rescuing her from?" Nolan asked.

The Gorgon went to the magic mirror on the wall. "You heard the Question, glass-face," she told it. "Answer."

"Necessary background," the mirror answered. "Centurion Centaur was sent to eradicate a dragon menacing a village. But the dragon turned out to be a human-dragon crossbreed named Pallorjade, who could assume the forms of her ancestry and also had the talent of being able to remedy any abuse. When Centurion arrived she changed to lovely human form, flashed her panties at him, seduced him, and then married him. So he did eliminate her as a threat, but not in the manner anticipated."

"Hey, centaurs don't fall for panties," Nolan protested. "They prefer fillies of their own species."

"Centurion is himself a human-centaur crossbreed," the mirror retorted. "His human component was susceptible to human blandishments, and in any event Pallorjade considered his interference with her teasing of the villagers to be an abuse, so she remedied it in her fashion. He was up against formidable magic. Actually he was well off, because she turned out to be a good wife."

"Point made," Nolan agreed with a faint odor of disgruntlement. "Go on."

"Their son was Cenpal, who was thus a handsome human-dragon-equine crossbreed, with the ability to assume those forms. His parents wanted him to marry an equivalent crossbreed, but there were none readily available, and fewer yet were smart and pretty in any of their forms. So they abducted Mnemonica from the Queendom of Thanx and locked her in a chamber of their isolated castle, pending her agreement to marry Cenpal. There she remains because she can't escape, despite her ability to change forms, but refuses the nuptial. Thus she needs to be rescued."

"I should think so," Apoca said. "No daughter of mine is going to be forced into a marriage she doesn't want."

"Nor mine," Nolan agreed. "She deserves the best."

They shared another glance, this one tinged with dawning passion. Their future daughter was already drawing them together. They had a mutual interest in signaling for her.

"Cenpal agrees with you," the mirror said. "He wants to choose his own wife, not have her selected by his parents, however meritorious she might be. But he, too, is captive to their will, in significant part by the excellent estate he will inherit if things remain sanguine, and if Mnemonica should change her mind and flash her panties at him, he will be lost, as his father was."

Apoca nodded. Men seldom realized the power over them that women had when they chose to exert it. Cenpal was lost the moment Mnemonica decided. If she decided. That had to be her own decision.

"As it should be," Nimbus said.

"We need to rescue her soon," Nolan said.

"Prince Dolph will take you there," the Gorgon said.

"Oh?" Apoca said. "I thought the parade of early characters was over."

"It is, except for this one last task." The Gorgon raised one hand and snapped her fingers.

In roughly two and a third moments a wraith phased through a wall and shifted into human form. His shape-changes were more versatile than she had realized. "Hello again, folks," Dolph said. "What can I do for you this time?"

"You can deliver these folk to Centurion Castle," the Gorgon said. "They are ready to rescue their daughter, Mnemonica, from dire distress."

Apoca was not at all sure they were ready but knew they would have to do it somehow. Their daughter!

They walked to the central courtyard, where there was room for a roc bird. There was a basket just big enough for a man, a woman, and two bugs if they squeezed together compactly. They climbed in, not much bothered by the squeeze. Apoca didn't mind if her buxom parts were pressing against Nolan. They were after all part of the process.

Dolph changed. This close he looked even larger than he had when dealing with the ogre. He set his huge talons carefully through the upper webbing of the basket, spread his wings, and sprang into the air.

"Oh!" Apoca exclaimed as the basket lurched violently upward. It felt more precarious than Gina Giant's glass had. Could a bad pitch hurl them right out of it? "Would you mind—"

"Gladly," Nolan said, throwing his arms around her as he anchored himself in place with his spread knees. She knew he was not just being gallant. He really did want to be holding her like this, and she really wanted to be held. Why be coy? They were falling in love in concert. Maybe knowing that their marriage was inevitable helped. They were not going to abolish Mnemonica.

Their faces were now close together. Nolan looked at her with increasing intensity.

Ask her, you idiot! Aurora's thought came. Apoca realized that she picked up on it because of her close physical contact with Nolan.

"Would you—" he started.

"Gladly," she replied, and plastered a kiss on him. It wasn't as universal as the one with Chaos had been, but it had one thing that one had not: burgeoning love.

Then the big bird was descending. Had it made the journey in less than half a moment, or had their kiss been timeless? Did it matter?

"To be continued," Apoca told Nolan as she drew her face from his.

"You didn't use your power."

"Are you sure?"

He laughed. "Not quite." He knew she would not use it on him, preferring to win him naturally. He also knew that it hardly made a difference, since he had been primed for love anyway.

They were approaching a castle perched on the pinnacle of a tall mountain. "Surely she could escape that," Apoca said. "Isn't the flying fish one of your forms?" Because any form he could assume, his daughter would be able to emulate.

"It is. There must be a reason."

She peered closely. "The windows appear to be barred, with mesh between. But it could be poked out so a serpent could slither out."

"Yet the mesh remains intact."

Then they heard a buzzing. It seemed to emanate from the castle. It got louder as they got closer. This was curious.

A biting fly landed on the rim of the basket. It glared at them, showing relatively big teeth. Then it launched at Apoca, jaws gaping.

She was ready for it, or rather Nimbus was. The nickelpede gaped her own mouth and took it in as it tried to land on Apoca's shoulder. Apoca had not been bugged by bugs since teaming with Nimbus.

But now the background hum increased. Half a squintillion flies were orienting on them. Nimbus would not be able to protect them from such a swarm. They would get eaten alive.

The roc veered outward, escaping them. But now it was clear why Mnemonica didn't try to poke out the mesh and fly away from the castle. No living form would stop the bugs.

The roc glided down to a ledge safely away from the castle. It set the basket down, then reverted to man form. "There are vermin that need cleaning out," Dolph said. "I will do it as you handle the rescue."

"Uh, thank you," Nolan said.

"I will not return here. It will take time to drown the flies."

"Drown the flies?" Apoca asked.

But he was already in motion. He jumped off the ledge and changed in midair to a weird, winged creature, like an ugly butterfly as big as small house. The wings were paper thin and glistened with brown goo, which slowly dripped as the thing flew clumsily toward the castle. There was a faint sweetish smell, as if it were edible.

"What is it?" Nolan asked.

"I have no idea."

They watched the thing lurch on into the swarm. The flies dived in for their feast, landing all over the wings. The first ones stayed there, while more piled in.

"That's odd," Nolan said.

"The creature?"

"That too. I mean the flies don't seem to be departing, just coming in. It's as if they are stuck there."

"Fly paper!" Apoca exclaimed. "It attracts flies but is so sticky they can't take off again. They stay there until they die."

"Or are drowned," he said, catching on. "When he has a full load, he'll fly to a lake and plunge in."

"Meanwhile we need to get inside, unobserved, so we can advise Mnemonica the bugs are gone."

"There must be access via the mountain," he said. "Caves, tunnels, and the like."

Apoca spied a hole in the ledge they were on. "Indeed."

They walked into the hole, which obligingly widened into a tunnel with faintly glowing fungus on the wall so that they could see their way.

"This can't be here for us to use," Nolan said.

"It is for the rats," Nimbus said. "So they can forage outside. We nickelpedes are familiar with such devices."

"Also to lure unwary creatures in so they can be swarmed and consumed," Apoca said. "We fire ants have used them."

Apoca paused. "Which would be why this passage is human-sized instead of rat-sized. We may be regarded as prey."

"As with the biting flies," Nolan said. "A pack of vicious rats. Too many for us to handle before we get eaten."

"Which explains why Mnemonica doesn't sneak out this way," Apoca agreed. She glanced at Nolan. "Would you be able to catch a rat without killing it?"

"In my serpent form? Yes. But why?"

"If you catch the king rat, I will kiss him."

He nodded. "I will be jealous."

"Not of this kiss."

He laughed. "I will soon be immune to that kiss."

She smiled. Natural love did nullify the love-slave kiss. He was telling her that he was getting there. Well, so was she.

"Maybe it is time to stop flirting and get on with the mission," Nimbus said.

"Or we'll start dream-kissing him," Aurora said, flashing her nude human persona.

"Together. You take his upper half," Nimbus said, flashing her own bare dream form. "I'll take his lower half."

Apoca stepped briskly forward. They were teasing, but she preferred not to risk it.

Soon, plus a moment or two, they were in a spacious cavern. Rats appeared all around its edges, cutting off their retreat. The trap had sprung.

Nolan became the serpent, big enough to gulp down a rat or three with a single strike. But there were hundreds of rats, and they looked to be ready to take a few losses for the sake of their feast.

The snake formed into a hoop and rolled rapidly toward the king rat. Apoca admired the way he could assume any form of serpent; this was a hoop snake. The other rats were unable to swarm him while he was in motion. He reached the king, unwound, and caught the rat in his jaws. Then he hooped again and rolled back to Apoca. He unwound and held the king up, unhurt, for her. The rat looked distinctly nervous, but realized it was not being eaten, so maintained its regal bearing. Apoca knew how it was; she had to do much the same herself on occasion.

Apoca leaned forward and kissed the king on the snout. She felt it take; he was now her love slave. "Direct your troops to form an honor guard for us," she told the king, knowing that Nimbus and Aurora would project her thoughts to the rodent's mind. "And lead us to the castle dungeon in our-sized passages, unobserved by any guards."

Nolan set the king down. The rat promptly ran off to rejoin his fellows, squeaking authoritatively. They formed into a troop that marched on down the largest tunnel exit, leaving the way behind them clear.

"We work well together," Nolan remarked as they followed.

"We do."

Then they were in the dungeon. "Thank you," Apoca told the king. "Wait for our return, so you can escort us back out."

The king nodded royally, amenable to her slightest whim. The rats would wait.

They made their way up the stone steps of the dungeon. At the top was a brief landing and a locked door. "Barred from the outside, of course," Nolan said. "But there's a small window for the passage of food."

"SOP," she agreed.

He changed to serpent form, lifted his head, and slithered through the barred window. Then he changed back, heaved up the bar, and opened the door. "Madame may pass," he said with mock gallantry.

She walked through. "And here is your reward." She kissed him without the magic power.

"He's mostly gone anyway," Nimbus said.

"We heard that," Aurora said. "But it's true."

A guard appeared, evidently having heard the door opening. "Hey! What's happening here?!" He actually managed to convey both units of punctuation. Then he recognized her type. "You're another Lips!"

Apoca stepped in toward him and kissed him, this time with the power. "Be silent," she commanded the man. "Lead us to Prince Cenpal."

Nolan glanced at her questioningly. "I want to know what kind of man is being thrown at our daughter," she explained.

He nodded, amenable to that.

The guard led them up a winding stairway to a comfortable suite. There was the prince, handsome in man form. "Greetings, parents," he said. "I am glad to meet you. We have a discussion to negotiate."

"You know of us?" Apoca asked, surprised.

"I am a multiple crossbreed. I recognize the type. I saw you coming, in a manner, when the flies got taken out and the rats stopped scuttling. I knew something was up. You have to be here to rescue your daughter."

"And you did not sound the alarm?"

"Why should I? We have a common cause."

Apoca was taken aback. "We do?"

"Come in. Make yourselves comfortable. Yes, I don't want to marry Mnemonica any more than she wants to marry me. I want to make my own choice, as does she."

Now, that's interesting, Nolan said silently.

"So the two of you have more in common than being multi-crossbreeds," Apoca said.

He smiled ruefully. "We do. My parents chose well. But we can't agree to a forced marriage."

"How well do you know her?"

"We share meals. This because it is the only way for us to eat; the food is secured. I could depart the castle and forage elsewhere, but Mnemonica can't, and I don't want to go openly against my parents' wishes. They want us to associate regularly, in the hope that we will be attracted to each other."

"And are you?" Apoca asked alertly.

He hesitated. "She is a fine young woman, smart, pretty, and talented. Any man, crossbreed or not, should be glad to marry her. But she is indomitable in her resistance to being forced, and I have to respect that."

Apoca found herself liking this candid young man. He really was a good match. "Was he fooling her?" Nolan asked via the bugs, suspecting that there was more interest here than was being expressed.

"Maybe," she answered the same way. Then, to Cenpal: "You did not answer my question."

He shook his head. "You remind me of her, by no coincidence. You even seem to be close to her age, surprisingly. I do know better than to kiss her."

Because they were in timeless Limbo, their ages not changing with the settings. In effect they were time travelers. "I am perhaps older than I look. You still have not answered."

"I already told you I don't want a forced marriage."

Apoca was losing her patience. "Do I have to kiss you to make you answer?"

He laughed. "Then I would be your love slave, not hers."

She reached out and put her hand on his. "You called my bluff. I will not steal my daughter's prospect. You have nerve."

"It comes with my centaur ancestry."

"He loves her," Nimbus reported. The physical contact had enabled her to read the man's mind, as Apoca had intended. "They have not kissed."

So it was natural. That was best. The attraction was surely mutual. As was their resistance to being forced. They were two of a kind in mind as well as ancestry, different as that was. Apoca had not yet met her daughter but admired her steadfast attitude. Too bad the two had been brought together the wrong way.

She squeezed the man's hand. "Tell her."

Cenpal realized she knew. "She would just think I was doing what her captors wanted. That would really turn her off."

"It would," Nolan agreed.

"Tell her after we rescue her. Then it won't be forced."

Cenpal was surprised. "You approve?"

Apoca nodded. "It is a good match. We want what's best for her."

"Come to our residence in Thanx," Nolan said. "Or intercept us anywhere else. We will talk to her."

"I will do that."

Apoca let his hand go and stood to depart. "We are glad we talked."

"So am I," Cenpal said, clearly gratified.

"Mnemonica's suite," Apoca told the guard. He led them on to a high tower. It was clear there was only the one access, and it was locked. She was indeed a prisoner.

An elegant woman appeared, clearly no servant. Apoca almost collided with her but managed to stop with only the brushing of shoulders. "The dragon lady," Nimbus said.

"Madame," the guard said, clearly surprised.

"Step aside and pause," she told him. Then she faced Apoca. "You have to be her mother."

There was no question whom she meant. "I am."

"I am Pallorjade, *his* mother. I do want what's best for him, and Mnemonica is exactly what he needs, and I would like to have her in the family, but I see now that abducting your daughter was an abuse. My talent is to remedy any abuse. Therefore I will exercise my power to remedy this one. Do your thing; I will not interfere. It will work out." She walked away.

Did this make any sense? Apoca had a gut feeling that it did.

"Nolan agrees," Nimbus said.

The guard unlocked the door, stood aside, and they entered.

A young woman appeared. She had fair hair, fair eyes, a fair face, and a fair figure. "Mother!" she exclaimed, coming to hug her as her hair flashed plaid. "You seem so young!"

"It's a long story," Nolan said. "Collect your things. We are taking you home."

"But the locks, the flies, the rats!"

Why was she protesting? "She hankers for him too," Nimbus said, having read her mind during the contact.

"We have them abated for now," Nolan said. "We are here to restore your freedom, but we must act before the proprietors catch on."

"Yes, of course, Daddy," the girl agreed halfheartedly.

The guard led them down to the dungeon. There were the rats. "Oh!" Mnemonica exclaimed, dismayed. "I thought you meant they were gone."

"I kissed the king rat," Apoca said.

The girl's hair darkened with distaste. "Oh. Of course."

Apoca kissed the guard again, this time with her nullifying version. "Go your way," she told him. "Do not tell anyone of your part in this, lest you be hanged as a traitor for helping us. Resume your normal routine. If anyone questions you, refer him to Cenpal. He knows what's what."

The guard nodded, looking slightly disappointed. "He rather liked being your love slave," Nimbus explained. "No woman ever kissed him before, let alone that way."

The rats conveyed them in style through the passages until they emerged at the original ledge. Apoca gave the king rat a kiss of release, and the swarm disappeared into the mountain. They stepped out.

A dragon was just arriving. They stepped back into the cave, which was too small for the creature, though if it was a fire breather that might not be enough.

The dragon landed on the ledge and transformed to a man. "Hello, three!" he called.

It was Cenpal.

"For pitiful sake!" Mnemonica exclaimed. "What are you doing here?"

"Helping you escape. You and your father can handle the descent from the ledge by changing forms, but not your mother. I will give her a ride, as I know a navigable route." He transformed into a centaur. "She can kiss me if she wants to be sure of my reliability."

Apoca noted that the dragon had been much larger than the man, as was the centaur. Evidently the rule of preservation of mass did not apply to Cenpal. That probably meant that the dragon was the size of his mother's dragon form, and the centaur matched his father's form. Which meant in turn that he probably had no separate talent the way Nolan did, because magic tended to even out. Nolan's talent was seeing the imaginary, while Cenpal's would be changing mass.

"You are helping me escape?" Mnemonica demanded incredulously.

"Yes."

"Why?"

Cenpal glanced at Apoca. "Because I love you."

"Have you lost your mind? You should want to keep me at the castle, where you can ravish me if I don't accede to your will." She hardly seemed to fear that fate.

"No. I love you for your indomitable spirit. You will never accede, any more than I will. I wish we had met in other circumstances, where perhaps you could have loved me. But as it is, at least I can help give you the chance to find your happiness elsewhere."

Her hair became a tangle of kaleidoscopic colors. "You want me to love whom I please?"

"Yes," he said sadly. "Whoever else it may be."

Her hair firmed on green. She had made her decision. "Then I suppose I will have to marry you."

He stared at her incredulously. "I never knew you to be a cruel tease."

"I'm not. I am making an unforced choice."

"But that can't mean—"

She stepped over to him and kissed him. Little hearts flew out.

She broke the kiss. "I have wanted to do that for some time, but circumstances prevented. I did not use the power."

He laughed ruefully. "That's what you think." Then he reconsidered. "Did Mother intervene?"

"No."

"Yes," Apoca said.

He looked at her, assimilating that. "Then it must be all right."

Apoca turned to Nolan, her own hair turning green. "I think our job here is done."

He nodded. "Of course that means that we accept this timeline, with all that implies. Unless you prefer more time to—"

She stepped over to him and kissed him. More little hearts appeared.

She drew back her head. "I did not use the—"

"That's what you think."

They both laughed.

Mnemonica turned to Cenpal. "You'd think after twenty years they'd stop being mushy."

"Will we stop then?"

She laughed. "Touché."

Cenpal glanced at Apoca. "See you at the wedding."

Apoca and Nolan exchanged a glance and a thought. They knew they would soon be out of Limbo. But their later selves would still be there in this reality.

"We'll look older then," Nolan said to Cenpal and Mnemonica.

Then Cenpal became the dragon. Mnemonica became the serpent. She coiled around his torso, nonconstrictingly, so that he could safely carry her. He spread his wings and took off, flying toward the castle. She would be there, but no longer captive.

"The three romances in chaos had a common theme," Apoca said. "He desired her, and had the means to win her, once he discovered it. This seems similar, but I'm not sure what he had. I know that his mother has a talent, but I think it had to be more than that."

"Abject devotion. Her will will govern them."

"That would do it," she agreed.

"Is there a larger message for us?"

"There must be. Once we discover it."

He took her in his arms. "I think we don't need to go meet our older selves."

"We have our own memories to make," she agreed.

Then, looking over her shoulder, he spied something set in the outer wall of the mountain. "What is that?"

"You don't mean my supple torso?" she inquired archly.

"It's a tablet," Nimbus said.

They looked at it more closely. It was an octagonal metallic plaque with copper letters spelling out the words NOT HERE.

He laughed. "What we have in mind to do together, we'll do elsewhere, in privacy."

"And it won't be commemorated by a plaque," Apoca agreed.

They kissed again. This time a single heart appeared. It expanded to carriage size and took them in. It flew back whatever way they had come. The scenery around them blurred. It hardly mattered; they weren't paying attention to their environment.

Chapter 7

IMAGINATION

Nolan looked around when their timeless kiss finally timed out. They were back in the Fire Sail Boat, with Vinia, Gent, Gina Giantess, Dolly Llama, Ghorgeous Ghost, Squid, and an unfamiliar young woman. Had their whole adventure in Limbo been just another instant?

"And is Mnemonica just a figment of our imagination?" Aurora asked, relaying Apoca's thought.

"She can't be!" he replied aloud. "We'll make sure of that." He was courting Apoca, but now he knew he loved her, and that she loved him. He couldn't wait to signal the stork with her, especially knowing the result.

The faces around them were blank.

Apoca looked around. "Have we been gone long?"

"Most of a moment," Squid said. "You blinked out, then reappeared in a heart-shaped bubble. Did you settle with the Good Magician?"

They did not know about Limbo? "I think we have a long story to tell," Nolan said. "The gist is that we not only saw the Good Magician, we met a number of historical figures and rescued a maiden in distress."

"Who happened to be our grown daughter," Apoca said.

"A grown daughter!" Ghorgeous exclaimed. "I envy you."

"Was there a boyfriend who wanted her, and you helped him get her?" Vinia asked.

"Something like that," Nolan said, smiling. "It does seem to be a theme."

Apoca glanced at the young woman, who looked to be about fourteen, with long blue-black hair, pretty and shapely. "Have we met?"

"This is my friend Laurelai," Squid said. "Her talent is to change her age, so she can appear adult if she chooses."

"She's pretty close now," Nolan said appreciatively. Apoca elbowed him in a rib.

"I should explain," Laurelai said, smiling. "I have a device that enables me to change genders at will. Normally by day I am more comfortable female, and am Squid's friend, but at night or on special occasions I turn male. Then the Demon Chaos takes over the body and is Squid's boyfriend."

"I like the one," Squid said. "I love the other."

Dolly Llama had mentioned this. Now it was personal. "Thank you for that clarification," Nolan said.

Then Apoca spied something. "Gent and Gina—are you holding hands?"

The two looked. "Why, so we are," Gina said, not letting go. "I think it's a leftover from that kiss."

Nolan remembered that the two had kissed when everyone else did. He himself had kissed Squid. It didn't necessarily mean anything beyond the compulsion for everyone to be kissing at that moment.

"But the two of you are from entirely different venues, regardless how you appear at the moment!" Apoca protested. "You're an invisible giantess with a boyfriend of your type, and he was my love slave."

"We have no past and no future together," Gina agreed. "But that kiss made our present romantic. We'll soon enough get over it." She smiled. "Especially when I revert to my own size and appearance. Or, more correctly nonappearance."

Gent nodded. "Know zoom."

"No hurry," she translated. They already understood each other.

There was a ripple in the air. The face of Ghorgeous Ghost appeared. "What's next?"

"We resume our Quest," Nolan said.

He looked at Vinia. "If your paths are ready."

The girl looked into space, checking the paths. "Not quite," she said, surprised. "They're mixed but I think will clarify in a moment."

Nolan glanced at the baton, which had been hovering as usual, observing without participating. It seemed confused.

Gina looked at Apoca. "Is your time capsule vacant?"

"I suppose it is," Apoca agreed, surprised in her turn, because the heart-shaped bubble had remained in place instead of fading out when they arrived. It had merely become temporarily invisible.

Gina faced Gent as they still held hands. "My invisible giant boyfriend and I are only dating. He gets together with other invisible girls on occasion, to my annoyance. I think I am entitled to a passing tryst of my own."

Gent grinned, catching on. "Eye know femfiend."

"You have no girlfriend." She glanced around. "We'll be only a moment, I think, outside." She led him to the heart, and they stepped in and disappeared. It seemed it was possible to see out from inside, but not in from outside. It occurred to Nolan that that was just as well; he and Apoca had been handling each other as well as kissing and would have been chagrined had strangers along the route observed. Still, he would have liked to see into it now. How did invisible giantesses make out? Did they remove their clothes?

Exactly one moment later the two reappeared and stepped out. His shirt was askew and her hair was mussed, but both looked quite satisfied. They had evidently spent somewhat more than a moment in the heart. Just as the Fire Sail Boat was larger inside than outside, the heart bubble was more timely inside than out.

"There's a green path," Vinia said. The moment of indecision had been expended. Maybe the paths had known about the passing tryst.

The baton seemed reassured. Now the narrative was proceeding as it should.

"I must get outside," Gina said, using a comb to unmuss her hair. "I feel the transformation spell coming to an end. I will hold up the glass cup."

Nia accompanied her up the ladder and onto the deck. The others followed, not looking up until the skirts cleared. There was the cup hovering beside the boat. Gina was of course invisible again. Was she clothed or unclothed?

"You are thinking too much about another woman's body," Aurora said. "Apoca is annoyed."

He kept forgetting he was bugged. Then he saw Apoca's quirk of a smile and realized he was being teased. Apoca would surely show him her body soon enough.

The cup came to rest on its side on the deck, and they marched in. It tilted slowly upright and they slid to the bottom in half a tangle of limbs. Then the cap closed it off and it rose into the air.

Dell, Nia, Squid, and Laurelai (after a nudge from Squid) waved farewell. Even the baton bobbed, though probably they couldn't see it. Nolan, Apoca, Gent, and Vinia waved back. They were on their way.

"The bugs are relaying my picture of the greenest path," Vinia said. "It will be a while before we reach the nexus. Will you tell us what you did?"

They told, as the scenery rushed past outside the glass. "Then Mnemonica decided to marry Cenpal after all," Apoca concluded. "Once she wasn't forced. Then we kissed and rode the heart bubble back to rejoin you."

"Twenty years hence," Dolly said. "Is this another hint for your Quest?"

"It does match the theme," Nolan said. "He wanted her and finally found the way to get her."

"As the Dwarf Demon of Talents wants the Dwarf Demoness of Transcription," the llama agreed. "But what does he have that she wants? That is the mystery. Solve that, and you should have a better chance to persuade him to resume his job."

"But why is the answer so obscure?" Nolan asked, frustrated.

"Because Demon protocol requires that one Demon not mess with the domain of another. Chaos can't influence your Quest directly, other than by ensuring that the Dwarf Demon play fair, but Squid wants him to help more, so he is doing it via obscure hints. That way your Quest is your own doing and he is just a bystander."

"Some bystander!" But it did make obscure sense. The universe would be a hopeless mishmash if the Demons who ran it did not honor their agreed conventions.

The baton seemed relieved. Maybe the Demon Chaos's influence had been changing the story, confusing it.

"Figure out what DD Talents has that DD Transcription truly wants, so he can win her," the llama said. "Then all should be reasonably well."

Now Nolan wondered how Dwarf Demons did it. That session with Apoca had revved him up.

"Her too," Aurora confided. "She's revved." Nolan liked that news.

"Could it be something we have, that we can give him?" Apoca asked.

"It could be," Dolly said. "You provided the key input in more than one of the examples."

"Yet even a Dwarf Demon has so much power compared to what we have, this seems unlikely."

"There must be something," Dolly insisted. "Demon Chaos did not strike me as a tease, and he truly wants to please Squid. She may be an imitation girl, but she is a good person. She likes you, and of course your Quest is important. She does not want her own children to be delivered with the talent of conjuring mud pies or worse."

"No woman does," Apoca agreed, and Vinia nodded. "It's hard on cleanliness."

"Or man," Nolan said. "He wants unique children." Like Mnemonica, though there was no issue of talents there.

The baton nodded.

"Something else," Nolan said. "We saw a plaque that said NOT HERE. We took that to mean we should not become unduly affectionate at that locale. But now I wonder."

"You should," Dolly said. "That more likely refers to Dwarf Demon Talents, whom you seek. Demon Chaos may be providing you with a hint of the proper path."

Nolan's glance collided with Apoca's glance. Of course! They had been in Limbo to rescue their daughter, not to find the Dwarf Demon. It was a necessary bypath. Now they needed to get back to the Quest.

"We will keep an eye out," Apoca said.

The passing scenery slowed. The cup descended. They landed at a nexus of six diverging paths.

They scrambled out, except for Dolly, who would return to the pundemic region with her new friend, Gina.

Gent had been silent throughout. He looked longingly at the cup as it lifted into the air, and Nolan knew it wasn't the llama he was missing. He was remembering his tryst. He was a man in need of a woman.

"These paths must represent our possible routes to Dwarf Demon Talents," Nolan said. "He has to be on one of them, and not necessarily the last one we take. This must be the real start of our journey."

"Where's the green?" Apoca asked Vinia.

"The colors are muddled. None of them are pure green."

"What does that mean, normally?"

"That we are missing something. But I don't know what it is."

"So DD Talents is fudging the trail, blocking the colors," Nolan said. "But the plaques will clarify it. If we can find them."

"He is quietly trying to cheat," Apoca said. "And Chaos is quietly preventing it. But we still have to do the brute work ourselves."

The baton was restless, as if the script were going astray again.

Ghorgeous formed a face. "Maybe we're looking in the wrong direction. Is there green behind you?"

Vinia turned around to face a path wandering away. "Yes," she said, amazed. "Sort of. It's not completely clear. But that's the way we came."

Nolan got a notion. "Not necessarily. We came through the air, not on a trail. This may be a group of seven trails, not six. We just happened to be facing the other six."

"It occurs to me that the Dwarf Demon may not be able to outright cheat," Apoca said. "But he may be able to distract. He may be at the end of the least likely trail."

"But the green should show the way," Vinia protested.

"To a reluctant Demon? Messing up colors, or at least fudging them a bit, could be, well, child's play for him."

Vinia nodded thoughtfully.

The baton was wavering uncertainly. What was its problem?

"I think it wants to intervene in our choice," Aurora said. She could see the baton because Nolan could; she was reading his mind. "I think it wants us to take the seventh path."

Now, this was really interesting. Was the baton trying to become part of the story, instead of merely observing and recording it? Why? Wouldn't that be a breach of its protocol? That made him really curious.

"Let's try this one," Nolan said.

They tried the seventh path. The baton relaxed.

At first the way was routine. It wound around assorted trees growing shirts, trousers, dresses, shoes, and hats. Nolan saw Apoca pause by a shoe tree, tempted but not yielding. Then came a grove of pie plants bearing apple, peach, cherry, and humble pies. Then a marshy area with milkweeds, the bottles full and fresh. Then beerbarrel trees filled with fine boot rear. Gent was tempted by those. Then pungent cookie flora of all types. Vinia dawdled briefly, then impulsively picked a fudge-mint cookie. Then a pantree, growing pans. Another pantree grew pants. And panties. That made both men pause. How would Apoca look in a pair of those?

The baton seemed impatient.

It occurred to Nolan that these were distractions. Was the Dwarf trying to divert them so that they feasted, drank, and dressed instead of getting on with their mission? It was probably best to ignore even incidental temptations.

Then they passed through a misty glade, where nude nymphs were dancing. They twirled, flung their hair about, screamed cutely, and kicked their shapely legs high. One of them looked directly at Nolan and smiled as she inhaled, getting set to do her dance right up close.

He felt Apoca's firm hand on his elbow, steering him onward. He wasn't freaking out, was he? After all, the nymphs wore no panties. Not that that would stop some men from freaking. Nolan's eyeballs were steaming, but he wasn't freaking, quite. He realized that the baton must have alerted her. For some reason women seemed not to like their men peering too closely at other women, even if they were only scintillationly bare nymphs.

After that was a copse of TreeVees, with moving pictures on their shiny trunks. Nolan knew that if they watched more than half a moment the story lines would catch them and hold them until the shows were over. Mundanes were known suckers for that sort of thing.

And a field of vines bearing big green gourds. Hypno gourds! "Don't look," Apoca warned; the peepholes would hold the attention of those caught indefinitely as their minds meandered in the hypnotic inner geography of the gourds.

These were definitely distractions. "Stay on the path," Nolan warned. "DD doesn't want us reaching the end."

They focused on the path, ignoring the further beguilements along the way. Once they did that, the path promptly ended, disgusted. They were where it led.

They stood before an array of containers, each of which held a special object. The nearest was a model of a winged Mundane horse. It was glossy black with white wings, mane, and tail, a lovely sculpture. The box was labeled CREATIVITY.

The others seemed unimpressed. "Why are these empty boxes here?" Vinia asked.

"Maybe raiders took their contents," Apoca said.

They could not see the horse? Then Nolan realized that it was imaginary, thus only he could see it. "It's a winged horse, symbolizing creativity," he explained. "Invisible to most folk, as the baton is."

The baton nodded.

"A horse?" Vinia asked, her eyes starting to glow. "May I see it?"

Nolan put his hand on her shoulder so that Aurora could extend her telepathy to the girl, enabling her to see what he saw.

"Ooooh!" Vinia exclaimed. "What a beautiful creature!"

Apoca joined them, resting one hand on his arm so that she could see too. "A magnificent stallion."

"It's just a statue," he said. He had never understood what girls saw in Mundane animals.

The horse spread his wings, flapped them, and rose up out of the box, expanding as it did. It was becoming a full-size stallion.

"Ooooh!!" both girls oohed together.

"Well, I *thought* it was a sculpture," Nolan said, taken aback. "A symbol of creativity."

The baton danced, indicating that there was something he was missing. Ah—if this was like the baton, it was more than a symbol. It was Creativity itself, coming to folk who needed it.

The horse flew up into the sky and away, soon disappearing behind a passing cloud.

"Why didn't it stay?" Vinia asked.

"And where is it going?" Apoca asked.

"And why did it wait for us to see it before it left?" Nolan asked.

"It received a call for its service," Gent said, his pun curse abated in this setting. "It is going to do its job. There must be a reason for us to witness that call." Gent was evidently getting over his tryst with Gina and returning his focus to the Quest. Presumably the giantess was reorienting similarly.

"A reason," Apoca said thoughtfully. "I smell another Demon hint."

So did Nolan. He suspected that they would not catch up to DD Talents until they knew how to handle him. He understood why the hints could not be too obvious, but he was experiencing some underlying frustration.

Apoca leaned close to him. "Me too." She kissed his ear.

Nolan's frustration segued from the Quest to romance. He wanted more than an ear kiss, but this was not the time for it.

The box became a three-dimensional picture of a dull Mundane man sitting at a desk. There was a keyboard before him, and an oblong screen. The screen was blank.

What was it? The picture seemed to make little sense.

"It is a Mundane writer," Gent said. "Trying to think of an original story to type. Mundanes like to read imaginative stories."

So they did, Nolan remembered. Their lives were so deadly dull that they had to escape into pretend stories about more interesting folk, such as those in the Land of Xanth. The absence of routine magic was the abiding curse of Mundania. No one would live there if they had any sense. Which was of course the thing about Mundanes: they lacked sense. They were also chronically boring.

So why was this animated picture here? Even as a passing distraction it was too dull to be useful.

The flying horse arrived at the scene, visible only to them, the watchers. It was now relatively tiny, no bigger than the Mundane writer's head. The writer seemed not to be aware of it.

There was a bookshelf beside the desk, filed with suitably dull tomes like *A History of Imaginative Writing* and *P's and Q's of Syntax*. Obviously they were not doing this writer much good. A few Mundane coins were on a shelf just above the writer's head as he sat. Nolan recognized several pennies. He remembered that in Mundania pies did not grow on trees but had to be purchased from stores, weird as that seemed; maybe these were for the writer's next meal.

The horse landed on that shelf, folded its wings, sniffed the coins, then turned around and faced away from them. Had it checked them out and lost interest? Nolan doubted that. There was too much purpose in its actions.

Suddenly the horse kicked back with its hind hooves, scraping them along the wood. The pennies shot off the shelf, right at the writer's head. They plunged into the man's forehead and disappeared. How could that be? They should have bounced.

No, Nolan saw now that the pennies remained on the shelf. It was their shadows, or rather their spirits that had flown, assuming that coins had spirits. The invisible essence of the pennies had gone to the man's mind.

Vinia tittered. "He just knocked some cents into the writer's head!"

"Some sense," Gent said, interpreting the unconscious pun.

The writer clapped a hand to his forehead. "That's it!" he exclaimed. They might not have heard him sonically, but they picked up his thought. "My writer's block has ended. The most original, imaginative, evocative story idea ever! Boy meets Girl, Boy loses Girl, Boy recovers Girl. It's never been done before, in all the history of literature!"

Apoca shared a querulous glance with Nolan. This was originality in Mundania?

"I understand it's the template for their entire Romance genre," Nolan said. "Variations on the fundamental theme."

"I always thought Mundanes were dull," Apoca said. "Now I know it."

"Whatever works," Vinia said wryly.

The horse flew away. Its job was done.

The writer started pounding the keys on his keyboard, his inspiration unchained. Words appeared on the screen before him. He was in the throes of imaginative creation. Indeed, the Winged Horse of Imagination had done its job.

The words formed sentences. "Everyman saw Everywoman as she waited at the street corner for the light to change. She was gorgeous! He knew in that moment that they were destined to be together."

Apoca grimaced, her hair flashing plaid. "All that counts is her appearance?"

"Maybe in Mundania," Nolan said. "Not here." But it was uncomfortably close to Xanthian reality too. He had never seen an ugly nymph.

The sentences fuzzed and expanded, forming into the scene of a city street at an intersection. There was the man and there was the woman.

And Nolan found himself drawn into the scene. Not the writer in his room; the picture forming on the screen. The story being told. He was sucked into the form of the man. There before him stood the woman: Apoca in all her beauty.

The red light turned green.

He stepped forward, guided by the ongoing narrative. "Miss, let me help you! There's a nasty puddle."

Apoca looked down. Indeed, she was about to step into an ugly pool.

Nolan ripped off his jacket coat and with a flourish spread it on the muck. Then he took her hand and guided her as they stepped together onto the jacket and safely crossed the mess.

"You are so gallant!" she exclaimed as they crossed the street.

That was the commencement of a wonderful association. Apoca was all Nolan had ever dreamed of in a woman, and he labored assiduously to persuade her that he was her dream man. Things looked good.

Until the Evil Wizard NoGoodNick spied Apoca one day outside his Sinister Magic Shoppe. Smitten by her beauty, he assumed his Harmless Old Man guise and invited her in. He proffered her a vial of Enchant Him Instantly perfume, a favorite of women ready to settle down to housewifery with the right man. She took a single sniff and fell into his arms, unconscious. "Oops," he muttered in mock chagrin. "I must have gotten the wrong bottle. This is Knock Her Out Instantly perfume." A favorite of men not about to settle down yet.

When Apoca woke, she was locked in a windowless, doorless pink padded cell, naked except for bra and panties. She wasn't sure how she had come there or how she had lost her clothing, and she preferred not to conjecture. Her only remaining possessions were her decorative earrings.

She stood and looked around. There was no apparent exit, only a screen set in one wall. So she was being observed. Par for the sneaky abduction course. "Who are you, and what do you want with me?" she demanded of the screen. Of course, there was only one thing a nasty old lecher ever wanted of a lovely young woman caught in his clutches, but she needed to learn more about the rest of her situation.

A face appeared on the screen. It was the store manager. No surprise there. "I am the Evil Wizard NoGoodNick. You are beautiful; therefore I want to marry you and sire my evil progeny in you. If you don't agree to this reasonable proposition, I will simply tie you down and ravish you endlessly until you wear out and have to be replaced by another pretty girl. Choose!"

Apoca realized that she was in trouble. So she burst into tears and tore her hair, the way any captive maiden would. But while her hair masked her face she activated her special earrings and called Nolan. "Help! I am captive and about to be cruelly ravished until I wear out."

Nolan's Smart Ring chimed. That was Apoca's bell! He lifted it to his ear. ". . . about to be ravished until I wear out."

Horrors! He was the only one entitled to do that, when the time came. "I'll be there pronto!"

"Don't let him know you're my boyfriend. He has Knock Out Vapor, and probably magic defenses all around his store."

"I'll be sneaky," Nolan agreed.

He zeroed in on her location, which was a back room of the store. He got there in no more than a pronto, as promised. He put on his best Innocent Customer manner and entered. The store was empty, but he knew the proprietor was close. He marched up to the service desk and bonged the bell.

"Oh, bleep!" NoGoodNick swore villainously in the background. "A customer."

"They happen at the least convenient times," Apoca said sweetly as she emerged from her torn hair. "I will wait." She knew Nolan was on her case.

NoGoodNick was not much amused. "Indeed you will." His face disappeared from the screen.

Nolan looked up from his ring as he muted it, leaving the connection to Apoca so she could hear. "Ah, there you are, Nick. I am looking for a woman, Apoca. She was last seen in this area. Have you seen her?"

Of course the man had, right down to her underwear, which had not freaked him out because this was drear Mundania, where men appreciated well-filled panties and bras but merely labored to gain possession of them and their contents. "Maybe. What is your interest in her?" He was cautious because he did not want his dastardly deed to be found out; it would take an awful lot of bribes to cover it up.

Now Nolan got clever. "Oh, nothing much. She owes me for a meal I bought her back when we were dating."

"You dated her?"

"Yeah, once."

"Why did you stop."

"She was too ticklish."

The Evil Wizard was intrigued despite himself. "What's wrong with tickling?"

"She's too ticklish. She couldn't be touched. I couldn't even dance with her without her going into a screaming fit of laughter. You could hear it all the way outside the building. It was embarrassing."

"No, I haven't seen her," NoGoodNick lied.

Nolan shrugged. "Thanks anyway. I'll keep looking." He turned about and departed the store. The seed had been planted.

The Wizard promptly returned to his control center. "Feathers," he directed, "do your thing."

A flurry of feathers flew into the padded cell. They tickled Apoca mercilessly, brushing every part of her exposed body. She shrieked piercingly, trying to avoid them as she danced about, bouncing off the padded walls, leaving smears of spittle. Indeed, she could be heard outside the building.

NoGoodNick hastily nulled the feathers, and Apoca collapsed in a shuddering heap. A padded door opened and she scrambled out. The Wizard was quietly getting rid of her, as it would be hazardously complicated to try to ravish her. He did not want to alert the neighborhood to her captive presence.

She ran around the corner, where Nolan waited with a large shawl and a quaint Mundane vehicle called a car. She bundled into both and they sped off.

"Thank you for rescuing me," she gasped.

"Well, I didn't want anyone to ravish you before I did."

"Nobody did, thanks to you."

"Good thing he didn't know you aren't at all ticklish."

They laughed together. "I'm more of an actress. I'll keep the secret if you will."

"I'll keep it if you marry me."

"I'm thinking about it." But it was clear that Boy had regained Girl.

The story came to THE END.

They emerged from the scene and watched while the narrative went into fast-history mode. The story was published by a Mundane genre magazine, was an instant success, widely praised for its originality, and won the coveted Nebulous and Huggie Awards. Boy meets girl, boy loses girl, boy regains girl; who would ever have anticipated that? The author was a success, thanks to the nudge by the Invisible Flying Horse of Imagination.

"Something seems almost familiar about the theme," Nolan said.

"He had what he needed to save her and win her," Apoca agreed. "In this case a clever take on her supposed ticklishness."

They were back with the others. The baton was getting impatient. It was time to move on.

The next section was an array of Mundanish books on a shelf labeled FUNDAMENTAL ANSWERS. The title of one book was *Why Is There Something Rather Than Nothing?* Another was *What Is the Nature of Ultimate Reality?* A third was *What Does Woman Want?* Then *Is There a God?* And *What Is the Secret of Consciousness?*

"Who cares about such dull stuff?" Vinia asked impatiently.

Nolan picked up the book about Woman. "There might be something interesting here."

Apoca slapped it out of his hand. "I'll let you know in due course."

They went to the next section. This showed a series of plaques bearing obscure statements, such as THIS STATEMENT IS FALSE, or YOU DO NOT EXIST, or THE FINAL DIGIT OF PI, or THE EXACT FIGURE FOR THE SQUARE ROOT OF MINUS ONE, or HOW CAN COMPATIBLE PEACE AND FREEDOM FOR ALL BE ACHIEVED?

"Boooring," Vinia said.

"Do you see a green path?" Apoca asked her.

The girl brightened. "Yes."

"Follow it," Nolan said. If what they had seen so far were incidentals, he was ready for the essence. Baton wanted them here; there had to be a reason.

Vinia led them to—another baton. This one seemed female, having tresses on her head, tied back by a pink ribbon. She was floating in an alcove, evidently waiting for her next assignment. She seemed to be asleep.

Baton flew up to Batoness. He bobbed before her.

She woke with a start. A little speech balloon appeared just over her head. Words materialized within it. "What do you want, bulbhead? You know I'm not interested."

So Baton had a would-be girlfriend! Did he think Nolan could help? That was chancy indeed.

Baton nodded in the direction of Nolan.

Batoness did a start of surprise so sharp her ribbon almost fell off. "You brought a mortal man here? What were you thinking of? You know they're not even supposed to be aware of us."

Baton bobbed.

"And the mortal can see us? This is way beyond the pale!" Nolan noted the spelling; she was not referring to a bucket.

Apoca touched his shoulder so that she could see what he saw; the bugs must have been sleeping and forgotten to relay the sight. "Wow!" she murmured.

In the better part of a moment Vinia and Gent were touching Apoca, forming a kind of chain. "Oops," Aurora said. "Nimbus and I got distracted by the weirdness. We're back on duty now."

The chain separated, now that the others could see the action.

Batoness flew out of her alcove and hovered before Nolan. Her speech balloon fairly quivered with ire. "Baton tells me you can see the imaginary, including us. It's your talent. You're a born snooper. So you tell me: what are you doing here?"

Suddenly he was on the spot. He had little or no idea what he was doing here, maybe even less. But he was a prince; he had learned never to show indecision. So he parried with a question of his own. "What is your problem?"

"What the bleep do you care?" The bleep symbol looked like a coiled Mundane rattlesnake that had just been trodden on, seething with righteous rage and dripping poison.

There had to be a reason that both the baton and the green path had led them here. In some devious manner this setting had to relate to the accomplishment of the Quest. Nolan was not at all sure that Demon Chaos had tuned out yet. Was there another important hint, if only they could comprehend it?

Baton hovered, nodding. There was relevance here.

Nolan parried again. "Maybe I can do something for you. What do you want?"

"What do I want?" the batoness's print fairly screeched, flashing into italics, then capitals, before reverting to normal. The speech balloon was looking bedraggled; soon it might burst and spray words and letters across the landscape. "I want to get the bloop out of this Protagonism business and do something interesting for a change. Have you any idea how dull it can be?" Now her bleep was the color of poop.

Protagonism was dull? That must depend on perspective. "No. Can you show me?" That sent the mud-ball back to her.

"Here is a recording of one of my early assignments, 'Little Red Riding Hood.' Hang on and watch."

Batoness dissolved into mist, in the manner of a Demoness. An image formed from that mist, a three-dimensional picture. Apoca was sucked into it, becoming a girl wearing a red cape with a hood, the Protagonist. Batoness hovered discreetly overhead, now an image within the story. Nolan became an invisible observer.

The girl walked through the woods, carrying a covered basket. Soon she came to a cottage labeled GRANDMOTHER'S HOUSE. She knocked on the door, then pushed it open without waiting. "Hello, Grandma," she called gaily.

A figure was in bed, wearing a shawl and tight cap that concealed her head except for her projecting muzzle. "You look good enough to eat!" she said.

The girl peered more closely. The woman did not look familiar, though she did wear her regular shawl. "Oh, Grandma, what big teeth you have."

"The better to eat you with, my dear." The figure flung off her shawl as she leaped out of the bed and was revealed as the Big Bad Wolf. He had eaten Grandma and taken her place. The girl was able to get out only half a scream before the wolf was on her, gulping down the other half of the scream.

But the wolf had reckoned without Apoca. She grabbed his nose with both hands, forced his jaws together, and kissed him on the tip of his snout, making him her instant love slave. "Now, cough up Grandma," she told him.

The wolf hacked and coughed up Grandma, intact. "Why, thank you, dear. It was getting a bit close in there," Grandma said, bringing out a little mirror and resettling her hair, which had gotten sadly mussed.

Apoca uncovered her basket. "I brought you a basketful of cookies, Grandma."

The old woman smiled. "What a wonderful present, dear."

They sat down on the bed and ate the cookies, letting the wolf have the fallen crumbs. After all, love slaves needed to eat too.

The scene dissolved. Batoness reappeared. "That wasn't quite the way it happened, but I like this version better, though it is still pretty dull. Here is another, the Pied Piper of Hamelin." She dissolved into mist again.

A new picture formed. This was of a town overrun by rats. They were everywhere, stealing the children's food, intimidating the cats, and pooping on the couches. The city fathers realized that something had to be done.

Nolan was sucked into the scene. He became the Pied Piper. "I can rid your town of rats," he said. "All I want in return is a bushel of gold and your fairest maiden for my wife." He glanced at Apoca, standing beside and slightly behind the mayor, being his dutiful daughter. "She'll do." Apoca smiled shyly.

"Done," the mayor agreed. "Payment on completion."

Nolan brought out his pipe and started playing. Immediately the rats took notice. They swarmed toward him, mesmerized by the music.

Nolan turned about and marched out of the central square. The rats followed. He walked all the way out of town and to the bank of the river that happened to be passing by. He waded in, and the rats followed, diligently swimming. Why did anyone think a rat would drown if caught in water?

The river narrowed, channeling into a culvert that did not have an end. Instead it descended deep into the ground, never to be seen again. Garbage was conveniently disposed there. Nolan came to straddle the hole, playing his pipe, and the rats swam through obediently, right into the opening. When the last one disappeared, he stopped playing the compelling music and put away his pipe. His job was done. Maybe the rats would discover some sunless sea and be happy there. Regardless, they would never bother the town again.

He returned to the central square, his trousers sodden. It was empty. The mayor and townsmen were gone. There was no bushel of gold. He was being stiffed.

He sighed. This sort of thing had happened before. He had worked out a way to handle it that made other towns hesitate to renege on the deal. This was a new area, but word would get around soon enough.

He lifted his pipe to his mouth and played a different melody. Suddenly children appeared, boys and girls of all ages from two to teen, scrambling out of their houses to run toward him, screaming gladly. And one more: Apoca. "I am one week short of maturity, still technically a child," she explained. "I feel the call. I suppose I could resist it, but why should I pass up a man as handsome and talented as you?"

There was something about her he liked, apart from her appearance.

Nolan turned about and walked away from the square, playing the compelling music. Apoca walked beside him. The children followed. They went to a nearby mountain cliff. A door opened in the stone wall. They marched in to discover a marvelous realm of toys, pet bunnies, amusement park rides, and free candies. When the last child was in, Apoca closed the door behind them. The children were sealed in. If any of them noticed, they didn't care.

Nolan stopped playing. The children exploded into an orgy of fun.

Apoca approached him. "I may be a child for one more week, but I do know how to kiss." She demonstrated, and Nolan was of course happily lost. In real life Apoca was no teen, but that hardly mattered for the story.

The scene dissolved. They were back in Xanth, with Batoness hovering before them. "Again, I like your version better," her speech balloon printed. "Mine lacks the romance. Here's another." She misted. Nolan fell into the scene.

Good King Nolan Wenceslas looked out on the Feast of Stephen, where the snow lay round about, deep and crisp and even. Loudly howled the wind that night, and the cold was cruel. Then a hooded poor man came in sight, gathering winter fuel.

"Hither, page, and stand by me," Nolan said.

The page came, and he saw that it was Vinia. Well, why not? Pages could be male or female. They were merely animating an existing story with a set plot.

"If thou knowest it, telling," he continued. "Yonder peasant, who is he? Where and what his dwelling?"

"Sir, she lives a good league hence, underneath the mountain," she answered. "Right against the forest fence, by St. Agnes's Fountain."

She? Well, peasants were of both genders too. It was necessary so that they could reproduce their kind. Vinia went on to describe the peasant residence in more detail.

Nolan made a decision. "Bring me flesh and bring me wine," he ordered. "Bring me pine logs hither. Thou and I will see her dine."

Then the two of them bundled up and went outside, determined to locate the peasant and bring her to the palace for a good holiday meal. Page and monarch forth they went, forth they went together, through the rude wind's wild lament and the bitter weather. The snow had already filled in the peasant's tracks they tracked, but Vinia followed the green that only she could see.

The deep snow and cutting wind soon proved to be too much for the page. "I can go no further," she gasped. "There's snow in my boots."

"Nonsense, child. Tread thou in my footsteps."

She did, carefully, dubiously, and heat was in the very sod he had printed. They made it to the peasant's rickety shack, where the poor shivering, bundled woman was trying to light a fire in the aged stove. They brought her back to the palace, where they all unbundled in preparation for the meal. Lo, she was uncommonly fair as her face and figure emerged from the masking hood and cloak. In fact she was Apoca, animating the role.

"Thank you so much, sire," she said, smiling. "I'm starving."

That smile dazzled him. He leaned across and kissed her.

The scene exploded into smithereens. "That's not how it goes!" Batoness's speech balloon printed. Then she reconsidered. "But I do like it better."

"So do I," Apoca said, forming an air kiss with her lips. The kiss floated across to catch him on the nose, then dissipated in a fragrant little pink, heart-shaped cloud.

"Wow!" Vinia said. "That's the first time I was ever in someone else's story."

They discussed the larger situation. The batoness was stuck with common old tales ad infinitum and was sick of it. She craved original, interesting, exciting stories, rather than SOS—Same Old Stuff. The last word was printed sloppily, as if it had been overwritten from another word before realizing there was a child present.

Baton bobbed agreement. He wanted to help her but didn't know how. That was why he had brought Nolan here.

A bulb flashed over Nolan's head. Batoness was a kind of Damsel in Distress! She was what these mini tales had in common. Baton wanted to rescue her and win her love, such as it might be, but didn't know how.

But Nolan knew how. He faced Batoness. "Go see Squid, the cuttlefish girl. Make yourself visible to her alone, and introduce yourself via your speech balloons. Tell her how you met us via Baton. Then ask her for a favor. She can't do it herself, but she has a friend who can. Tell her you want to join our narrative as a Co-Protagonism Batoness. We have a much more original, interesting, and exciting story. It's not about dull fairy tales but about tackling a balky Dwarf Demon. There could be real trouble. You won't be bored with us."

Baton looked excited. This was how he might win her company.

"Genius," Apoca murmured appreciatively.

Batoness's hair flared. This interested her. It might indeed get her out of her dull track. Then she vanished.

Ghorgeous Ghost appeared. "You're shmarter than I took you for, Nolan."

"Thanks, I guess."

"You had no business kissing me in that Xmas story," Apoca said.

"I apologize. You just seem to be made for kissing, regardless of the role."

"I am." She closed on him and kissed him with magical passion. But this time he didn't float.

"I'm immune," he said. "You know why." Because he had fallen in love with her naturally, and that was more potent than love slavery.

"I do. But I will turn up the power." She kissed him again. This time his feet did leave the ground.

Batoness returned. "I did it," her balloon printed. "And her friend did it, after her girlfriend became a boyfriend with him inside the body. That was weird. I am now part of your narrative." She considered briefly. "He's some person, if that's what he is. I felt the awesome power as he twitched one finger."

"He's her boyfriend," Apoca said. "Let it go at that."

Sage advice.

Nolan looked around. There, on the trunk of a nearby tree, was the plaque with the words NOT HERE. Too bad it couldn't have been at the beginning of the path, instead of at the other end, saving them a fair amount of hassle.

"I see it," Apoca murmured. "I'm not sure it was there before."

Or was there reason? Could part of their progress be to pick up something that might help them further along the way? Like the batoness?

Chapter 8

ZOMBIE

Batoness was hovering close to Apoca. Then Baton winked out.

Apoca was startled. "What happened to Baton? He just winked out. I thought he wanted to romance you."

The speech balloon appeared, and the print formed in it as Batoness answered. "Not while we're on duty. Because there are now two of us, we can alternate, and the one not on duty can go elsewhere to relax. It is your turn to protagonize, and I will handle it unless you object."

"I don't object. I like being able to talk with you. Nolan sometimes wonders what Baton wants, as he doesn't speak."

"Males tend to think of themselves as strong, smart, silent types, but sometimes they are simply silent."

"Amen to that! But without them there'd be no one to admire our special qualities." Apoca inhaled, emphasizing a quality. Sure enough, Nolan's eyes sneak peeked.

"True. They are useful to that extent. That just about makes up for their liabilities."

They were walking back along the seventh path. Soon they came to the nexus. There were the other six paths, each leading into the unknown.

Apoca sighed. "DD Talents is bound to be on the least likely path. But these all look similarly unlikely. I fear there could be NOT HERE plaques on every one of them. I wish they were labeled."

"There are hints. The nearest one has a loose screw on the ground that a robot must have lost. The next one has a torn strip of a sheet that a ghost could have left. Another has a rotting piece of flesh, evidence of the passage of a well-aged zombie."

Apoca shuddered. "I don't much like zombies. I don't want to go there." She paused, reconsidering. "Which may make it the least likely path."

"Bleep," Nolan muttered. He of course had heard their dialogue, because of his talent.

Apoca sighed. The one thing about that was that to do it properly she had to inhale fully, compelling Nolan's attention.

They took the path. It soon took them to a sign saying ZOMBIE COUN-TRY—ABANDON LIFE ALL YE WHO ENTER HERE.

"Ignore that," Nolan said. "The zombies just want to scare off raiders who otherwise might steal their goods."

"It is after all the border," Batoness printed.

He nodded. "All the same, let's check first. Ghorgeous, can you—"

The ghost appeared, deep cleavage first, then face. "I can fhirm up anything you want to get your hands on." She had been flirting with him ever since kissing him, to Apoca's muted annoyance.

"—verify what's ahead and let us know?" he continued with only a trace of a pause.

"Just enough pause to make a mental snapshot of that mountain valley she flashed, that he can process later when you aren't close," Nimbus said cynically. "I doubt it was that impressive when she was alive."

Apoca nodded. Ghorgeous lacked substance but had malleable appearance.

"I hear and obey." The ghost was gone, leaving behind only a trace of evocative perfume.

Apoca adjusted her own cleavage. The living could play that game better than the dead could, when they had the mountains.

They gazed across the border. A zombie shuffled along it, dropping bits of rotten flesh, which seemed to regenerate so that he remained repellingly intact. He was probably a border guard. The trees were zombies, too, with moldy trunks and spoiling leaves. There was even a zombie bird, a vulture, pecking at one of the pieces of rotten flesh the guard had left behind.

Apoca shuddered. She did not like to think of herself as prejudiced, but this was not a region she liked.

In due course, perhaps a little longer, Ghorgeous was back, this time appearing tight-skirt first before her full thighs descended into legs and reached the ground. "There's an imprisoned living phrince," she reported. "In a haunted-house cellar, alone. No jailers, just strong bars. There must be an interesting story there."

"Of course there is," Batoness printed. "Protagonism guarantees it."

Apoca wished they could just get on with their mission somewhere else. But things were seldom that simple when they were in a narrative.

"I'll go check him out," Nolan said. He was never hesitant about getting things done.

"You do that," Apoca said. "I'll rest here. I'm not keen on haunted houses, other than yours in Thanx, Ghorgeous."

"I will show you the way, Nholan," Ghorgeous said, walking ahead, her hips flexing sexily. Apoca realized she had made a tactical error, letting him go alone with the ghost, but she was stuck with it. Not that she thought he would stray. Just that she was coming to resent his receiving the attentions of any other woman, particularly a comely one. She had never thought of herself as a jealous woman, but it seemed she had the potential now that she had a man to care about.

They departed, but Gent and Vinia remained. They got about exploring the local terrain. Apoca realized that they were giving Apoca and Batoness time to get to know each other better.

"I am new to this scene," Batoness printed. "I don't have background information. Normally I start at the beginning of a story, not in the middle. Do you care to fill me in?"

"Gladly. Nolan asked the Good Magician who his ideal woman was, and that turned out to be me. So he came to court me, and I believe he is winning his case. We already have a future daughter. But his service for his Answer is to solve the problem of talents, so that all new children don't have the same one, that of conjuring pies. I am helping him in significant part because I don't want our child to be stuck with that talent." She paused about two-thirds of a moment, then resumed before the moment could be complete, hoping she wasn't unkindly teasing it. "I don't think she does have that talent, or any other, so it seems we will succeed, in a manner. But the way is unclear. It appears we must enable the Dwarf Demon of Talents to win the Dwarf Demoness he fancies. We are being subjected to repeated stories of romance involving males winning females who had seemed to be out of reach. Boy gets Girl. There is evidently a clue there, but so far we have been too dull to catch on to it. So we are plodding on, perhaps until we do somehow catch on. You may be an example: Baton wanted you, you did not want him, but now he can court you."

"Oh, he's all right. But I was unwilling to remain in my dull routine with the fairy tales, and he was part of that routine. But joining him in a narrative relating to capital-D Demons transforms that picture. So yes, Baton will get me, in due course, just as Nolan will win you. We females are prizes that can be won when the offer suffices." Batoness paused the remaining third of the moment. "But maybe we can change the script a bit. How about enabling Girl to get Boy?"

Apoca was intrigued. "Can we do that? Change the script?"

"I'm not sure. But I'm tired of following scripts. They tend to be repetitive and dull. Let's look for an opportunity to make the change."

"Let's," Apoca agreed. She began another moment of pause. "Starting with what Nolan is up to now. I'll wager it's another Boy/Girl story. Let's see if we can flip it to a Girl/Boy story."

"Let's," Batoness agreed, adding a pleasure emoticon.

Apoca glanced at the nickelpede on her shoulder. "Nimbus?"

"Connected," Nimbus said. "Aurora and I thought you'd never ask."

The picture formed before them: what Nolan was seeing. Immediately before him was the evocative outline of Ghorgeous, now not bothering to form the image of a dress. She had evidently been flashing him with her backside throughout. How long could he ignore that? Fortunately she lacked the substance to make her whole body visible; an outline was all it was. She had also forgotten to form panties. As temptation went, this was minimal. He seemed to be handling it well enough, knowing that it had no more reality than a picture. In any event, he was not interested in forming a more durable interest in a ghost. She hoped.

They were approaching what appeared to be a haunted jailhouse. It was decrepit, with dirty walls, cobwebs, and broken glass on the floor. Eager weeds crowded it. But there was one reasonably clear path to the front door. Ghorgeous faded out, recuperating from her efforts of guidance and presentation.

Nolan navigated that path, opened the rickety door, and went inside. It was gloomy but roomy. Inside was a barred prison cell, with a single prisoner lying on a plain cot, asleep.

"Hello," Nolan said.

The man woke. He sat up, put on his crown, stood, and approached the gate. "I haven't seen you before."

"I am Prince Nolan Naga, passing through."

"Ah. I am Prince Morose of the Mini Kingdom of Modicum."

"This is zombie country, but you don't look like a zombie."

"I'm not. I hate zombies. Neither am I a criminal. It's a dull story."

"I will be happy to hear it." Nolan reached for the gate.

"Nuh-uh!" Morose warned. "Don't touch it. It's spelled to give a hor-rible shock, so I can't escape."

Nolan jerked his hand away. "Now I really want to hear your story. Why should a living prince be locked into a cell in zombie territory with-out even a guard to watch him?"

Morose went back to sit on the cot. "I am of age to marry, and of course I have to marry a princess. But when I looked over the local princesses my parents selected for me, I rejected them all. So now I am confined in uncomfortable quarters and fed gruel twice a day, in the hope that I will change my mind."

"Like Mnemonica," Apoca said, knowing the bugs would not relay their dialogue. "Only this is a male."

"We must be alert to convert it to a female variant."

"Princes are generally expected to marry princesses," Nolan said. "I faced the same situation. Now I am courting a queen my age, and we expect to have a lovely daughter in due course. Why don't you want to marry a princess? It is generally expected of princes, as commoner maid-ens, however alluring they can be for passing dalliances, lack the training and connections to benefit the kingdom."

Morose smiled. "So you really are a prince. I'd be happy to marry a princess. But the selection is poor. One is so ugly she looks like a pig. Another is old enough to be my mother. Another is crazy; she thinks she's a dragon, but she's no crossbreed. Another is gay, wanting nothing to do with a man. One is a sadomasochist, preferring the sadist role. One is so lazy they have to bring her meals to her bed and dump her potty for her. Another is so stupid she can't figure out whether it is morning or eve-ning, let alone how to handle a routine royal audience. Not one of them is appealing for a virile young man."

"He's got a point," Apoca said. "I faced a similar problem with prospective princes or kings, once I had time to consider prospects. I am fortunate Nolan entered my scene."

"You are," Batoness agreed. "He is handsome, apart from being otherwise qualified. That helps."

"It does, much as it annoys me to admit it. Now I can't be sure his appearance isn't blinding me to his defects."

"What defects?"

"That's the problem. He must have some, but I am blind to them."

"You may have to search beyond the local kingdoms," Nolan said. "I did."

"That's one problem with being the prince of a mini-kingdom. Only other minis are interested, and distant minis can't afford far-flung liaisons. As a naga prince you have far more clout than I do."

"True," Apoca said.

"Perhaps," Nolan agreed.

"So I simply had to balk," Morose said. "It has been good to talk with you but you can't help me, unless you have a pretty naga princess sister who would be interested."

"I have no sister, and the naga princesses I know are taken. So I regret you are correct. I am unable to help you. Can I at least bring you anything?"

Morose laughed humorlessly. "Maybe some rat poison? The rats seek to nibble my toes when I sleep, and I can't get rid of them." Indeed, there were rats lurking balefully in the shadows.

"Maybe I can scare them off." Nolan changed to serpent form and launched at a shadow, catching a rat by surprise. He flung it across the room. Then he changed back. "Listen, rats, it annoys me to have my friend harassed. Don't make me have to return here."

There was the scratching of rats' feet over broken glass as the vermin scrambled to depart, terrified.

"Why does that remind me of Mundanian literature?" Batoness asked.

"Who cares?" Apoca said. "They're all hollow men."

"I am impressed," Morose said. "I had thought those rats were fearless."

"Naga and rats have a long history. The rat who doesn't fear a naga soon becomes the naga's next meal."

"It's true," Apoca said. "I've seen him eat a pie rat."

"I owe you a favor," Morose said. "If we should meet again."

"No need." Nolan departed.

Outside, Ghorgeous reappeared, this time her face and décolletage. "I could see myself being his princess, assuming I had the rank and substance."

"You really want to be real again? I mean, physically?"

"I'd give anything to be physical again. I lost my body at the height of my maidenly appeal. I could give a man so much, if I only had it to give."

"I'm almost sorry for her," Apoca said. "She flirts with Nolan because flirting is all she can do."

The scene with Nolan faded. He was on his way back.

"That gives me an idea," Batoness printed. "We need to find a princess for Prince Morose, played from her perspective."

"There don't seem to be many likely prospects."

"Maybe Ghorgeous can help. Contact her via your telepathic bugs. Nolan doesn't need her to show the way back. She can do a spot search."

"And we don't need her to show him more of her back," Apoca said with some asperity.

In less than half a moment the bugs had contacted the ghost, explaining what was wanted: a suitable local princess, if any existed. "I'm on it," Ghorgeous agreed.

By the time Nolan returned, Ghorgeous had a prospect. "I found the perfect princess. Beautiful, smart, motivated, and well connected. Only two problems."

"There's always a problem," Apoca said tiredly.

"She's two weeks underage."

"Time will take care of that." She smiled. "About half a month."

"And she's a zombie."

Oops. Time would not take care of that. "He hates zombies. That's why they put him in zombie territory. To wear him down faster."

"Why do you even mention her?" Batoness asked.

"Because she's a very fresh zombie. No sign of rot. She could pass for a live girl, at least for a few more days." The ghost paused a ghost of a moment. "One problem there, though."

"Let's have it," Apoca said.

"She's honest. She refuses to pretend to be something she's not."

"Like a living girl," Apoca said.

"Yes."

"So again, why do you offer her as a prospect?"

"Dead folk can do a lot, when circumstances are right. My ghost friends and I helped save the Queendom of Thanx from the invaders. Now we are citizens of Thanx, with our very own haunted house there that children like to visit. They know that not all ghosts are spooky, apart from the show we put on for the house."

"That's right," Vinia said. She and Gent had returned from their exploration. "The kids really like the spook shows, so long as they know the ghosts are faking it and won't really scare anyone to death."

"So what can a zombie do?" Apoca asked. "Morose doesn't need to be spooked."

"She can free him. That magic electric shock hurts only living folk. A zombie could open the gate and let him out."

"That still won't solve his problem. He needs to marry a princess, or be forever in trouble with his family. He'll never be King of Modicum without a wife."

"I am thinking that he might be just a wee bit peeved by the requirement, at least when it means marrying an unattractive woman. Maybe even enough to mess them up by openly marrying a zombie, if he liked her. That would pay them back, no?"

Apoca considered. "Could he come to like her?"

"If he got to know her well enough. Alive she would be perfect. Dead she is still almost perfect."

"For a few more days."

"Here's the thing about that. If there is the one thing that will preserve a zombie, it is the knowing love of a living person. It can't cure the zombie, but it can prevent her from deteriorating any further, as long as the love lasts. She could be a passable queen."

Apoca was becoming intrigued. "Odd couples can fall in love."

"Like Squid and Chaos," Vinia agreed. "She's a cuttlefish and he's the strongest Demon ever, but their love is real."

"A live man and a beautiful zombie," Apoca said. "Men don't necessarily care much what's inside a woman, so long as what's outside looks good. But it's likely to take a while, with close association. That needs to be arranged."

"If something should block off the front door, they might have to use a more devious route to escape the prison," Ghorgeous said. "There are dangerous caverns."

"Struggling through together," Apoca said. "So they really have to depend on each other. That can evoke feelings."

"That gradually intensify," Batoness printed. "I have seen it many times."

"I have experienced it once."

The four of them, a woman, a girl, a ghost, and a Batoness of Protagonism, settled down to their devious design. The poor prince hardly had a chance.

Soon they had their plan. "But we want to see it happen," Vinia said.

"Baton will help, if I ask him to," Batoness printed. "He is free now, since he is off duty."

"Contact him," Apoca said. "Use your feminine persuasion."

"Baton," Batoness printed, "will you grant me a favor? I would be most appreciative." She paused a full pause. "Yes, for this favor I would return my favor." Her speech balloon assumed the shape of a heart, then became an outline of a curvaceous bare woman, similar to what Ghorgeous had shown Nolan. It was symbolic, but she was promising a lot.

There was another pause. The outline moved as if being embraced and kissed. Baton was definitely interested. He was a typical male.

"After the job is done," Batoness printed.

The next pause was disappointed but resolute.

"He'll do it," Batoness reported. "He will animate protagonism for Prince Morose."

"Now we need to get the zombie princess there," Apoca said. "How close to the prince is she?"

"Too far," Ghorgeous said. "It will take her a wheek to trek there."

"By which time she'll be well rotted," Vinia said.

"We need her there within the hour," Apoca said. "Can we arrange transport?"

"I will notify the local zhombie king. He'll support our effort, because his kingdom could bhenefit significantly by a living phrince marrying a zhombie." She faded out.

"And ask him where the plaque is," Apoca called after her. "You know: NOT HERE."

"I will," her fading voice came.

Prince Nolan arrived. "I have news."

"Of a prisoned prince," Apoca said. "The bugs relayed the sequence."

"Oh, of course. I forgot."

"Forgiven." Apoca stepped up to him and kissed him, reminding him that whatever a ghost might hint, there was a woman in his life who could do more than hint. "You are in time to watch our plot unfold." She caught him up on the details.

He shook his head. "You girls are dangerous!"

"Of course we are. Don't you dare blab the secret. Now, make yourself comfortable for the show."

He looked around. "I can fetch some cushions to sit on."

"No need." She sat down and leaned against the trunk of an element tree, the kind that made complicated things seem simple. She beckoned him down. "I am soft enough."

Lying beside her with his head on her lap as she stroked his plaid hair, her full bosom close above his face, he was happy to agree.

The ghost reappeared. "The zombie king is dispatching a dragon. He says he'll show us the plaque if we make this liaison work. Now I will notify the princess." She vanished.

Well, that was progress.

There was a delay of an indefinite time, but Nolan seemed quite content to wait. Apoca had suspected that would be the case. Men were malleable in the hands of women, especially when the women showed enough feminine flesh.

Ghorgeous appeared. "I will animate the scene in outline while I report the dialogue. Your imagination can fill in the details."

Apoca focused, as the ghost misted and the outline formed from the vapor. It was a lovely young woman lying on a royal bed, her eyes closed. She was alone.

"Zoila." That was Ghorgeous speaking to her.

The eyes flickered open. The mouth moved. "Wha?"

"You are not all the way dead. You are a zombie."

The mouth opened to scream, but only a bit of a sigh emerged, because she was unable to take a sufficient breath.

"Listen to me, Princess Zoila. I am Ghorgeous Ghost. I was cruelly killed, as you were. I died all the way, but my spirit could not depart until I avenged my murder. Then I decided to stay with my ghost and living friends. I would dearly like to be alive again, but that is not an option. At least I get to tease a live man on occasion. Now I am here to help you. Your prospects in this regard are better than mine."

The princess moved the fingers of one hand. "No dea?"

"Not dead," Ghorgeous agreed. "Merely living impaired. Sometimes people don't die all the way. We don't know why some become zombies. The Zombie Master used to animate the dead, but he's not here. It seems to be random. Normally the zombies slowly deteriorate, rotting on their feet as it were, until there's not enough of them left to get around. It's an unpleasant fate. But here's the thing: you don't have to go that route. You can't become alive again, but you can halt your decay. You can be most of the person you were in life. What you need is the sincere love of a living man who knows you for what you are. It is rare for a living person to love a zombie, but it can happen. It is an avenue you may be able to follow, if you choose."

Now she had the zombie's full attention. "Haw?"

"How?" the ghost echoed. "By going to a man who truly needs you and winning his love."

"Buh Im dhead!"

"Freshly dead. You died yesterday. Your body hardly shows it. You remain a lovely young woman, and a princess."

"Yeth, buh—"

"Yes, but you know of no ordinary man who would want a zombie, let alone a prince. But there may be one. Zoila, you have no future here in your own kingdom. They will give you a fine and tearful funeral, seal you into a crypt, and slowly forget about you."

"Yeth." She tried again. "Yess."

"There is a live prince imprisoned in a zombie kingdom because he won't marry an unattractive local princess. You don't have that problem. You are highly attractive."

Zoila grimaced. "Buh dead."

"Yet because you are a fresh zombie, your body remains whole and your mind remains functional. You can act to secure what you have. But you must do so promptly, before the rot progresses too far."

"Haw?"

"By traveling to the prince, freeing him from his cell, leading him back to his own land of the living, and winning his love. His love will preserve you as you are now. I don't think you'll be able to order a baby from the stork, because they ignore zombies, but you can go through the motions, which well may suffice. He is, after all, a man. They care mostly about those motions."

"A mahn," the zombie agreed, understanding. "Buh—but how doo I ghet to him?"

"A zombie dragon will take you. We'll go out for it now."

"A drhagon!"

"A tame one. They like carrying maidens. You'll be safe enough."

Zoila considered. She took a conscious breath, and it worked. She was able to talk more normally. "Why am I dhead?"

Ghorgeous paused a fair portion of a moment. "Why, I don't know. Since there is no mark on your body, I suspect you were poisoned."

"Poishoned!"

"It's just a conjecture. Do you have enemies?"

"Nho. Nhot that I khnow of. I was about to mhake my preshentation as a marriage prospect, and seek a good alliance for my khingdom."

"I'm sure you would have done well. Beauty, smarts, and royalty make you an ideal prospect."

The zombie frowned. "Until I died."

The ghost considered another portion of the moment. "Maybe we can find out. Do you have a magic mirror?"

Zoila made an effort and sat up. "Yes. On the wall there."

Ghorgeous saw it. "I doubt it will answer me. But it should still answer you. Ask it."

"Yes." The zombie got up unsteadily and made her way to the wall. She faced it. "You know me," she told it. "Princess Zoila. I am dead. Who killed me, and why?"

"You were the prettiest princess extant," the mirror replied. "Other princesses knew that the moment you came on the scene, they would have no chance with the handsomest or most powerful princes. Even some kings had their eye on you. So your rivals conspired to take you out of the picture. They obtained poi-daughter and sent it to you as a gift, trusting that you would not recognize its nature."

The zombie was taken aback. "I thought it was play cookie dough, misspelled! I baked it and took a bite or three. It was delicious."

"So they were correct about your ignorance," the mirror said, a generous trifle smugly. "You should have asked me before using it. Poi-son and poi-daughter, most effective on sons and daughters respectively. You are the king's daughter. It took you out instantly."

"Ask who did it," Ghorgeous prompted her.

The mirror eyed her. "Wow! You're as pretty as she is, ghost. You died for a vaguely similar reason, a jealous suitor. Bemused by your beauty, I will answer you. Here are the names." It rattled off three names.

The fair ghost turned to the fair zombie. "Do these mean anything to you?"

"Yes! They are princesses in adjacent kingdoms. I thought they were my friends."

"So maybe you have a score to settle, in due course."

"Maybe I do."

"After you win your prince and gain power in the living realm."

"Yes."

"Thank you, Mirror," Gorgeous said. "This way to the dragon."

They made their way quietly out of the room and down to the ground floor, avoiding the palace servants. There was no point in shaking things up with the appearance of a ghost and a zombie, even if they were lovely. "Couldn't I just have jumped out the window?" Zoila asked. "Since I'm already dead."

"Yes. But you might have broken some bones, making progress difficult. Certainly you would have mussed your hair."

"Mussed my hair!" the zombie repeated, horrified.

The dragon was waiting, a large female. "Hello, dragon lady," Ghorgeous said. "This is Zoila Zombie, a princess on her way to meet a living prince. You have the address."

The dragon nodded. The zombie climbed on and sat between the wings. Soon they took off.

"Now, let me give you some pointers on drawing in a man, even when you're dead," Ghorgeous said. "And on the devious route you must take as you lead him back to his kingdom. You have to engage him long enough for him to be sufficiently attracted to you. It's like reeling in a fish on the line, when the fish could readily break the line if it caught on. Victory is when it no longer wants to escape. It's an art."

"An art," Zoila agreed.

"Beginning with your breathing. You don't need to do it now, except to talk, but you will make a man nervous if you don't do it regularly. You need especially to inhale when he is looking at your chest; that emphasizes your bosom."

"Inhale," the zombie agreed, doing it.

The scene dissolved. "And she is now on the verge of introducing herself to him," Ghorgeous Ghost concluded. "Time for Baton to take over."

"I present Prince Morose, Protagonist," Batoness printed. The picture appeared. Apoca stroked Nolan's head as he watched from her lap, keeping him pacified.

"Hello, Prince Morose."

The prince sat up on his bunk. "What?"

The dulcet voice came again from the darkness of the shadow beyond the cell. "Hello, Prince Morose. I am Princess Zoila."

He got up and approached that corner, peering into the gloom. He saw an extremely lovely figure. "Is this a joke? I am not allowed visitors, apart from the jail master and his servant who brings my daily gruel and replaces my filled potty. And stray zombies, whom I refuse to count. Especially not permitted are pretty foreign princesses." Then he amended himself. "Actually I did have a visit, but that was a naga prince just wandering through. He got rid of the rats for me. But he would have been in trouble if they had caught him."

"This is not a joke. I am here to rescue you, in more than one sense."

He remained suspicious. "Are you an apparition? A will-o'-the-wisp sent to tempt me into doom? It won't work because I can't get out of this cell alive."

"I am no apparition, though I am not exactly what I appear." She stepped gracefully forward. She was clearly a princess, because she wore a delicate silver crown and an elegant royal-purple robe that showed off the finest slender figure he had seen. Her hair was a rich gray, not that of age, and her eyes matched.

"You are lovely!" he exclaimed. "So is this illusion, and your real appearance is ugly?"

"No, this is my proper aspect. I am, however, two weeks under the age of eighteen."

He laughed. "That will soon abate."

"Perhaps."

"Then what's the catch? You said you are not what you appear."

"I am a zombie."

He froze. This was zombie country! How could he have forgotten that detail? "Bleep! I hate zombies."

"So I understand. I am nevertheless here to rescue you, as I said."

"In more than one sense," he agreed. "I presume one sense is physical, somehow getting me out of this cell. I do want that. What is the other?"

"I want to marry you, so that you can assume your rightful place in your society, and eventually become king of Modicum, no pariah anymore, and I will be your queen."

"No offense intended, but I can hardly think of a female I less want to touch, let alone marry, than a zombie."

"No offense taken. I hope to persuade you to change your mind."

He gazed at her. Bleep, she was beautiful! "So the parameters have been established. You offer me escape and recognition. I must say, you don't appear to be rotten."

"I am quite fresh, though I am cold. I have been told that the love of a living man can sustain me in my present condition indefinitely. I hope to win your love, not entirely for that purpose."

"Even if you succeeded, you could not bring me an heir."

"Unless the storks decide to recognize our signal. They might make an exception to their policy of ignoring zombies if the signal were forceful enough."

He declined to argue that case. "So whatever rot you suffer is not visible outside your clothing."

"I have no rot anywhere on my body as yet. I will show you. Forgive my immodesty, but I know no other way to make my case." She stripped away her robe, which was all she wore, and stood naked, a perfect figure of a woman. She turned around so that he could see every delightful part of her. "Do you wish to see more?"

He had nearly freaked out. What a sight, even without bra or panties! She was perfect in every detail. "No. So the rot must be internal."

"Not there either, yet. Not ever, if I win your love. I have an almost completely functional body." She put her robe back on.

His feelings were mixed. He was severely tempted. But she was a zombie!

"I see you hesitate. Do you wish to touch me?"

"No!" But he realized as he spoke it was a lie. One part of him wanted to take her in his arms, stroke her, and kiss her. Yet his mind remained repelled. "Or maybe just your hand. But the bars are magically electrified. Don't touch them."

She walked around to the front gate. She put her hand on the bar that sealed it shut. The current flashed, making her whole body glow. Smoke rose from her singed robe. She ignored it. "I am not hurting," she said. "I am dead, or as I prefer to put it, living-impaired, and feel no pain."

So it seemed. "I see, amazed."

She drew the gate open and stood there. "Now you may touch my hand."

He nerved himself and stepped forward. He took her extended hand. "It's not cold!"

She looked at it, surprised. "Oh—it must be the current. It heated me."

He had to smile. "That must be it. I will take your word that you are normally cold."

She smiled back. "Thank you. My body is cold, but not my spirit."

That unnerved him further. He liked her smile and her spirit. Only how could he, given his distaste for zombies?

So he changed the subject. "We need to get out of here. The jail master keeps irregular hours and can come at any moment."

"The back way is best. I know a devious route."

"But it is bound to be haunted by zombies. This is zombie territory."

She merely looked at him.

Oh. He had forgotten for the moment that she was a zombie. He spread his hands apologetically. "Lead on, princess."

She led the way to the rear chamber of the jail. "When I spot researched, I learned that this was once a fort, before a truce was established between the dead and the living. There are secret tunnels leading every which way. I know an avenue. Stay close to me because if you deviate, you could get lost."

Ordinarily that would be no chore. But close to a zombie? Yet this zombie remained treacherously appealing. "I will stay near," he agreed.

Zoila went to a faded picture on the wall. She touched the frame, and it swung out to reveal an opening. She held on and lifted a leg high to climb in. Not only did the robe press tightly across her bottom, her thigh showed up to the nonexistent panty line. That turned him on. He had seen her naked, but this inadvertent flash compelled his attention anew.

By the time she scrambled through the hole, she had flashed not only her thigh but her cleavage and much in between. Was she doing it on purpose? Did it matter?

She stood on the other side. "Your turn."

That jolted him out of his momentary trance. He quickly climbed through himself, then reached behind to draw the framed picture back into place. He turned to face her. She was quite close, as the tunnel beyond was narrow.

"Honest disclosure," she said. "I knew you were looking, and I did nothing to hide my assets. I am trying to arouse your desire, so that you will forgive my zombie status."

She was making progress! He wanted to take her into his embrace. But she was dead! Or living-impaired. "I appreciate the warning."

"Anything you may want of me, at any time, is granted. I am in effect courting you. But I will not pretend to be what I am not: alive. My flesh is cold, outside and inside."

"You might make better progress if you did pretend."

"Perhaps. But I refuse to sacrifice my integrity."

"As you wish." The fact was, her integrity was more seductive than her flashes. Integrity's absence was a significant part of his objection to the run of princesses he had encountered. He strongly suspected that some of them would stoop to foul means to achieve their devious purposes.

Zoila turned and led the way down the tunnel. Glowing fungus lighted the walls, so that he could see the way reasonably clearly. He could also see how smoothly her slender hips swayed as she walked. Zombie or not, purposefully or not, she was stunning.

There was a commotion behind them. "I think the jailer has returned," he said.

"Then we should hide, lest he search and discover the tunnel before we exit it." She turned quickly into a side passage he hadn't noticed that led to a closet-sized chamber. They squeezed in, and she drew a sliding panel across to mask their hideout. "They will not discover this," she said. "It is spelled to be unnoticeable by living folk."

Now they were in full torso contact. She was indeed cool, but not actually cold; it was as though she had just come in from a chill outdoor day. He discovered that one of his hands had gotten under her robe and was against her bare back. He was not at all repulsed.

"I apologize for my inadvertent intimacy," he said.

She took a breath so she could talk. He noticed the motion as much as the words. "As I said, you may have all the intimacy you want. But I think first it would be better for us to get to know each other. We have a mutual need which we can fill, for legitimacy, but that may not suffice for a long-term relationship."

"You are surprisingly sensible, and not just for a zombie."

She smiled, and he found he liked it very well up close, just as he liked her intermittent breathing. She clearly did not need air to sustain her body, only for communication, but it made her seem more animate. "I am a princess. I have had the proper training in the protocols. I know how to appeal to a man. I merely did not anticipate getting murdered before I had a chance to impress and to marry."

"You were murdered?" He had wondered how she had died so young.

"Jealous rivals poisoned me."

He could see how she would incite jealousy. But that was not worth dwelling on at the moment. "My talent is to enter any mirror and to exit from another. They do not need to be magic. I can travel almost anywhere that has mirrors. They made sure there were no mirrors anywhere near the jail."

"That is an excellent talent. Can you take things or people with you?"

"Yes, if they want to go. But I use it cautiously. There could be danger if a mirror broke while I was using it."

"I would like to travel that way with you, the slight risk notwithstanding." She paused a fraction of a moment. "If we should have a relationship."

He saw that she really wanted this. The fact was that she was more of a woman than any living one he had encountered, of any age. But he remained cautious. "That remains to be determined. Zoila, I like you personally, but I remain highly uncertain that I should connect with a zombie."

"I understand," she said sadly. "I was wary of zombies, too, before I became one." She took another intriguing breath, seeming to remember to do it when he was watching, as if she needed prompting. "My talent is capturing sickness and plague in books. Those volumes are not safe to open." She smiled grimly. "I may in due course send some books to the shrews who poisoned me." She looked at him from her adjacent range, kissably close. "Does this sentiment disturb you?"

He had to force himself to focus on the question. "Not at all. I believe in eye-for-eye, tooth-for-tooth justice. It is the royal way."

"Then we align in that respect. That is good."

They aligned in more than that. "Your talent—you retain it in death?"

"Yes. Talents attach to bodies or to souls. Those that attach to souls remain with the spirit when a person dies. Even some ghosts have talents. Mine is a soul attachment."

"So you can be dangerous in life or death."

"Yes. But I would not abuse it, any more than you would abuse yours. It is a matter of princessly ethics."

Princely ethics too. She was his kind of woman, through and through. If only she weren't dead!

"Bleep," he muttered.

"I think I know what you're thinking. You wish I were alive." She inhaled beautifully for a sigh. "So do I."

Morose suffered a surge of emotion. "Kiss me," he said.

"I will if you wish. But are you ready? I remain a zombie. I will never deceive you on that or anything else."

He did not argue the case. He kissed her.

She kissed him back warmly. Little hearts flew out. Some were living, some dead.

He drew back just enough so he could talk. "You are warm!"

"Why, so I am," she agreed, surprised again. Then she saw the hearts. "I fear I have fallen in love with you, and that is heating me. I do remain dead physically, if not emotionally."

That did it. She was honest even when love was on the line. "And my love will sustain you. Marry me and be my zombie queen. It will serve my folks right for trying to force the issue. The requirement is a princess; it is not specified that she be alive."

Tears came to Zoila's eyes, something that only a very fresh zombie could manage. "Oh, Morose! I do agree."

"We will tackle the matter of stork signals. Any two species can make crossbreeds; why not a living-dead crossbreed?"

"Why not?" she agreed. "I shall be happy to go through the stork-signaling motions as many times as you wish." They kissed again. She heated further.

"It has been quiet in the hall," he said. "It should be safe to resume our trek."

"Yes. Also, I believe I know where there is a couple-sized mirror, so you can take us directly to the Palace of Modicum."

"There will surely be a hassle, but we can prevail if we stand firm." Then he thought of something else. "They will seek technicalities to try to disqualify you. Are you a virgin?"

"I am, though that is increasingly difficult to maintain when I am this close to you. My only possible disqualification is my absence of life."

"Your life *impairment*," he corrected her, smiling.

The scene dissolved. "The issue is settled," Apoca said. "Girl got Boy."

"Which is satisfying," Ghorgeous said. "But what is our larger business here in the zhombie realm? This can't be a random incident."

There was the sound of a slightly spoiled drum. The ghost flicked out, then returned. "Zombies are approaching us. It looks like the zombie king."

"And that may be our answer," Batoness printed. "We have just done the zombies some good."

"It's green here," Vinia said. "No danger."

They held firm, Nolan rising to his feet with his hand near his sword, just in case. He lacked experience with zombies and did not completely trust them.

The zombie troupe arrived. It was indeed the king, looking moderately fit, with his ragged courtiers. "Ghreeting, live vhisithors. Our dhragon reported," he said.

Apoca realized they had forgotten the zombie dragon. Of course it had returned to the one who sent him, and it seemed was smart enough to tell what he had done. "We meant no harm to your folk," Apoca said cautiously.

"Yhou enabled a zombie princess marriage to a live prince. Unlives matter! This will combat anti-zhombie prejudice in Xhanth."

"I suppose it will," Apoca agreed cautiously. Did this prospect upset the king?

Nolan was more direct. "What is the purpose of this visit?"

The king nodded, shaking loose a section of skin from his forehead. "Whe whill dho yhou a rheturn favor. Here is your phlaque." A zombie soldier laid the moldering octagon down before them. It said NOT HERE.

"Thank you," Nolan said. Apoca suspected that he was as relieved as she was that the Dwarf Demon was not hiding in the zombie realm.

"Ahnd here is Rocker Robot." The king gestured.

An odd device with four wheels set around its pyramidal-shaped body rolled squeakily forward. It was caked with dirt and cobwebs, and its struts were rusty. It looked as if it had been buried a long time.

They simply stared at it, unable to make much sense of it.

"Yhou're whelcome," the king said, and departed with his retinue.

They looked at one another, perplexed. It seemed they had inherited a zombie robot.

Chapter 9

ROBOT

Nolan took stock. First things first: where were they going next? "Let's return to the nexus and consider paths," he said. "Um, Gent, can you see that the robot follows us?"

Gent hesitated until Apoca cast him a glance. He took orders from her, not Nolan, regardless of who was the protagonist. Then he walked over to the machine, which stood about waist-high to him. "Thistle weigh," he told it and started walking. The robot followed. At least it seemed to understand him. Nobody commented.

They walked back the way they had come, trooping along the path, Nolan and Apoca first, accompanied by their bug friends, then the two batons, then Gent and the robot, then Vinia and Ghorgeous. Soon they reached the nexus and paused.

"Um, before we choose a new path, let's see if we can learn more about the robot," Nolan said. "In case we decide to tackle the robot territory next. Maybe it will help." He glanced at Vinia. "Is the green near it?"

"Mixed," the girl said. "Green background, meaning it means us no harm, but there are patches of fiery red, meaning danger. So we need to be careful around him."

They considered the mechanism more carefully. It was about a yard tall, long, and broad, each blank side triangular so that no matter which way it might fall, there was always a supportive triangle at the base. This was an all-terrain machine. The rust, cobwebs, and faded paint indicated long disuse, but it did seem functional in its fashion. It was a zombie? How could something that had never been alive be one of the walking dead?

Nolan broke the silence before it could coagulate. "Can it communicate?"

Ghorgeous floated close. "Let me explore." She siphoned herself right into the machine, which seemed vaguely startled but not annoyed. Its top wheel spun in the air as if seeking to propel the body somewhere. Infusion by a ghost could have that effect.

In a moment and a half she emerged, and the wheel stopped spinning. "A small-*d* demoness animated him for a time," she reported. "He loved her, but she was frivolous and deserted him for a more advanced device. Some trace of her remains behind, just enough to leave him partly animate and longing for more. He really is a zombie machine."

"So that's how a robot gets zombied," Apoca said. "I wondered, since robots aren't alive to begin with, so can't be only partly alive." That had been Nolan's thought, which perhaps showed how close the two of them were getting.

"That's how," Ghorgeous agreed. "Demons are spirits, like ghosts. They have more substance than ghosts, and more magic, so can become temporarily solid, while ghosts are mostly appearance, physically. But ghosts are souls, whereas Demons are not, so have more conscience, not that it does us much ghood." She sighed. "I wish I had my body again. I'd be such a good girl." She formed a flash of bare torso in a provocative pose that suggested otherwise.

"How about the robot body?" Vinia asked. "Would that do you much good?"

"I suppose, in a manner. But I'd really prefer a living body. One that could please a live man."

"If the robot is male, he might like it if you animated him."

Apoca chimed in. "You might also be able to make him more responsive, so we can find out exactly what he is good for."

The ghost considered. "I might," she agreed. "I suppose I can stand animating a male host for a while for the good of the mission. It can hear and understand okay, but it has no voice box, so I'll need someone to translate at first. Once we know what's what, I'll leave it to speak for itself in its own way." She siphoned back into the machine.

"I'll do it," Vinia said. "Translating is fun." She put a hand on the machine's surface, between wheels.

In the remaining half moment left over from the ghost's prior exploration, the zombie robot animated. It clicked.

"That's how it communicates," Vinia said, picking up Ghorgeous's message. "One click for Yes, two clicks for No, three for Maybe, four for It's Complicated, and five for Get Out Fast!"

"How's that again?" Apoca asked. "That last sounds dangerous."

Vinia listened to the ghost. "It seems this robot was designed to be a bomb sniffer for a Mundane country at war. It smells explosives and leads soldiers to them, so they can be defussed."

"Defused," Apoca said. "Bombs have fuses to set them off."

"Defused." The girl was still learning spelling. "So the soldiers don't get blown up. It even eats explosives; that's what powers it physically. But it seems the robot got too close to a bomb, and the thing exploded and knocked out its computer brain. That's a known risk, in that business. So it was dead, and they junked it. Then the demoness came and animated it—there's not much magic in Mundania, but there are some Demons and ghosts hiding in the background—Ghorgeous was one—and made it roll to Xanth. She must have known a route that we don't."

"Maybe via NoName Key," Apoca said. "There's a connection there, though the Mundane government won't admit it."

Vinia looked up. "Maybe they're afraid that all their citizens will flee to Xanth, if they knew."

"Of course they would," Apoca said. "Nobody would stay in drear Mundania if they had a choice."

Nolan cleared his throat.

"Back to work," Vinia agreed. "Then the demoness tired of the novelty and deserted him, leaving him desalted."

"Desolate," Apoca said.

"The regular robots didn't want a zombie, so he wound up in Zombie Land. But I guess the zombies didn't want him either, because he's a machine, so they gave him to us," Vinia concluded, translating for Ghorgeous.

"So at last he is ours," Nolan said. "At least now we know his background."

The ghost emerged. "Rocker's not a bad sort. He just wants to do his job. Now that he's animated by magic rather than Mundane science, he's lonely. He likes our company and will help us any way he can." She made half a pause. "And there's something else, but I couldn't quite suss it out."

"Anything dangerous?" Apoca asked.

"Maybe. It relates to explosions, but not the ordinary ones. The rest is vague."

That meant that Nolan had to make a decision. Ditch the zombie robot, or gamble that they could handle whatever it was. But if there were danger, it might be present regardless of Rocker. Also, he didn't like turning away anyone or anything that felt lonely. He had on occasion felt lonely himself, until Aurora became his companion.

"Thank you," the ant said. "Me too."

Maybe there was a compromise. The ghost had come to understand the robot reasonably well, and it surely liked her company. "Suppose you stay with Rocker, Ghorgeous, and keep alert for any such danger. Maybe he will help us see it coming."

"Will do." She siphoned back inside. This did give her a kind of physical body, which had to be slightly better than nothing.

"Now, Rocker, you may come along with us and do your thing. Ghorgeous will be with you. Let her know of any danger you discover."

The robot clicked once. Good enough; it was operative and responsive, at least to that degree.

"Ides deer," Gent said. That meant "idea."

Apoca looked at him. "Yes?"

He made a gesture of kissing his own hand, then touching the robot's metal surface.

"Kiss Rocker!" Vinia exclaimed. "That might unfry his brain."

Again Nolan's glance collided with Apoca's glance. Her kisses had power, positive and negative. Could they negate the lingering influence of the demoness, or possibly restore some of the lost function of his original brain? It seemed worth a try. What harm could it do to an already largely wasted machine?

Apoca went to the robot and kissed him in the middle of a triangular side panel. The top wheel spun again, and a speaking grille made a squeal as of electrocution. There was a low hum. Then it clicked four times. Something complicated had happened.

Vinia touched the panel. "Wow! Ghorgeous says its battery is recharged and its brain circuitry is humming. It's almost better than new. But she still doesn't know what five clicks really means."

"Stay the course," Nolan said. "Maybe events will clarify it."

"Thank you for your suggestion, Gent," Apoca said, and the man smiled. He lived to please her, at present.

"Eyed ear."

"Another idea?" Apoca said. "Let's have it."

Gent pointed to her shoulder, then to Nolan's shoulder. He made a zipping motion across his mouth.

"The bugs should maintain telepathic silence," Apoca translated. "In case the robots have special sensors and can hear them. So that we maintain a hidden resource, just in case."

Nolan nodded. So did Vinia. Rocker clicked once.

"We agree," Aurora said. "We will alert you only if we spy something critical."

"Thank you again, Gent," Apoca said, and the man basked in her approval. Nolan noted privately that Gent was smart, behind the mask of his curse.

They took the Robot path. Soon they came to a colony of old-fashioned wood-burning robots. They were of several types, wheeled, tracked, and stick-legged, small, medium, and large, some with speaker grilles and others with lighted screens. Some had tools built into their limbs, while others had weapons: clubs, knives, whips, stun probes, squirt nozzles, or guns.

Nolan glanced at Vinia. "Two questions," he murmured. "Is this the way we should go? Is it safe?"

"Yes and yes." She glanced at Rocker. "But it's greenest around him. He can help us, I think, now better than ever."

Nolan approached Rocker. "Come with me."

Together they walked up to the chief wood robot. "We are passing through your territory on a mission of our own," Nolan said. "Is there any problem we can help you with?"

The chief puffed a cloud of woodsmoke. "One of our newer models would like to join your party," his speaker grille said, "to tour the other sections, before settling down to dull wood-chopping here."

And Rocker clicked five times.

Uh-oh. "Let me consult with my companions," Nolan said diplomatically.

They retreated to where Apoca, Gent, and Vinia waited. "We just got five clicks," Nolan said. "Vinia, is it dangerous here?"

"No. The path is green."

Was Rocker malfunctioning? "Ask Ghorgeous if she knows."

The girl put a hand on the robot's panel. "Wow! There's no physical danger, as the wood-burners are friendly. But there's a social peril. If we let one wood robot join us, a dozen more will want to, and others in the other robot zones, until we are swamped and won't be able to complete our search for the NOT HERE plaque."

Apoca shook her head. "How can Rocker know this? It's not a bomb."

Vinia listened some more. "It's a social explosion. Rocker orients on any explosion, not just physical ones. A bomb is a potential material explosion. A robot fellow traveler is a potential cultural explosion. That's something my paths can't track."

Nolan whistled. "Rocker may turn out to be more useful than we thought."

"We'll have to tell the chief no," Apoca said.

"That may be mischief of its own. Leaders don't like to be balked."

Nolan lifted a hand. "I'll tell him."

Apoca nodded. "And I'll kiss him if I have to."

Nolan and Apoca returned to the chief. "We regret that we are unable to take any other robots along."

The chief puffed a villainous cloud of smoke, and his eye pads glowed red. But before he spoke, Apoca stepped forward and kissed him smack on the faceplate.

The smoke dissipated. "As my lady decrees," the chief wooder said.

"Continue your business here," Apoca said. "Spread the word."

"I will."

They moved on, the crisis defused. "I think I like Rocker," Vinia said.

"Ditto," Apoca agreed.

Nolan also liked the way he and Apoca had handled the chief. They made a good team.

They walked on through the wood-burning sector, noting how many of the trees had been cut down. In time there would be none left, and the robots would have to move to a new locale. But that was their problem.

The next section was for the coal-burning robots. There were more trees standing here, but there was a huge ugly pit where the buried coal had been dug out, and the air pollution was just as bad.

A coal boss approached them. Rocker started clicking. "If you want to pass through here," he puffed, "you will have to—"

Apoca stepped forward and kissed him. The clicking stopped, and the coaler retreated.

The next section was for the gasoline-powered robots. Oil wells littered the landscape, and there were huge tanks of fuel. The air was foul.

Then they came to a refreshingly different landscape. Windmills dotted it, and the air was clean. This was the region of wind-powered robots. They wore sails on their heads, and little propellers on their hands. It was clear that their batteries were charged by the generators at the windmills and supplemented by the personal sails and propellers.

Next was a sunny, bright section with vast arrays of solar panels, and the robots wore smaller panels on their heads and backs. The air was clean here too.

Then a problem developed. One of Rocker's little wheels jammed. Evidently an old internal bearing had gone bad. He flipped over to put another panel down so that he had a functioning triad, but now the top wheel was unable to spin, and his occasional clicks sounded pained, which tended to dampen his personality.

"We had better get his wheels replaced," Nolan said. "We don't know when another bearing will go."

Apoca agreed. So they took a detour, following a new path Vinia discovered. This led to a robot repair shop.

Nolan approached the proprietor, a sturdy machine with arms like iron bands. "Our zombie robot is in need of repair. One wheel is jammed, and others may be vulnerable. Can we make a deal?"

"Yess," the central grille said without hesitation. "Find our lost adapter. We had it yesterday, and today it is gone. We fear theft."

So there could be dishonesty among robots, maybe even crime. Nolan glanced at Vinia.

"This way," she said, orienting on a new path. She set off, and they followed along with a lady solar robot helper assigned by the shop master.

They knew she was female because of her delicate construction and aesthetic lines. Rocker remained at the shop, waiting.

They came to a shed where supplies were stored. There was the adapter; the helper recognized it instantly and picked it up.

An alarm sounded and lights flashed. Wind robots converged. But the helper stood up to them, making angry beeps as she held up the adapter for them to inspect. They scanned its serial number, verifying its identity. It was Solar property.

"Apology," the Wind subchief said. "This was taken by a new one, not yet fully programmed. He will be punished by a dose of rancid oil. There will be no recurrence."

The helper thanked him with a metallic kiss on his propeller housing that flashed a blue spark. He plainly liked it. She was evidently pretty, in robot terms.

"An errant child stole it," Apoca murmured. "It figures."

They returned to the shop, where the proprietor was pleased to have his adapter back. Then he gestured to Rocker, who now had four new wheels. The top one was spinning happily, and the clicks were serene. The repair was complete.

"I think I like doing business with robots," Nolan murmured. "They are straightforward." The others agreed.

They resumed their trek along the original path. They had learned something about the robot society. It was like human society, in its fashion.

Next was a mountainous section with dammed rivers to generate power from the flowing water. This was near the sea, and there were giant paddles in the water that moved with the tides and generated more power for the Hydros.

Then a region with pipes delving deep down into the ground, bringing up heat, with generators on the surface, and a network of cables to distribute the canned power. This turned out to be the section of the geothermal robots.

After that there was the New Clear Fission section, but Vinia's path steered them away from those robots because some of them were radioactive, not healthy for live folk.

Finally they came to the New Clear Fusion section, where the robots glowed with the energy of the sun. These were clearly the dominant tribe, having phenomenal power without the need for distributive cables, and they did not radiate.

Here a robot guard blocked the path. Rocker's clicks sounded; this was not an entity to be balked. Yet they needed to proceed.

"Take us to your leader," Nolan said.

That worked. The guard led the way along what Vinia signaled was a green path.

In due course they were ushered to the leader, the Emperor Fusion, in a reasonably elegant palace meeting room. Rocker's muted clicking continued: there was social danger here. The emperor was in handsome human form, with a fitted purple robe and a small conservative crown. "What is your purpose here, travelers?" he inquired mildly, not seeming dangerous at all, but subtle menace surrounded him. He was obviously a potent leader. He glanced at Rocker. "Cease your alarm, zombie; I do not abuse my power."

The clicking stopped. That did not reassure Nolan.

"We are looking for a plaque that says either HERE or NOT HERE," Nolan said cautiously. "If it is the latter, we will move on out of your domain."

Fusion smiled. He was clearly a sophisticated machine, seeming quite human with his expressive plastic face, with no metal showing. "As it happens, we know of such a plaque. It appeared recently in our domain, and we wondered what its purpose was."

"If you value it, we will not take it. Simply tell us which of the two types it is."

Fusion frowned. "I think not. We will fetch it for you so that you can see for yourself and be satisfied. But first you must render us a service. That will make it a fair exchange."

Nolan felt Apoca's gaze on the back of his head. She knew this was mischief. They did not need the clicks or the bugs to warn them. But how were they to handle it? The robots were a bartering society. So—carefully.

"We may be happy to oblige you," Nolan said. "But it depends on the service. We are not interested in hurting anyone or anything, or in compromising our larger mission. We just want to get along."

"Which mission I understand relates to the talents of living children," Fusion said. It seemed he had his sources. "We lack that problem, but sympathize. Our request is merely a matter of observation and instruction. We wish to establish closer relations with our neighboring living human kingdoms, who are understandably wary of robots. You, as full humans, can teach us how to become more presentable."

The zombie's muted clicks resumed warningly. A glance from the emperor silenced them again. Caution enough.

"Perhaps," Nolan said. "But we lack experience in robot culture."

"You did well enough with the zombies. Royal human-zombie liaisons are rare. Perhaps you can enable us to arrange a royal human-robot one. It is our impression that human prejudice against robots is generally less than that against zombies. Your success with the zombie connection augurs well for your ability with robots."

"Even so, the nuances can be awkward to convey," Apoca said. "Particularly in romance."

"Indeed," Fusion agreed. "We have discovered that there are subtleties that can torpedo a romance that may not be noticeable to us in ordinary discourse. Our students are apt; they can learn quite well by example. But as yet we have not had that example."

"It is clear that you are able to craft humanoid robots that could be mistaken for living humans," Nolan said. "But we are not sure we wish to help you deceive humans. This might be considered a betrayal of our species, even though I myself am a crossbreed in human form rather than a native human."

"Understood. We have no intention to deceive. We merely desire to become sufficiently adept in the human manner so that neighboring human kingdoms will be comfortable with us, even to the point of open intermarriage, thus forming enduring associations in the human manner. We prefer them to see us as a variant of human, knowing our nature."

"No deception," Apoca said thoughtfully. "So that just as I might consider knowingly marrying a form-changing naga prince, a human princess might consider doing the same with a robot prince, fully understanding his nature."

"Exactly." It was indeed what he had said.

They considered that, still uncertain.

"Aye dear," Gent said.

"Say it."

"Yew & hee, & row butt M U lotions."

Apoca required much of a long moment to sort that out, but she got it. "Me and Nolan and robot emulations."

This was beginning to seem feasible, but Nolan retained one reservation. "You can surely craft realistic emulations of the two of us, and we could interact with them, exploring the nuances. But can you guarantee that they would always be identifiable as robots, no matter how realistic in other ways? So that no deception is possible?"

"Yes." Fusion snapped his fingers. Two people approached, a man and a woman. He was handsome, and she was shapely.

"Oh my," Apoca gasped.

Then Nolan recognized what his mind had momentarily resisted. They were Nolan and Apoca, complete in every detail. Except for the bugs on their shoulders, which the robots either hadn't noticed or considered irrelevant.

"Wrists, please," Fusion said.

The two held out their left arms. There on their wrists were metal bracelets, inset bands, part of their arms. One said NOLAN ROBOT and the other said APOCA ROBOT. Very solid identification.

Nolan laughed. "Hello, robot selves."

Robot Nolan laughed exactly the same way. "Hello, human selves."

"You're lovely," Apoca said to her opposite, smiling graciously.

The other Apoca smiled equally graciously. "Thank you."

"We have a guesthouse for the other members of your party," Fusion said. "And a palace suite for you, if you are ready to start."

Apoca glanced at him, and the robot edition did the same thing, perfectly. They were indeed apt learners. "All you require is our observation, guidance, and report, so that other folk will see them as metal humans with complete social graces?"

"That's all," Fusion said. "A day or so should do it. To demonstrate our good faith, and knowing that you are creatures of honor, we will show you the plaque now." He gestured, and a courtier approached carrying a plaque that said NOT HERE.

"Thank you," Nolan said, relieved that they could leave once their observation was over. This monarch was too pushy and powerful to associate with too long.

A robot courtier went to Gent, Vinia, and Rocker, to conduct them to the guesthouse. These robots certainly were efficient! Nolan knew that Ghorgeous would emerge from the zombie robot and alert him if anything untoward happened. With luck these robots did not know about her or the bugs.

Robot Apoca stepped forward and took his arm. "This way, dear," she said.

What? Dear? He saw that Robot Nolan was taking Apoca's arm. Well, the purpose was to educate them in the nuances of interpersonal interaction, including romantic. They were clearly eager to learn. So it was best to get it over with. Nolan suffered himself to be guided to the suite.

It turned out to be palatial, a whole complex in itself. There was a living room with a window overlooking the colored spires and turrets of the rest of the palace, a kitchen, and even a marvelous pool with literally sparkling water.

Nolan Robot saw his look. "Special effects," he explained. He touched a button, and the sparkle became a miniature rainbow, then a starry sky right there inside the chamber. The water changed colors and showed the images of fish. Multicolored bubbles appeared, rising slowly to the surface and on into the air before popping. The pool border became a sandy beach complete with old seashells and tufts of sea oats. Currents appeared, with green water swirling against blue water. Then it took on a viscous semblance, as if it were thickening gelatin. Finally a fountain appeared, splashing into the surface like rain. "Our guests generally enjoy the variations."

So they had entertained living visitors before, not necessarily human.

"But enough distraction," Apoca Robot said, taking his arm again. "We have more interesting business."

Nolan Robot did the same with Apoca. They moved on to the sleeping quarters.

He found himself in a private bedroom with the female, who looked and sounded so much like the real Apoca that he wanted to hug and kiss her. That was dangerous. He was thankful for the wrist ID. "Now, let's make love, dear," she said as she stepped out of her clothing and stood gloriously nude.

He did not need to hear Rocker's clicking or Aurora's warning to know that this was treacherous ground. But he did not want to risk offending the robots by an outright refusal. "Um, not so soon." Was the male making a similar advance to Apoca? It was past time to get this under control. "Human couples don't generally just jump into bed with each other, let alone with others. There are protocols."

She smiled prettily. "I apologize. I merely wish to learn how to please a man most efficiently."

He smiled back, knowing that his expression was no more sincere than hers. "Efficiency is not the point. Romance is not efficient, it is emotional."

"Emotional," she repeated, as if slightly hurt. Bleep, she was good!

He realized that he was overlooking something. "You're a robot. A machine. Do you even have emotions?" He remembered how Rocker seemed to have different moods, but that was not necessarily the same.

"We have emotion circuits we can invoke."

"That's a start. But Apoca Live can clarify that better than I can. Let's join them for this discussion."

She looked demurely regretful but walked over to the wall and tapped on it. A panel slid open. Beyond it was the next room, where Apoca and the male robot sat on the bed beside each other. Apoca glanced their way and frowned.

Nolan remembered belatedly that Apoca Robot was now gloriously nude. He covered the awkwardness by speaking. "We need your input on emotion."

Apoca smiled wryly. "So I see."

She knew him well enough to be sure he had not done anything with the robot. "I have explained that romance is more complicated than merely stripping and getting into bed," he said. "Especially royal romance, which has political complications. This is one aspect our companions need to pick up on. They have emotion circuits, but they lack nuances. Can you show her how to proceed with an interested human prince?"

Apoca stood. "This way." She stepped toward him, drawing him in close. "Shall we dance, Prince Anonymous?" she inquired archly.

For the moment both robots were nonplussed. Nolan faced them. "Surely you have programs for formal human dancing. Download them."

There was a pause of only half an instant. "Done," Nolan Robot said.

"Thank you, NR," Apoca said.

Then Nolan and Apoca danced a slow waltz. He loved it. Not only was she his beloved, she was supple, graceful, and knew exactly how to do it.

They took a turn around the room, then split. Nolan went to Apoca Robot—AR—and Apoca went to NR. The robots' programs were good; they had the moves down perfectly, and AR was exactly as light on her feet as Apoca. She also remained excitingly nude.

"Very good," Apoca said after the turns. "This is an expedient way to get close to your opposite without alarming him or her." She returned to Nolan. "Next stage. Shall we kiss, Prince Anonymous?" She smiled invitingly.

"You are beautiful, Princess Obscure," he said. "And marvelous to hold." Of course she was actually a queen, but these were roles.

"Thank you." Her arms tightened around him, drawing them closer together.

Their faces moved slowly, slowly toward each other, closing the gap with tantalizing deliberation. Then they kissed fleetingly. Nolan loved this too.

Apoca turned to her double. "The first time is generally minimal, so that neither feels forced. They will talk further and hold hands, gradually becoming more comfortable with their closeness. It may go no further than this, the first day. He may desire her, but she will be more cautious. In due course they will kiss more passionately. Do not hurry it. It can take time for the hormones to be stirred."

"I should not have removed my clothes," Apoca Robot said.

"Yes. You do not want to seem overly eager. Let him take the lead, and yield cautiously to his advances. The initiative is normally his. Then you may invoke your hormone emulation circuits to accommodate his growing desire." She disengaged from Nolan. "Now, you try it, AR."

The robot came to join Nolan, and they went through the same motions. Exactly the same. Then Apoca tried it with NR. Both robots had the moves and expressions down perfectly.

After that, the robots did it with each other, and it was supremely realistic. They were indeed apt learners.

They continued the demonstrations, covering variations of motions and dialogue, until they were ready for the next stage. "What we have covered is called necking," Apoca said. "Because much of it occurs above the neck. The next stage is petting, which occurs mainly between the neck and the waist." She took Nolan's hand and threaded it under her shirt so that he could feel her bare bosom. It was, of course, a phenomenal turn-on for him, and perhaps for her. "This will increase his interest, but she will demur when he wants further action. The limits are hers, and she may set them wherever she pleases. He will honor those limits, lest he annoy her and lose any chance for further progress."

Then Nolan got to do the same with AR, which he found almost as guiltily exciting as he had with the original. He knew that the robot had no true emotions, but she was a superlative actress, and her nuances were perfect. But it bothered him privately that Apoca was now doing the same with NR.

"Hereafter it can become nude, for both, in bed," Apoca said. "But it must be voluntary, at least for the female. The male will always express interest, and be quite ready to follow up, but the female must acquiesce before any stork summoning occurs. Violation of this principle will likely cause immediate cessation of the relationship. If the female is really interested, she may even take the initiative, and seduce the male. That is her prerogative. Do you understand, in part or in whole?"

"We understand," NR said. "Your instructions have been excellent."

"But will they work on other royals?" AR asked.

"They should, if you are patient. Remember, do not rush it. Give them time to adjust to the idea of personable robots."

"Also," Nolan said, "a romantic association, even including seduction, does not guarantee a marriage. That may require a prolonged courtship."

"It took me time to adjust to the idea of marrying a naga prince," Apoca said. "I suspect it would have taken longer for a robot prince."

"Thank you for this lesson," NR said. "We have learned much that was not in our programs."

"I think we are done here," Nolan said. "We must return to our group."

"Please, not yet," AR said, frowning prettily. "We will practice by ourselves but may yet encounter unanticipated nuances. We prefer to have you stay the night, to be available for our possible questions. We want to be perfect."

Nolan exchanged a glance with Apoca. She shrugged. "Why not? We want the emperor to be satisfied."

"Thank you so very much," AR said warmly. Even her gratitude echoed Apoca's perfectly.

"Now we must use the sanitary facility," Apoca said. "We living folk have biologic needs you robots lack."

The two robots exchanged a glance exactly the way Nolan and Apoca had. They were still picking up nuances. "We understand," NR said. "Here is the facility." He opened another door, and there was a nice bathroom complete with sink, tub, toilet, and accessories. "And this is the pantry." He showed them another chamber stocked with assorted foods and beverages.

"Thank you," Nolan said, impressed anew.

Then NR and AR opened the invisible door and went to the other bedroom, holding hands. They had practicing to do. The door closed behind them and disappeared.

Apoca stepped into the bathroom while Nolan sat on the bed and munched on tasty crackers and sipped excellent wine. The robots did know how to entertain guests. Surely they had done it before, repeatedly. That would explain their amazing ability to tune in on the nuances.

Nolan relaxed. It had certainly been a day, and they were ready to rest, physically and emotionally.

In due course Apoca emerged, prettified, and Nolan took his turn. When he emerged, Apoca was seated where he had been, nibbling on more crackers and sipping wine. He joined her, and she handed him a cracker. "Confession," she said, blushing slightly.

"If it is that you regret having to demonstrate intimate touching with me and NR, I understand. I felt awkward doing it with AR. But we had to do it right, while they watched, or there was no point in the exercise."

Her blush deepened. "That too."

This was more than interesting. She was an extremely self-possessed woman, not much given to embarrassment, and they had not crossed any taboo boundaries. "There is more?"

"The demonstrating turned me on."

He smiled. "Me too. I kept wishing we were alone together."

"We are alone together now." Her blush continued as her breathing deepened.

Oh. "You mean you want to—"

She cut him off with a passionate kiss. It seemed she did want to.

What more could he ask? He kissed her back, then stood so he could get undressed. She did the same, then drew back the blanket and sheet. He had never seen her more lovely and had never been more ready himself.

"Nolan," Aurora said mentally.

He answered her the same way. "Can it wait? I'm busy at the moment."

"That is not Apoca. It is the robot."

That froze him. "But there's no wristband."

"They abolished them."

"But she was eating crackers."

"Robots can, when they need to. They can also drink and pee."

"And she blushed." But he knew that could be programmed into sophisticated machines. Aurora was contact telepathic, and he had been touching Apoca. Apoca Robot. The fire ant knew.

"I am in touch with Nimbus. She is telling Apoca."

He realized that the robots had pulled a stunt, switching places with the real people and pretending to be the originals. It might be their ulti- mate test; if they could fool their living partners into complete seduction, they would prove their mastery of the form and manner. The ultimate nuance.

They might even have succeeded, but for the bugs. AR had indeed fooled him. Had aroused him. She had played the role perfectly. Even knowing he was with a machine, he had to concede that this thing before him remained infernally sexy. He well might have bedded her and never known the difference. If NR was as good with Apoca as he surely was, the two of them could have had their first complete intimacy without ever knowing of the substitutions. The robots would truly have passed their final exam, as it were.

The easiest course was to play along, pretending never to know, and resume their search for the right plaque in the morning, leaving the robots well satisfied. Too bad Nolan was not that good a sport! He was sure Apoca had a similar objection.

"Why do you hesitate, dear?" the pseudo Apoca asked as she spread her lovely legs, her concern manifest. Bleep, she was good!

They had to get out of this! But how, without blowing up the deal? If they called the robots on their fakery, that could be taken as proof that their instruction of those robots was incomplete. That more was needed. But to go through with it was not acceptable either. It was an impasse.

He needed time to think this through. So he temporized. "As you know, Apoca, we have not before been intimate. We have merely held each other and kissed. This is a significant step. Are we sure we want to do it at this time? We are not yet married."

Her face crumpled into horror. "Are you saying that you don't love me?"

Bleep, she was good in that too! His continued reluctance could be taken as lack of passion. Even knowing it was an act on her part, he felt guilty for even making such an implication. He surely could enjoy doing it with AR. But he had to fight it through. "I am suggesting that we may prefer to wait until we are married. For one thing we don't want the storks to bring our daughter prematurely." That put the ball, as it were, in her corner. She could not point out that there was no danger of any signal reaching the Stork Works, because machines did not order from the storks. New robots were constructed, not signaled for. Machines sent no three dot ellipses. This tryst had no substance other than pleasure.

She smiled. "I came prepared. I am wearing an internal barrier of the type used in Mundania that will prevent any signal from getting through to the storks. I will remove it when we marry."

Bleep again. She had refuted him. But he got another idea. "Nevertheless, it remains a significant step, emotionally as much as physically. Let's ponder it a while, just to be sure. We do have all night, assuming we don't get interrupted by questions from the robots."

She yielded gracefully. "If they are doing what we are doing, they will not break off for questions." She of course knew that the robots would not be interrupting anything. They wanted to complete the action, thus proving themselves.

They lay side by side, holding hands. Now Nolan had a chance to think. How had the robots made the exchange? The bathroom had to be the key. When Apoca used it, her door must somehow have exited to the companion bedroom, so that she joined NR, who would have been eating crackers. AR had then stepped into this bedroom. This must be a sophisticated suite, with a movable bathroom.

Could he and Apoca work a similar exchange? Not via the bathroom, which they did not know how to move. But some other device?

Then he got it. The swimming pool! With its naughty colors. Get all four of them in it together, color it, and make the switch with the guidance of the bugs. With luck the robots, intent on their personifications, would not know.

"Aurora, can you put me in touch with Apoca? We have a plan to work out."

In barely a moment Apoca's mental voice came through. "I hope your plan is apt, Nolan. I don't want to have to become intimate with a machine."

She, of course, had had relations with other partners, as had he. He had fond memories of seductive nymphs and mermaids, and she could have any man she wanted for a temporary tryst merely by kissing him. That was not the point. They wanted their first intimacy to be their own. That was not something the robots needed to understand.

"The pool. With its lights, textures and bubbles. Have a splashing party with the machines, and quietly switch places to be with each other, leaving them to seduce each other. We, too, if we want. If they are good enough to fool us, they may be good enough to fool each other."

"Problem," she said. "We are supposed to think they still have their ID wristbands on. It will be apparent that they don't."

Oops.

"Problem," Aurora said. "The pool is presently being serviced, as it is nightly when not in use. Corrosive chemicals are flooding it."

Oops again.

Nolan spurred his reluctant brain to special action. And got a flash that solved both problems.

"I saw that flash," AR said. "You have an idea."

"I do," he said, knowing that Aurora would relay his words to Nimbus and Apoca. "I want to have this first fling, but I want to make it special. Like no other, so as to be truly memorable. I have thought of a way."

"This sounds like fun."

"I want to do it in the pool, with the lights, bubbles, and colors. To make it super special, have the two robots participate, making it a two-couple foursome. It will also show them how far the niceties can stretch, so that they will not be caught off guard if they later encounter living royals who have specialized romantic tastes. The final nuance." He knew she could not turn down a nuance.

"Um, I understand that the pool is cleaned and refurbished at night," she said. "Caustic fluid fills it, before fresh water is restored for the next day. It is not suitable for swimming."

"Oh, bleep! I did so want that nuance." His disappointment was artificial; this was a key aspect of his plan. "But I have a notion: let's don wetsuits and goggles to protect us from the chemicals, so we can splash all we want. Suits that fit so well anatomically that they will not interfere with our intimacy. The boys can wear blue suits, and the girls red suits, making it a really colorful occasion." The suits would also conceal the robots' lack of wristbands.

"Genius!" Apoca murmured. Her genuine appreciation thrilled him.

"Let's do it," AR said, her unvoiced objection nulled. She knocked on the wall. "Robots, don wetsuits and meet us at the pool for a wild splash. Blue for male, red for female."

"Will do," NR called back.

They repaired to the supply closet, then to the pool. There they were met by the other couple, supposedly both robots. Apoca looked gorgeous in the tight wet suit. Of course she was playing along. If the true robots had had any time to consider more fully, they might have realized that a living woman playing a robot was suspicious at this moment. No, she would have been told that the other couple were the robots.

The water was a dilute gray, because of the cleaning fluid. But then the special effects came on, independent of the water, and the pool came alive, complete with the fountain. They waded in, and soon were swimming, then splashing one another like children.

"Get behind the fountain," Nolan told Apoca via the bugs. "When I join you, swim underwater to the far side."

The other Apoca splashed her way to and through the fountain. Nolan held his breath and dived, tackling her underwater. She dropped down and swam beside him. They came up together and looked back. The other two were still splashing each other. Then they broke off and kissed. It was working! They had succeeded in switching partners.

They wasted no time. Nolan and Apoca kissed, knowing they were the right ones. Then they made love in the water, in wetsuit fashion, without actual physical contact. No actual signal went out to the Stork Works. Now this first emulation could never be taken from them.

Then they rejoined the robots. It no longer mattered as much who was with whom; they had had their experience.

Nolan and Apoca changed out of their wetsuits and returned to the bedroom. "This is AR again," Aurora said.

Nolan sighed inwardly. It seemed that the robots had managed to switch back.

"I proffer you this deal," AR said. "If you will tell me how you knew I was not your living partner, I will leave you alone romantically and cause you no mischief. The same goes for NR with Apoca. Evidently our performance has been imperfect."

So she knew he knew. "Is it safe to tell her?" he asked Aurora.

"We are in touch with Ghorgeous and thus Rocker and Vinia. They indicate that it is safe. The region is green, and the clicks are routine. The robots mean us no harm. They just want their emulations to be perfect."

"Deal," he told AR. "We have telepathic bugs that enable us to communicate with each other. Mine is Aurora Ant. She read your mind when we touched, and knew it wasn't alive. She told me. It was no fault in your presentation; you had me fooled. As far as I am concerned, you have learned well enough to succeed in your relations with living kingdoms. Especially since you will not be trying to deceive them about your nature." That last was a reminder of their promise to be open.

AR nodded exactly as Apoca would have. "This is interesting. I would like to meet her." She was avoiding the issue of deception.

Nolan put his hand on his shoulder, and the ant stepped onto it. "This is Aurora," he said, holding her up. "She is accompanying me while she looks for a suitable new home for her nest. We get along well."

"She is telepathic? I would like to communicate with her directly."

"I don't know if that is possible, as you are not alive."

"Why should that make a difference? I am conscious and feeling, when the key circuits are invoked. Don't those qualities count?"

Did they? He had not considered this aspect before.

"Aurora?" he asked.

"She does have a mind. It is foreign to any I have encountered before, but there is a glimmer there."

"She says there's a glimmer," he told AR.

"Maybe I can adapt an empathy circuit so as to tune in better." The robot focused.

"Getting warmer," the ant said. "Touch her so I can read her better."

"Keep tuning," Nolan said, taking AR's hand.

The focus continued.

"There!" AR and Aurora said together.

A picture formed in the air between them. In it appeared the robot facing the ant, adjusted to be on a similar scale of size. "I am so glad to meet you, telepathic companion," AR said.

"Likewise," Aurora said. Then both turned to Nolan, looking at him from the picture. "We have established mental contact," the figures said together. "Now, let go of the hand."

He let go. "That's great! I hope you like each other."

"We do," they said together, and laughed. Clearly the telepathic contact remained.

"With assistance like this," AR said separately, "we could make progress approximately 2.75 times as rapidly as before. We must contact the bugs in our domain."

"Only a few will be telepathic," Aurora said. "But you should be able to scout them out if you use your present empathy tuning. They will not be just ants and nickelpedes; telepathy seems to be randomly scattered among species, with perhaps one in a hundred individuals having the capacity for it."

"We will give all robots the telepathic setting, now that we know it," AR said. "What can we offer the bugs in return for their assistance?"

"Recognition as sapient species. We are long since tired of being considered vermin and put in chronic danger of damage or even extermination."

"We will gladly grant that. A bug representative will have a place in the court, and the emperor will heed her advice. All extermination will halt."

"You can say that?" Nolan asked, surprised. "An ordinary fusion robot?"

The robot's expression changed. "She can," the emperor's voice said from her mouth.

Oh. The robots had better interpersonal connections than he had realized. Had the emperor been watching as AR tried to seduce him?

AR's body spoke again with the emperor's voice. "Nolan, you have perhaps inadvertently delivered to us significantly more than our bargain required. We owe you one. Here is our repayment, in the form of advice. You may be about to take the path leading to the realm of madness. Avoid it, despite the temptations it may proffer, as things are not merely crazy there. You will lose your living minds and be unable to escape it or to complete your Quest. The other paths are safer, though they have their challenges."

"He knows what he is talking about," Aurora said. "He may have saved your sanity."

"Uh, thank you," Nolan said, taken aback.

"Honor requires fairness. Quo pro quid." Then the robot's expression reverted to normal. The emperor was gone.

"Now rest and sleep, preparing for the morrow," AR said. "I will leave you alone, or oblige you in any manner you desire, or return your fiancée to you."

"The last," Nolan said, relieved.

The robot got up and went to the door. She opened it to admit Apoca, then stepped on out.

Apoca flung herself into his embrace. "The bugs kept me informed. Just hold me." She kissed him, her face wet with her tears of relief. She seldom showed the softer emotions, but this seemed justified at the moment.

"This is the real Apoca," Aurora said unnecessarily.

They spent a chastely passionate night, still leaving the stork out of it. Any question of their commitment to each other had been banished.

In the morning they kissed once more, got up, cleaned, dressed, and went to the living room to bid parting to the robots, who now wore their ID bracelets again. "We very much appreciate your instruction," AR said warmly. "We hope to establish excellent relations with the Queendom of Thanx and the Kingdom of Naga in due course."

"We will be glad to see that happen," Nolan said.

A picture appeared above the two robots. "You too, Aurora and Nimbus," AR said from it. "Our discovery of you marks a turning point in robotic history."

"You are welcome," Aurora said.

Then the four of them went outside, where the other members of the Quest stood, including Rocker Robot, whose surface was now clean and shiny. It seemed he had been serviced too. His clicks were even, signaling no problems. Vinia was wearing a cute new dress, and Gent a handsome new suit. They had evidently enjoyed the Fusion hospitality.

"May we?" AR asked as they were about to part.

Nolan shared a quick glance with Apoca. Then they each accepted their robot double's parting embrace and kiss.

It was time to move on.

Chapter 10

COVEN-19

Back at the nexus they considered paths. Apoca's batoness was glowing, which meant that a new chapter was starting, and she was the protagonist. She hoped her chapter wasn't as nervous as parts of the last one had been. Fortunately being the protagonist did not mean she was required to make all the key decisions. She was happy to leave that to Nolan. For now.

Or was it going to be that easy? The batoness was hovering close, as if concerned about something. It was not safe to ignore her concern, whatever it was. "Talk with me privately," Apoca said. "What is agitating you?"

The speech balloon appeared. "I have a sense when my protagonist is about to enter a more dramatic story. There is a portent of danger and opportunity. Tread carefully. Protagonists are not guaranteed successful outcomes."

Fair warning, indeed! "I will tread carefully," Apoca agreed.

The next path was nicely manicured and girt with pretty flowers. There was even soft music in the background. A handsome man appeared, looking her way invitingly.

Apoca glanced at Vinia, who shook her head violently no. At the same time Rocker Robot sounded two emphatic clicks. This was definitely the wrong one to take. It was already time to tread carefully. But was this the extent of it?

"No," the batoness printed. "This is a several-decision crisis."

"Emperor Fusion didn't know we had warnings of our own," Nolan murmured. "But his point was well taken. We don't want madness, however appealing the access may seem."

A nymph appeared, bearing a dish piled with chocolate cake and vanilla eye scream. "Bleep," Vinia muttered. "The spooks are playing to my weakness."

A stunningly manly ghost formed, making gestures of holding and kissing. "And mine," Ghorgeous said from a momentary cloud. "I'd give my all to suffer the romantic attention of a truly virile man. But this is not real, even in ghostly terms." She returned to the robot.

An image of a lovely valley appeared, replete with standing firewood, firebirds, firedogs, firemen, and a blazing firestorm in the background. Nimbus relayed Aurora's reaction. "And mine." Naturally the fire ant longed for a setting like that for her nest to occupy.

"But it is madness," Apoca said firmly.

"Madness may offer potent temptations," Nimbus said.

The path beyond was lined with egregious puns, like a man whose toes were little rockets. "Missile-toes," Gent murmured. Stones in the form of keys. "Rocky." A bear wearing a fancy band on one toe. "Bearing." A male deer without clothing. "Buck naked."

Apoca quailed at the very thought of returning to the pundemic zone. A bird appeared at her feet and took flight. A quail, of course.

The next path had a sign: WITCHES BEST? But Gent was silent. Which meant it was not a pun for "Which is best?" Which meant in turn that this one led to witches. Almost as bad.

Nolan turned to her. "I think I'd rather face witches than more egregious puns."

"Me too. But if the plaque is negative, it will have to be the pundemic again."

He looked at Rocker. "How are chances among the witches?"

The robot clicked thrice. It didn't know. Apoca realized that it figured that the paths were resistive to useful details, except for the one for madness.

"Oh, well, not all witches are old and ugly."

She shot him a dark glance, in part because she was not completely sure he was joking. Had he had a witch among his bygone girlfriends? She did not care to ask.

They set off along the path. Soon a branch led to a section labeled COVEN-1. It actually looked reasonably attractive, with a neatly trimmed hedge and a field where cute kittens played. Vinia's green indicated that was not where they should go. The kittens might be slated to become familiars. That was fine for witches, but not so much for travelers.

"Unless you count bugs as familiars," Nimbus said.

"We count you as friends."

The next branch led to a far spookier landscape, labeled COVEN-2, with a haunted house in sight. That was not the one either. "Fake," Ghorgeous said after investigating. "No real ghosts there. Maybe it's a trap ghostwriters use."

Apoca wasn't sure what danger there could be for unwary ghosts, and decided not to ask. Probably they would simply be forced to write spooky scenes so the writers could take time off.

The third branch, labeled COVEN-3. looked diabolical, with statues of horned, tailed demons doing nasty things to innocent people. The figures were so realistic that they seemed ready to come to life at any point, screaming. That was not green either, to Apoca's relief. She feared that the demons were real, lurking for foolish folk to come close enough to grab and torture. She suspected that demons, like mortal folk, came in a wide variety of types, and it was best to stay clear if possible. And what about Demons, one of whom they were seeking? Was their whole Quest a mistake?

The fourth one looked nice at first, with a calm lake. But when Nolan threw a stone into it, a lake monster shot its ugly head up and snapped it out of the air. Only to spit it out a moment later, disgusted, sending a glare Nolan's way; it was a rotten piece of gravestone. This one, too, was not right.

The branch-offs continued, none of them appealing, though of course that was not the point. Where was the plaque?

The main path terminated beside an inlet of the sea, where there was a temporary shelter marked COVEN-19. Several witches were there building a fire for their huge cauldron. They wore the standard black cloaks and pointed hats but appeared normal otherwise.

This was their destination, on this path, unless they needed to strike out into the wilderness. Vinia's green indicated that this was indeed the place. Rocker's clicking was routine. The bugs were picking up no hostility. The batoness had no further input. So what was the sinister portent?

This did not seem like much danger or opportunity. There wasn't even any ominous background music.

The witches ignored them, busy with their own tasks. Each wore an ID tag bearing a number, one through thirteen. Apoca knew that the higher the number was, the greater the seniority within the coven; she had encountered occasional witches before. As a general rule they minded their own business unless accosted, and their specialty brews, like love potions, could be useful.

Well, time to tackle the witch by the broomstick, as it were. Individual witches could be nice or nasty. It was best to assume nice, until corrected. Apoca girded herself and approached the senior witch, Witch Thirteen, while the others waited close behind, just in case things got complicated. The old witch was standing beside the bubbling cauldron, directing younger witches as they added ingredients like baboon blood, eye of newt, and tongue of dog. The main item was a slowly cooking fatted prig, probably slated for the evening meal.

"Pardon me, please," Apoca said to Thirteen. "I am Apoca from the Queendom of Thanx. I have a question."

"Thanx!" young and pretty Two exclaimed before being reproved by a Senior Glance. So it seemed that word of the new feminist establishment was spreading.

"A greeting, Apoca," Thirteen said evenly. "Our complement is complete. You will have to seek some other coven to join. Not that you'd want to join this one."

This was interesting on one and a half grounds. Normal women were becoming witches and joining covens? And what was wrong with this one?

"We are the last coven to form in this territory," Thirteen said, knowing what question was coming. "We got the site none of the others wanted, because of its history. It is isolated, its house is haunted, it is subject to lout raids, and it requires an annual sacrifice of a tender maiden. In addition, no warlock will join us or even visit us because we are feminists."

Feminist witches. Interesting indeed! Naturally they would be aware of the queendom. A haunted house hardly mattered; Ghorgeous could readily check that out. Lout raids? One Lips kiss would level a lout. But maiden sacrifices? Warlock exclusion? The challenging nature of this excursion was coming into view. "We are just traveling through, not intending to join any coven. We are looking for a special plaque that says HERE or NOT HERE. Nothing else. Have you seen it?"

"No, but I know where it would be. Where everything of any interest to anyone is: the haunted house."

"Then may we check that house? Once we find it we'll be on our way and won't bother you anymore."

Thirteen shook her head. "You'd be welcome, as far as we're concerned. The ghosts are not a threat. They are the spirits of the maidens sacrificed over the years. But you can't get there. It's on a little island in an inlet of the sea. Loan sharks patrol it. We can cross over on our brooms, once we decide to tackle it, but unless you can fly, or back off the sharks, you're out."

Apoca thought of Nolan. He could handle a loan shark, and since they normally attacked one at a time, he could intimidate them all in turn. But that reminded her of the other water challenge. The maiden sacrifice. "What is this annual event?"

Thirteen paused half a witchly moment. "You really are interested?"

"Yes. We don't much like sacrifices of people."

"Then be our guests tonight, you and your troupe, and we will acquaint you with the whole story."

Apoca was surprised. "You invite passing strangers into your abode? Male, female, and robot? Is that safe?"

"One member of our coven suffers premonitions. She said that visitors were coming who could solve all our problems. I am cautious, because though there is always substance to her visions, their proper interpretation can be devious. But I have a certain feel for character, and you strike me as worthwhile. Your reference to Thanx helps. Perhaps you are merely passing travelers, but there is an even chance that you are the party of the premonition, and if that is true, it is more than worth the gamble."

"She is serious," Nimbus said.

Apoca glanced at Vinia. The girl nodded; this course was green. Rocker's clicks were even. The bugs were not alarmed. Even Gent, who suffered the curse of a witch, did not seem wary of these ones. Maybe he was distracted by pretty Two, who was shyly smiling at him. The absence of a warlock might be making outsiders look good to her.

"Then we accept your offer. We will acquaint you with our people and mission, to the extent that interests you, and you will inform us about your situation. If it turns out that we can do each other some good, so much the better."

Ghorgeous went off to check the island house and ghosts, while the others chatted with the witches as they worked on their several routine tasks. One was good with children, and Vinia liked her. One was scholarly, compiling a spot history of crossbreeds, and Nolan was glad to update her on his naga and mer ancestry. Another specialized in machines; she found Rocker very interesting, and he seemed to like the attention. Apoca observed a carpenter witch constructing a wharf intended for fishing. Her talent was to join wood together magically so that she needed no hammer or nails. Another witch was practicing her illusion, trying to imitate the wood planking, though of course it could not be walked on. She was one of the younger ones, pretty but not yet broadly skilled. The other witches had other specialties. They called it a coven, but it was really a small cooperative community.

"I never thought about joining a coven," Vinia said. "But I can see it wouldn't necessarily be a bad thing."

"People are people, whatever their association," Apoca said. "It's generally better to get to know them before making a judgment."

Ghorgeous returned. "Those are all nice ghosts," she reported. "They showed me where the plaque is hidden in the attic. It says NOT HERE."

"So now we know," Apoca said, relieved. "But we're still going to help this coven."

"Of course." The ghost faded out.

Thus it was that Apoca and the other members of the Quest found themselves eating what turned out to be truly delicious gruel and crockery cakes, in the close company of the full coven of witches. The women formally introduced themselves in ascending order, from the youngest and fairest to the oldest and ugliest, all of them friendly. Then the members of the Quest did the same, including the bugs, Ghorgeous Ghost, and Rocker Robot, omitting only the two batons, as they were imaginary. Nolan explained their mission to contact the Dwarf Demon of Talents and try to get him to resume doing his job.

"This is important," Thirteen said. "We hope to have children in this coven, in due course, and do not want them limited to mud pies. We will help you if we can."

Then she clarified the dire situation of Coven-19, which felt like being stricken with a bad-tempered plague. The worst of it was the sea monster who visited each year and required a succulent young maiden for his meal. When he ate her, he guaranteed the safety of the island for the coming year, as not even the loan sharks dared cross him. Which related to the witches' temporary shed. They weren't quite sure they wanted to make the sacrifice to attain the house on the island. Witch One, being the youngest, had volunteered for the good of the coven, but not only was she their prettiest girl, she was also their nicest. No one wanted her to die. So they were pondering passing up the island house, with its protection, in favor of the crude shore structure. They could use illusion to at least make it look decent.

But that would bring other problems. The best foraging was on the island, with fine year-round pie plants and a great old ale barrel tree. Sweet-smelling flowers were everywhere, and the wild herbs were the best. The house was comfortable, with self-fueling fireplaces and magic-mirror windows that could picture any outside view a witch wanted. The ghosts were not bad; as the spirits of witches, they could be good company on lonely nights. The shore dwelling, in contrast, would be uncomfortable and drafty, and the foraging was so-so.

"The lout raids," Apoca prompted them.

Thirteen nodded. "Roving bands of men who somehow obtained light armor that is proof against witchly magic. They raid our supplies, steal our trinkets, and ravish our younger members. The other covens defend themselves with fortifications, prickle burrs, foul smells, and some of their warlocks are warriors. But we have not yet had time to establish effective barriers. There is hardly a stink horn to be found. We shall have to hide, but that may not be effective. We are bound to take losses, and any maidenly innocence any of us may have is at peril. On the island we can avoid that. But that means the sacrifice. It is due tomorrow."

Apoca appreciated the grim choice. Ravishment of the younger witches or sacrifice to the sea monster. Too many men regarded witches as fair game. That was only the start of it. A witch's lot was not a happy one.

Number Ten, the lookout, glided down on her broom with a grim report. "Louts incoming. They spied activity on the path and figured something was up. Estimated time of arrival within one hour. Less if they hurry. I had to sweep one who tried to grab me."

"Sweep?" Apoca asked Nimbus.

"Their brooms are useful for more than flying," the nickelpede replied, reading the information from the witch's mind, which it seemed could be explored from a short distance. Were witchly minds more open than others? Did it matter? "They can deliver a nasty kick when swung against an opponent. They call it—"

"Sweeping," Apoca agreed, catching on.

"The sea monster is also approaching, slightly ahead of schedule." Ten took off again, to continue her watch. Her short skirt fluttered up as she maneuvered, flashing a shapely thigh, and Apoca saw both men take note. Fair game indeed.

"Oh, bleep!" Thirteen swore. "We're not nearly ready. We'll have to scatter and hide. They'll probably burn down our shelter when they don't find us."

Apoca glanced at Nolan, whose own glance had been hovering in the vicinity, once the lookout departed, waiting on her. He nodded. So did Vinia. The bugs agreed. The robot issued a single click. All of them approved, knowing her thought.

"We'll help you solve your problems," she said.

"But our problems are immediate and huge, and we have little to offer in return."

"We are not making a deal; we are simply being neighborly. It's our fault the louts are here, because our arrival alerted them. But you will need to cooperate."

Now the glance careened around the witches, almost knocking some hats askew. "We will," Thirteen said guardedly. She had surely picked up on the men's reactions to the younger members of their coven; women did. Cooperation could be euphemistic for suffering male attentions.

Apoca went into organization mode. She was a queen; she had managed campaigns before. Especially against obnoxious males. "First we need to get you girls to the island, where you will be safe."

"But the sacrifice!" Thirteen wailed.

"We will handle the sea monster. None of you will get eaten. Or ravished."

The witches plainly were uncertain about this reassurance but had little choice at the moment. They fetched their brooms.

"I need more than this," Thirteen said grimly. "The island will protect us from the louts, who are afraid of the ghosts, but how do you propose to handle the monster? Once we're on the island, we're committed."

"I will kiss it."

"Kiss it! It will gobble you down as a sacrifice."

Apoca smiled. "In which case you will have a year's reprieve, no? Trust me."

"I do," she said dubiously.

It was now dusk. Sure enough, the louts were arriving, and the monster was surely not far behind. They needed to act swiftly.

"Four, Eleven," Apoca rapped, before they could get airborne. "I need your talents at the shore."

The designated witches joined her, fastening their brooms to their backs with spot harnesses. These were the young illusionist and the carpenter Apoca had watched in the afternoon.

"Add some quick planking to your wharf," she told the carpenter. "So that it projects farther across the water."

"It can't possibly cross to the island in such a brief time," the witch warned.

"It doesn't need to. This is a special purpose device." She turned to the other witch. "Stand at the edge of the wharf and make an illusion of it extending the rest of the way across to the island. Can you do that?"

"Yes, I think so. But no one could actually use it to cross."

"No one will cross. Can you maintain the illusion without staying right beside it?"

"Yes, but not for very long."

"That will be fine. Can you use your illusion to mask yourself, to become invisible, so others can't see you?"

The girl laughed. "I do that all the time. My sister witches aren't much amused when I spy on them."

"Can you do both illusions at once?"

"No, only one at a time."

This was going to be tricky, but it should be feasible. "I will direct a little charade here, when the louts come. Follow my directions, then be ready to fly out of danger."

Four and Eleven got to work. In a generous moment there was a new plank attached, and the illusion of more planks extending all the way across the inlet to the island. The other witches stood at the shore, watching with confused interest. What was the point in presenting a causeway that couldn't be used?

The louts arrived, charging almost mindlessly ahead in the dusk. "Now we need to lure them onto the apparent causeway," Apoca said. "We want to seem to be three stranded witches crossing the water via the planks. You, Four, can hide by disappearing. I can't. May I borrow your broom?"

The younger witch looked at the older witch, who nodded nervously. Four handed over her broom. "You control it mentally. Think 'Fly,' and it will. Then hang on."

"Thank you."

Apoca stepped onto the last of the solid planks and faced the oncoming horde. She ripped off her clothing, jammed it into her purse, squeezed the purse to mini nut size, put it into her mouth, and stood naked, holding only the broom. She knew she presented an alluring figure for men intent on ravishment. The two witches stood on either side of her.

"I think I am seeing the plan," Eleven said, removing her own clothing to reveal a solid but shapely torso garbed only in white bra and black panty. "They think the causeway is real."

"They're not thinking rationally," Apoca said. "That's part of the point of our exposure."

Four caught on. "They'll get dunked!" She doffed her own clothing except for the pink panty and stood as a tempting nymph.

"Yes," Apoca agreed. "But make sure they don't actually get their lusty hands on you."

Four got into the act with relish. She waggled her hands beside her ears. "Nyaa! Nyaa! You can't catch me!" She did a little jump that made her assets bounce dangerously.

The louts spied them and charged in a lascivious phalanx. In barely (so to speak) two moments they were close enough to see what wasn't there.

The ones to the left spied Four's panty, freaked out, and fell to the left side. The ones to the right spied Eleven's bra and panty and fell to the right side. But the ones in the center, orienting on nude Apoca, no panty, did not freak; their eyeballs merely glazed somewhat. Their reprieve, however, would be temporary.

Apoca inhaled. Then the louts in the center freaked out and fell, causing the ones following them to trip over their bodies. There was a pile of louts, with arms and legs projecting at odd angles.

But soon they scrambled back to their feet and resumed their charge. "Let them get close, then fly your broom low over the illusory causeway," Apoca told Eleven. "So they think it is supporting you."

"Got it."

"And you vanish at the last moment," she told Four. "Maybe wade through the shallower water. The sharks won't see you. We want the louts to follow Eleven and me until they splash."

"Splash," the young witch agreed. She was enjoying this. So were the witches on the island, who were now stripping and flashing galore with multicolored underwear. It looked as if the causeway would lead the oafs right to them.

Now the louts were hard upon them. "Eeeeek!" Apoca screamed with five e's, as if trapped. Five e's was standard for distressed maidens. Louts typically could not count beyond that.

A lout leaped for her. She grabbed the broom. *Fly!* she thought fiercely.

The lout barely (so to speak again) missed her as the broom lurched upward, hauling her after it. She tried to get her legs around it, but missed, then dangled precariously. She glimpsed the clods staring at her thrashing legs and toppling into the sea. Somewhere in the background was a generous hint of pride that she was able to freak them out without panties despite being over a dozen years beyond teendom.

She clasped the broom handle tightly as it zoomed on up into the air. She got a leg up over it so she could ride it more properly, but the thing plunged back toward the sea. She wrestled it around to point back up, but it bucked as if trying to throw her off.

As if? "I read its mind," Nimbus said. "It doesn't like being ridden by a stranger."

"Well, tell it to behave, or I'll break it into splinters!" She put her hands on the handle so firmly that it was evident she could make a good try at breaking it.

That threat was effective. The broom started flying straight. Even objects had some instinct of self-preservation, especially when they were magic.

Apoca looked down at the scene beneath her. The illusory causeway was gone, which was okay because it had done its job. Most of the louts had charged into the water, and the loan sharks were trying to take an arm and a leg from them. The witches ashore were watching and applauding. They loved seeing the louts get ravished or ravaged for a change.

Most of the louts managed to scramble to the shore and escape the sharks. They didn't stay. They fled back the way they had come, deserting their comrades.

Apoca smiled. She doubted that any of these cretins would ever return. Word would spread, and the witches would have one less threat to face. That had been her larger purpose: not merely to thwart the immediate attack but to stop future attacks. That much seemed to be successful.

But now a lout leader appeared from the rear. He was evidently smart enough to avoid the vanguard, as cunning leaders were. He harangued the fleeing louts and made them stop. "Bleep," Apoca muttered. "They'll reorganize."

"There are ants and nickelpedes there," Nimbus said. "I sensed them as we passed. Fly down and I will contact them. There's good eating available, if they get on it immediately."

Apoca hadn't thought of that. She flew the broom back to the shore and landed where Nimbus told her.

"Bugs!" Nimbus called mentally. "Pests, vermin, rabble of low degree! You are good for nothing but to annoy. Here is your chance. These louts are not witches. You have no truce with them. Bite them, sting them, harass them, and the witches will be your friends. Get in their pants and give them bleep!"

There was a surprised pause. The bugs were not telepathic but could receive Nimbus's projection, as Apoca did. Only they thought it was their own idea.

Then the louts started dancing and slapping at themselves. "Yow!"

They had ants in their pants and worse. Soon they fled, their leader included. "It's almost as if they don't like getting bitten and stung in the rear," Apoca said, smiling.

"Almost," Nimbus agreed.

This time the louts really departed. They had a bellyful of reason.

Apoca took off again. "Thank you, Nimbus. You finished the job for me."

"That's what a friend is for. I am sorry only that I could not get a butt to gouge myself."

"Maybe another time."

She glided down to the island and landed. "This is Four's broom," she said, handing it to Thirteen. "I hope you will return it to her with my thanks."

"I will. That was a marvelous show."

"Nimbus contacted the local bugs and got them to chomp the louts in their most private parts. We promised that the witches would be friends with the bugs hereafter."

"We will be." Thirteen beckoned to another witch. "Seven, you specialize in nature. The local bugs have just done us a favor."

Seven smiled. "I saw. They taught the louts to dance."

"We will befriend them. No more stepping on them or poisoning them. They are now our friends."

"Got it." Seven went to spread the word to the other witches of the coven.

Another witch approached. She whispered in Thirteen's ear, then walked away.

Thirteen frowned. "But Ten reports that the monster has arrived, and now we are committed to offering the sacrifice. We were so distracted by your performance that we forgot to depart the island in time."

Apoca had forgotten too, but she knew what to do. "I will take care of that detail now. Where is the sacrificial spot?"

"This way." Thirteen led her to a stone landing, where the poor girl One stood, hunched in fear. She was terrified but plainly determined to fulfill her role. Her stalwart attitude was to be admired.

Apoca walked up to her. "Move over. I will handle this."

Numbly, the young witch obeyed.

Apoca glanced at Nolan, who had crossed to the island on his own, probably by turning fish and reverting to human at the shore. He had no fear of sea creatures. He nodded; he knew what to do. He went to Vinia and got a vial from her. Then he walked to the bank and dived into the sea, changing to serpent form in midair. He splashed in, disappearing as the younger witches gaped. He was a handsome man, and he had flashed them for half an instant as he lost his clothing.

The sharks converged, each one wanting to be the first to brace this new mark. Then they backed off in half a hurry. Apoca wasn't sure what kind of fish he had changed into, but it surely had ferocious teeth and an attitude to match.

Meanwhile, the sea monster was coming in. It was huge and ugly, with a mouth just big enough to swallow a tender maiden without straining. It paused, as if a distraction had drifted by, and put its head under the water to investigate. After four-fifths of a pause the head lifted back into the air and the monster resumed forward motion. But it seemed slightly dazed, as if rethinking its purpose. Just so; Nolan had done his bit. In fact, he was now emerging from the water, flashing the witches again before shaking himself dry and dressing. She suspected he liked doing that, seemingly inadvertently, but she was in no position to fuss at him, considering her own dishabille, to put it euphemistically.

Apoca lifted a hand and waved. "Yoo-hoo, big boy! Over here!"

The creature spied her and swam in, all several coils of it. It lifted its head clear of the sea and over the landing, slavering. It gaped its ponderous and marble jaws to take her in.

She stepped forward and kissed the giant lower mandible, putting her power into it.

The monster froze in place. So did the witches. They had never seen this happen before. It didn't like this succulent morsel?

Apoca smiled. "Let me explain what just happened," she told the monster, knowing the witches were almost equally interested. "My friend Nolan Naga became a fish and fed you a dose of pacification elixir, so you were slow to tackle me. Then I kissed you on the jaw, using my power as a Lips woman. You are now my love slave. Do you understand?"

The monster hesitated. This experience was evidently new to it. Then slowly it nodded.

"You will do whatever I ask of you, because you now have no purpose other than doing my will. Here is my will: you will no longer eat any human maidens. When you come here each year, you will kiss them instead. Or rather, accede to their kissing your closed snout. Then you will be rewarded with some other succulent morsel, perhaps an oink or a baby dragon, which you will consume, then go your way, satisfied. You will continue to guard this island, and the witches on it, ensuring that no louts, oafs, or clods boat across to annoy the residents. Any who try it are your fair game. They may not taste as good as maidens, but there is some nutritional value even in louts. Got it?"

The monster nodded.

Apoca glanced at Thirteen. "That fatted prig. Feed it to the monster, who is now your friend."

Thirteen glanced at Two. "Do it."

Two bestrode her broom and flew across the sea to the cauldron. She hauled the heavy morsel out of the hot water and dragged it to the shore.

Apoca gestured toward that scene. "There's your meal, serpent, nicely cooked and flavored. Enough to feed thirteen witches or one sea monster. Go for it."

The monster went for it. Two heaved the prig up and into the maw. The monster lifted it high, then let it slide down its long throat. It returned sinuously to Apoca.

"That is the future way of it," she said, petting it on the snout. "I won't be here, but my word remains. Do not make me return here to see to it; that would annoy me."

The monster bowed its head. It did not want her to be annoyed.

"Now, go about your business. You surely have other inlets to terrorize." The monster obeyed.

"I never saw the like," Thirteen said. "Your kiss tamed the terror."

"That's two of your problems solved," Apoca said briskly. "Now for the third."

The witch was blank. "The third?"

"You are being boycotted by the warlocks, remember? Will a man enchanted by a witch do?"

"I suppose. Our interest is in the stork, not the man. Some of those warlocks are creeps."

"I will lend you my former love slave Pun Gent, if he agrees. He is cursed to speak only in puns or the equivalent, but in other respects he is all man. Set aside a room in your new home for that matter." She beckoned Gent, who was always close when not on a task. "Tonight you will serve the witches. They will tell you what to do. You should like it." He nodded.

The witch smiled. "It will be done." Thirteen lifted her voice. "One!"

The youngest witch, One, scampered close. "Yes?"

"You were ready to be sacrificed. Now you face a different kind of sacrifice. Take this man to the master bedroom in the haunted house and signal the stork with him. The ghosts will show you where it is. You do know how?"

"Oh, yes. I have never done it, but we have all studied the moves." She blushed fetchingly. "You know, in case a warlock should come." One turned to Gent. "This way, please." She took him by a hand and led him toward the house. It was clear that she preferred this sacrifice to the other type. Gent, glimpsing her splendid nude body, seemed not at all averse. Apoca had been pretty sure that would be the case.

She spat out her mini purse, expanded it to convenient size, took out her clothing, and dressed. She, Nolan, and Vinia went with Thirteen to the haunted house. The machine-oriented witch was seeing to Rocker Robot. She was Nine, good at making mechanical things, ranging from self-propelled wagons to simple toys. She was clearly intrigued by the robot.

The remaining group of them settled into the main room of the haunted house. Eerie light illuminated it, and it was clean and comfortable throughout. There was even a supply of food stored in stasis, tasty as the day it was enchanted. They had a marvelous meal to replace the one they had given the sea monster.

"I don't know how we can ever repay you for the favors you have done us this day," Thirteen said. "You saved our cursed coven from ruin." The other witches murmured agreement.

"Just establish amicable relations with the Queendom of Thanx. We support feminism wherever we may find it."

"We will certainly do that!"

There were thirteen bedrooms in the house. Apoca and Nolan used the one that would be assigned to Witch One. It was very nice, with its programmable window looking out at a starry sky.

But Nolan was restless. "I am concerned about what happens when we find the HERE plaque, which is bound to be soon because we are running out of paths. How do we handle that? Our mission depends on it. I can't sleep yet."

"I share your dread," Apoca confessed. "I have no idea how we can persuade a balky Demon to do his job."

"Which gives me a notion. If we could get his would-be girlfriend to commit to him, then he might cooperate."

"Which merely moves the challenge over one square. How to persuade a balky Demoness to suffer the attentions of a Demon she's not interested in."

His mouth quirked. "I find a balky Lips woman plenty of challenge. A Demoness might even be worse."

"Might," she agreed wryly. "Yet there must be a way. If there's one thing I retain from my kiss with Chaos, it is that a way exists. We have merely to find it."

"That's been a common theme in our adventures," he agreed. "Boy seeks Girl and has the means to win her, if he can only figure it out."

"Or zombie girl seeks living boy and wins him."

"That one is obvious. She kept flashing him with her body until he capitulated. She did have the body, and it wasn't always cold."

She smiled. "I gather you noticed, as he did. But it turned out that he did want to get back at his pushy family, and marrying a zombie was a way."

"So it fits the formula," he agreed. "But the humanoid robot scenario doesn't. They did not succeed in seducing us, though they came close."

"I'm not sure that particular aspect is the point. We turned out to have something the robots as a whole really needed: the bugs."

"So we did. And we had things to really help the witches, like your expertise and Gent."

"I am getting a glimmer," she said. "Maybe the message is that we have something that will enable the Demon to get the Demoness."

"And if we can just catch on to it, voilà! Victory!"

They looked at each other. "That rings true to me. Chaos is not supposed to cheat, but hints may be okay. All we have to do is figure them out."

"We have a man who can see imaginary things," he said. "A woman with a powerful kiss. A girl who can see paths. A man cursed by a witch."

"A lovely ghost," she added. "A zombie robot. Two telepathic bugs."

"And two batons," he concluded. "Which of these people and things is what a Demoness might want, that she couldn't conjure for herself?"

Apoca sighed. "Which, indeed."

"Actually, the batons and the ghost might be beyond her reach. But why would she want them?"

"Why, indeed," she repeated tiredly. Her brain felt as if it were beginning to freeze up.

"If there are hints for us to pick up on, we must be too dull to do it."

It was time to change the subject. Her eyes flicked around the room as if searching for inspiration—and found it. "That window—I am curious. What other scenes can it show?"

"I have no idea."

"Maybe we should ask a ghost," she said half-facetiously. As if they hadn't had enough of that subject already.

"We do know one."

"I mean a house ghost. They know what's what here."

Nolan lifted his voice. "Hello! Do we have a resident ghost for this room?"

There was flicker as a ghostly face appeared. "I am heere," she wheezed.

Could a ghost be sick? "Is there a problem?" Apoca asked.

"Yess. I am not uused to appearing or taalking."

Ah. Apoca remembered the problem Ghorgeous Ghost had marshaling her very limited substance. "Could you use my body for a while, if I let you?"

"Yess, maaybee."

"Then come on in," Apoca said, opening her mind. It helped that she knew the resident ghosts were female and friendly.

The ghost floated up to her head, then filtered in through her nose. Apoca felt like sneezing but suppressed it. Then the presence expanded, finding the controls. The eyes focused, the ears oriented, and the mouth opened. "Oh, it is so good to feel alive again, if only for a little while!" her voice said.

Nolan seemed nervous but handled it. "You are the ghost?"

"Yes. I am Zelda, short for Griselda, meaning 'The Heroine.' I was one of the early sacrifices. I have been dead for over a century. I was twenty when I died."

"Hello, Zelda! So you are twenty, or a hundred and twenty, depending."

"Forever twenty, I prefer." The head turned to face him. "Oh, you are a handsome man! I was beautiful, when. You would have liked me, then."

"I like you now," he said gallantly. "What you did, becoming a sacrifice for the benefit of your coven, that was noble. But I won't touch you. My fiancée wouldn't understand."

She certainly wouldn't, Apoca thought.

"Why did you call me?" Zelda asked.

He paused an instant short of a moment, finding his mental place. That was still most of a moment too long for Apoca's taste. He was distracted by the presence of a younger (as it were) woman in bed with him. Men could be maddening that way. "The window!" he said, remembering at last. "How does it work?"

"Oh, we rub a bit of our spirit off on the frame, so we can control it," Zelda said. "Then we paint the surface with our imagination. I was an aspiring astronomer, so I put stars in mine. But I can do other pictures too. What do you want?" She inhaled, using Apoca's lungs, and Nolan's eyeballs inflated correspondingly, because she wasn't using a nightie. Apoca stifled her annoyance; it was, after all, her own body he was admiring.

"A scene with dancing nymphs." Then he caught himself, realizing that he had spoken a private thought. "I mean—"

But his correction was too late. The starry night flickered and became a green glade with nude nymphs dancing with abandon, flinging their long tresses about, lifting their shapely bare legs high, and screaming seductively as they bounced.

"I mean formal dancing," he said quickly. But it would have been better if he had clarified it before the nymphs appeared. "As in a ballroom."

A ballroom formed around the scene. Music sounded. The nymphs took fauns as partners and danced with them. Still nude. Still bouncy. Still youthfully enticing. The fauns clearly loved it; their hands were everywhere. The nymphs screamed ticklishly, not withdrawing at all.

Apoca was disgusted. Still, it did demonstrate the potential of the screen.

"I understand that in Mundania they have windows or mirrors that show whole little stories," Nolan said, perhaps trying to recover from his verbal slip, or maybe just trying to pacify Apoca.

The picture changed to an ogre twisting saplings into knots and frightening young dragons. Print appeared, superimposed on the scene: *Ogre, Ogre: A Romance*.

Well, now. That was one of the historical stories. Apoca was familiar with it. A human girl had won the love of an ogre, and he had become almost human. It would do. *Leave that on*, she thought forcefully. *And go about your business.*

Zelda got the message. She siphoned back out via the nose and faded, leaving them to enjoy the show.

They fell asleep in each other's arms well before the story ended. That was fine. Apoca was satisfied that they had learned about the windows. She also reflected on the visit by the ghost Zelda, letting her body be used by the spirit of another woman. That was interesting, but she wasn't sure she would care to do it again.

In the morning they got up, used the attached little bathroom, and dressed. Zelda appeared and ushered them to the dining room, where Thirteen and Vinia were waiting. "We have ghost toasties and evaporated milk," the witch said. "This house is well stocked. Thank you so much for enabling us to take possession; the witches all love it."

"I shared a room with Three," Vinia said excitedly. "She's good with children, and I'm a child. She told me wonderful witch stories, and the ghosts animated them."

"That's nice, dear," Apoca said. She had an idea how the ghosts animated stories. She turned to Thirteen. "How did Gent work out?"

"Excellently. One says that there's no way the stork will ignore her signals. There might even be triplets. Two is ready for tonight, and Three tomorrow."

"Tonight? Tomorrow? I thought we would be moving on today, now that we know your coven is secure."

"Oh, you must stay longer! The girls are so thrilled to have this chance. We will try so hard to make it worth your while."

"Three is so nice," Vinia said. "It is only fair that she get to order a child."

"But we need to complete our mission," Apoca protested. "So that your children won't all have the same talent."

"That is true. But I consulted with Twelve, who has the premonitions. They apply only to our Coven-19, which incidentally is why you turned out not to be in so much danger. Your own forebodings were for us rather than you. But we got around that by focusing on our future children. That turned out to be a huge uncertainty; we don't know how they'll be talented, because there is no guarantee your quest will succeed. But our auspices suggest that your result is most likely to be positive if you tarry here three days."

Apoca digested that. Vinia's paths could select the best routes but did not predict the future. Rocker Robot could warn of danger, in his fashion, but again, that was the present, not the future. The bugs were telepathic, but again that was limited to the present. The Quest's best indication was the Witch Twelve's premonition, uncertain as it was.

Nolan and Vinia were looking at her with what the Mundanes called poker faces. She knew they wanted to stay. What could she do? "Three days," she agreed with resignation.

Vinia clapped her hands. "Goody! I get to see more stories."

"And I get to see more shows," Nolan said.

"And we get to order our first children," Thirteen said with satisfaction.

Apoca hoped that was all there was to it. The secret truth was that she herself was satisfied to wait that time, now that she had a solid pretext, because the prospect of facing the evasive Dwarf Demon of Talents terrified her. The Kiss had shown her the magnitude of a Demon who she knew was on their side; what of one who was not?

"We truly appreciate what you are doing for us, in more than one venue," Thirteen said. "You have enabled us to become a coven worthy of respect. You ask nothing in return, but we believe we owe you a giant favor. Twelve says an occasion will soon come. Do not hesitate to ask."

Apoca knew it would be undiplomatic to dismiss this offer. "We shall do that, when," she agreed.

"And of course we will send a witch as liaison to the Queendom of Thanx. Maybe Nine, who can make excellent toys. She should be popular with Thanx children."

Their Quest related to children, though in another manner. "I'm sure that will be appreciated."

Gent and One showed up, both looking well rumpled. Gent also looked as if he would be well satisfied to marry a witch, were he free to do so.

"Thank you ever so much for saving me from the sacrifice," One said to Apoca. "I was ready to do it, but I really didn't want to."

"You're welcome," Apoca said. And wondered whether the Quest was heading into what well might be a similar sacrifice.

Chapter 11

HERE

Back at the nexus, they found three paths remaining. They recognized the ones to Madness and to Pundemonium but hadn't considered the last one before. Could it be worse than the other two?

It turned out to be clearly labeled HELL. There was a paved path, each tile labeled GOOD INTENTIONS. There was even a demon handsomely garbed in a tuxedo, smiling, ready to help them travel along it.

Nolan did not need to share a glance with Apoca to know that this was not their preferred path, however good their intentions. So, reluctantly, he turned to the one leading to the pundemic. It was the least worst.

"Get lost, foul spirit," Apoca said as they changed direction.

The demon frowned, and smoke curled up from his ears. Hell had no fury like that of being scorned by a woman.

They collectively gritted their teeth and walked along the path to Pundemonium. A chill gust of wind blew, making Vinia shiver. She spied a jacket tree and went to harvest a nice yellow one her size.

Rocker Robot clicked thrice.

Vinia paused. "This?"

One click.

"Yellow jackets sting the wearer," Gent said, talking normally now that they were back in punnish territory.

"Oh. Of course." She carried the jacket back to its tree and hung it up. She believed in neatness. Fortunately the chill wind had passed, its purpose nulled.

They walked through a field of saw grass, careful to avoid the assorted saws as they waved in another gust of breeze. The clapping hand saw, carefully coping saw, and dancing jig saw weren't too dangerous, but the chain saw with its sharp whirling chain was ugly, and the see saw was looking for vulnerable flesh.

The next section was marked PROFESSIONAL NAILS. Large nails with little arms and legs were busy doing assorted things, such as assembling a structure made of wood. "Carpenter nails," Gent explained. "Roofing nails. Finishing nails." Indeed, the indicated ones were putting a roof on the structure, while the last were completing the job.

Nolan managed to stifle his groan. It wasn't as if he hadn't visited the pundemic zone before.

They came to a king-sized bed that a king must have discarded, maybe because the foot of it had king-sized feet. "That looks tempting," Apoca said. "I'd like to lie down on it. But I won't."

"Why not?" Vinia asked.

"Two reasons. First, I don't trust anything in the pun zone. Second, it's king-size, and I'm a queen. Those big feet might kick me out. Punishment."

Nolan concluded that made sense, in this region.

They walked on, guided by the route and Vinia's green path. Then she stopped. "Oh!"

They had come to a corral enclosing a horse with a marvelously colorful mane. Vinia was a girl. Horses had a similar effect on girls as panties had on men. She was fascinated. So, to a lesser extent, was Apoca.

A sign on the gate said FREE RIDES, FRIENDLY HORSE, HUE MANE. Nolan glanced at Rocker. The robot clicked thrice. He didn't know what problem there might be.

Nolan gave in to the inevitable. "Ride him. Then we'll be on our way."

With a squeal of delight, Vinia opened the gate, slipped through, and approached the horse. She petted him on the neck. He nuzzled her hair, and his mane brightened. It was clearly love at first sight.

Then she scrambled up onto his back. There was no saddle, no reins, but they were not needed. The horse walked slowly around the corral, carrying the girl with no problem for either.

Something bothered Nolan. After a fair-size moment he realized what it was: where was the pun? Hue Mane, for humane, but was that enough?

They returned to the gate. Vinia slid off and landed neatly on her feet. "Thank you, Hue. That was a lovely ride. Now I must move on."

Rocker clicked twice.

Vinia glanced at him. "You say no? I say yes. I loved it." She stepped away from the horse. And paused, confused. "My paths are gone."

Uh-oh. "Your paths?" Apoca asked.

"Well, they're there, spreading out every which way, but the colors are missing. I don't know which is green."

"The horse is another color," Gent said.

Indeed, the horse's mane was twice as bright as before. It had stronger hues.

"The horse took your colors!" Nolan said. "You left, but the hues stayed."

Rocker clicked once.

"And there is the trap," Apoca said ruefully. "The horse is a magnet for hues. That's the rest of the pun."

That was why the zombie robot had clicked only when Vinia stepped away. That was when it happened. The puns were not always harmless. The horse had meant no mischief; it was just its nature.

"You have two talents," Apoca said. "Did it steal your telekinesis too?"

Surprised, the girl glanced at a stone on the ground before her. It rose into the air, looped about, and landed in her hand. "No," she said relieved.

"So it is only colors it takes."

"Yes, I guess. But my tele won't show the way to the plaque."

"Still, that's better than losing it."

"I guess," the girl agreed, not fully satisfied.

So it was not a total loss, Nolan thought. But what were they to do now? Without her paths, they were almost literally lost.

"Maybe her colors will revert when she's away from the horse," Gent suggested.

Nolan doubted it and saw that Apoca did too. But what choice did they have?

They walked on, following only the visible path they were on. Nolan had forgotten how much they depended on Vinia's vision of the green. He felt almost naked. Who knew what they might encounter, unguided, or what threats they might fail to avoid? Their very mission might be in peril. He saw that Apoca was similarly nervous, and of course Vinia was on the verge of hysteria.

Ghorgeous appeared, faintly. "I don't like this. We've lost our compass."

"We just have to hope we recover it."

"Rocker thinks there's a game changer in the vicinity. But he has no idea of its nature."

"Is it dangerous?"

"No, merely obscure." She flickered out, then in again, her way of pausing. "He also thinks that I have something vital to contribute to the larger mission. But that may be only because I am the ghost in his machine."

"You have already contributed. You enabled Zoila Zombie to find her living prince."

"More than that. Something I can do that can change everything. If only I knew what it was."

"That seems to be the theme of this Quest. We can maybe change whatever, if only we knew how."

She smiled ruefully. "Exactly." She faded out.

"If only," Apoca murmured sympathetically.

That note of sympathy touched him. "You know what I'd like to do right now?"

"Do it."

He took her in and soundly kissed her. A little heart flew out, got caught in the breeze, and drifted away.

"Exactly," she repeated.

Neither Vinia nor Gent commented.

They came to a device lying on the ground. It was made of some kind of metal, with a glossy screen facing upward. "What is this?" Nolan asked warily.

Rocker clicked thrice. This type of machine was evidently beyond his experience.

"That is Com Pewter, the nefarious electronic device that can change reality in its immediate vicinity," Gent said. "But it can't change itself; otherwise it would no longer be made of cheap tin alloy and be helpless to move physically on its own. It appears to have been dumped here, perhaps as outdated trash."

Nolan realized that the thing was a pun on the word "computer," a kind of advanced Mundane calculator. That was why Gent recognized it.

"I have heard of it," Apoca said. "It resides in a cave. What's it doing here?"

"I will ask it," Gent said. He stood over the screen. "Pewter, are you still operative, or are you useless junk?"

Printed words appeared on the screen: I AM OPERATIVE, YOU IDIOT EX–LOVE SLAVE.

Gent smiled, not entirely nicely. "Then why are you out here lying on your tinhorn backside emulating junk?"

IT IS A MEDIUM-LENGTH STORY, IGNORAMUS.

A bulb flashed over Apoca's head. She had gotten an idea. "Let's set you upright, Pewter, introduce ourselves, and exchange stories. Maybe we can do each other some good."

DON'T KISS ME, VILE FEMALE.

Nolan had to smile. So the machine knew her nature.

"I won't kiss you if you behave," Apoca said evenly. "You need help, we need help, so it makes sense we explore the situation."

Nolan knew she had an idea she was working toward. But what was it?

Com Pewter paused much of a microsecond, then printed AGREED. He evidently realized that it was better to cooperate with a Lips woman than to oppose her.

They got to work. When Pewter was upright and the members of the Quest introduced, and their mission clarified, Pewter explained that a Mundane trucker had gotten badly lost and wrecked in the pundemic, spilling computer parts across the landscape. Pewter knew that an excellent upgrade was there for the taking, if he got there in time. So he took his magically propelled wagon and headed into the zone. Unfortunately his route took him across the path of a herd of bulls that were immune to hostile magic. They had solid herd immunity. Some were bullheaded, some were unmanageabull, and some were downright horribull. His traverse spooked them, and the herd stampeded. They bore right down on him. He tried to throw up a bullwark to fend them off, but they were immune to what they took to be hostile magic, and crunched him under-hoof, wrecking his wagon. The wagon was in an adjacent gully upside down. It could be righted, but its magical power had been stomped out of it by the magic-resistant hooves; now it was just wheeled scrap. Thus he was stranded without transport, to say nothing of his parts upgrade.

"You can change reality in your immediate vicinity?" Apoca asked.

YES, TO A DEGREE. BUT THE HERD WAS IMMUNE.

"Can you restore a lost talent to a person?"

Nolan saw Vinia perk up. Suddenly Apoca's idea was coming clear.

TO AN ORDINARY PERSON, YES.

"Vinia rode the horse Hue Mane, and it stole her talent of seeing colored paths. Can you restore it to her?"

YES. THAT IS JUST A MATTER OF DRAWING IT BACK TO HER FROM THE HORSE.

Apoca nodded, gratified. Vinia looked about ready to faint from relief. Nolan was silent, letting her handle it as she chose. He was privately proud of her queenly ability to handle a situation. He knew she would be an effective negotiator.

"Now, about our return favor," Apoca said. "You are in trouble. We can get you out of it. In fact, we can leave you better than before. Are you interested?"

The machine was cynical. SUCH A CLAIM MUST BE DOCU-MENTED.

"Of course. We can provide you with a mode of travel that will not only haul you wherever you wish to go but can also be your companion, to the degree you choose. It will even warn you of danger."

SHOW ME THAT MODE.

"Rocker Robot, come forth." The robot obeyed. She had kissed it and it answered to her command. "Rocker, check your awareness. Would association with Com Pewter be beneficial to you?"

The robot clicked once.

"Then if we make this deal, I will kiss you farewell and you will go with Com Pewter, to serve him and profit by his magic. He can surely improve you by enhancing your details. You will in turn haul him on his wagon, protect him from explosions both physical and social, and engage in such dialogue as the two of you care to have. You do have something in common, both being odd machines. You will both be better off." She turned to Pewter. "Deal?"

DEAL. The device was smart enough to recognize a really good bargain.

She went to Rocker and kissed his panel. Nolan pictured sparks flying as the love spell was nulled. "I release you. I thank you for your service to us and wish you well hereafter."

The robot blushed. Apoca could have that effect on males of any variety, even without using her power.

Ghorgeous appeared and went to him next. "I have appreciated working with you, Rocker. You're a good contraption."

The robot blushed again.

She floated on to Pewter, touching his screen with a gossamer finger as she formed an image of herself leaning forward, flashing cleavage. "Treat him right."

The screen went momentarily blank, then formed a brief smiley face. This machine, too, was not entirely immune to human female beauty, even ghostly.

Then they hitched the robot to the wagon, using the harness that Pewter's reality change conjured, and lifted the machine onto it. They were good to go.

"Your turn, Vinia," Nolan murmured. He wanted to be sure the deal was complete.

Vinia went to stand before Pewter. The screen blinked, then printed COLOR VISION RETURNS.

She slapped her forehead. "It's back! I can see the green!"

Nolan's knees felt weak.

Apoca smiled. Her deal had restored their main asset.

ONE FAVOR, Pewter printed.

Apoca looked at him, a frown hovering near her face. "You want more?"

MY WAGON KNEW THE ROUTE TO THE WRECK. THAT IS GONE, ALONG WITH ITS BRAIN. VINIA CAN SEE THE WAY.

Apoca glanced at Nolan. He nodded. For one thing, it would verify that Vinia's path sense really was operating again. "Agreed," she said.

IN RETURN I GIVE YOU THIS NEWS. WHEN GHORGEOUS GHOST TOUCHED ME, I READ HER REALITY. THAT IS WHAT MADE ME BLINK. SHE IS VITAL TO YOUR QUEST IN A WAY YOU DO NOT YET KNOW. I DO NOT KNOW THE DETAILS, BUT THIS IS IMPORTANT.

This was confirmation of Rocker's belief. "Thank you," Apoca said thoughtfully. "We do appreciate the news."

Nolan mulled that over. How could the ghost be so important? She had no substance and no special expertise.

"I don't know either," Ghorgeous whispered in his ear. "But I promise I'll do everything I can to help the mission, whatever it may be." She kissed the ear. It warmed with pleasure.

Vinia pointed across the field where the tracks of the herd remained. "That way to the Mundane wreck. And our destination, too, farther along. Green all the way."

They walked across the field, pacing Rocker as he hauled the little wagon along. They found a navigable path. It was, coincidentally, green.

The path wound through hill and dale, forest and field, sand and stream, avoiding the stenchiest puns, until it found the wreck.

A small dark cloud formed beside Nolan. "Well, now, handsome naga prince. You must be up to something nailing."

"Something what?"

"Fastening, bolting, securing, screwing, hammering—"

"Riveting?"

"Yes," it agreed sourly. "Or at least interesting."

A talking cloud with a speech impediment? What kind of pun was that?

"No kind of pun, Nolan," Ghorgeous said in his ear. "That's the mischievous demoness Metria. She's chronically bored and always on the prowl for something interesting but tends to garble her vocabulary. She loves to flash her hot panties at innocent men, spoiling their innocence. Ignore her so she'll go away."

"And hello to you, Ghor," the cloud said. "Are you dating crossbreeds now? You must be desperate. This is really gross."

"Engrossing," the ghost said quickly, cutting off the threatened game of words.

"Oh, bleep!" Apoca swore. "The fiendish fiend. I'd rather swallow a pun."

"And suffer emnudifying pundigestion? You're bluffing, hot lips."

Emnudifying? Then Nolan caught on: her version of embarrassing.

"So would I, cloudbrain," Vinia said.

"You too, jailbait? This is bewitchifying."

"Ignore her," Ghorgeous repeated. "It's the only way to get rid of her."

THE GHOST IS CORRECT, Pewter printed. THE DEMONESS KNOWS BETTER THAN TO COME WITHIN MY REALITY RANGE.

"I sure do, Tin Ear. You'd gander me if you had a hand. If I put my bottom close." The cloud formed momentarily into a floating human bottom.

Gander her? Goose her. "Got it," Nolan muttered. Metria evidently existed for distraction, regardless of the subject.

"Yes, ignore me, prince." The cloud poked out a pair of well-formed and silk-stockinged human legs right under his nose. More of them emerged, leading toward their intriguing juncture.

"Avert your gaze!" Aurora warned. Thus advised, he managed to look away just before the mesmerizing panties showed. They would have fried his brain from this point-blank range. The naughty spirit really was mischief.

"Bleep!" This time it was the demoness. "A telepathetic ant, of all things. This is the most intriguing party I've happened across in epochs."

"Ages," Apoca said.

"Wow!" Vinia said. "Polka-dot panties with no material in the dots."

"My specialty. They used to drive Professor Grossclout wild when I flashed them in class."

"I wonder if I could get some like that, for when I'm old enough to flash."

"Maybe your friend Hilda will sew you some."

"Yeah, maybe."

The two seemed to be becoming friends. But this was wasting time. Nolan cleared his throat.

"Okay, here's a deal," Metria said. "I'll put on dull clothing for the nonce. Tell me what you're up to, and I'll leave you lonely." Apparently Vinia's interest had mollified her.

"Deal," Apoca said quickly.

Now the full demoness appeared, intoxicatingly shapely but fully covered. "All her clothing is just part of her demon substance," Aurora said. "So you are seeing as much of her as ever."

"But some presentations are more compelling than others."

"Maybe next time I assume dream-girl form," the ant said, "I'll wear panties like that."

"I'm looking forward to it." They were teasing each other, as fast friends did.

Meanwhile, Apoca was telling the demoness about the Quest and its complications. When she finished, Metria nodded and faded out as promised.

"But she's still here," Aurora told him. "She didn't promise to depart, only to leave us lonely, that is, alone. Ignore her."

They walked on. Nolan wondered whether he could get Apoca to don polka-dot panties with holes. "She's planning to, Nimbus says. But not while Metria is watching."

In due course, maybe even overdue course, they reached the wreck. The Mundane truck lay on its side, with the hardware spewed across the landscape. They helped Pewter assemble it and set up. Soon he had multiple screens, each showing a different aspect of his capacity. The new equipment enabled him to find routes the wagon had found before, so he could travel with confidence. That was only the beginning of it. He was about as happy as an emotionless machine could be.

Then Rocker, Pewter, and the new instruments departed, as the pundemic could be wearing even on machines. "That contraption isn't as bad as I thought," Apoca confessed as they moved on.

Nolan wondered whether the same was true for the demoness Metria.

They came to a swampy region. "There's something ahead," Vinia reported. "Big but not dangerous to us. The green leads right to it."

"I will investigate," Ghorgeous said. "That's what I'm here for, I think." She vanished.

"That makes me wonder, again," Apoca said. "Are we missing something about her? She is helpful, yes, but Rocker and now Pewter seem to think it is more than that."

"They do," Nolan agreed. "But I just can't figure out how."

"We know the common theme. Somebody needs somebody else, who isn't much interested, but there's a factor that can help."

"If the somebody can only figure it out."

"I am feeling stupid. It's probably in plain sight, and maybe relates to Ghorgeous, but we can't see it."

"I'm feeling stupid too," he said.

"Me too," Vinia added.

The ghost returned. "There's an invisible giant caught in slowsand."

"In what?" Vinia asked.

"Slowsand. There's regular sand, quicksand, and slowsand. Regular sand gets in your shoes, quicksand speeds you up to a blur, and slowsand slows you down so you can take a month to make a single step. That giant won't be getting out of there soon. Fortunately it's not our business."

"But if that's where the green path goes, and I think it does, then it is our business."

The ghost showed shoulders shrugging. "Then we'll have to figure it out."

"What does a giant in slowsand have to do with our Quest?" Apoca asked.

Nolan mimicked the ghostly shrug. "We may have to figure it out."

They walked on into the swamp, watching their footing carefully. There was a fairly firm bank, and of course Nolan could turn serpent or fish if necessary. But that would not help Apoca or Gent, and in any event, slowsand would trap him regardless of his form.

Vinia's green path led to a bank beyond which it was all slowsand. "Right ahead," she reported. "The green stops here. But there's a patch of green over the muck."

The giant must have walked this way and stepped off, intending to wade on through to the other side, then been caught by surprise. It might not even realize how much it had slowed.

It was definitely slowsand. Assorted creatures were mired in it, apparently unmoving. There was a green alligation, a Welsh rabbit, and a maidserpent, all oblivious. The sand didn't hurt them, merely slowed them.

Apoca looked at Nolan. That meant the next decision was his. He marshaled his balky brain before it could sneak off and hide behind some other subject. "The bugs! Let them read the giant's mind, and maybe tell it how slow it is if it doesn't know."

"Is that feasible?" Apoca asked. "Maybe its mind is frozen too."

"No," Vinia said. "When the six princesses Prince Ion and Princess Hilda rescued were frozen in storage, being crystallized, one was telepathic, and I was able to talk with her. Their bodies were in stasis, but their minds could be wakened as if in a dream. The bugs may be able to connect us to its mind."

"Let's do it," Nolan decided.

He and Apoca stood together at the bank, extremely careful to go no farther, while Aurora and Nimbus reached out mentally. Working together they were able to do more than either could alone, reaching out without direct physical contact. And they connected! Nolan could feel the huge mind of the invisible giant, asleep at the moment but not frozen. The enormous invisible man was male and adult. In fact he was dreaming of an invisible giant woman, whose name was—

"Gina," Apoca said. "This is her boyfriend, Geode."

"He could have been here some time," Nolan said. "Maybe that's why she hadn't heard from him recently."

"We have to help him."

"Maybe that's why the green is here," Vinia said. "It knew we had to help a friend."

That made Nolan pause. The involvement of the green path meant it was not coincidence. They should indeed assist, but there was a complication. "How do we help a frozen invisible giant?"

Apoca spread her hands. "I fear we'll need more magic than we have."

"The coven!" Vinia exclaimed. "Didn't they say they owe us a favor? Maybe this is it."

"Maybe it is," Nolan said thoughtfully.

"I'll go tell them," Ghorgeous said. "Or at least I'll tell the ghosts, and they'll relay it."

"That should do it," Apoca agreed.

The ghost popped off. Meanwhile they explored Geode's mind in more depth.

Indeed, he did not know that he was in effect stalled in place.

"Geode," Nolan said, the bugs relaying his thought to the giant so that it seemed as if they were talking normally, apart from the fact that one was a multiple crossbreed and the other an invisible giant in stasis. "This is not a dream. I am Prince Nolan Naga, one of the small visible folk. Do you hear me?"

"I hear you, naga," Geode replied, surprised. "But I don't see you."

"Here I am." Aurora generated a dream picture of Nolan standing at the bank, a bit more handsome than he was in reality. "I was passing through and discovered you stuck in slowsand."

"Slowsand! I avoid that stuff."

"There is a patch of it here in the swamp we didn't know about. You stepped in it and got caught. Now you are standing in place."

"This is hard to believe."

"Would you believe that we are friends of Gina Giantess, who misses you? By the time you wade on out of this muck, she may be an old maid."

That got to the giant. "I prefer her as a young maid. Of all the women I have known, she is the best. How do I get out of this?"

"We are checking with a witch coven we know. Maybe they will have helpful magic."

"Why would witches help an invisible giant? We seldom if ever interact."

"They owe us a favor because we helped them."

"Why would you help an invisible giant?" Geode was not stupid.

"We are friends with Gina, as I said. We got to know her at the invisible mountain, and she carried us to our next stop. We know she is a good woman. We'll do it for her, because she would be desolate without you." There was no need to mention Gina's passing liaison with Gent.

"Point made. Get me out of this, and I will owe you one giant favor."

"We will do our best." Then he thought of something else. "Did you happen to see a plaque lying around?"

"I did. I didn't know what it meant, as I can't read, so I put it in my pocket. Maybe Gina will read it for me."

So now the plaque was invisible, and unreachable, until they could recover it from Geode.

Nolan tuned out, knowing that the giant would take hours to even miss him.

"Ghorgeous is back," Apoca said.

A ghostly mouth appeared. "I am," it said. "The coven is sending a party to investigate. I will guide them in." The mouth closed and faded out.

"Well, now," a witchly voice said.

It was Two, the young witch who had assisted at the cauldron. She was sitting cross-legged on a flying carpet, her nice bare legs trying to extend from under her black cloak and succeeding nicely. Behind her sat Witches One and Three, similarly cross-legged. They were the three youngest and prettiest of the coven, and evidently liked to display their forms when not under the censorious eyes of Thirteen.

"Two has a magic carpet," Aurora said. "It's safer for longer hauls than their brooms, and they can carry more."

"Gent!" purple-haired Three cried. "Fancy meeting you here!"

They were incidentally the three who had nighted with Gent. That had to be why they had volunteered for this spot mission. They also cast covert glances at Nolan, just in case. Three also exchanged a glance with Vinia, whom she had helped at the coven.

Apoca assumed a stern expression very like that of Thirteen. "You are here on business. That is your first priority."

"Yes'm," One agreed contritely as the three got off the carpet and their shapely legs retreated under their cloaks.

"Have you a sufficient notion why you are here?"

"To investigate the situation and report back so that Thirteen can assign the appropriate personnel," One said.

Apoca glanced at Nolan. He was on protagonist duty again. "We have here an invisible giant by the name of Geode. He is bogged down by slowsand. He has the tablet we seek. But mainly we want to help him so he can return to his girlfriend, Gina. Do you know how to extricate him from his plight?"

"Darn," Two said. "We were afraid that would be it. We'll have to contact Sandy."

"Who?"

"Sandy is a sand witch," Three said. "But she's not in our coven. She's a loner, not part of any coven, and tough as thumbtacks. It will be bleep to deal with her."

"A sand witch," Apoca repeated. "She makes sandwiches to eat?"

Nolan saw the obvious pun. This was after all the pun zone.

Three smiled. "No, she works with sand."

"We don't need more sand, we need less."

"She has power over sand," Three explained, as if talking to a child. "She can change slowsand to quicksand."

Oho! "We'll negotiate with her," Nolan said. "There must be something she really wants that we can provide."

Three glanced at him in a purple-eyed way that made Apoca frown. "What every witch wants. A man of her very own. Not a lout, not a visiting warlock, but a real man, like you. Not for a one-night stand, but to keep indefinitely, always at her beck and scream. But she's not young and sexy, so men are scarce. She's more like Thirteen."

Uh-oh. "She's right," Aurora said. "You'd be perfect for Sandy. Three is a good judge of that sort of thing. She sees adults as matured children, and that's a fair guide."

"I am not available," Nolan replied grimly. Were he uncommitted, a witch like Three herself could have been tempting, and not just because of her lovely hair and eyes, but a witch like Thirteen, competent as she was, not so much.

"We seem to be at an impasse," Apoca said. Nimbus was surely keeping her abreast of the private dialogue.

A mouth appeared by Nolan's ear. Not Ghorgeous's mouth. "You are missing the oblivious," Metria's voice said.

"Oh, for bleep's sake!" Nolan swore. "You were supposed to be gone, demoness."

"I was supposed to leave you solitary. That's not the same. Now I can help you. Then you will owe me one."

"Owe you what?" Apoca demanded grimly.

"Let's bargain. One night with Nolan, my inaugural?"

"Initiative," Gent supplied.

Apoca looked as if she wanted to chomp someone's tail. "One second with him."

The bargaining was on. Nolan stayed out of it. He hadn't realized that the demoness had any such interest in him. Maybe she didn't and was just mischievously teasing to make Apoca jealous. Maybe.

"One hour?" the demoness bid.

"One minute."

"One kiss?"

Apoca hesitated. She had, after all, phenomenally kissed the Demon Chaos, so was in an awkward position to deny Nolan that. "A shallow one. Lasting no longer than a minute."

"Done."

"After you help us," Apoca said. "And it had better be good."

"Here is the obvious you missed," Metria said. "There is a spare fusion-powered robot crafted in Nolan's exact likeness and manner. It can't change to serpently or fishly forms, but it can emulate his human form marvelously well, and can be programmed to become a virtual love slave to Sandy Witch. Ask Emperor Fusion for it."

Apoca clapped her hand to her forehead. "Bleep! That's it!"

Metria turned to Nolan, her hair, eyes, and lips turning a shade of purple. What a tease she was! "One minute," she murmured. There was something portentous in her tone.

A deal was a deal. The demoness had earned it. Apoca was holding a start watch. It was his turn to deliver. Nolan took the marvelously supple figure in his arms and kissed her evocative lips.

She kissed him back, steamy heat radiating from her mouth. Her compelling torso pressed against his, feeling amazingly close. In fact, he realized that her cloak had dissolved where it touched him, forming into wondrously firm bare breasts where they didn't show to others, and impure nudity below.

Then her face changed, becoming that of another woman, a weirdly fascinating one. "She got stepped on long ago by a sphinx," Aurora reported, reading the demoness's mind. "That split her into three forms. Metria with the speech impediment, Mentia who is slightly crazy, and a sad child named Woe Betide. This is Mentia."

Indeed, the torso was massaging his body, even through the clothes he wore, in ways no sane body could. The sex appeal was, well, demented.

Then it changed again. He found himself intimately kissing a child. Woe Betide was taking her turn. He tried to pull back his face, but now her hand was behind his head, holding it firmly in place. He was stuck in seeming violation of the Adult Conspiracy. Fortunately he knew the demoness was eons old, regardless of her form.

"Time!" Apoca rapped.

The creature disengaged, now the fully clothed Metria. "Thank you for an adorable happening," she murmured. "Mayhem we will meet again, off-camera." For an instant the face of Mentia flashed, licking her plaid-colored lips, her eyes pools of passionate madness.

"Now, fade out," Apoca said tightly. Had the bugs relayed the details of the kiss to her? He feared they had. He couldn't blame her for being annoyed. Metria was not in the same league as Chaos, but she had her moment, or rather minute.

The demoness faded. The last thing to go was her satisfied smile, floating above her chasm-deep cleavage. She had had her will of him, in her fashion.

They got busy. Ghorgeous popped off to see Emperor Fusion while Nolan joined the three witches on their carpet, heading for the sand witch. They placed him in the center and pressed closely on three sides, their crossed legs forming a six-way knee brace against his body. No panties showed, quite, but they were threatening. "We don't want you falling off," Three explained.

Apoca did not look thrilled but did not protest. She trusted him. It was the witches she didn't trust.

They took off with a jerk like that of a tablecloth yanked off the table, leaving the place settings unmoved. Nolan would have been left behind if the soft bodies of the witches had not braced him as they leaned forward and clasped hands around him. He tried to avoid looking down into their drooping necklines.

Then they sailed up, up, and away, flying high into the sky. The landscape of Xanth coursed below them. Not that he could see it well, past the close trio. There was entirely too much to see already.

"Uh-oh," Three said. She was clearly the senior witch here. "Fracto."

Fracto. That meant the mischievous storm cloud, Cumulo Fracto Nimbus, who liked to rain on parades and anything else festive. How had he known they were here?

"He must have seen us coming in," One said.

"And known we'd be skyborne soon again," Two said.

"He always did like to play wettee shirt with young witches," Three said.

"Not that we minded much," One said.

They raced the carpet forward, but the storm angled across to intercept them. Violent gusts battered them so that they had to cling close around Nolan to hold him in place. They did not seem to mind doing this. Actually, neither did he.

They did manage to outpace the storm but did get caught by a soaking splash of rain. Wettee shirts indeed! They looked phenomenal, but he pretended not to notice. Not that he was fooling them.

"We'll have to dry off," Three said with cheerful resignation. "We hope you don't mind."

"I'm a naga. I'll change to serpent mode so my own clothes can dry. Assuming you don't object to having a big snake on your rug."

"We understand," Three said, sounding faintly disappointed. Had they really expected to have him naked in man form on their carpet? Amid three naked girls? All pressed together as they flew?

"They had hoped," Aurora said. "But they're good sports. They appreciate what you did for the coven, including their nights with Gent. They just wanted more if they could get it. So did Metria."

Nolan had gathered as much. Witches and demonesses were notorious in that respect. Seduction was part of their nature.

He changed, and they extracted his wet clothing from the pouch, stepping over his coils without aversion. They held his things up to the sunlight along with their own clothing. Aurora remained hidden in the pouch. That was just as well, as she knew the effect the bare bodies had on him even in serpent form. "Not that I would tell," the ant said, amused.

The sun was bright, and soon everything was dry. Then they dressed, and he changed to man form and dressed, providing them an unavoidable peek or three in the process. They pretended not to notice, per the protocol.

Just in time, for now they were gliding down to the sand witch's abode. "No need to mention the weather on the flight," he said.

"No need," Three agreed. Hopes and games were fun, as were sneak peeks, but nobody else's business.

They landed on the small beach of what had evidently once been a sea. As the climate changed the sand had blown into dunes. Atop one dune was an old house, not exactly haunted but in significant disrepair. Behind it was a grove of witch-hazel shrubs and trees. This was obviously the place for a sand witch.

"This you must handle on your own," Three told him. "She does not much like coven witches, but she does like men."

"Thank you. Wait here for my return." Nolan marched up the dune toward the rickety house, putting on his most princely mien.

The witch surely saw him coming but elected not to respond. He came to stand at the front door. "Ho, honored Sand Witch," he called. "I am Prince Nolan Naga, and I have need of your assistance. May I enter your domain?" He was pretty sure his appearance and manner would impress her.

It did. She appeared at the door, a witchly hag in a typical black cloak and hood, her broom at her side. He knew she was ready to use it on him if he made a wrong move. "What do you want with me, crossbreed prince?"

"I want to rescue an invisible giant who is stuck in slowsand. Is this something you can handle?"

"Certainly. But I do not exert myself for nothing. What do you offer in return for my expertise?"

"She is already half-smitten by your handsomeness. She's hoping for romantic interest," Aurora said. "But she knows this is unlikely, especially since you aren't just any man, you're a prince. Her forbidden fancy is warring with her realism."

Just so. "I have an unusual offer, which requires some explanation. Why don't you invite me inside, put on your pretty face, and we'll talk."

She cackled. "You have dealt with witches before."

"I have. Some of them have impressed me." Such as the three who had brought him here.

"I'll bet. Very well, come in and make yourself at home. I will be with you as soon as I change." She stepped back from the door, muttering a null spell so that he could pass through without injury.

He did so and found himself in a comfortable chamber with a pleasant couch. He eased himself onto it and waited.

A mature but lovely woman appeared, garbed in clinging black lace. This was Sandy with her pretty face, magic common to witches. Her pointed hat was now a lacy little bonnet, her scraggly tangle of hair now glossy black tresses curling languorously down past her tiny waist, and her warty beak nose was straight and small. Her baggy front had become a bold bosom showing just enough curvature inside the low neckline to invite closer attention. The broom had been replaced by a miniature of itself, on a delicate necklace, suspended over a compelling chasm.

"Allow me to compliment you on your presentation," he said, reaching out to touch her hand in appreciation. That also provided Aurora with a stronger connection. "You would be tempting indeed, were I on the market."

"Thank you." She took an impressive breath. "What is the nature of your offer?"

"I tease myself that I would like to get to know you more intimately, circumstances being otherwise, and that you might even be amenable to such an association."

She laughed, and this time it was like the musical tinkling of little bells. "What is the nature of your offer?" she repeated. Translation: stop teasing and get on with it. She knew he was here for business, not flirtation.

"Recently I passed through the territory of the robots. Are you familiar with them?"

She crossed her legs under her brief skirt, providing him another potent flash. "Wood-burning all the way through fusion. We have had peripheral dealings."

"I encountered a fusion emulation of my fiancée that was so apt it almost fooled me. Similarly, my fiancée was with one that emulated me with corresponding accuracy. They were attempting to deceive us and seduce us without our knowing that we were not with each other."

"They are good at simulations," she agreed. "How did you catch on?"

"We are bugged. Allow me to introduce my companion, Aurora Ant."

Aurora showed herself on his shoulder, then formed a dream picture of herself as a lovely woman. "I am telepathic, which is why I can read your mind and form a fantasy picture you can see."

"Ah. I have encountered your kind also." She glanced at Nolan. "She is the reason you are targeting me so accurately."

"Yes. You can't have me, but the robots owe us a favor and we may be able to borrow the robot that simulates me. He would not be able to change to my ancestral forms as I do, nor would he have a telepathic bug as his companion. He would be relatively limited. But he could be programmed to adore your every nuance, whatever your appearance, and to be chronically eager to make love to you. He could also serve as a guard by day and night so that you would not have to keep your broom close at hand when dealing with strangers."

She smiled brilliantly, her teeth actually sparkling. "I will make your deal, with two caveats. First, get me that robot, appropriately programmed, on indefinite leave. Second, kiss me."

Victory! But he was cautious. "My fiancée might not understand that latter."

"The queen of the Lips tribe will understand perfectly and be annoyed. But she is realistic, as queens are."

So the witch had her own sources of information. Apoca would indeed understand, and be annoyed, as she had been with Metria, but she would tolerate it.

"Agreed." He stood, she stood, and they approached each other. He braced himself for a kiss to rival that of Metria. He took her in his arms, lowered his face to hers, and kissed her.

Her kiss was almost chaste, with no erotic undertones. It was as if she had never been kissed before. How could that be?

It ended and they separated. He looked at her, unsettled.

"I have kissed many times before," she explained. "For business, never for romance. With you I prefer to pretend that we are as we look, an innocent maiden and an interested prince. Not an ugly witch and a crossbreed male in human guise. Let me have my moment of fond illusion."

"She is telling the truth," Aurora said.

"I like your moment," he said candidly. "Now I must contact the robots. This may take a while."

She reverted to hag form. "First we rescue the giant."

He was surprised. "You don't want payment in advance?"

"I trust you."

"Truth," Aurora said. "She knows you are a creature of your word. So is she."

Nolan suffered a pang of appreciation. "Bear with me, please." He took the crone in his arms and kissed her passionately. Now she was the one surprised. She was stiff for half an instant, then melted.

They broke. She took an unsteady breath. "That never happened before to that aspect."

Then he realized that her appearance had changed again. She was now an ordinary woman, neither hideous nor exquisite, with an average broom. "Your real appearance," he said, catching on. "Both witch and beauty are simulations."

"Your gesture jolted me out of simulations for the moment. I will remember it in my dreams." She shrugged as realism reasserted itself. "Time to get on with business."

They left the house and walked down to the three young witches. "Sandy, these are One, Two, and Three, from Coven-19. They brought me here. Girls, this is Sandy Sand Witch, who has agreed to help the giant escape the slowsand."

"So nice to meet you, witches," Sandy said with cold formality. "Thank you for bringing the prince here. Now I will follow you to the giant."

The three, surprised, made a place for him on the carpet. They took off, and Sandy followed on her broom.

"She doesn't look nearly as bad as we expected," Three said.

"She has a hag form she uses for business, but we compromised. She's actually a decent sort."

Fracto, the cloud they had outraced, remained where they had left him. He spied them and swelled ominously. This time it had the way securely blocked. They were in for another wetting and maybe a windy dumping.

Sandy circled past them and flew to intercept it. "Begone, foggy-bottom!" she screeched. "Don't make me hex you again."

Fracto, evidently cowed, withdrew. They passed him without even a nasty gust. He was afraid of Sandy.

"She can conjure up a sandstorm that will really sandbag him," Aurora reported.

"She *is* a decent sort," Two said, surprised.

"More likely she didn't want to get drenched herself," One said. But she, too, seemed impressed.

They came to where Apoca, Vinia, Gent, and Ghorgeous waited. There were quick introductions. Then Sandy strode to the verge of the slowsand. She brought out a small bag of powder and blew it into the breeze over the sand. It drifted down onto and into the sand around the invisible giant. The sand seemed to boil, at first on the surface, then deeper down. "Talk to him," she told Nolan. "Tell him the slowsand is changing to quicksand, so he can wade out faster."

Aurora renewed the connection. "Geode!" Nolan called. "The slowsand around your feet is changing to quicksand. You will be out very soon. Go see your girlfriend, Gina."

"After I do you a return favor. What is it?"

"Take us to the robot domain," Aurora said for Nolan. "We have business there."

Suddenly the sand sucked downward with a loud slurp as the giant stepped out of it at warp speed. "He's out and back to normal as he sheds the quicksand," Aurora said. "He is putting a hand down." She made a dream picture of the hand.

Nolan, Apoca, Vinia, and Gent climbed onto the hand, where Ghorgeous joined them. The three witches flew their carpet to the other hand, and the sand witch joined them there. Then Geode lifted them all up, curling his fingers so they could grab on to them for steadiness.

"The bugs updated me," Apoca murmured. "You were right to kiss her, both times. She's lonely. She will never forget."

"You're not annoyed?"

"Are you annoyed when I kiss males?"

"That's business."

"Just so."

Aurora guided the giant, who strode at high speed to the robot domain. As they neared it, the bugs reached out to the newly telepathic robots and advised them of the situation. When they arrived most of a moment later, the fusion emperor and his retinue were assembled in the main square.

"He has an ant!" Aurora exclaimed. "Adora Water Ant."

A powerful mind impinged on Nolan's own. The dream image of a spectacular queenlike human woman appeared, complete with a crown of watercress and a liquidly clinging dress. "Hello, handsome crossbreed." Her long tresses were translucent, concealing none of her fine lines.

"Hello, pretty ant," Nolan replied. "You must give the emperor seductive dreams."

"Like none he ever before imagined. He wanted to understand what living men see in women. He is learning."

"He clearly has an excellent teacher."

Nolan and Apoca Robot were there. "We are happy to return the favor you did us," the emperor said. "The set of them are now programmed to serve Sandy Witch."

"All I asked for was the male robot," Sandy protested.

"But you can surely also use a maidservant to accomplish the household chores, fetch wood for the cauldron, stir potions, sew patches, and such," Apoca Robot said. "Not to mention distracting brute males who come to make demands. While you are occupied with your own passions."

She glanced meaningfully at Nolan Robot, who refracted it to Sandy with candid male interest. The glance glanced off the side of her face but evidently had an impact.

Sandy opened her mouth to protest further, but as the advantages sank in, she stifled it. She looked directly at Nolan Robot, who returned a look of ardent desire. "Welcome to the household, both of you."

Meanwhile, the three young witches were admiring the other male robots, who were returning the looks with dawning appreciation. "Maybe we'll visit a night," Three said. "Are any of you interested in witchcraft?"

"We are interested in establishing relations," the emperor said. "We have accommodations available at the palace."

The three gladly accepted the fellowship of three humanoid robot males and accompanied them to the palace.

"Thank you," Nolan said to the emperor. "We are quite satisfied with our exchange."

"As are we. Our acquisition of telepathic communications is significantly helping our situation, along with our dreams." The image of Adora reappeared, this time with her decolletage dissolving into colored water.

"You bet he dreams," Aurora said.

The emperor departed, along with his retinue. They seemed interested in getting to know the young witches better.

"I am ready to return home," Sandy said, unlimbering her broom. "Do you robots have traveling mechanisms?"

"We do," Nolan Robot said. A hatch on the top of his head slid open, and a propeller emerged. It broadened to umbrella size and revved up to high velocity. He rose slowly into the air. Apoca Robot lifted similarly.

Sandy mounted her broom and took off. The two robots followed, pacing her. In four-fifths of a moment the three were disappearing over the horizon.

Nolan and Apoca connected another glance. They had had no idea the robots could do that. They had been in bed with those machines?

They returned to the giant's hand, along with Gent and Vinia. In the remaining fifth of the moment they were on their way.

Soon they were back in the swamp where they had rescued the giant. He set them down carefully. "Now I will visit Gina."

"She will be glad to see you, if you can see each other," Apoca said. "Give her our good regards."

"I shall." He reached into a pocket, then set something down and departed. The bugs showed him in faint outline.

"The green path is this way," Vinia said, stepping forth. Then she halted. "Oh."

They looked. There was the object Geode had put on the ground.

It was the plaque they had momentarily forgotten about. It said HERE.

Chapter 12

DEMONS

They gazed at the plaque. "It marks the path," Vinia said. "Bright green. The Dwarf Demon of Talents must be at the end of this one."

"And we still have no idea, really, how to handle him," Apoca said. The batoness had lighted as they saw the plaque while the baton went dark. She was now the protagonist. It must be a new chapter of their story.

"I'm excited," Batoness printed. "Not necessarily positive interaction with a capital-D Demon. There's no telling what he might do, that you will be powerless to prevent."

"Exactly," Apoca agreed sourly.

She looked at Nolan. "Are we ready for this?"

"Do we have a choice?" He looked no happier than she felt.

"Not really." Because they still had no idea how to handle the Dwarf Demon.

She turned to Gent and Vinia. "It may get dangerous. If you prefer to exit the Quest at this stage, feel free."

"My path is green," Vinia said. That meant she was staying.

"I go where you go," Gent said.

"I will release you, Gent. You have served well and do not need to be exposed any longer." She stepped up to him and kissed him with the counter-kiss. She felt the energy crossing to him, nullifying the special kind of curse she had put on him, returning his natural emotion to him.

He swayed half a moment as the power of the kiss took hold, then steadied. "Thank you. It has been a pleasure serving you. I am no longer compelled. But this Quest is essential and still needs to be accomplished. I will see it through."

Surprised, she nodded. "You're a good man." She turned to Nolan. "The presumption is that we will survive because we have a daughter in the future."

"I agree. But she has no talent apart from the Lips kiss and the ability to assume the forms of her ancestry. We need to be sure others have different talents. The Quest continues."

"Lead on, Vinia."

The girl walked on along the path. It led quickly out of the swamp and into a jungle. Sinister trees crowded in, and there were ominous sounds, as of hungry dragons and muck monsters. Large wide-set eyes appeared in the shadows, staring speculatively at them. Apoca tried to mask her shiver.

Now there was a sign: YOU ARE ENTERING THE NEVERGLADES.

"Why are they called that?" Apoca asked.

"Because once you enter them, you may never get out again," Gent said.

"That's encouraging," she said wryly.

"This is the route," Vinia said. "Green as long as we stay right on it."

They kept going. What other choice was there? Their challenge was not the path but the Demon at its end.

Nolan reached out and plucked a small fruit from an offering branch. "Nuh-uh," Vinia said. "That's red."

"But it's brown," he said, for the moment forgetting her talent.

"It is a back date," Gent said. "A time-traveling fruit. You don't know when it will take you."

Oh. he was also forgetting that they were in the pundemic zone. They had not run afoul of too many puns yet, but it was bound to get worse as they approached the Demon. Talents was hiding where no one in his right mind would go, because the puns were bound to make it wrong.

The path wound around to a halfway pleasant cottage set on an island in the swamp. A little old lady was working in her garden. "Hello," Apoca called as they went, being sociable. "We are on a Quest, just passing through. I am Apoca of the Lips tribe."

"Hello, Apoca," the woman replied. "I am Aunt Ti Dote. But I don't have the remedy for your notorious kiss."

"Antidote," Gent murmured. "She surely sells cures for routine ailments."

"But I do have a body." She stood up straight to show off her fine figure.

"Auntie body," Gent said. "Antibody."

A pun person galore. "I won't kiss anyone in your area," Apoca promised. They walked on.

Then came a man with a pile of papers. "Get your ballots here, for the big election," he called. "Vote by male, vote by female. I have male-in and female-in ballots."

Apoca repressed a groan, knowing they could not afford to let the puns get to them. "Thank you, but we are outsiders, not voting." They hurried on.

The forest closed in on the path, the trees all colors. They looked like pines or firs, except for that.

"Ever trees," Gent said. "Evergreens, everreds, everoranges, yellows, blues, whites, blacks, browns, tans, purples, silvers—"

"We get the picture," Apoca said.

A man ran by, looking ill. "Help! I'm covid with germs!"

"Go see Aunt Ti Dote!" Nolan called after him.

How much more of this could they take?

Then a boy ran up to Apoca. "You're a Lips woman!"

She was cautious. "So I am. Are you looking for a kiss?"

He laughed. "No! But I'm a fan of yours. My name is Tom."

"Fan Tom," Gent murmured. "Phantom."

Oh. a spook masquerading as a person. "Thank you, Tom. Now, get on home."

The spook realized he had been discovered. He faded out.

Vinia halted. "The green goes straight through the jungle, but it is tinged with red. I don't think it's completely safe, even if we stay on the path. The green shows the best way, but it can't make the best way risk-free."

Apoca had been afraid of that. So far the puns had been fairly innocent, but that would not always be the case. Some places or some folk simply were not benign; Dwarf Demon Talents was surely an example. She turned to Nolan. "It seems we'll have to gamble, if we want to continue."

"Then gamble we shall, in the interest of completing our mission." He grimaced, as tired of the puns as she was. "I can change to serpent form. Not many creatures of any size will care to take me on because some serpents are poisonous. But that may not completely protect you or the others."

She agreed with his assessment. "I think we need to go outside the box."

"Your saying that makes me nervous."

She laughed. "Maybe you're coming to know me too well. I can indeed be a devious female. That is surely part of what you like about me." She saw his agreement in his posture. "Here is my notion: you change to that serpent form and hiss for serpent company. Can you do that?"

"Yes. There's no guarantee the serpent will be small or friendly."

"Exactly. We want a big one. A monster one that moves well."

"Maybe an ATV?"

"A what?"

"An Awful Toothsome Viper. They're the worst. They can handle any terrain. Nothing can escape them."

"That's ideal. Then you distract it so I can kiss it."

"Oho! Like the sea monster."

"Yes. Only this one's to ride."

He frowned. "Kissing it may be difficult. They can be cunning brutes."

"That's why I need the distraction."

He sighed. "I guess it makes sense. But be ready to dodge. This ain't widdlytinks."

"It sure ain't," she agreed with a grim smile.

He looked at the others. "Seem like a plan?"

"Just be careful," Vinia said nervously. "The colors around you are wildly mixed."

So was her hair, Apoca suspected. "You too, bugs. Do you have any input?"

"We can read a monster's mind," Nimbus said. "But monsters typically don't have real minds. They are driven mostly by hunger, fear, or lust."

"So maybe the viper won't see the trap coming."

"Maybe," she agreed uneasily.

"An ATV is too big for me to toast," Aurora said. "My fire would only annoy it, if it felt it at all."

"But maybe you bugs could project something interesting to it, like a female viper."

"If the ATV is male," Nimbus said.

"Let's hope." Nolan changed to serpent form. Then he issued a kind of hissing whistle.

"We can enhance that mentally," Aurora said from the protective pouch. "Make it seem female."

"Good idea," Apoca said.

The hissing continued. "Something hears it," Nimbus said. "It's coming."

The hissing continued. So did the sounds of an approaching monster. Apoca gestured Gent and Vinia back to hide behind a tree.

Ghorgeous appeared. "It's an enormous serpent, a slavering monster. It's making its own trail."

Then the creature burst into sight. Apoca was dismayed. The ferocious head was lifted well above her reach, dripping venom. She couldn't kiss it!

The viper advanced on Nolan, towering above him. The moment it realized that he was not an appealing female serpent, it would be enraged. It could take his whole body in its gaping mouth. And yes, it had awful yellow fangs.

Apoca knew she had to act swiftly. But what could she do?

"Go for what you can reach," Nimbus suggested. "That's what we nickelpedes do. When we attack."

Apoca followed that advice. She lunged forward, threw her arms around the nearest section of the closest coil, and kissed the scaly skin. She delivered her most potent magic, hoping it would work. It had, after all, worked on the zombie robot.

It did. The giant snake froze in place for a good three and a half instants, uncertain what had happened. Then it whipped its fearsome head around to investigate.

Apoca acted almost without thought. She leaped at the coil, and clambered onto it, bestriding it as if riding a Mundane horse. She was able to extend her legs down either side, and that same scaly skin held them in place without slipping.

The serpent could have flexed and thrown her off. It didn't. The head could have chomped off her body above the waist. It didn't. The coils writhed horrendously, in front and in back, but her section was quite still. It looked as if she were in the middle of a big bowl of boiling spaghetti, but she herself was untouched. She had no trouble staying on.

"It doesn't want to bite itself," Nimbus said. "Your kiss made that section your love slave. To bite you would be like biting itself. And the body can't do anything to hurt you. You've got a steed. But only that section, maybe an arm's reach before and back of the kiss."

"Well, now," Apoca said, assessing the possibilities. "Is it safe for other riders?"

"Only right here. The rest of the monster is as savage as ever."

"That will do." She lifted her voice with both hands. "Nolan! I have tamed this part of it. You can safely join me." She looked at the other two behind the tree. "You too."

Nolan made a different hiss. "He's keeping his serpent form, just in case," Nimbus translated. "But he'll be close by."

Vinia and Gent ran to join her, bravely dodging the spaghetti coils. Vinia scrambled up just in front of her, and Gent got just behind her, both of them close enough to be in the tamed zone.

Ghorgeous formed faintly beside Apoca. "I checked. DD Talents is in the vicinity. He is in a pleasant little thatch cottage made of turf, the down-to-earth kind he would like to share with Dwarf Demoness Transcription. He really doesn't seem to know much about mortal accommodations or women of any type." She formed a translucent smile. "Even I could teach him a thing or three about that, ironically. The surrounding terrain is challenging, to ensure his privacy."

"Can the viper reach it?"

"Yes, if we guide it along the correct access trail. Vinia's paths will identify that."

"I think we have our ride," Apoca said. "Now, how do we tell it where to go?"

"The bugs," Vinia said. "I'll watch for the green path, which isn't exactly on the physical trail, and the bugs can relay it to Viper's mind, making him think it's his own idea."

"Whatever would I do without you? Do it."

Vinia concentrated. The two bugs focused in tandem because the serpent's mind was as large and savage as a jungle, and it took two signals to steer it.

The viper moved. The head rose high, the end of the tail sank low, and there were several writhing coils in between, but their tamed saddle area never faltered. It moved grandly forward with never a rise, dip, or quiver.

Nolan, in his own serpent form, followed closely. No other animals threatened; the viper was not a creature to mess with. Thus in this weird but effective manner, they advanced toward the Dwarf Demon Talents.

They passed a pasture where a male bovine stared at them, snorting, not believing what he was seeing. "Incredibull," Gent murmured.

So they hadn't escaped the puns. Apoca sighed inwardly.

The jungle gave way to a ragged valley carved out by a fiercely flowing river. The viper splashed into and through it without hesitation, swimming by undulations. Even the savage river didn't mess with this monster. Their saddle region remained above water and steady; they didn't get their feet wet. "I like this ride," Vinia said. She was a girl, and girls liked riding, even when the steeds were strange. Apoca was enjoying it too, now that the threat was gone. But what about the Demon? This was hardly in the class of Demon Chaos, but it was still a formidable challenge. She knew better than to think she could kiss the Dwarf Demon into submission. So what remained?

With all this time and challenge just getting to the Dwarf Demon, one might have thought that they would have devised a plan to make him heed their plea. Might have thought. Now they would have to wing it ignorantly. They were, in the end, complete amateurs.

The viper emerged from the river and plunged into the jungle on the other side. This was so thick that the light of the sun did not find its way to the ground. They were in a dark tunnel formed by large tree trunks and overhanging branches festooned by moss, mold, and cobwebs. Fortunately, the viper had no problem with it, being guided by smell and sound as much as by sight, and Vinia's green assured them that this was the way.

Plants of the night radiated their dim illumination in green, blue, yellow, and plaid. That last made Apoca's hair turn plaid with her mixed feelings. "Nolan! Are you seeing that?"

"I see it," he replied, the bugs translating his thought to spoken language, since hissing was not adequate. "I like this jungle. I assume it bodes well."

She stifled her doubt. They needed encouragement wherever they could find it. "Let's hope."

A deer with antlers stood in their way, but the viper undulated to the side and avoided it.

"We passed the buck," Gent said.

The tunnel path made a sharp turn to the left, then to the right, skirting a cypress tree busy pressing cy. This resulted in printed news bulletins, the business of the press. "Oh, I like this," the batoness printed. "They are talking my language."

Apoca read a random bulletin but quickly quit. It was all bull, of course. Bull for bulletin.

Knees were all around the tree, struggling to kick their legs out of the muck, without much success. She wondered why a tree would have knees, but that was not her concern. It could do what it wanted, here in the pundemic zone.

Then the path dived into a hill, becoming a real tunnel. A dragon lurked there but hastily got out of the way of the viper. Then they emerged from a hole in the side of a vertical chasm. This might be an offshoot of the huge Gap Chasm, wide enough to discourage jumping, deep enough to discourage surviving. The viper angled to the side, where there was an almost hidden fragment of a trail that only serpentine scales could cling to.

Was the path trying to shake them off? It was reckoning without Vinia's green.

They passed a man holding his thumb up: a hitchhiker. That had to be a pun.

"He's all thumbs," Gent said.

Now Apoca saw that was literally true. The man had five thumbs on each hand.

Finally they came to a glade in a relatively ordinary forest. There was the cute little cottage. It looked completely innocent.

This was the place.

"Can you continue to track the viper?" Apoca asked Nimbus.

"Yes, if it stays within range."

"Forage within range," Apoca told the middle section of the viper as she dismounted. "In case we need you again." The rest of the monster might not care, but it could not leave its middle behind.

The creature considered half an instant, which was the limit of its attention span, digesting that. Then it slithered back into the forest.

Nolan changed back to human form. "That was a nervous trail, even for a serpent."

"I trusted the green." She gave Vinia half a glance. "Thank you."

The girl managed to catch what there was of it. "Okay. Have you figured out what to say to Dwarf Demon Talents?"

"Not a clue." Apoca clamped down on her burgeoning qualms and marched toward the cottage. The others followed. If any qualms got loose and fell by the wayside, no one was unkind enough to pick them up.

"You've got nerve," Ghorgeous said, flickering back into faint sight.

"I'd trade it for more smarts."

The ghost laughed a bit hollowly. "I know the feeling. I'd trade my all for another chance with a solid body. But we're both stuck with what we have."

They reached the front door. Pretty flowers grew beside it, some of them plaid. "It's hard not to like the D Demon," Nolan remarked. "He has good taste."

"Are we ready?" Apoca asked.

"No," Nolan answered, and the others made silences of abject agreement.

"That's what I thought." Apoca lifted a knuckle or four and knocked on the door. They waited tensely.

Nothing happened.

"Is he in there?" Nolan asked.

"Yes," Ghorgeous replied. "But not moving."

"The green leads inside," Vinia said.

"Maybe he doesn't want visitors," Apoca suggested.

"So do we go away and leave him alone?" Nolan asked.

"Bleep no!" Apoca said, and pushed open the door. "Dwarf Demon Talents, you have visitors," she called.

There was still no response.

"This is getting weird," Vinia said.

"*Getting?*" Nolan asked.

"I mean, weirder than it was before."

"Enough stalling," Apoca said, her hair flashing angrily. She strode boldly on into the house, hoping that nobody else would notice that her seeming courage was an act. Any real boldness she might have had was hopelessly lost in the forest. The others followed.

There in the main chamber sat a garden-variety man figure, the kind no one would notice in passing. She wasn't even sure what color his hair was, and she was looking right at it. He was motionless, staring straight ahead. Across the room was a picture of a ravishingly beautiful young woman in an evening gown.

"That must be Dwarf Demoness Transcription," Nolan said as he gazed at the picture. "As he sees her."

"As he would like her to be," Apoca said. "So he got a pin-up picture to use as a model. Demons can assume any form they want. He hopes she will copy that."

Nolan nodded. "He has good taste in women too."

Apoca thought of sending a glare his way, but it was too much effort. For one thing, he was right: the picture could hardly have been prettier. "Maybe."

Nolan glanced at Vinia. "Which way is the green?"

"It's all around here, with deeper puddles around the Demon and the picture. We seem to be where we are supposed to be."

"Huge help," Apoca muttered. This whole business was weird.

"Perhaps we are thinking too literally," Gent said. "The key may not be physical so much as mental."

Apoca knew that here in the pundemic zone he did not have to speak in puns or malapropisms. Still, it was a surprise to hear him being so rational. "What do you mean?"

"Demons of any type, small or capital *D*, are mostly minds without substance. They can form physical bodies, but it's not their natural state. DD Talents here has condensed into the form of a nondescript man, but his essence is clearly elsewhere. His attention is focused on the female of his dreams, the Dwarf Demoness Transcription. To communicate with him we need to go through her. That can only be through her mind, as she has no physical presence here."

He was making sense, she hoped. "And how might we reach her mind?"

"Perhaps by meditation, or the equivalent."

"You mean by thinking relevant thoughts?" Nolan asked.

"Perhaps. We might try it and be guided by what we find."

Nolan was plainly as vague on this as she was. Even the batons seemed dubious.

Now Apoca glanced at Vinia. "How's the green?"

"Now there's a puddle of it around Gent."

"We'll try it," Apoca decided. "We'll sit in a circle on the floor and think of Dwarf Demoness Transcription."

They sat down cross-legged and closed their eyes. Apoca focused on DDT . What was she like as a person? Was she worthy of DD Talents's adoration? Why did she ignore him?

She picked up a wisp of something. A faint presence. Demoness?

Who seeks me?

Well, now. Was she getting somewhere, or just imagining it? *I am Apoca, a mortal woman. I need to talk with you.*

I am busy at the moment, but maybe you can help. Come to me at the Dragon Sanctuary.

Dragon Sanctuary? Helping a Demoness? As if she could do any part of that! Apoca opened her eyes. The other three were sitting with their eyes closed, evidently not connecting. As might be the case if this were pure imagination.

Then Vinia's eyes popped open. "A blotch of green just hit you. Go for it!"

Apoca went for it. She closed her eyes again and concentrated on the Demoness. The presence remained. She oriented on it as if grabbing hold of a dangling rope. It gently hauled her through the wall and out over the glade, then just over the jungle. She was definitely going somewhere, and not by her own direction; it was like riding the hand of one of the giants, seeing the passing landscape. The batoness paced her, having no trouble following her thought.

"There is something," Nimbus said. So the nickelpede was along on this excursion. Perhaps that was not surprising, since it was a mental one. Apoca knew her body still sat on the floor of the cottage, unmoving. She was physically safe, at least from falls from the sky. She was glad to have the nickelpede's company.

"Definitely something," Ghorgeous Ghost agreed. So she was along too. Maybe that was not surprising, as this was a ghostly excursion.

She came to a flying dragon, a small one. A steamer. It seemed to be injured. Its wings were functioning, but there was blood on its breast and its breathing was labored. There was barely any steam, only driblets of condensation. It also seemed to be lost. It would not be able to remain airborne much longer.

"Poor thing," Ghorgeous said. "It needs help."

"Maybe it's looking for the sanctuary," Nimbus said.

A sanctuary. For dragons. The Dwarf Demoness had mentioned it. Could that be true? Apoca gambled that it was.

Dragon! she called mentally. *Follow me!*

The creature heard her. It turned to follow her mind.

She pursued the signal, which was growing stronger. It led her across hills and valleys, streams and fields, even an isolated village. Then it descended into a circular indentation, maybe an old volcano crater, long since overgrown with greenery. Green, indeed.

There were dragons there, of every description. Large, medium, small, and pocket-size. Fire breathers, steamers, smokers, and some she did not identify. Flying, walking, swimming in the adjacent pond, and, could it be, burrowing? She had never before seen such an assembly. They were not fighting or sleeping; they seemed to be there under some kind of truce.

And there was the Demoness, a nebulously shining presence forming arms and hands for physical work, dispensing dragon food consisting of barrels of fish, chunks of raw meat, and a pile of beefsteak tomatoes. The dragons were waiting their turns as she walked among them. Now Apoca saw that their pacifism was at least in part because most were in poor health. Some were injured, some sickly. They needed help, and they were receiving it. Some had bandaged limbs; others just lay on the ground, unable even to crawl to her for food.

Transcription spied Apoca's presence. "Ah, the human woman," she called, now seemingly audible, perhaps because of the proximity. "And you brought friends and a client." She indicated the dragon who had crash-landed behind Apoca.

"It was looking for you but got lost," Apoca explained. "So I led it in. It seems to have a chest injury."

The Demoness came and checked. "A bad bruise. It will survive. I will delete the pain." She touched the creature's chest, and it relaxed, at peace for the moment.

Apoca waited while the Demoness saw to the remaining patients. Some became well enough to depart. Some rested on the ground, still recuperating. Some she put in improvised nests for a longer recovery time.

Then she gave Apoca more of her attention. "Thank you for bringing in that steamer. You did help." She made a small gesture, and a house formed around them. "You were looking for me. Why?"

"This is moderately complicated."

"You were at DD Talents's domicile. Does it relate to him?"

"Yes. He defines the talents our children receive. Each child is supposed to receive a different talent. He has stopped doing his job. Now all children are getting the same talent. That is awkward. We want him to resume."

The figure nodded. "I thought it might be that." She did not volunteer more.

Apoca was cautious about pushing too hard. This Demoness could obliterate her with a blink, and that would not solve the Talents problem. It was better to change the subject, for the moment. "Why are you ministering to dragons? I never knew of anyone caring for the welfare of such monsters."

Transcription formed a human face and smiled. "That is why they need help. Humans don't care about them, and most other animals are their prey. I saw the need and am trying to address it. I wish I could do more, but I am not a creature of Xanth and must not interfere unduly."

"You're a good person!" Apoca exclaimed, amazed.

"Some Demons are. Is that a fault?"

"Not at all. Merely a surprise." Actually Chaos seemed to be good, but she had assumed that was because of the influence of Squid. As far as she knew, Chaos had not cared at all about the universe until he encountered Squid. Then, associating with a creature with a soul, he had changed. Souls were as powerful in their fashion as Demons were in theirs.

Transcription picked up on that thought, perhaps not surprisingly, since this whole scene was mental. "Yes, it was the child's soul that captivated him. I wish I had a soul. Dealing with the souls of nascent children made me become aware of things like conscience and decency. That is why an aspect of me is here, trying to do a bit of good."

Then Apoca returned her attention to the mission, encouraged by the Demoness's attitude. She liked doing good? There was more good to be done. "DD Talents is mooning for you. That's why he is neglecting his job. Why do you reject him?"

"He is talented with his talents, marvelously apt in creating and assigning them. I doubt any other Demon could do that job as well as he. But he is selfish and ultimately irresponsible, as can be seen by his disregard for his assignment. His proximity to the children's souls has not affected him. That is not my type."

Apoca was taken aback by the accuracy of the assessment. She could not refute it. DD Talents seemed to be indifferent to the mischief caused by his neglect of his job, concerned only about his personal interests. DD Transcription could surely change that, simply by agreeing to be with him if he returned to that job. But why would she want to do that, given that he was hardly her type? Why would any female want to be stuck with an unworthy male? Yet how then could Apoca accomplish their mission and restore talent normalcy to the children? She seemed to be up against an impossible challenge.

"Bleep!" Ghorgeous whispered in her immaterial ear. "We're stuck."

"If only we could think of whatever it is we're supposed to have that would enable us to succeed," Nimbus said.

That was indeed the problem. Ever since Apoca had kissed Chaos, she had been aware that success was within their grasp, had she but the wit to recognize the key. There had been repeated hints. Somehow Boy could after all get Girl and be transformed.

Transformed. Almost like Transcription. Transcription transformed. Somehow. No pun.

What Demon Talents really needed was a closer relationship with a soul. So he could be more like the Demoness. That might make him worthy. If there were any soul available. If he had any interest.

But what could a mortal woman like herself do, given that she was not smart enough to recognize what was within her grasp?

"Or a bug," Nimbus agreed, following her thought and sharing her frustration, her inadequacy. "Telepathy is not enough."

"Or a ghost," Ghorgeous added, similarly balked. "A soul without substance."

Then Apoca got an idea that flashed so brightly that the impact blew the roof off the little house. That was possible, given that the house was merely mental. A thought had as much reality as the structure did.

"Wow!" the batoness printed.

"My," Transcription remarked, impressed. "I am interested in your revelation. It is surely a potent one."

"It is indeed," Apoca said, dazed by the wonder of it. "It is the answer to the problem of the Quest. I—wait, our whole group needs to hear this. Can you transport us back to the cottage, Demoness?"

Transcription smiled. "You never left it. I will join you. Open your eyes."

Apoca's mental eyes were open, but not her physical ones. She opened those, and found herself back in the cottage room, sitting on the floor with Nolan, Vinia, and Gent. Nimbus was back too, and Ghorgeous, and the batoness. Dwarf Demon Talents remained frozen, freaked out by the picture.

"Wow!" Vinia said. "The batoness faded out, so I knew your mind was elsewhere. You're the Protagonist; we don't count when you're not with us. Now it's back."

"It's back," Apoca agreed, smiling.

"You are densely green. You're into something huge."

"I must be," Apoca agreed, half-dazed by the revelation. The assorted hints had finally coalesced into an insight. It had been there all along, just waiting to be grasped.

"What is it?" Nolan asked.

Apoca organized her discovery. "Folks, I finally caught on to the answer we were missing. But first, let me introduce Dwarf Demoness Transcription. She is a significant part of the key to the solution. Demoness?"

The Dwarf Demoness formed with a roughly human aspect, a woman whose details somehow escaped notice. "Hello, Quest."

"Hello, Demoness," they chorused back, fascinated by her presence.

"Here is my capsule summary," Apoca said. "DD Talents is not at his post because he has a crush on DD Transcription, but she sees their relationship as business, not romance. If she were to become romantic and tell him to get back to work, he would do it immediately. We need to persuade her to romance him."

"Obese fortune," the Demoness muttered. "Or in your dialect, fat chance."

"Every entity has his or her price," Apoca continued evenly. "Demoness, what would you give to have close, continuing contact with a soul?"

"Just about anything. Any Demon would. But this is academic, because a soul cannot be coerced. It has to want to associate, and only it can decide. I have no more chance of persuading a soul to companion with me than you have of persuading me to romance this oaf." She indicated the tuned-out Dwarf Demon. They were treating him as if he wasn't there, because he really wasn't there. Only his formed body, a shell to be animated as convenient.

"Exactly," Apoca said. "The challenges are parallel." The others looked at her, perhaps wondering exactly how far away her lost mind was. "Ghorgeous."

The ghost formed a faint image of a face. "Yes?"

"What would you give to have a physical body again, shaped to your image as you were when you died?"

"Anything. But only by joining someone else's living body is that possible, and then it would be her image and initiative, not mine."

"You are in effect a disembodied soul."

"I am a disembodied soul. No 'in effect' about it. That's my problem."

"If DD Transcription condensed into a physical body, in your image, would you be willing to animate it?"

"Yes," Ghorgeous whispered, amazed. "But why would she ever want to waste her effort that way?"

Apoca looked at the Demoness. "I think you know the price of her."

The Demoness looked at the ghost. The ghost looked at the Demoness. Then the two of them moved together, overlapping.

Ghorgeous Girl formed, nude, breathtakingly beautiful. In fact, she put the pin-up picture to shame. Her dark hair flowed curvaceously past her full bosom, tiny waist, compelling hips, perfect thighs, and exquisite legs to her dainty feet. She smiled, and the room brightened, literally. "Hello, all. I am now physical."

"Who are you?" Apoca asked, just to be sure.

"I am Ghorgeous." Then her dazzling face changed expression. "And Transcription. We have merged. We are compatible. We each have what the other most ardently desires. Ghorgeous will handle things when there are mortal matters to attend to, as she is conversant with the mortal realm. Transcription will attend to Demon duties." She looked at the Demon. "Including the chores."

"There is more," Apoca said. "Another potential conversion that may alleviate that chore. Put on some clothing." She was not even taken aback by the fact that she was giving orders to a Demoness.

A conservative dress formed around the figure, together with dainty gloves and slippers, masking its attributes without diminishing its appeal by more than a whit or two.

"More?" Nolan asked with barely suppressed amazement.

"In a moment." Apoca looked at the woman. "What DD Talents needs is discipline, integrity, and decency. With those attributes he would be an acceptable partner."

"He would," Transcription agreed. "But that would require a massive infusion of responsibility."

"That would require a soul."

Ghorgeous laughed, her whole body quivering delectably. "He can't have mine."

"Gent," Apoca said.

The man managed to haul his eyes away from the fabulous woman and met Apoca's gaze. "Yes?"

"How would you like to be the male equivalent to that female?"

He did not smile. "What is the price?"

"You must share your body with Dwarf Demon Talents, lending him your conscience, which is something he presently lacks, and your familiarity with mortal matters such as eating, sleeping, and, um, digestion. You will have control, in the mortal realm, but there will be the job of crafting and assigning talents for new children. In return you will have magic such as you have never known and the physical aspect of that female to love."

He looked again at the figure. "I have come to know Ghorgeous Ghost. I would be delighted to have her as my girlfriend regardless of her appearance. Is the Demoness of good character?"

"Yes. I am impressed with the work she is doing to help a species that has little sympathy elsewhere. In addition, she handles a vital aspect of processing orders for creating babies, and she has not neglected that. I do believe she is a good person."

"Then I will be glad to share my body and soul with the Demon."

Apoca nodded. "You?" she asked the woman.

"I have come to know Gent too. Behind the facade of the witch's curse, he is an informed and honorable man. I am not forgetting that he elected to remain with the Quest when he no longer had to, despite its dangers. He will do."

Apoca was not surprised. She had come to know both of them herself. "It is time for that merger. Transcription, if you please, wake Talents. Make the deal."

The woman walked over to the picture and stood in front of it. "Wake," she murmured.

DD Talents snapped out of his trance. "What?"

"I am Transcription. I will be yours if you join with a soul."

He was plainly mesmerized by her identity and appearance. "How?"

She reached out and caught Gent's hand. "Merge with this mortal."

The Demon did not argue. He dissolved into mist, floated forward, intercepted Gent, and faded into him. Gent straightened, firmed, and glowed faintly. "We are merged." It hardly mattered which of them spoke.

"Kiss me," Ghorgeous said.

He kissed her. A little heart sailed up, a precursor of many more to come. It was done.

He whispered in her ear. She shook her head. "Not before marriage. I was a virgin when I died, and I mean to be one when I finally do marry." That was clearly the recently mortal woman.

He backed off. There was a Demoness enforcing her stance.

Then something else occurred to him. "I need to be rid of this pun curse. Otherwise when it comes to the wedding I will say 'Eye dew.'"

"Not so," Apoca said. "You now have a thousand times the magic the witch had. You can burn that curse to a crisp with just a thought."

"So I can," he agreed, realizing. He focused and a wisp of smoke rose from his head.

"Now catch up on those talents," Transcription said.

"Yes, dear," he agreed meekly. He vanished. He had Demon work to do.

The woman turned to Apoca. "Thank you from both of us. You have given us each what we most craved."

"It was the Quest." But she was inordinately pleased, not only for succeeding in that, but for helping two friends to improve their lots significantly.

"We will remember. Now I sense an ailing dragon." Then she, too, vanished.

"You did it!" Vinia said. "You saved the talents, and maybe some dragons too! You are soaked in green."

"You certainly helped. So did Nimbus and Aurora. Their telepathy was invaluable." The girl and the bugs radiated pleasure for the recognition.

The two batons bobbed, contented with the outcome of what had turned out to be a significant story.

Apoca glanced sidelong at Nolan. "You too. It was really your Quest."

"I did it so I could court you. You were always the center of this story. There is more to you than your constantly changing hair, though I do like it."

Apoca didn't argue as her hair flashed plaid. It was a mixed case, but she was well satisfied overall.

Chapter 13

IT BETTER BE YOU

Nolan's baton glowed. That meant he was back as the protagonist. He had rather thought that their story would end with Apoca's victory, as there was nothing but routine details remaining. Why was this continuing?

"Do you know?" he asked the batons. They didn't answer. Evidently Baton didn't know, and Batoness didn't print her speech for him, anyway, only for Apoca. He was on his own. Well, along with Apoca, Vinia, and the bugs. Their Quest group was smaller than it had been, but that was fine; their mission had been accomplished.

"We have to take Vinia back to Thanx," Apoca said. "Also return Nimbus Nickelpede to her hive. And you still have to find a new home site for Aurora Ant."

"Details," he agreed. "We shall attend to them."

"You had better," Aurora said severely. But there was a curtain of humor in her background. He knew she had enjoyed the adventure and valued Nimbus as a friend. This escapade had changed all of them, including the bugs.

Apoca smiled. "Then we can visit your Naga Kingdom so I can meet your folks, and you can court me full-time."

"I look forward to that. We can fade into character obscurity together."

"In relative privacy. I have been a trifle reticent about our personal relations, not from any caution about you but because some of what I have in mind is too hot for a volume of the annals of Xanth history. Sometimes children get hold of those editions."

"And our children should have brave new talents."

"Indeed."

"The green leads to the viper," Vinia said. "But it's admixed with purple. I don't know what that means."

"Purple is a mixture of red and blue," Apoca said. "Red means danger, blue means peace. Dangerous peace?"

"Or a phenomenal challenge that has its rewards," Nolan suggested. "As long as we are in it together."

"We'll be together," Apoca said. "Close together." She squeezed his hands between hers suggestively. "You may not have known what you were getting into when you courted me. I am not exactly an innocent nymph."

He smiled appreciatively. "I am eager to find out."

"I wish you two would stop flirting and get on with our return trip," Vinia said, frowning cutely. "I've got a boyfriend of my own to catch up with."

They all laughed. They had not said so, but handling two Dwarf Demons had had its scary aspects. It was an enormous relief to have things successfully concluded.

They walked out to the glade and found the viper waiting. "Give us a ride to Thanx, and I will release you," Apoca told him. The serpent looked relieved. Having one of his coils be a love slave to what would otherwise be prey was probably embarrassing. What would other awesome, toothsome, vicious serpents think?

They rode in style back to the queendom. They dismounted, and Apoca smooched the coil with her negation kiss. Free at last, the viper launched back into the jungle, obviously glad to be rid of them. It would probably never tell other ATVs. Queen Demesne appeared before them. Vinia ran to hug her. "Mesne!"

"There is News," she said around the girl.

"We succeeded in our Quest," Apoca said. "Talents will be restored."

Vinia dashed off to rejoin Prince Ion, who had surely missed her.

"Oh, they already are," Demesne said. "Children are being delivered with wondrous talents. One can't talk yet, but he can make cartoons in the air, little pictures with blanks where the words will be when he learns to talk. A girl can reverse the talents of others. A boy can turn anything into antimatter. Really potent talents, of types rarely if ever seen before. We're going to have to set up a preschool just to teach these tykes caution before they inadvertently destroy things. But that's not the big news."

"Not?" Nolan asked blankly.

"It's that there's going to be a Demon wedding right here in Thanx. It seems that our residents Pun Gent and Ghorgeous Ghost have somehow made associations with Dwarf Demons and are eager to get married. Everyone will be attending."

"All the citizens of the queendom?" Apoca asked. "That's nice."

"No, everyone who is anyone. Including the Demons. Like Xanth, Fornax, Chaos, and all. It seems they like ceremonies like this, where they can dress up and show off, as it were. Demons do have their foibles." She disappeared, being a Demoness.

Dressing up? Showing off? It occurred to Nolan that there were ways in which Demons rather resembled mortals.

"That's because they are learning mortal ways," Aurora said; she had read bits of the Demon minds in passing. "Like vanity. They discovered how much fun it can be. Frivolous fun is a novelty to their kind."

Which in turn reminded him. "Nimbus's nickelpede colony lives here at Thanx. Maybe your anthill would find it suitable too."

"I was hoping you would think of that. That way I can be close to you without advertising that I have a foolish crush on you."

Nolan felt a surge of realization. "I like you too, Aurora. I wouldn't mind if you stayed with me. Not just because your telepathy is a real help."

"I thought you'd never ask. Not just because you can see imaginary things. Nimbus wants to stay with Apoca too."

"We'll remain bugged."

"We will," Apoca agreed. "Nimbus, maybe you could become the official nickelpede emissary to the Naga Kingdom."

"And Aurora can be the fire ant emissary to the kingdom," Nolan said. "Besides being our friends."

"You two human variants deserve it," Nimbus said. That was a compliment. Nickelpedes and fire ants seldom made friends outside their cohorts.

They walked to the nickelpede field. Nimbus ranged out mentally and contacted their queen, Nitro Nickelpede. "Here is my friend Aurora Ant. Her colony needs a new home. Would you object to them settling in the adjacent empty field?"

There followed a brief mental dialogue. They negotiated a mutual-assistance pact. Nickelpedes would not gouge ants, and fire ants would not scorch nickelpedes. Neither would hurt citizens of Thanx. All other creatures had better beware.

Now all that was needed was a means to safely transport the fire ant hill to Thanx. "Ghorgeous?" Aurora called mentally.

Immediately the potent presence was with them. Nolan was reminded that Ghorgeous was no longer a merely a ghost but the physical manifestation of a Demon. She was also friends with the bugs. "I have cleared it with Queen Demesne. I will move them here." She vanished.

Then, as they watched, the entire ant mound appeared on the adjacent field, undisturbed except for the abrupt change in locale. That mission, too, had been accomplished.

Queen Antonia Fire Ant emerged and made a formal visit to Queen Nitro Nickelpede, establishing amicable relations. The ant royal guard fired a torch salute that lighted the air above the field, while the nickelpede royal guard made a serenade of clicking. It was a nice occasion.

Queen Demesne of the Queendom of Thanx appeared. She congratulated both bug queens. Then she oriented on the remnant of the Quest. "The wedding is tomorrow. You bugs are of course invited."

"We'll be there," Aurora agreed. "With our associates." She made a dream flash image of Nolan and Apoca.

Things happened fast when Demons were involved.

Apoca smiled. "How can we decline? They're our friends."

They spent the night in the pleasant little suite normally reserved for guests of Queen Apoca. This time Nolan was the guest and she was the host. They kissed chastely and slept. Their time would come, once things settled down and they were safely anonymous, with the two batons supervising other characters. Nolan knew that he and Apoca were already well on the way to the background. Probably they remained protagonists mainly to view the gala wedding. It seemed that readers of Xanth history volumes liked weddings almost as much as warfare.

In the morning they rose, cleaned, dressed neatly, ate the occu pie and boot rear provided, kissed, and went out to assist the ceremony. Things were already progressing. They felt halfway anonymous already.

"There you are!" Vinia said, intercepting them. "How are you with animals?"

"Animals?" Nolan asked blankly. "This is supposed to be a wedding."

"Yes, a really truly big, fancy one. They want music, background, and of course the wedding march. They demand the very best. So they are importing a small herd of unicorns."

"Unicorns!" Apoca exclaimed. "What do they have to do with a wedding?"

"These are special. They're from Phaze."

"From where? Faze?"

"Phaze. It's the magic half of a planet, maybe one of Ida's moons, I don't know. Ion's mom, Ida, has all these worlds orbiting her head—"

"I know about Queen Ida's moons. Some have unicorns. But that doesn't answer the question."

"Yes it does. Phaze is where the unicorns live. They look like garden-variety 'corns, but their horns play music. Each horn is a different instrument. Most are wind instruments, like the harmonica, flute, oboe, bassoon, or trombone. But some are percussion, like drums or xylophones, or string, like violins or guitars. They have really melodic magic. They're the best."

"I suppose," Apoca said uncertainly. "But you know, unicorns and virgins. I'm not exactly a—"

"Phaze unicorns are different. They don't care about that sort of thing. In fact, they can change forms, sometimes to human form, and do it with people they like. They're as smart as people. The point is, they are the best musicians, because their horns are not separate instruments, they are part of the unicorn. They don't have to learn to play their horns; they *are* their horns. A herd of them makes the best orchestra there is, with the beat of their hooves keeping the cadence. That's why the Demons want them here."

"How do you know all this," Nolan asked. "When it's new to us?"

"My fiancé Ion knows just about everything about everything, and he has tools to find out what else. I asked him, and he told me." She smiled. "I'm a girl. I like unicorns even better than horses. I never thought I'd get to meet a Phaze unicorn."

"So the Demons are importing a herd of them for the occasion," Apoca said. "Where do we fit in? We don't know peas about that breed."

"Well, I volunteered to escort them here. But the Demons want adult supervision. So—" She managed a small blush.

Nolan and Apoca laughed together. "So you are recruiting your adult friends," Apoca said.

"Who you know won't turn you down," Nolan added.

The blush expanded to middle size. "Yes."

"Smart move," Apoca said. "We're here to help. Show us the way."

The girl's relief practically made her float. In fact, her feet did rise a bit from the ground. "This way."

They followed her to Prince Ion, who had a set of boxes in hand. "Set one up here," he told them, opening out a box that quickly expanded to barn-door size. "Take the other to Phaze and set it up there. The unicorns can step into one and emerge from the other. When they return, it's the same process. Just make sure that no one moves a portal or collapses it back to miniature size before the excursion is complete."

"We will need to set guards by them," Nolan said. "Who would do it?"

"Fire ants," Aurora said.

"Nickelpedes," Nimbus said.

"Both," Apoca said. "We can leave a mixed contingent at the near portal and another at the far portal, and bring them back when the portals are shut down."

"Sounds like a plan," Nolan said.

They went to the two fields housing the ants and the nickelpedes. Brief dialogues with the two queens quickly produced contingents of a hundred of each kind of bug. The nickelpedes climbed onto Apoca without gouging her, and the fire ants got on Nolan without scorching him. They walked to the field beyond the two used by the bugs and set up the first portal. Fifty fire ants and fifty nickelpedes unloaded, taking up stances on either side of it. Nobody was about to mess with this item.

Then Ghorgeous ex-Ghost expanded to giant size and picked up Nolan and his ants in one hand, and Apoca and her nickelpedes in the other. Vinia clung to a finger near Apoca. They were on their way.

Ghorgeous strode to the Kingdom of Adamant, to the royal palace. She set them down and faded back out of sight, preferring to be anonymous for this side trip.

Queen Ida came out to meet them, having been advised mentally. Her little moon Ptero orbited her head and seemed curious about this meeting. "It is good to see you again, Vinia. And your friends, who are . . ." She delayed artfully to give them time to introduce themselves.

"Prince Nolan Naga," Nolan said. "And my fiancée, Queen Apoca Lips."

"Oh, the ones who saved the talents!" Ida exclaimed. "We are so grateful."

Apoca laughed. "We did not realize news had already gotten around."

"Folk knew the moment the pie conjurings stopped. The prior ones have been retroactively changed to other talents. You are incidentally famous. The messed-up talents have been a horror." She made a small queenly gesture of changing the subject. "What brings you here?"

"Nolan and Apoca are helping me with a detail for the big wedding," Vinia explained.

"Ah, yes, we received an invitation. But I am not clear exactly whom the parties are. One reading suggests a mortal man and a ghost. Another suggests two Dwarf Demons."

"Both," Vinia said. "The Demons merged with the man and the ghost because they wanted to experience mortality and souls. Now they are marrying, to experience I have no idea what."

Ida smiled, knowing that the girl was not nearly as innocent as she pretended. The Adult Conspiracy was sharper on appearances than on reality. "To be sure. Perhaps my prior question was unclear. What is it that brings the three of you here, plus so many ants and nickelpedes? Not to mention the ineffable personage who brought you."

Nolan realized that not only was Ida a Sorceress in her own right, relating to imagination, she was a pretty sharp observer. He liked her.

"We need to visit the world of Phaze," Vinia said. "For a herd of unicorns."

"Phaze," the queen repeated thoughtfully. "That's one of the alien planets, not readily accessible. It resides mainly in an alternate framework."

"Yes. But you have every planet, somewhere along the line."

"So I do. But some are dangerous to visit without protection."

"We have protection."

Ida smiled. "I thought you might. Then here is the route." Ida proffered what looked like a length of string.

"Thank you." Vinia took the string. She turned to the others. "The other end of this will be on Phaze, near the unicorns. All we have to do is follow it."

Nolan did not know how that worked but was sure Vinia did. Her green path surely followed the string.

Ghorgeous picked them up again. They sailed up, up, into the sky, for Ghorgeous was no longer a ghost but a Dwarf Demon with relatively boundless powers—and there was the moon of Ptero, looking ever larger as they approached it. They zoomed across its landscapes until they came to a version of Castle Roogna, following the string, and there in her room was Queen Ida again. Except that her orbiting moon was Pyramid, with four triangular faces colored blue, red, green, and gray respectively. They soared to the blue face, to a lake with an isle, where there was another Ida. Her moon was a torus, or shaped like a doughnut. There they crossed the Sarah Sea to the Isle of Niffen, where Ida's moon was Cone, with the center filled with water hosting sea folk who were eagerly meeting with land folk at the shore. "I have no idea what they're doing," Vinia said, which suggested that it was covered by the Adult Conspiracy to Keep Interesting Things from Children. They plunged into the water and dived down all the way to the base of the cone, where Ida lived. Her moon was Dumbbell, where everyone seemed to be working out with weights. Ida was in the center of the bar, the most muscular woman of any age Nolan had seen. Her moon was Pincushion, with residences on the huge pins stuck in the center. Ida was on the rounded end of the planet. Her moon was Spiral, like a tiny galaxy, with Ida in the center. Her moon was Tangle, like a knot in a messy ball of string, with her in the center. Her moon was Motes, which was a cluster of planetoids, she in the center of it all. And on through Trapezoid, Shoe, Implosion, Puzzle, Octopus, Tesseract, Fractal, Zombie, Dragon, Green Goo, and so many others that Nolan had to stop watching lest he expire of dizziness. As it was, he was feeling a bit motion sick. What a panorama!

At last they homed in on Phaze, which from a distance looked relatively ordinary. Ida was on an island in a sea near the West Pole. This time they did not go on to the next moon but crossed the Translucent Demesnes—Nolan was reminded briefly of the Queen of Thanx—to find a herd of grazing unicorns. Now all they had to do was make the deal to borrow some for the wedding and set up the portal.

Ghorgeous set them down on the edge of a green field, where a colorful herd of unicorns was grazing. It consisted of about fifty mares and one stallion.

"Your turn," Vinia said as Ghorgeous faded out.

The mares ignored them, but the stallion spied them and trotted up, his hooves beating the cadence to the vibrant sound of double-bass strings. He was large, muscular, and his hide was plaid. "Well, now," Apoca gasped.

Nolan realized that it was probably not coincidence that they had been brought to this particular herd, of all the herds on this world.

The stallion stopped before them with an impressive terminal musical chord. He changed form to a naked man, as well endowed in his various aspects as the unicorn, with plaid hair like Nolan's and the stub of his horn at his forehead. "Well, now," Apoca repeated. Vinia was silent, but it was clear that she was admiring both forms of the unicorn, in all aspects. The Adult Conspiracy was surely shuddering, but it lacked force on this distant world.

Nolan stepped forth. "I am Prince Nolan Naga." He made a spot change to serpent form and back to illustrate his identity. "This is my fiancée, Queen Apoca Lips." Apoca smiled. "This is Vinia, the fiancée of the human Magician Prince Ion."

The man nodded. "I am Player Plaid, the stallion of this herd. To what do I owe the honor of such a royal interplanetary visit?"

Nolan glanced at Vinia. She took it from there. "Two Dwarf Demons are getting married today. They want the finest music for their wedding. We would like to borrow a few of your herd to play that music, including the Wedding March. Can we make a deal?"

"What do you offer?" So there was to be bargaining.

Now Apoca spoke. "We can provide bales of the finest alfalfa hay. Buckets of sugar cubes. The adoration of maidens and children." She paused. "Do they all have to be virgins?"

"Not a problem. None of my mares are."

Nolan saw that the mares within range were pausing in their grazing. They understood what was being said and were interested.

"A guided tour of the local area of the world of Xanth," she continued. "Plus the honor of the occasion and plaudits for your participation in it."

Player nodded. "It will do. Next question: transport. We can't gallop to neighbor worlds."

"We have a portal that connects," Nolan said. "We can set it up, and transport will be instant, there and back." He smiled. "There is powerful magic in the background."

"So it seems." Player looked at the herd. "I will select a suitable variety of instruments. There will be no problem on that score."

"We will set up the portal. Vinia will lead you through. She has a feel for paths."

Then Player thought of something. "Is there a limit on the number?"

"I don't think so," Apoca said. "Your whole herd could visit, if they care to."

Nolan saw ears perk up. They cared to.

"You have handsome hair," Player remarked to Nolan.

"You have handsome hide."

Then Player changed back to his natural form and trotted among the herd, his vibrant music spreading the word. The humans set about setting up the portal.

A blue mare approached with the sweet sound of a harmonica. She changed to nude maiden form, her hair and eyes blue. "Player designated me as liaison. I am Bluette. How can I help?"

Vinia seemed mesmerized.

"I doubt you can help with the portal," Apoca said. "But Vinia would like very much to get a ride. Is this permissible?"

"Yes." Bluette changed back and waited while Vinia mounted her, bareback. Harmonica music resumed the moment the mare moved. It seemed it tied in with their breathing, and motion accelerated that. They went to circle the herd, the girl plainly thrilled.

"That was nice of you," Nolan murmured.

"Vinia's my friend. I know what she likes."

He did not argue the case. He liked the way Apoca looked out for her friends.

They completed the portal and set the bugs to guard it, explaining that aspect to Player. The unicorns were already lining up, directed by the basso notes of the stallion. Then Vinia, riding Bluette, led the way, disappearing as they stepped through the seemingly open framework. The others followed, until only Player, Nolan, and Apoca remained.

"Who's next?" Apoca asked.

The stallion became the man. "The two of you." Then after half a pause, he asked "Is it true what they say about Lips women?"

"It is true," Nolan said. "Don't kiss her or any of them. I understand that unicorns are resistive to outside magic, but it's not worth the risk."

"Surely not." But he looked as though he would have liked to test it. He had forty-nine mares to breed with, but a human woman was its own challenge.

Nolan and Apoca stepped through and were immediately back in Thanx. Sure enough, girls and children were massed, adoring the unicorns, and some were riding them. It seemed the unicorns liked girls almost as much as girls liked unicorns. Queen Demesne was watching with pleasure.

The stallion came through next, in man form. Nolan introduced them. "Player, this is Queen Demesne of the Queendom of Thanx, our host for this occasion. She is a lowercase demoness in human form at the moment." The queen obligingly became a purple cloud for two and a half instants, then reverted to human form. "Demesne, this is Player, the herd stallion, in man form at the moment." The unicorn shifted to stallion mode, then back. They were not showing off; they were demonstrating their natures, per socially accepted convention.

"Oh my," Demesne whispered, seeming quite taken. Player was also admiring her form, perhaps picturing her as a unicorn mare.

"Give her a ride," Apoca told Player. "In demon terms she's still a girl."

In barely three-fifths of a moment, the demoness was riding the stallion, both theoretically directing their contingents, both loving the contact. Girlhood did not necessarily end with maturity.

The site for the ceremony had been set up during their absence, a virtual stadium with separate sections for each type of guest. In the center was a stand for the key participants. The furnishings were elegant. Demons evidently rated the best.

Then the guests began to arrive. The first was Demon Xanth, in his ass-headed dragon guise, accompanied by his beauteous human consort,

Chlorine, whose talent was the distinctly run-of-the-mill poisoning of water. Nolan understood that it had been a fair story how the unlikely two of them had gotten together, something about a Demon contest requiring a human tear of love or grief. But romances could be fashioned from the least likely pairs.

Then came Demoness Fornax, whose sphere was Antimatter, with her consort the Demon Nemesis, whose domain was Dark Matter. Both were in human guise, though there were a few sparks where bits of airborne dust collided with their ambiance. Nolan suspected that they had interesting nights together, possibly generating larger sparks.

Then came Demon Chaos, with Squid on his arm. He was humanly handsome, having learned the art of appearances, and she was on the verge of bursting out of childhood, a lovely girl. Nolan and Apoca went to greet them. "No kissing!" Squid said as if alarmed, and the four of them laughed. But there was something about a look Chaos gave Nolan, not in the least threatening, merely unfinished. Was Nolan missing something? It hardly mattered, as the couple was soon gone, joining the others in the Demon section.

The other guests filed in, slowly filling the stadium. There were assorted royals from several kingdoms, including Queen Ida and her twin sister, King Ivy. The citizens of Thanx occupied their section, and their surrounding kingdoms had sent representatives. There were the fire ants, the nickelpedes, the ghosts, and the dragons, all well behaved. Also a few zombies, robots, and witches. There were a number of folk Nolan didn't recognize, but he was sure they were important in their own stories.

And of course the unicorns, coming to stand in their own section: forty-nine mares and the herd stallion. Many eyes admired them, as unicorns were not common in Xanth, and these were spectacular with their myriad colors and the muted sounds of their horns as they moved. It hardly seemed to matter who was getting married; the audience alone was spectacular.

Nolan and Apoca joined the Lips section of the queendom contingent and took their seats. It was just about time. Nolan was reminded of their own wedding to come, which would be barely an echo of this one, but just as meaningful to them personally. They were of course not Demons, merely mortal royalty.

Then the music started, at first subdued, then expanding to fill the stadium. It was authoritative and beautiful; any question anyone might have had about the melodic skill of the unicorns was banished with the first notes. A hush fell on the throng; it was time to pay attention.

The music hushed as a figure appeared at the central dais, male and forbidding. "A greeting, all. I am the demon Professor Grossclout, here to officiate at the marriage of the human manifestation of the Dwarf Demon of Talents, otherwise known as Gent, and the human manifestation of the Dwarf Demoness of Transcription, otherwise known as Ghorgeous." He paused, and the stadium was silent, for his talent was Intimidation. "Participants, show yourselves."

The couple appeared. He was stunningly handsome in a form fitting dark suit, and she was of course gorgeous in a tiara and wedding gown that seemed almost ghostly in the way it displayed her spectacular face and figure. There was a subdued sigh in the audience as every man wished he could have married a creature like that, and every woman wished she could have been a creature like that. Which was of course the point of the outfit.

"Are you ready?" Grossclout glowered.

"We are," the groom and bride answered together, suitably cowed.

"Are the accouterments in order?"

"Here!" Vinia called as she hurried up. "A set of magic rings that guarantee, well, you know." She was unable to finish because she was underage.

"Fertility," Grossclout said, annoyed. "The Adult Conspiracy is overdue for an update, as it obstructs clarity." He let loose a token glower. "Very well. The bride will go to the far side of the hall, at the end of the red carpet." The carpet appeared. "The Wedding March will start, and she will commence her walk. Once the music begins, the ceremony *will* proceed to its inexorable conclusion. If you have any doubts, speak now or forever hold your idiotic peace."

They would not have dared to have any doubts.

Ghorgeous took her place at the far end of the long carpet, while Gent and Vinia waited beside Grossclout. The evocative theme of the Wedding March began. The guests watched and listened, fascinated, and a number of the women were tearful. It seemed that unicorns were not the only thing that truly moved the fair gender.

Then something off-script happened. A small flying dragon appeared, making its way erratically to Ghorgeous. "Help! A dragnet is attacking the Dragon Refuge! It is sweeping up all the ill dragons, who will surely be compacted into canned spam. Only I escaped to cry the alarm!" Having done that, it dropped to the floor, its flame expiring.

"Canned spam? The bleep it will," the Demoness swore, only the word she used wasn't quite covered by the bleep. An *h* showed at one end, and an *l* at the other. Then she vanished, leaving her clothing behind. There were dragons to save!

The groom, observing that, hastened to join her, vanishing himself, leaving his suit behind.

The music paused in place, prolonging a single note. The Wedding March had commenced; it could not be stopped, only paused.

"It seems we have a problem," Grossclout said, issuing a medium-sized glower. "There has to be a wedding. The ceremony cannot be abated at this stage." He paused a good quarter of a moment to let steam out of his ears. "Have we a volunteer?"

There was a disorganized silence in the rest of the audience, fitting neatly around the sustained note. No one else had come here to get married.

The Demons in attendance sat without reacting. There was an obscure hint of a suggestion of a smile hovering near Chaos's face. What was he thinking?

Then a young woman appeared before Nolan and Apoca. "It better be you," she said grimly.

"Mnemonica!" Apoca exclaimed, recognizing her daughter-to-be. "What are you doing here?"

"I got an ugly premonition. It made me feel only partially real. I went to Squid, who exists through to my time, and she gave me a pass through Limbo. I have to promote a wedding. My existence depends on it."

This was weird. "What are you talking about?" Nolan asked.

She gave him a stare so direct it almost tanned his hide. "I know the date and hour of your wedding. There's a commemorative plaque because the two of you are known for saving the talents. It is today and now. You have to do it, and follow through in proper fashion tonight, or you will change history and I will never exist. Now, get out there and do it." She raised a hand to signal the professor. "Volunteers!" She pointed to the two of them. "And don't ever mention this to me as a child. I will remember when the time comes. Paradox, you know."

"We won't," Apoca promised, amazed.

The audience broke into applause, grateful to the volunteers. "Get in your places," Grossclout snapped, more interested in the procedure than the participants.

What could they do? They stood, to more applause, and Nolan walked up to the dais while Apoca went to the far end of the carpet. They weren't dressed for the star roles. Nolan picked up Gent's dropped wedding suit. It magically enclosed him, replacing his own clothing, fitting perfectly, making him the Handsome Groom. Apoca picked up the wedding dress, and it enclosed her similarly. Suddenly she was a radiant bride, leaving only a few strategic shadows to the imagination in front and back.

She glanced Nolan's way. He nodded. They were committed. How could they deny their only daughter her existence? Then she stepped onto the carpet and marched forward. The music resumed, swelling into magnificence. She had indeed become the Bride.

Nolan looked where they had been in the audience, minutes or eons ago. Mnemonica was gone. She had done what she could and had to depart before the threatened paradox got worse. It was probably dangerous even to think about it too much. Paradox was treacherous stuff.

Apoca marched along the carpet. The wedding dress enhanced her, to be sure, but she was a spectacular woman in her own right. Her hair was flashing plaid with her tumultuous thoughts, contributing further to her perfection. Nolan absolutely adored her.

The music crescendoed as she arrived at the dais, then faded to a pleasant background. The unicorns were indeed the perfect musicians. "Very good," Grossclout conceded grudgingly. He went into the words of mutual commitment, which they dutifully echoed. Soon they had both I-do'd. Nolan was hardly picking up on the details, overwhelmed by the suddenness and completeness of the occasion. His courtship of his perfect woman was in abrupt culmination!

Then he saw half a tear in Apoca's eye and knew that she was as moved as he was. There was more to their union than occasionally matching hair.

"The rings," Grossclout commanded.

Oh, yes. They were forgetting that detail.

Vinia stepped forth, bearing the two rings on an elegant cushion. They went through the ceremony of putting them on each other. The moment his ring circled his wedding finger, Nolan felt an extra surge of desire for Apoca. He wanted to get to the privacy of their room and signal a thousand storks simultaneously. Oh yes, the ring ensured potency.

"Mnemonica, here we come," Apoca murmured.

Exactly.

"I now pronounce you woman and husband." This was after all the queendom. "You may kiss the groom."

Another detail they were forgetting in the wonder of the experience. They embraced and kissed, and the music surged into a climax, perhaps a bit of unicorn humor. Nolan was immune to her love-slave kiss, being already thoroughly enamored, but he thrilled to the reality of their union and knew that she did too. They had known they would marry but hadn't expected it on this day, at this hour.

There was a stir in the audience. The Dwarf Demons had returned! Transcription held the torn remnant of the dragnet, which would never threaten dragons again. It should have known better than to go after dragons protected by a Demoness. Meanwhile, a collection of injured dragons were taking an empty section of the stadium, beside that of the unicorns, who looked a trifle uneasy. They had become guests.

"Sorry about the delay," Talents said. "May we resume where we left off?"

Grossclout took it in stride. He had to, because while he was a fearsome demon, these were Demons, vastly more powerful. "You may. There has been a small change in the interim. You will need to generate new clothes and rings."

Nolan and Apoca backed off, satisfied to return the stage to its original actors. They stood beside the injured dragons, who seemed to recognize Apoca, though she had visited them only in a dream sequence.

Transcription took her place at the end of the carpet, garbed in a fresh gown. Talents stood beside Vinia in the center, whose cushioned rings had been regenerated. The music surged back to life. It had become a double wedding.

The ceremony proceeded as before. Nolan looked around and saw the Demon Chaos, whose smile now quirked near the corner of his lips. Suddenly Nolan knew that the Demon had known this would happen. Chaos had acted to save Mnemonica, probably at Squid's urging. It had not been coincidence. In fact, very little of what followed the Kiss might have been coincidence. They would never know for sure.

The Demons donned their rings and kissed. Sparks flew out, becoming little orbiting hearts. They, too, were now officially married, and learning the little signals of love. Their new souls made that important.

The occasion swung into the next stage, the Dance. The stadium was abruptly festooned with ribbons and softly glowing lights as the unicorn orchestra struck up the Purple Danube Waltz. "Get out there," Grossclout said as he appeared beside them. "You know the routine."

So they did. They embraced and danced. It was delightful. The other couple was also dancing. Then the music paused, and they changed partners.

Nolan found himself dancing with Ghorgeous, who was every bit as lovely in the flesh as she had been as a ghost and more graceful to hold. "Thank you for what you did," she murmured. "You gave me back my physical life."

"Actually that was Apoca who worked it out. She finally fathomed the hints we had been seeing. You were the key to our success."

"I'm not going to dance with her. I am thanking you as a couple." Her expression changed, becoming beautiful in a different way, and her eyes were shining little stars. "I thank you too," the Demoness said. "At last I have the soul I longed for, in effect. And the legal presence as a citizen of Xanth to enable me to help the dragons. The rest is incidental." She meant marrying Talents. The soul of the ghost was worth more to her than the Demon.

"You're welcome, both of you," Nolan said. "You did us a return favor when the dragons interrupted you, enabling me to marry my beloved." And save Mnemonica from nonexistence, but they were going to be silent about that aspect. Any incidental mention might wipe out a precious life.

The music paused again. Now the other female guests were taking their turns dancing with the grooms, while Apoca and Ghorgeous danced with the men. Nolan liked the idea of dancing with the women but wasn't sure about his wife dancing with the men.

In the next stage the men got to kiss the brides, and the women kissed the grooms. Ghorgeous/Transcription gave him a kiss of gratitude that would have floated him out of the stadium on any lesser occasion. Oh yes, he loved Apoca, but Ghorgeous could have taken him had he not been committed elsewhere. She was all woman and more than woman. Gent/ Talents were lucky males.

And the Banquet. There were all the usual foods, such as beefsteak from tomato plants, pied pies, boot rear and beau tea to drink, and eye scream and electric currants for dessert.

Then came an announcement by Queen Demesne. "It has been proposed that the portals that admit the unicorns be left in place after the festivities. It seems that the women and children of Thanx and the unicorns of Phaze enjoy each other's company and would like to perpetuate it. All in favor, say Aye."

There was a loud chorus of ayes, admixed with a few I's and eyes and aye-ayes. The portals would stay. That saved Nolan and Apoca the chore of taking down and bringing back the one on Phaze.

At last the day wore out, and the celebrants dispersed. It had been a momentous occasion that all the guests had enjoyed, especially the girls riding the unicorns. The Dwarf Demon couple disappeared, surely compelled by their wedding rings. Nolan knew exactly how that felt. He was more than ready to be with Apoca.

Then they were alone together in their bedroom. "Tomorrow we travel to visit your Naga Kingdom," Apoca said as she stepped out of her clothing. "So your folks can see what you found and captured in your travels."

"It better be you," he said, and they laughed.

Then they set about making sure Mnemonica was properly ordered. It was quite a night. Their daughter would be lucky if she didn't turn out to be twins or triplets or worse.

The two batons had stayed in the background throughout the ceremonies. Now they came forward together. "Your story is ended," Batoness printed. "We must leave you now."

"Maybe that's just as well," Nolan said.

"It has been a great adventure," Apoca agreed. "But we shall be happy to recover our privacy."

"We value our privacy too."

Nolan wondered what the batons needed privacy for. Did they have rituals for reproduction, the way mortals did? He was tempted to ask, but the batons faded out and . . .

Author's Note

My life progresses novel by novel. During the last novel, *Six Crystal Princesses*, my wife, Carol, died. We had been married sixty-three years, but few things last forever apart from Death, Taxes, and the Puns of Xanth. It was an ugly shock, but it had been long in coming and was not a surprise. I knew I did not want to live alone, and that Carol was not coming back, so I invited a long-term correspondent, MaryLee, age sixty, to come be my companion, perhaps more. She is another writer, so understands the devious ways of writers. I told her that I might not be much, at age eighty-five, but we had these warm Florida winters. She came to visit, stayed, and it got serious. It is said that love is friendship that catches fire. It caught fire. We married and she is now my wife. So that is part of the legacy of this novel. There sort of had to be a wedding in it. There may be a bit of magic in Mundania after all.

Things have changed, as there is now a new sheriff in town, as it were. I no longer wear suspenders or socks with my sandals, as these, MaryLee informed me, made me look my age of eighty-five, now eighty-six. I discovered that new marriage is bleep on a schedule. We also undertook a massive house and property cleanup and got new trails carved in the tree farm to make every part of it accessible. Now we can get out to see the shores of Lake Tsala Apopka, the Mundane version of Lake Tsoda Popka in Xanth. We live in backwoods Florida, with oak, pine, and magnolia trees admixed, and saw and sabal palmetto trees throughout. The saw palmetto is a tree that crawls across the ground until it finds a good place to stand; then it angles up into the sky. The sabal palmetto starts with a single spear of a frond poking up from the ground, then expands into a bushy mass of fronds, then grows into a tree whose trunk resembles a wickerwork basket, and finally sheds the crisscross decoration and becomes a normal palm tree. It is the state tree of Florida. We were married before a handsome sabal palmetto beside our driveway. So there is magic in the backwoods too. We live in a subtropical paradise, apart from the mosquitos.

We were also subjected to the coronavirus pandemic, which started in China and spread to the world, becoming the worst global medical and economic crisis since the Spanish flu a century before. It might have been stifled at the outset by scrupulously restricting traffic from infected areas, except for ignorant politicians who first pretended it was fake news, then tried to use it to cull minorities. MaryLee and I stayed home and used masks for things like doctor visits, escaping it. I had hoped to take her to restaurants, beaches, movies, Disney World, maybe a scenic train trip for our honeymoon. Alas, all gone; the honeymoon was obliterated. But we found that it's not such a bad thing, being housebound for months while newly married. Kisses, hugs, and secrets of the Adult Conspiracy can make up for a lot. If you noted peripheral references to the pandemic in the novel, such as the pundemic zone or the witches' Coven-19, those were probably not coincidental.

Another significant change is the keyboard. I touch-type on the Dvorak keyboard layout, which was designed to be efficient. The QWERTY layout was designed to be inefficient because in the early days of mechanical typewriters, the keys could jam if the most used letters were too close together. So the most used keys were spaced far apart from each other. This made sense, then. But the advancement of technology eliminated the jamming problem; you can't jam adjacent computer keys by rapid typing. But the public remains locked into the horse-and-buggy inefficiency, other than a few sensible folk like me who moved to Dvorak. Except that the computer industry stuck its finger in our eye by changing the punctuation keys about. So I found myself spelling words like "isn;t." Since I believe the machine should serve the user, rather than the other way around, I had to get programming to change the keys back. So naturally, software updates messed that up, making it increasingly difficult to work. I needed a programmable keyboard that the computer programmers couldn't mess with. But I also use an ergonomic keyboard, because that abates the carpal tunnel syndrome I got touch-typing on the cramped regular keyboard.

Sure enough, there was no programmable ergonomic keyboard. But now at last there is. Mine is Ergodox, at ergodox-ez.com; there may be others. The forces of darkness can no longer mess with me. I hope. This novel was typed on the new keyboard; if it stinks, blame the—never mind.

Another change was the vegetation. Our swimming pool had long since reverted to nature, with frogs colonizing it, so we converted it to our Sunken Garden. We had the torn enclosure screen replaced and trimmed back encroaching trees that had actually poked their branches through. We got the water drained and replaced with earth. Then we planted it with assorted shrubs and flowers, mostly shades of purple because that's MaryLee's favorite color. What's my favorite color? I'm not sure, but it could be plaid, Mela Merwoman's panties having fried my brain. But there aren't many plaid flowers. We transplanted several plumeria plants. We also planted a pink hibiscus shrub. That dates from several hibiscus plants we got a couple years back and planted outside, only to have the caterpillars and such destroy them. One branch of the pink one got accidentally broken off during the planting, so I put that in a pot and it survived, better protected, and now it is about eight feet tall and flowering in the garden. Also a papaya plant, of similar height. Plus tomato plants we started in a hydroponic Aerogarden, but they outgrew it. Plus a number of flowering weeds. The definition of a weed is a plant where you don't want it, but I prefer to call them volunteers. We'll add more plants as we think of them.

And the credits for the puns. As my critics know, I have little or no imagination; my ideas come from my readers. I try to use ideas by new suggestors before having several by old ones, but I also need to work within the context of the story, so there are repeats. I have many more puns in store than I can use, so selection is essential. The entries are listed approximately in the order they appear in the novel, except that repeats are grouped with the authors of the first ones used.

Credits:
Hide Armor—Naomi Blose
Swing Dancing—Emilio Ross
Ankle thinks it's a legend—Douglas Brown
Power Plants—Misty Zaebst

Stick-hers—Meeran

Babies delivered all with the same talent—Cheryl Jacob

Swearing a blue streak; crazy house; nervous wreck; saw grass; foot of the beds; cartoon talent; Incredibull; all thumbs—Mary Rashford

Conjuring pies of any type; Add, Minus, Multiply, Divide Dresses; Lip stick, lip branch, lip tree. Mouth stick, face stick. Weap-puns, A-bomb, F-Bomb, H-Bomb, etc.; the sun sick with the corona virus; talent of physically entering one mirror and exiting another, that works for any mirror, not just magical ones; poi-son and poi-daughter; zombie unlives matter: a movement to combat anti-zombie prejudice in Xanth; missile toes; rock keys; bearing; buck naked; Hue Mane; herd immunity; back date; Aunt Ti Dote; vote by male, female; male-in and female-in ballots; ever trees of all colors; covid with germs; Fan Tom—Tim Bruening

Up to your ears in corn—Christina McQuirk

Gas cap, screw cap, abundance, fence post—Cal Humrich

Slow Djinn, necromance, aphrodisiac wormwood, electric currants—Richard Van Fossan

Abacuss—George Pope

Dolly Llama—Misty Zaebst

Pie Rat; talent of capturing sickness in books—Laura Kwon Anderson

Nimbus can't hurt his namesake; the Kiss affects all Xanth; Coven-19—MaryLee Jacob

Centaur/Dragon crossbreed—Jesse Amal

Pallorjade, the human/dragon crossbreed—Jennifer Morris

Early characters reappearing—Kathy Hendricks

Yellow jacket—Guinevere Stoops

Professional nails—Mamie and Willa Wolfe

Mundane truckers' parts upgrade Com Pewter—Owen Gray

Talent of reversing the talents of others; talent of turning anything into antimatter—James Beardsley

Aunti Bodi—Ellie Kerans

Passing the buck—David Seltzer

And credit to my proofreaders: Scott Ryan and Doug Harter.

This was Xanth #47. Will there be a #48? Well, I am making notes for one tentatively titled *The Ugly Nymphs*, which I thought of when Nolan had never seen an ugly nymph. Nymphs are supposed to be beautiful, empty-headed, scream cutely, kick their bare legs high, and fling their hair about. But suppose some aren't, or don't? There could be a story there. I will find out.

About the Author

Piers Anthony is one of the world's most popular fantasy writers, and a *New York Times*–bestselling author twenty-one times over. His Xanth novels have been read and loved by millions of readers around the world, and he daily receives letters from his devoted fans. In addition to the Xanth series, Anthony is the author of many other bestselling works. He lives in Inverness, Florida.

THE XANTH NOVELS

FROM OPEN ROAD MEDIA

INTEGRATED MEDIA

Find a full list of our authors and
titles at www.openroadmedia.com

FOLLOW US
@OpenRoadMedia

EARLY BIRD BOOKS

FRESH DEALS, DELIVERED DAILY

Love to read?
Love great sales?

Get fantastic deals on
bestselling ebooks delivered
to your inbox every day!

Sign up today at
earlybirdbooks.com/book

CPSIA information can be obtained
at www.ICGtesting.com
Printed in the USA
JSHW022032230123
36651JS00002B/2